ROSE OF ACADIA

BY
MARGARET
MARSHALL SAUNDERS

INTRODUCTION BY
GWENDOLYN DAVIES

Formac Publishing Company Limited
Halifax

Copyright © 2002 by Formac Publishing Company Limited
All rights reserved. No part of this book may be reproduced or transmitted in any form or by any means, electronic or mechanical, including photocopying, or by any information storage or retrieval system, without permission in writing from the publisher.

Formac Publishing Company Limited acknowledges the support of the cultural affairs section, Nova Scotia Department of Tourism and Culture. We acknowledge the financial support of the Government of Canada through the Book Publishing Industry Development Program (BPIDP) for our publishing activities. We acknowledge the support of the Canada Council for the Arts for our publishing program.

Cover illustration from W.H. Bartlett, *Windsor, Nova Scotia*, (1842).

National Library of Canada Cataloguing in Publication Data

Saunders, Marshall, 1861-1947
    Rose of Acadia / Margaret Marshall Saunders.

(Formac fiction treasures)
First published 1898.
ISBN 0-88780-571-X

    I. Title. II. Series.

PS8487.A867R62 2002   C813'.4   C2002-903375-6
PR9199.3.S248R6 2002

Originally published as *Rose à Charlitte* in 1898, L.C. Page & Company, Boston
Series editor: Gwendolyn Davies

Formac Publishing Company Limited
5502 Atlantic Street
Halifax, Nova Scotia B3H 1G4
www.formac.ca

Printed and bound in Canada

Presenting Formac Fiction Treasures
Series Editor: Gwendolyn Davies

A taste for reading popular fiction expanded in the nineteenth century with the mass marketing of books and magazines. People read rousing adventure stories aloud at night around the fireside; they bought entertaining romances to read while travelling on trains and curled up with the latest serial novel in their leisure moments. Novelists were important cultural figures, with devotees who eagerly awaited their next work.

Among the many successful popular English language novelists of the late 19th and early 20th centuries were a group of Maritimers who found in their own education, travel and sense of history events and characters capable of entertaining readers on both sides of the Atlantic. They emerged from well-established communities which valued education and culture, for women as well as for men. Faced with limited publishing opportunities in the Maritimes, successful writers sought magazine and book publishers in the major cultural centres: New York, Boston, Philadelphia, London, and sometimes Montreal and Toronto. They often enjoyed much success with readers 'at home' but the best of these writers found large audiences across Canada and in the United States and Great Britain.

The Formac Fiction Treasures series is aimed at offering contemporary readers access to books that were successful, often huge bestsellers in their time, but which are now little known and often hard to find. The authors and titles selected are chosen first of all as enjoyable to read, and secondly for the light they shine on historical events and on attitudes and views of the culture from which they emerged. These complete original texts reflect values which are sometimes in conflict with those of today: for example, racism is often evident, and bluntly expressed. This collection of novels is offered as a step towards rediscovering a surprisingly diverse and not nearly well enough known popular cultural heritage of the Maritime provinces and of Canada.

Margaret Marshall Saunders (Courtesy: Acadia University)

INTRODUCTION

On the evening of December 29, 1923, poet, novelist, and cultural entrepreneur John Frederic Herbin was found dead in the snow on a lane leading to his home in Wolfville, Nova Scotia. His cigar tossed aside, his duck hunting equipment around him, he died of a heart attack after a day spent on the dykelands developed by his Acadian ancestors two hundred years before. As he had noted in an interview in the *Boston Sunday Herald* in 1905, the lane that ran by his house "was used by my ancestors three or four generations back to haul hay from the salt marshes." Across the Minas Basin from his home had "sailed the ships which took the Acadians away" in the *grand dérangement* of 1755. Thus, for Herbin, every aspect of the landscape in the Wolfville/Grand Pré/Minas Basin area resonated with memories of his displaced ancestors. "I am never tired of wandering through these lanes," he told the Boston journalist in 1905, "and I would be ashamed to tell you how much time I waste going down to the spot on the beach from which it is known my people were forced to embark, and trying to imagine myself in their place. I imagine the anguish of my great-great-grandfather as he was made to leave the home he loved and the farm where he had worked for so many years, and go away to a strange land. I can almost hear the crying of the mothers separated from their children, and I realize standing on that beach, more than at any other time, the injustice and the awfulness of it all."[1]

John Frederic Herbin's lifelong "mission to work and write, to preserve for the interested the name and memory of my people, 'the terribly wronged Acadians,'"[2] echoes the passion of the Acadian lawyer and historian, Agapit LeNoir, in Marshall Saunders' *Rose of Acadia*. Published in Boston and London as *Rose à Charlitte* in 1898 and 1899 respectively, the novel was renamed *Rose of Acadia: A Romance* in L.C. Page's second American edition in 1898. The opening chapters counterpoint Agapit's impassioned denunciation of the deportation against the ancestral guilt of Vesper Nimmo, a descendant of the 1755 New Englanders who executed the official policy of dispersion. Startled to realize that two suicides and a fiery death at sea have been the legacy of an Acadian curse upon his family, Nimmo leaves his privileged Boston home for Nova Scotia to find the descendants of his ancestors' cruelty. The process not only brings him face to face with the intense nationalism of Agapit Le Noir but also plunges him into a convoluted love affair with Rose à Charlitte, a figure reminiscent of the heroine of Henry Wadsworth Longfellow's 1847 poem *Evangeline*.

Despite a certain antipathy between the two men early in their relationship, Nimmo comes to appreciate the dedication of Agapit to the distinctiveness and resilience of Acadian culture. He also recognizes the threats facing the Acadian community as it enters the twentieth century. Bicycles, telephones, automobiles, visiting journalists, travelling salesmen, touring photographers, and merry-go-rounds from Boston all speak of the external forces breaking down community boundaries. As Nimmo prepares for a picnic, he contrasts the simplicity of Madame Pitre "in her hood-like handkerchief and plain gown" with her daughters Diane and Lucie, factory girls from Worcester who return on holiday as "overdressed birds of paradise, in their rustling silk blouses, big plumed hats, and self-conscious manners" (167). "Our children ... They donno' w'at

INTRODUCTION

they are," Mr. Watercrow (formerly Corbineau) laments as Nimmo moves along Saint Mary's Bay to visit an anglicized community: "They are not French, they are not Eenglish. They 'ave no religion." "W'y do they teach Eenglish to the French?" he adds, as he recalls his schooling, "the words was like fish 'ooks in my flesh" (275).

Saunders highlights these threats to Acadian language and culture partly through Nimmo's growing sensitivity to them and partly through the politicization of both Agapit Le Noir and the "modern Evangeline," Bidiane LeNoir. Yet she also shows the adaptability and business acumen that will enable Acadian society to survive. Not only does Rose à Charlitte go to Boston to study culinary strategies for the success of her inn but she also advertises successfully in *L'Evangeline* in order to attract a clientele of salesmen and tourists. Schooners travel frequently from Weymouth to the Boston states to sell the fish that will fund bicycles, sewing machines, Boston cooking ranges, and other commercial goods. Moreover, Agapit LeNoir and Bidiane both study outside of Nova Scotia, bringing back to the district of Clare ideas that will inform Acadian life. In one sense, Bidiane is typical of other Saunders' heroines such as Berty in *The Story of the Graveleys* (1902) and Patty in *The Girl From Vermont* (1910) in her insistence that women should vote, be community active, and not rush into marriage ("Just fancy having to ask a man every time you wanted a little money" (445)). On the other hand, she brings a new dimension to the politicization of Saunders' feminist protagonists by insisting on Acadian politicians for Acadians. Moreover, it is she in the novel who celebrates the fact that Sir Wilfrid Laurier, "the Premier of the Dominion is a

Frenchman ... and we are proud of him" (415).

In introducing Acadian nationalism into her novel, Saunders was responding to the temper of the time. Both she and her father, the Halifax-based Reverend Edward Manning Saunders, were familiar with John Frederic Herbin's initiatives to generate a spirit of pride amongst the Acadians, and she fittingly introduced a number of the novel's chapters with Herbin quotations.[3] Moreover, as a fluent French-speaker who had studied as a teenager in Orleans in France, Marshall Saunders clearly felt comfortable with moving to the district of Clare in the summer of 1897 in order to experience at first-hand the character of the community. A surviving letter to her from Placide Gaudet, a well-respected Acadian historian, journalist, and genealogist who taught at College Sainte Anne in Church Point from 1895 to 1899, reveals that he had read sections of *Rose of Acadia* in progress.[4] Although he reacted against Saunders' literary liberties in depicting the Acadians, he nonetheless approved of her ridiculing those Acadians (such as the Watercrows) who abandoned their religion and language for the sake of expediency: "je vous remercie bien sincèrement de les flageller si vertement."[5]

Saunders was both a novelist and a sometime journalist. Fresh from spending 1895-97 in Boston where she had researched two novels and had written occasional pieces for the *Halifax Herald*, she followed with interest issues pertaining to Acadian culture. As the novel indicates, she was already familiar with the Acadian newspaper, *L'Evangeline*, and the historical memory that she develops in Agapit, the parish priest, and the old men at the picnic reflects the nationalism of the Acadian conventions of 1881, 1884 and 1890 where cultural

INTRODUCTION

distinctiveness from Quebec had been vociferously discussed. At the conventions, as historian Naomi Griffiths has pointed out, Acadians resisted pressure to adopt Quebec symbols such as the feast day of Saint Jean-Baptiste and the fleur-de-lis flag, opting instead for August 15th, Assumption Day, as their national holiday and the "stella maris" as their own distinctive tri-colour flag.[6] Also emerging after the 1860s was the centrality of the 1755 deportation as the single most important determinant in shaping cultural identity. Griffiths quotes Jean-Paul Hautecoeur in pointing out that phrases such as "le Grand Drame, le Grand Dérangement, la Tourmente, la Grande Tragédie, le Démembrement, l'Expulsion, la Dispersion, La Déportation" cemented the image of a harmonious, Edenic community of over 10,000 Acadians violently torn apart by their expulsion from Maritime Canada between 1755 and 1763.[7] In the first Acadian National Convention in 1881, Senator Pascal Poirier identified the Acadians as the sons of the martyrs of 1755.[8] The spirit of J.F. Herbin's poetry and prose helped to reinforce this sentiment, as did the literary model for it, Henry Wadsworth Longfellow's 1847 poem, *Evangeline*.

In speaking of cultural roots and nation-formation, theorist Benedict Anderson has argued that "no more arresting emblems of the modern culture of nationalism exist than cenotaphs and tombs of Unknown Soldiers."[9] In many respects, Longfellow's *Evangeline* filled this role for the Acadian nation, providing it at a critical mid-nineteenth century point in its rehabilitation with a seemingly viable image of what Anderson calls an "imagined community."[10] Central to this "imagined community" was the iconographic figure of Evangeline, saint-like for those seeking religious confirmation from the poem, martyr for those seeking political validation from the text. None of this mythologizing had been anticipated by Longfellow who, captivated by a good love story, had perceived in Evangeline a symbol of women's fidelity.[11] As his son recalled events, the catalyst for the poem occurred on October 27, 1846, when

> Mr. Hawthorne came one day to dine at Craigie House, bringing with him his friend Mr. H. L Conolly, who had been the rector of a church in South Boston. At dinner Conolly said that he had been trying in vain to interest Hawthorne to write a story upon an incident which had been related to him by a parishioner of his, Mrs. Haliburton. It was the story of a young Acadian maiden, who at the dispersion of her people by the English troops had been separated from her betrothed lover; they sought each other for years in their exile; and at last they met in a hospital where the lover lay dying. Mr. Longfellow was touched by the story, especially by the constancy of its heroine, and said to his friend, "if you really do not want this incident for a tale, let me have it for a poem;" and Hawthorne consented. Out of this grew Evangeline.[12]

Saunders' Rose is a re-writing of the Evangeline myth. Saintly, passive and stunningly beautiful, Rose yearns for Vesper Nimmo's love while loyally waiting for her missing partner Charlitte. Like Longfellow's heroine, she also inspires devotional responses in those around her. In a scene reminiscent of the poem, Nimmo "surreptitiously" lifts " a fold of her dress to

INTRODUCTION

his face" as he murmurs, *"Au revoir,* my sweet saint" (207). Bettina Tate Pedersen has noted that, as the novel progresses, Rose is "consistently described in terms of her deepening spiritual beauty."[13] Viewed by Nimmo at the beginning of their relationship as a "grieving Madonna" (126), she is, by the conclusion, such a "pure saint" (511-12) that

> She only raised her eyes from her prayer-book to fix them on the sky. She alone of the women seemed to be so wholly absorbed in a religious fervor that she did not know where she was going nor what she was doing.[14]

As his Christian name suggests, Vesper Nimmo is open to the influence of Rose's spirituality. Even though he is absent from the Bay for a major section of the novel, the reader is aware of his nurturing background role in providing love for Rose's son, educating Bidiane into her French heritage, encouraging Agapit through correspondence, and honouring Rose's devout Catholicism until she is free to marry him. He also expiates the guilt of his ancestor. In a sense, Nimmo, like Rose, becomes an allegorical figure whose goodness and self-control no doubt encouraged the *New York Times* in 1898 to review the book as more idyll than story.[15] The marriage at the end is highly symbolic, uniting the two solitudes of New England and Acadia through the birth of "a tiny creature—a little girl whose eyes and mouth are her [Rose's] own, but whose hair is the hair of Vesper" (515). In a sense, the Evangeline story promises to be yet again rewritten.

For Saunders, however, *Rose of Acadia* was a flesh-and-blood tale. Initially entitling it *Down the Bay*, she saw it as "a story of

Acadian life — of the French in Nova Scotia who are the descendants of the people mentioned in the poem of Evangeline. It is written from a French & Catholic standpoint."[16] As a practising Baptist who in 1894 had successfully published her award-winning novel *Beautiful Joe* with the American Baptist Publication Society in Philadelphia, she felt obligated to offer *Down the Bay* to the Society. However, by emphasizing that it "is an Acadian novel ... very favorable to Roman Catholics,"[17] she successfully convinced A.J. Rowland, Secretary of the APBS, that "it would hardly be worth our while to examine it, as we could not publish anything here which was at all favorable to Roman Catholics. A considerable part of our constituency would raise such a howl if we were to do this that it would injure our Society."[18] Rowland's response freed Saunders to complete publication negotiations with L.C. Page & Company of Boston who offered her ten per cent on the first two thousand copies, fifteen per cent on the next three thousand, and twenty per cent after that. Eager to promote *Rose à Charlitte* in England and "willing to take any kind of a story that I offer him,"[19] Page even sent a special illustrator, H. DeM. Young to Nova Scotia to develop visuals for the book.

It was Saunders' ability to occasionally introduce irony, social criticism or caricature into *Rose of Acadia* that saved the novel from disintegrating into stylized characterization and allegory. For example, as Vesper travelled to Nova Scotia early in the novel she cleverly revisited the stereotype of the fast-talking Yankee salesman first satirized in Thomas Chandler Haliburton's 1835 *Sam Slick* sketches, revealing that, fifty years after Sam tried to "gull the Bluenoses," the tension between money-getting and quality of life was still being debated as a

INTRODUCTION

distinctly American-Canadian cultural difference:

> "Upon my life, you can stand in the middle of Halifax, which is their capital city, and shy a stone at half a dozen banks and the post-office, and look down and see grass growing between the bricks at your feet."
> "Very unprogressive," murmured Vesper.
> The salesman relented. "But I've got some good chums there, and I must say they've got a lot of soft soap, — more than we have."
> "That is, better manners?"
> "Exactly; but" — and he once more hardened his heart against Nova Scotians, — "they've got more time than we have"(37).

She also integrated into the novel other cultural tensions existing within the province, including a moment of potential self-parody when Agapit rails against a woman journalist with a small dog who researches the Sleeping Water community throughout the summer and then subsequently writes about its "quaint" folk (85).[20] However, Saunders was clearly sincere in trying to capture the dynamic of Saint Mary's Bay. She accepted candid criticisms from Placide Gaudet about the caricatured dialogue that she gave to the Watercrows, her Protestant misunderstanding of Catholic terminology and her portrayal of "une vielle Acadienne avec la pipe *au bec*."[21] In the last case, Gaudet worried that "Les ennemis de notre race" would confuse Acadian women with "femmes indiennes"[22] if the scene remained in the novel. His reaction suggests both the inherent prejudice of late Victorian society and his obsession with constructing a socially acceptable Acadian identity. In this sense, Gaudet and Saunders were not much different. As Karen Sanders has pointed out, racism crept into Saunders' work as it did with other novelists of the period.[23] Thus, current readers of *Rose of Acadia* will occasionally notice that people of aboriginal and African descent in the story experience systemic racism in the homogenous environment of Saint Mary's Bay. For example, the child Narcisse becomes disconcerted when he meets a servant of African American descent in Nimmo's Boston mansion, and Bidiane is guilty of condescending middle-class attitudes when she enters the mixed race home of Nannichette and her Micmac husband at L'Eau Dormante.

In spite of Gaudet's anxiety that the Watercrow caricatures might undermine the public image of the Acadians, Saunders was sufficiently conscious of North America's literary taste for "local colour" to retain the flamboyance of characters such as Emmanuel, Mirabelle Marie, Nannichette and Bidiane in the novel. She was also sensitive to the public taste for stories of beguiling orphans, creating first with red-haired Bidiane Le Noir, and then in 1901 with *Tilda Jane*, two outspoken and scapegrace-inclined young women who demonstrated many of the qualities that would attract L.C. Page to *Anne of Green Gables* in 1908.[24] But Saunders' Bidiane is more than an interesting orphan. She is also a "modern Evangeline," one of the "new women" of the 1890s who demands a level of equality and social participation for women that the "old Evangeline," Rose à Charlitte, cannot envisage. With her propensity for whizzing off on her bicycle to all parts of the bay, organizing women into political action, resorting to headstrong language, and stirring up agitation, Bidiane is by far the most vital and

INTRODUCTION

memorable character in the novel.[25] As Elizabeth Waterston points out, she dominates the second half of the book.[26] That Saunders has her marry the controlling and somewhat misogynistic Agapit may surprise readers, but Bidiane goes into the marriage realistically as well as romantically, recognizing it as a union of interests, mutual Acadian commitment and strong wills ("I daresay we shall have frightful quarrels when we are married" (479)).

In many respects, *Rose of Acadia* is a problematic novel. But as an insight into the challenges facing Acadian society on the cusp of a new century, it contributed more than did the pre-World War I novels of Sir Charles G.D. Roberts and Carrie Jenkins Harris[27] to the rewriting of Longfellow's *Evangeline*. As well, *Rose of Acadia* was "classic Saunders," bringing into a novel of chaste romance her themes of social change, emancipation for women and the importance of the environment and children. With his precious phrasing and propensity for hugging trees, Rose's son, Narcisse, is a fey creature in this story, but he becomes a vehicle for Saunders in emphasizing her belief that children need balanced parental love, natural surroundings in which to play, encouragement for their appreciation of the environment and stimulation in their education. When, at the end of the novel, Vesper returns with Narcisse to Nova Scotia "to plant trees along the shore of the charming, but certainly wind-swept Bay" and to develop an electric railway (514), Saunders projects a blended world where New England and Acadia, in the words of J.F. Herbin, "set the bitter deed" of deportation "aright."

NOTES

1. "All Alone in his Native Land of Evangeline," *Boston Sunday Herald* (1905).
2. *Ibid.*
3. Edward Manning Saunders and John Frederic Herbin were both graduates of Acadia University and had an on-going association with the institution through its annual convocations.
4. See: Anselme Chiasson, "Placide Gaudent," *La Société historique acadienne*, 31ème cahier, vol. iv, no. 1 (avril-mai-juin 1971), 7-8. I wish to thank Patricia Belier, Humanities Librarian, Harriet Irving Library, University of New Brunswick, for providing me with this and other Gaudet biographical references.
5. "Marshall Saunders — Various," Osborne Collection of Early Children's Books, Toronto Public Library.
6. Naomi Griffiths, "Longfellow's Evangeline: The Birth and Acceptance of a Legend," *Acadiensis*, 11:2, (Spring 1982), 38-40.
7. *Ibid*, 40.
8. *Ibid.*
9. Benedict Anderson, *Imagined Communities*, London/New York: Verso, 1991, 9.
10. *Ibid.*, 6.
11. Griffiths, 41.
12. Cecil B. Williams, *Henry Wadsworth Longfellow*, New York: Twayne, 1964, 149.
13. Bettina Tate Pedersen, *Gendered and Regional Nationalities in the Fiction of Post-Confederation Canadian Women Writers, 1867 –1900*, PhD Dissertation, University of Illinois, 1996, Chapter 5, 53-54.
14. Pedersen, 53-58.
15. "Rose à Charlitte," *New York Times — Saturday Review of Books and Art* (30 July 1898), 501.
16. Marshall Saunders to A.J. Rowland, 13 December 1897, in Jacqueline Dawn Langille, *Letters From 1894 to 1906 Found in the Marshall Saunders' Collection of the Acadia University Esther Clark Wright Archives*, Unpublished M.A. Thesis, Acadia University, 1993, 188. Unless otherwise indicated, all references to Saunders' letters will be to this source.
17. Marshall Saunders to A.J. Rowland, Halifax, 19 January 1898,

NOTES

Langille, 192.
18 A.J. Rowland to Marshall Saunders, Philadelphia, 22 January 1898, Langille, 193.
19 Marshall Saunders to A.J. Rowland, Halifax, 19 January 1898, Langille, 192.
20 The fact that the woman journalist in the novel is accompanied by a small dog reinforces the impression that Saunders was aware of how the community may have been perceiving her in the summer of 1897. Forever associated with canines because of her award-winning 1894 novel, *Beautiful Joe*, Saunders was nearly always photographed in publicity pictures with one of her small dogs.
21 "Marshall Saunders — Various," Osborne Collection.
22 *Ibid.*
23 Karen Sanders, *Margaret Marshall Saunders: Children's Literature as an Expression of Early Twentieth Century Social Reform*, Unpublished MA Thesis, Dalhousie University, March, 1978, footnote 26, 137.
24 Among those who have seen Saunders' Tilda Jane and Bidiane as precursors to Anne of Green Gables, are Pedersen p. 59-60 and Carole Gerson, *Dictionary of Literary Biography*, 92, 329-30. Also see Elizabeth Waterston, "Margaret Marshall Saunders: A Voice for the Silent," in Carrie MacMillan, Lorraine McMullen and Elizabeth Waterston, *Silenced Sextet: Six Nineteenth-Century Canadian Women Novelists*, Montreal & Kingston: McGill-Queen's, 1992, 151-53.
25 See Pedersen, 63.
26 Waterston, 150.
27 Sir Charles G.D. Roberts was undoubtedly conscious of the popularity of *Evangeline* when he published novels such as *The Raid From Beauséjour* (1894) and *A Sister to Evangeline* (1898). Carrie Jenkins Harris published her novel *A Modern Evangeline* in 1896. Some years later, John Frederic Herbin retold the Evangeline story in *The Heir to Grand-Pré* (1907) and *Jen of The Marshes* (1921).

Dedication

I inscribe this story of the Acadiens to one who was their warm friend and helper while administering the Public Systems of Education in Nova Scotia and in New Brunswick, to a man whose classic verse is rich in suggestion caught from the picturesque Evangeline land, and who is a valued and lifelong friend of my beloved father, —

TO

Theodore Harding Rand, D. C. L.

OF McMASTER UNIVERSITY

TORONTO

BOOK I.

ROSE À CHARLITTE

CHAPTER I.

VESPER L. NIMMO.

"Hast committed a crime, and think'st thou to escape?
Alas, my father!" — *Old Play*.

"EVIL deeds do not die," and the handsome young man stretched out in an easy chair by the fire raised his curly black head and gazed into the farthest corner of the comfortably furnished room as if challenging a denial of this statement.

No one contradicted him, for he was alone, and with a slightly satirical smile he went on. "One fellow sows the seeds, and another has to reap them — no, you don't reap seeds, you reap what springs up. Deadly plants, we will say, nightshades and that sort of thing; and the surprised and inoffensive descendants of sinful sires have to drop their ordinary occupations and seize reaping-hooks to clean out these things that shoot up in their paths. Here am

I, for example, a comparatively harmless product of the nineteenth century, confronted with a upas-tree planted by my great-grandfather of the eighteenth, — just one hundred and forty years ago. It was certainly very heedless in the old boy," and he smiled again and stared indolently at the leaping flames in the grate.

The fire was of wood, — sections of young trees cut small and laid crosswise, — and from their slender stems escaping gases choked and sputtered angrily.

" I am burning miniature trees," drawled the young man; " by the way, they seem to be assisting in my soliloquy. Perhaps they know this little secret," and with sudden animation he put out his hand and rang the bell beside him.

A colored boy appeared. "Henry," said the young man, " where did you get this wood ? "

" I got it out of a schooner, sir, down on one of the wharves."

"What port did the schooner hail from ? "

" From Novy Scoshy, sir."

" Were the crew Acadiens ? "

" What, sir ? "

" Were there any French sailors on her ? "

" Yes, sir, I guess so. I heard 'em jabbering some queer kind of talk."

" Listen to the wood in that fire, — what does it say to you ? "

Henry grinned broadly. "It sounds like as if it was laughing at me, sir."

"You think so? That will do."

The boy closed the door softly and went away, and the young man murmured, "Just what I thought. They do know. Now, Acadien treelets, gasping your last to throw a gleam of brightness into my lazy life, tell me, is anything worth while? If there had been a curse laid on your ancestors in the forest, would you devote your last five minutes to lifting it?"

The angry gasping and sobbing in the fire had died away. Two of the topmost billets of wood rolled gently over and emitted a soft muttering.

"You would, eh?" said the young man, with a sweet, subtle smile. "You would spend your last breath for the good of your race. You have left some saplings behind you in the forest. You hope that they will be happy, and should I, a human being, be less disinterested than you?"

"Vesper," said a sudden voice, from the doorway, "are you talking to yourself?"

The young man deliberately turned his head. The better to observe the action of the sticks of wood, and to catch their last dying murmurs, he had leaned forward, and sat with his hands on his knees. Now he got up, drew a chair to the fire for his mother, then sank back into his own.

"I do not like to hear you talking to yourself," she went on, in a querulous, birdlike voice, "it seems like the habit of an old man or a crazy person."

"One likes sometimes to have a little confidential conversation, my mother."

"You always were secretive and unlike other people," she said, in acute maternal satisfaction and appreciation. "Of all the boys on the hill there was none as clever as you in keeping his own counsel."

"So you think, but remember that I happened to be your son," he said, protestingly.

"Others have remarked it. Even your teachers said they could never make you out," and her caressing glance swept tenderly over his dark curly head, his pallid face, and slender figure.

His satirical yet affectionate eyes met hers, then he looked at the fire. "Mother, it is getting hot in Boston."

"Hot, Vesper?" and she stretched out one little white hand towards the fireplace.

"This is an exceptional day. The wind is easterly and raw, and it is raining. Remember what perfect weather we have had. It is the first of June; it ought to be getting warm."

"I do not wish to leave Boston until the last of the month," said the little lady, decidedly, "unless, —unless," and she wistfully surveyed him, "it is better for your health to go away."

"Suppose, before we go to the White Mountains, I take a trial trip by myself, just to see if I can get on without coddling?"

"I could not think of allowing you to go away alone," she said, with a shake of her white head. "It would seriously endanger your health."

"I should like to go," he said, shortly. "I am better now."

He had made up his mind to leave her, and, after a brief struggle with herself, during which she clasped her hands painfully on her lap, the little lady yielded with a good grace. "Where do you wish to go?"

"I have not decided. Do you know anything about Nova Scotia?"

"I know where it is, on the map," she said, doubtfully. "I once had a housemaid from there. She was a very good girl."

"Perhaps I will take a run over there."

"I have never been to Nova Scotia," she said, gently.

"If it is anything of a place, I will take you some other time. I don't know anything about the hotels now."

"But you, Vesper," she said, anxiously, "you will suffer more than I would."

"Then I shall not stay."

"How long will you be gone?'

"I do not know,— mother, your expression is that of a concerned hen whose chicken is about to have its first run. I have been away from you before."

"Not since you have been ill so much," and she sighed, heavily. "Vesper, I wish you had a wife to go with you."

"Really,— another woman to run after me with pill-boxes and medicine-bottles. No, thank you."

Her face cleared. She did not wish him to get married, and he knew it. Slightly moving his dark head back and forth against the cushions of his chair, he averted his eyes from the widow's garments that she wore. He never looked at them without feeling a shock of sympathy for her, although her loss in parting from a kind and tender husband had not been equal to his in losing a father who had been an almost perfect being to him. His mother still had him,— the son who was the light of her frail little life,— and he had her, and he loved her with a kind, indulgent, filial affection, and with sympathy for her many frailties; but, when his heart cried out for his departed father, he quietly absented himself from her. And that father — that good, honorable, level-headed man — had ended his life by committing suicide. He had never understood it. It was a most bitter and stinging mystery to him even now, and he glanced at the box of dusty, faded letters on the floor beside him.

"Vesper," said Mrs. Nimmo, "do you find anything interesting among those letters of your father?"

"Not my father's. There is not one of his among them. Indeed, I think he never could have opened this box. Did you ever know of his doing so?"

"I cannot tell. They have been up in the attic ever since I was married. He examined some of the boxes, then he asked you to do it. He was always busy, too busy. He worked himself to death," and a tear fell on her black dress.

"I wish now that I had done as he requested," said the young man, gravely. "There are some questions that I should have asked him. Do you remember ever hearing him say anything about the death of my great-grandfather?"

She reflected a minute. "It seems to me that I have. He was the first of your father's family to come to this country. There is a faint recollection in my mind of having heard that he — well, he died in some sudden way," and she stopped in confusion.

"It comes back to me now," said Vesper. "Was he not the old man who got out of bed, when his nurse was in the next room, and put a pistol to his head?"

"I daresay," said his mother, slowly. "Of course it was temporary insanity."

"Of course."

"Why do you ask?" she went on, curiously. "Do you find his name among the old documents?"

Vesper understood her better than to make too great a mystery of a thing that he wished to conceal. "Yes, there is a letter from him."

"I should like to read it," she said, fussily fumbling at her waist for her spectacle-case.

Vesper indifferently turned his head towards her. "It is very long."

Her enthusiasm died away, and she sank back in her rocking-chair.

"My great-grandfather shot himself, and my grandfather was lost at sea," pursued the young man, dreamily.

"Yes," she said, reluctantly; then she added, "my people all die in bed."

"His ship caught on fire."

She shuddered. "Yes; no one escaped."

"All burnt up, probably; and if they took to their boats they must have died of starvation, for they were never heard of."

They were both silent, and the same thought was in their minds. Was this very cool and calm young man, sitting staring into the fire, to end his days in the violent manner peculiar to the rugged members of his father's family, or was he to die according to the sober and methodical rule of the peaceful members of his mother's house?

Out of the depths of a quick maternal agony she exclaimed, "You are more like me than your father."

Her son gave her an assenting and affectionate glance, though he knew that she knew he was not at all like her. He even began to fancy, in a curious introspective fashion, whether he should have cared at all for this little white-haired lady if he had happened to have had another woman for a mother. The thought amused him, then he felt rebuked, and, leaning over, he took one of the white hands on her lap and kissed it gently.

"We should really investigate our family histories in this country more than we do," he said. "I wish that I had questioned my father about his ancestors. I know almost nothing of them. Mother," he went on, presently, "have you ever heard of the expulsion of the Acadiens?" and bending over the sticks of wood neatly laid beside him, he picked up one and gazed at a little excrescence in the bark which bore some resemblance to a human face.

"Oh, yes," she replied, with gentle rebuke, "do you not remember that I used to know Mr. Longfellow?"

Vesper slowly, and almost caressingly, submitted the stick of wood to the leaping embrace of the flames that rose up to catch it. "What is your opinion of his poem 'Evangeline?'"

"It was a pretty thing, — very pretty and very

sad. I remember crying over it when it came out."

"You never heard that our family had any connection with the expulsion?"

"No, Vesper, we are not French."

"No, we certainly are not," and he relapsed into silence.

"I think I will run over to Nova Scotia, next week," he said, when she presently got up to leave the room. "Will you let Henry find out about steamers and trains?"

"Yes, if you think you must go," she said, wistfully. "I daresay the steamer would be easier for you."

"The steamer then let it be."

"And if you must go I will have to look over your clothes. It will be cool there, like Maine, I fancy. You must take warm things," and she glided from the room.

"I wish you would not bother about them," he said; "they are all right." But she did not hear him.

CHAPTER II.

A MESSAGE FROM THE DEAD.

> "The glossing words of reason and of song,
> To tell of hate and virtue to defend,
> May never set the bitter deed aright,
> Nor satisfy the ages with the wrong."
> J. F. HERBIN.

"Now let me read this effusion of my thoughtless grandparent once more," said Vesper, and he took the top paper from the box and ran over its contents in a murmuring voice.

I, John Matthew Nimmo, a Scotchman, born in Glasgow, at present a dying man, in the town of Halifax, Nova Scotia, leave this last message for my son Thomas Nimmo, now voyaging on the high seas.

My son Thomas, by the will of God, you, my only child, are abroad at this time of great disease and distress with me. My eyes will be closed in death ere you return, and I am forced to commit to paper the words I would fain have spoken with living voice to you.

You, my son, have known me as a hard and stern man. By the grace of God my heart is now humbled and like that of a little child. My son, my son, by the infinite mercies of our Saviour, let me supplicate you not to leave repentance to a dying bed. On the first day of the last week, I, being stricken down with paralysis, lay here on my couch. The room was quiet; I was alone. Suddenly I heard a great noise, and the weeping and wailing of women and children, and the groans of men. Then a heavy bell began to toll, and a light as of a bright fire sprang up against my wall.

I entered into a great swoon, in which I seemed to be a young man again, — a stout and hearty man, a high liver, a proud swearer. I had on my uniform; there was a sword in my hand. I trod the deck of my stout ship, the *Confidence*. I heard the plash of waves against the sides, and I lifted my haughty eyes to heaven; I was afraid of none, no not the ruler of the universe.

Down under the planks that my foot pressed were prisoners, to wit, the Acadiens, that we were carrying to the port of Boston. What mattered their sufferings to me? I did not think of them. I called for a bottle of wine, and looked again over the sea, and wished for a fair wind so that we might the sooner enter our prisoners at the port of Boston, and make merry with our friends.

My son, as I, in my swoon, contemplated my former self, it is not in the power of mortal man to convey to you my awful scorn of what I then was, — my gross desires, my carnal wishes. I was no better than the beasts of the fields.

After a time, as I trod the deck, a young Acadien was brought before me. My officers said that he had been endeavouring to stir up a mutiny among the prisoners, and had urged them to make themselves masters of the ship and to cast us into the sea.

I called him a Papist dog. I asked him whether he wished to be thrown to the fishes. I could speak no French, but he knew somewhat of English, and he answered me proudly. He stretched out his hand to the smoking village of Grand Pré that we were leaving. He called to heaven for a judgment to be sent down on the English for their cruelty.

I struck him to the deck. He could not rise. I thought he would not; but in a brief space of time he was dead, the last words on his lips a curse on me and my children, and a wish that in our dying moments we might suffer some of the torments he was then enduring. I had his body rolled into the sea, and I forgot him, my son. In the unrighteous work to which I had put my hand in the persecution of the French, a death more or less was a circumstance to be forgotten.

I was then a young man, and in all the years that have intervened I have been oblivious of him. The hand of the Lord has been laid upon me; I have been despoiled of my goods; nothing that I have done has prospered; and yet I give you my solemn word I never, until now, in these days of dying, have reflected that a curse has been upon me and will descend to you, my son, and to your sons after you.

Therefore, I leave this solemn request. Methinks I shall not lie easy in my narrow bed until that some of my descendants have made restitution to the seed of the Frenchman. I bethink me that he was one Le Noir, called the Fiery Frenchman of Grand Pré, from a birthmark on his face, but of his baptismal name I am ignorant. That he was a married man I well know, for one cause of his complaint was that he had been separated from his wife and child, which thing was not of my doing, but by the orders of Governor Lawrence, who commanded the men and the women to be embarked apart. But seek them not in the city of Boston, my son, nor in that of Philadelphia, where his young wife was carried, but come back to this old Acadien land, whither the refugees are now tending. Ah me! it seems that I am yet a young man, that he is still alive, — the man whom I killed. Alas! I am old and about to die, but, my son, by the love and compassion of God, let me entreat you to carry out the wishes of your father. Seek the family of the Frenchman; make restitution, even to the half of your goods, or you will have no prosperity in this world nor any happiness in the world to come. If you are unable to carry out this, my last wish, let this letter be handed to your children. Eschew riotous living, and fold in your heart my saying, that the forcible dispossession of the Acadien people from their land and properties was an unrighteous and unholy act, brought about chiefly by the lust of hatred and greed on the part of that iniquitous man, Governor Lawrence, of this province, and his counsellors.

May God have mercy on my soul. Your father, soon to be a clod of clay,

JOHN MATTHEW NIMMO.

HALIFAX, May 9, 1800.

With a slight shudder Vesper dropped the letter back in the box and wiped the dust from his fingers. "Unhappy old man, — there is not the slightest evidence that his callous son Thomas paid any heed to his exhortations. I can imagine the contempt with which he would throw this letter aside; he would probably remark that his father had lost his mind. And yet was it a superstition about altering the fortunes of the family that made him shortly after exchange his father's grant of land in Nova Scotia for one in this State?" and he picked up another faded document, this one of parchment and containing a record of the transfer of certain estates in the vicinity of the town of Boston to Thomas Nimmo, removing from Halifax, Nova Scotia, to the State of Massachusetts.

"Then Thomas got burnt for despising the commands of his father; but my poor sire, — where does his guilt come in? He did not know of the existence of this letter, — that I could swear, for with his kind heart and streak of romance he would have looked up this Acadien ghost and laid it. If I were also romantic, I should say it killed him. As it is, I shall stick to my present opinion that he killed himself by overwork.

"Now, shall I be cynical and let this thing go, or shall I, like a knight of the Middle Ages, or an adventurous fool of the present, set out in quest of the seed of the Fiery Frenchman? *Ciel!* I have already decided. It is a floating feather to pursue, an occupation just serious enough for my convalescent state. *En route*, then, for Acadie," and he closed his eyes and sank into a reverie, which was, after the lapse of an hour, interrupted by the entrance of the colored boy with a handful of papers.

"Good boy, Henry," said his master, approvingly.

"Mis' Nimmo, she tole me to hurry," said the boy, with a flash of his resplendent ivories, "'cause she never like you to wait for nothing. So I jus' run down to Washington Street."

Vesper smiled, and took up one of the folders. "H'm, Evangeline route. The Nova Scotians are smart enough to make capital out of the poem — Henry, come rub my left ankle, there is some rheumatism in it. What is this? 'The Dominion Atlantic Railway have now completed their magnificent system to the Hub of the Universe by placing on the route between it and Nova Scotia a steamship named after one of the heirs-presumptive of the British throne.' Henry, where is the Hub of the Universe?"

Henry looked up from the hearth-rug. "I dunno, sir; ain't it heaven?"

"It ought to be," said the young man; and he went on, "'This steamship is a dream of beauty, with the lines of an exquisite yacht. Her appointments are as perfect as taste and science can suggest, in music-room, dining-room, smoking-room, parlor, staterooms, bathrooms, and all other apartments. The cabinet work is in solid walnut and oak, the softened light falling through domes and panels of stained glass, the upholstery is in figured and other velvets, the tapestries are of silk. There is a perfect *cuisine*, and a union of comfort and luxury throughout.'"

The young man laid down the folder. "How would you like to go to sea in that royal craft, Henry?"

"It sounds fine," said the boy, smacking his lips.

"No mention is made of seasickness, nor of going

to the bottom. A pity it would be to waste all that finery on the fishes — don't rub quite so hard. Let me see," and he took up the folder again. "What days does she leave? Go to-morrow to the office, Henry, and engage the most comfortable stateroom on this bit of magnificence for next Thursday."

CHAPTER III.

FROM BOSTON TO ACADIE.

" For this is in the land of Acadie,
The fairest place of all the earth and sea."

J. F. H.

IT is always amusing to be among a crowd of people on the Lewis Wharf, in Boston, when a steamer is about to leave for the neighboring province of Nova Scotia. The provincials are so slow, so deliberate, so determined not to be hurried. The Americans are so brisk, so expeditious, so bewildering in the multitude of things they will accomplish in the briefest possible space of time. They surround the provincials, they attempt to hurry them, to infuse a little more life into their exercises of volition, to convince them that a busy wharf is not the place to weigh arguments for or against a proposed course of action, yet the provincials will not be hurried; they stop to plan, consider, deliberate, and decide, and in the end they arrive at satisfactory conclusions without one hundredth part of the worry and vexation of soul which shortens the lives of their more nervous cousins, the Americans.

At noon, on the Thursday following his decision to go to Nova Scotia, Vesper Nimmo stood on the deck of the *Royal Edward*, a smile on his handsome face, — a shrewd smile, that deepened and broadened whenever he looked towards the place where stood his mother, with a fluffy white shawl wrapped around her throat, and the faithful Henry for a bodyguard.

Express wagons, piled high with towers of Babel in the shape of trunks that shook and quivered and threatened to fall on unsuspecting heads, rattled down and discharged their contents on the already congested wharf, where intending passengers, escorting friends, custom officials, and wharf men were talking, gesticulating, admonishing, and escaping death in varied forms, such as by crushing, falling, squeezing, deaths by exhaustion, by kicks from nervous horse legs, or by fright from being swept into the convenient black pool of the harbor.

However, scorning the danger, the crowd talked and jabbered on, until, finally, the last bit of freight, the last bit of luggage, was on board. A signal was given, the ambulance drew back, — the dark and mournful wagon from which, alas, at nearly every steamer's trip, a long, light box is taken, in which one Canadian is going home quite still and mute.

A swarm of stewards from the steamer descended upon their quarry, the passengers, and a separation was made between the sheep and the foolish goats, in the company's eyes, who would not be persuaded to seek the fair Canadian pastures. Carefully the stewards herded and guarded their giddy sheep to the steamer, often turning back to recover one skipping behind for a last parley with the goats. At last they were all up the gangway, the gorgeous ship swung her princely nose to the stream, and Vesper Nimmo felt himself really off for Nova Scotia.

He waved an adieu to his mother, then drew back to avoid an onset of stolid, red-cheeked Canadian sheep and lambs, who pressed towards the railing, some with damp handkerchiefs at their eyes, others cheerfully exhorting the goats to write soon.

His eye fell on a delicate slip of a girl, with consumption written all over her shaking form; and, swinging on his heel, he went to stroll about the decks, and watch, with proud and passionate concealed emotion, the yellow receding dome of the State House. He had been brought up in the shadow of that ægis. It was almost as sacred to him as the blue sky above, and not until he could no longer see it did he allow his eyes to wander over other points of interest of the historic harbor. How many times his sturdy New England forefathers had dropped their hoes to man the ships that sailed over these blue waters, to hew down the Agag of Acadie! What a bloodthirsty set they were in those days! Indians, English, French, — how they harried, and worried, and bit, and tore at each other!

He thoughtfully smoothed the little silky mustache that adorned his upper lip, and murmured, "Thank heaven, I go on a more peaceful errand."

Once out of the harbor, and feeling the white deck beneath his feet gracefully dipping to meet the swell of the ocean, he found a seat and drew a guide-book from his pocket. Of ancient Acadie he knew something, but of this modern Acadie he had, strange to say, felt no curiosity, although it lay at his very doors, until he had discovered the letter of his great-grandfather.

The day was warm and sunshiny. It was the third of June, and for some time he sat quietly reading and bathed in golden light. Then across his calm, peaceful state of content, stole a feeling scarcely to be described, and so faint that it was barely perceptible. He was not quite happy. The balm had gone from the air; the spirit of the writer, who so eloquently described the lure of the Acadien land, no longer communed with his. He read on, knowing what was coming, yet resolved not to yield until he was absolutely forced to do so.

In half an hour he had flung down his book, and was in his stateroom, face downward, his window wide open, his body gently swaying to and fro with the motion of the steamer, the salt air deliciously lapping his ears, the back of his neck, and his hands, but unable to get at his face, obstinately buried in the pillow.

"Sick, sir?" inquired a brisk voice, with a delicate note of suggestion.

Vesper uncovered one eye, and growled, "No,— shut that door."

The steward disappeared, and did not return for some hours, while Vesper's whole sensitive system passed into a painless agony, the only movement he made being to turn himself over on his back, where he lay, apparently calm and happy, and serenely staring at the white ceiling of his dainty cell.

"Can I do anything for you, sir?" asked the steward's voice once more.

Vesper, who would not have spoken if he had been offered the *Royal Edward* full of gold pieces, did not even roll an eyeball at him, but kept on gravely staring upward.

"Your collar's choking you, sir," said the man, coming forward; and he deftly slipped a stud from its place and laid it on the washstand. "Shall I take off your boots?"

Vesper submitted to having his boots withdrawn, and his feet covered, with as much indifference as if they belonged to some other man, and continued to spend the rest of the day and the night in the same state of passivity. Towards morning he had a vague wish to know the time, but it did not occur to him, any more than it would have occurred to a stone image, to put up his hand to the watch in his breast pocket.

Daylight came, then sunlight streaming into his room, and cheery sounds of voices without, but he did not stir. Not until the thrill of contact with the land went through the steamer did he spring to his feet, like a man restored to consciousness by galvanic action. He was the first passenger to reach the wharf, and the steward, who watched him going, remarked sarcastically that he was glad to see "that 'ere dead man come to life."

Vesper was himself again when his feet touched the shore. He looked about him, saw the bright little town of Yarmouth, black rocks, a blue harbor, and a glorious sky. His contemplation of the landscape over, he reflected that he was faint from hunger. He turned his back on the steamer, where his fellow passengers had recently breakfasted at fine tables spread under a ceiling of milky white and gold, and hurried to a modest eating-house near by from which a savory smell of broiled steak and fried potatoes floated out on the morning air.

He entered it, and after a hasty wash and brush-up ate his breakfast with frantic appetite. He now felt that he had received a new lease of life, and buttoning his collar up around his neck, for the temperature was some degrees lower than that of his native city, he hurried back to the wharf, where the passengers and the customs men were quarrelling as if they had been enemies for life.

With ingratiating and politic calmness he pointed out his trunk and bicycle, assured the suspicious official that although he was an American he was honest and had nothing to sell and nothing dutiable in the former, and that he had not the slightest objection to paying the thirty per cent. deposit required on the latter; then, a prey to inward laughter at the enlivening spectacle of open trunks and red faces, he proceeded to the railway station, looking about him for other signs that he was in a foreign country.

Nova Scotia was very like Maine so far. Here were the Maine houses, the Maine trees and rocks, even the Maine wild flowers by the side of the road. He thoughtfully boarded the train, scrutinized the comfortable parlor-car, and, after the lapse of half an hour, decided that he was not in Maine, for, if he had been, the train would certainly have started.

As he was making this reflection, a dapper individual, in light trousers, a shiny hat, and with the indescribable air of being a travelling salesman, entered the car where Vesper sat in solitary grandeur.

Vesper slightly inclined his head, and the stranger, dropping a neat leather bag in the seat next him, observed, "We had a good passage."

"Very good," replied Vesper.

"Nobody sick," pursued the dapper individual, taking off his hat, brushing it, and carefully replacing it on his head.

"I should think not," returned Vesper; then he consulted his watch. "We are late in starting."

"We're always late," observed the newcomer, tartly. "This is your first trip down here?"

Vesper, with the reluctance of his countrymen to admit that they have done or are doing something for the first time, did not contradict his statement.

"I've been coming to this province for ten years," said his companion. "I represent Stone and Warrior."

Vesper knew Stone and Warrior's huge dry-goods establishment, and had due respect for the opinion of one of their travellers.

"And when we start we don't go," said the dry-goods man. "This train doesn't dare show its nose in Halifax before six o'clock, so she's just got to put in the time somewhere. Later in the season they'll clap on the Flying Bluenose, which makes them think they're flying through the air, because she spurts and gets in two hours earlier. How far are you going?"

"I don't know; possibly to Grand Pré."

"A pretty country there, but no big farms,— kitchen-gardening compared with ours."

"That is where the French used to be."

"Yes, but there ain't one there now. The most of the French in the province are down here."

Vesper let his surprised eyes wander out through the car window.

"Pretty soon we'll begin to run through the woods. There'll be a shanty or two, a few decent houses and a station here and there, and you'd think we were miles from nowhere, but at the same time we're running abreast of a village thirty-five miles long."

"That is a good length."

"The houses are strung along the shores of this Bay," continued the salesman, leaning over and tapping the map spread on Vesper's knee. "The Bay is forty miles long."

"Why didn't they build the railway where the village is?"

"That's Nova Scotia," said the salesman, drily. "Because the people were there, they put the railroad through the woods. They beat the Dutch."

"Can't they make money?"

"Like the mischief, if they want to," and the salesman settled back in his seat and put his hands in his pockets. "It makes me smile to hear people talking about these green Nova Scotians. They'll jump ahead of you in a bargain as quick as a New Yorker when they give their minds to it. But I'll add 'em up in one word, — they don't care."

Vesper did not reply, and, after a minute's pause his companion went on, with waxing indignation. "They ought to have been born in the cannibal isles, every man Jack of 'em, where they could sit outdoors all day and pick up cocoanuts or eat each other. Upon my life, you can stand in the middle of Halifax, which is their capital city, and shy a stone at half a dozen banks and the post-office, and look down and see grass growing between the bricks at your feet."

"Very unprogressive," murmured Vesper.

The salesman relented. "But I've got some good chums there, and I must say they've got a lot of soft soap, — more than we have."

"That is, better manners?"

"Exactly; but" — and he once more hardened his heart against the Nova Scotians, — "they've got more time than we have. There ain't so many of 'em. Look at our Boston women at a bargain-counter, — you've got a lot of curtains at four dollars a pair. You can't sell 'em. You run 'em up to six dollars and advertise, 'Great drop on ten-dollar curtains.' The women rush to get 'em. How much time have they to be polite? About as much as a pack of wolves."

"What is the population of Halifax?" asked Vesper.

"About forty thousand," said the salesman, lolling his head on the back of the seat, and running his sentences as glibly from his lips as if he were reciting a lesson, "and a sly, sleepy old place it is, with lots of money in it, and people pretending they are poor. Suburbs fine, but the city dirty from the soft coal they burn. A board fence around every lot you could spread a handkerchief on, — so afraid neighbors will see into their back yards. If they'd knock down their fences, pick up a little of the trash in the streets, and limit the size of their hotel keys, they'd get on."

"Are there any French people there?"

The salesman was not interested in the French. "No," he said, "not that I ever heard of. They could make lots of money there," he went on, with enthusiasm, "if they'd wake up. You know there's an English garrison, and our girls like the military; but these blamed provincials, though they've got a big pot of jam, won't do anything to draw our rich flies, not even as much as to put up a bathing-house. They don't care a continental.

"There's a hotel beyond Halifax where a big excursion from New York used to go every year. Last year the manager said, 'If you don't clean up your old hotel, and put a decent boat on the lake, you'll never see me again.' The hotel proprietor said, 'I guess this house is clean enough for us, and we haven't been spilt out of the boat yet, and you and your excursion can go to Jericho.' So the excursion goes to Jericho now, and the hotel man gets more time for sleep."

"Have you ever been in this French village?" asked Vesper.

"No," and the salesman stifled a yawn. "I only call at the principal towns, where the big stores are. Good Lord! I wish those stick-in-the-muds would come up from the wharf. If I knew how to run an engine I'd be off without 'em," and he strolled to the car door. "It's as quiet as death down there. The passengers must have chopped up the train-hands and thrown 'em in the water. If my wife made up her mind to move to this province, I'd die in ten days, for I'd have so much time to think over my sins. Glory hallelujah, here they come!" and he returned to his seat. "The whole tribe of 'em, edging along as if they were a funeral procession and we were the corpses on ahead. We're off," he said, jocularly, to Vesper, and he kicked out his little dapper legs, stuck his ticket in the front of his shiny hat, and sank into a seat, where he was soon asleep.

Vesper was rather out of his reckoning. It had not occurred to him, in spite of Longfellow's assurance about naught but tradition remaining of the beautiful village of Grand Pré, that no French were really to be found there. Now, according to the salesman, he should look for the Acadiens in this part of the province. However, if the French village was thirty-five miles long there was no hurry about leaving the train, and he settled back and watched his fellow passengers leisurely climbing the steps. Among those who entered the parlor-car was a stout, gentlemanly man, gesticulating earnestly, although his hands were full of parcels, and turning every instant to look with a quick, bright eye into the face of his companion, who was a priest.

The priest left him shortly after they entered the car, and the stout man sat down and unfolded a newspaper on which the name and place of publication — *L'Évangéline, Journal Hebdomadaire, Weymouth* — met Vesper's eye with grateful familiarity. The title was, of course, a pathetic reminder of the poem. Weymouth, and he glanced at his map, was in the line of villages along the bay.

The gentleman for a time read the paper intently. Then his nervous hands flung it down, and Vesper, leaning over, politely asked if he would lend it to him.

It was handed to him with a bow, and the young American was soon deep in its contents. It had been founded in the interests of the Acadiens of the Maritime Provinces, he read in fluent modern French, which greatly surprised him, as he had expected to be confronted by some curious *patois* concocted by this remnant of a foreign race isolated so long among the English. He read every word of the paper, — the cards of professional men, the advertisements of shopkeepers, the remarks on agriculture, the editorials on Canadian politics, the local news, and the story by a Parisian novelist. Finally he returned *L'Évangéline* to its owner, whose quick eyes were looking him all over in mingled curiosity and gratification, which at last culminated in the remark that it was a fine morning.

Vesper, with slow, quiet emphasis, which always imparted weight and importance to his words, assented to this, with the qualification that it was chilly.

"It is never very warm here until the end of June," said the stout gentleman, with a courteous gesture, "but I find this weather most agreeable for wheeling. I am shortly to leave the train and take to my bicycle for the remainder of my journey."

Vesper asked him whether there was a good road along the shores of the Bay.

"The best in the province, but I regret to say that the roads to it from the stations are cut up by heavy teaming."

"And the hotels, — are they good?"

"According to the guide-books there are none in Frenchtown," said the gentleman, with lively sarcasm. " I know of one or two where one can be comfortable. Here, for instance," and one of his facile hands indicated a modest advertisement in *L'Évangéline.*

> Sleeping Water Inn. This inn, well patronized in the past, is still the rendezvous for tourists, bicyclists, etc. The house is airy, and the table is good. A trustworthy teamster is always at the train to carry trunks and valises to the inn. Rose de Forêt, Proprietress.

Vesper looked up, to find his neighbor smiling involuntarily. " Pardon me," he said, with contrition, " I am thinking that you would find the house satisfactory."

" It is kept by a woman ? "

" Yes," said the stranger, with preternatural gravity ; " Rose à Charlitte."

Vesper said nothing, and his face was rarely an index of his thoughts, yet the stranger, knowing in some indefinable way that he wished for further information, continued. " On the Bay, the friendly fashion prevails of using only the first name. Rose à Charlitte is rarely called Madame de Forêt."

Vesper saw that some special interest attached to the proprietress of the Acadien inn, yet did not see his way clear to find out what it was. His new acquaintance, however, had a relish for his subject of conversation, and pursued it with satisfaction. " She is very remarkable, and makes money, yet I hope that fate will intervene to preserve her from a life which is, perhaps, too public for a woman of her stamp. A rich uncle, one Auguste Le Noir, whose beautiful home among orange and fig trees on the Bayou Vermillon in Louisiana I visited last year, may perhaps rescue her. Not that she does anything at all out of the way," he added, hastily, "but she is beautiful and young."

Vesper repressed a slight start at the mention of the name Le Noir, then asked calmly if it was a common one among the Acadiens.

The Le Noirs and Le Blancs, the gentleman assured him, were as plentiful as blackberries, while as to Melançons, there were eighty families of them on the Bay. "This has given rise to the curious house-that-Jack-built system of naming," he said. "There is Jean à Jacques Melançon, which is Jean, the son of Jacques, — Jean à Basile, Jean à David, and sometimes Jean à Martin à Conrade à Benoit Melançon, but" — and he checked himself quickly — "I am, perhaps, wearying you with all this?" He was as a man anxious, yet hesitating, to impart information, and Vesper hastened to assure him that he was deeply interested in the Acadiens.

The cloud swept from the face of the vivacious gentleman. "You gratify me. The old prejudice against my countrymen still lingers in this province in the shape of indifference. I rarely discuss them unless I know my listener."

"Have I the pleasure of addressing an Acadien?" asked Vesper.

"I have the honor to be one," said the stout gentleman, and his face flushed like that of a girl.

Vesper gave him a quick glance. This was the first Acadien that he had ever seen, and he was about as far removed from the typical Acadien that he had pictured to himself as a man could be. This man was a gentleman. He had expected to find the Acadiens, after all the trials they had gone through in their dispossession of property and wanderings by sea and land, degenerated into a despoiled and poverty-stricken remnant of peasantry. Curiously gratified by the discovery that here was one who had not gone under in the stress of war and persecution, he remarked that his companion was probably well-informed on the subject of the expulsion of his countrymen from this province.

"The expulsion, — ah!" said the gentleman, in a repressed voice. Then, unable to proceed, he made a helpless gesture and turned his face towards the window.

The younger man thought that there were tears in his eyes, and forbore to speak.

"One mentions it so calmly nowadays," said the Acadien, presently, looking at him. "There is no passion, no resentment, yet it is a living flame in the breast of every true Acadien, and this is the reason, — it is a tragedy that is yet championed. It is commonly believed that the deportation of the Acadiens was a necessity brought about by their stubbornness."

"That is the view I have always taken of it," said Vesper, mildly. "I have never looked into the subject exhaustively, but my conclusion from desultory reading has been that the Acadiens were an obstinate set of people who dictated terms to the English, which, as a conquered race, they should not have done, and they got transported for it."

"Then let me beg you, my dear sir, to search into the matter. If you happen to visit the Sleeping Water Inn, ask for Agapit Le Noir. He is an enthusiast on the subject, and will inform you; and if at any time you find yourself in our beautiful city of Halifax, may I not beg the pleasure of a call? I shall be happy to lay before you some historical records of our race," and he offered Vesper a card on which was engraved, Dr. Bernardin Arseneau, Barrington Street, Halifax.

Vesper took the card, thanked him, and said, "Shall I find any of the descendants of the settlers of Grand Pré among the Acadiens on this Bay?"

"Many, many of them. When the French first came to Nova Scotia, they naturally selected the richest portions of the province. At the expulsion these farms were seized. When, through incredible hardships, they came struggling back to this country that they so much loved, they could not believe that their lands would not be restored to them. Many of them trudged on foot to fertile Grand Pré, to Port Royal, and other places. They looked in amazement at the settlers who had taken their homes. You know who they were?"

"No, I do not," said Vesper.

"They were your own countrymen, my dear sir, if, as I rightly judge, you come from the United States. They came to this country, and found waiting for them the fertile fields whose owners had been seized, imprisoned, tortured, and carried to foreign countries, some years before. Such is the justice of the world. For their portion the returned Acadiens received this strip of forest on the Bay Saint-Mary. You will see what they have made of it," and, with a smile at once friendly and sad, the stout gentleman left the train and descended to a little station at which they had just pulled up.

CHAPTER IV.

THE SLEEPING WATER INN.

"Montrez-moi votre menu et je vous montrerai mon cœur."

A FEW minutes later, the train had again entered the forest, and Vesper, who had a passion for trees and ranked them with human beings in his affections, allowed the mystery and charm of these foreigners to steal over him. In dignified silence and reserve the tall pines seemed to draw back from the rude contact of the passing train. The more assertive firs and spruces stood still, while the slender hackmatacks, most beautiful of all the trees of the wood, writhed and shook with fright, nervously tossing their tremulous arms and tasselled heads, and breathing long odoriferous sighs that floated after, but did not at all touch the sympathies of the roaring monster from the outer world who so often desecrated their solitude.

Vesper's delicate nostrils dilated as the spicy odors saluted them, and he thought, with tenderness, of the home trees that he loved, the elms of the Common and those of the square where he had been born. How many times he had encircled them with admiring footsteps, noting the individual characteristics of each tree, and giving to each one a separate place in his heart. Just for an instant he regretted that for to-night he could not lie down in their shadow. Then he turned irritably to the salesman, who was stretching and shaking out his legs, and performing other calisthenic exploits as accompaniments of waking.

"Haven't we come to Great Scott yet?" he asked, getting up, and sauntering to Vesper's window.

Vesper consulted his folder. Among the French names he could discover nothing like this, unless it was Grosses Coques, so called, his guide-book told him, because the Acadiens had discovered enormous clams there.

The salesman settled the question by dabbing at the name with his fat forefinger. "Confound these French names, and thank the Lord they're beginning to give them up. This Sleeping Water we're coming to used to be *L'Eau Dormante*. If I had my way, I'd string up on these pines every fellow that spoke a word of this gibberish. That would cure 'em. Why can't they have one language, as we do?"

"How would you like to talk French?" asked Vesper, quietly.

The little man laughed shrewdly, and not unkindly. "Every man to his liking. I guess it's best not to fight too much."

"I get off here," said Vesper, gathering up his papers.

"Happy you, — you won't have to wait for all of Evangeline's heifers to step off the track between here and Halifax."

Vesper nodded to him, and, swinging himself from the car, went to find the conductor.

There was ample time to get that gentlemanly official's consent to have his wheel and trunk put off at this station, instead of at Grand Pré, and ample time for Vesper to give a long look at the names in the line of cars, which were, successively, Basil the Blacksmith, Benedict the Father, René the Notary, and Gabriel the Lover, before the locomotive snuffed its nostrils and, panting and heaving, started off to trail its romantic appendages through the country of Evangeline.

When the train had disappeared, Vesper looked about him. He was no longer in the heart of the forest. An open country and scattering houses appeared in the distance, and here he could distinctly feel a mischievous breeze from the Bay that playfully ruffled his hair, and tossed back the violets at his feet every time that they bent over to look at their own sweet faces in the black, mirror-like pool of water set in a mossy bed beside them.

He stooped and picked one of the wistful purple blossoms, then stepped up on the platform of the gabled station-house. Inside the kitchen, a woman, sitting with her back to the passing trains, was spinning, and at the same time rocking a cradle, while near the door stood an individual who, to Vesper's secret amusement, might have posed either as a member of the human species, or as one of the class *aves*.

He had many times seen the fellows of this white-haired, smooth-faced old man, in the Southern States in the shape of cardinal-birds. Those resplendent creatures in the male sex are usually clothed in gay red jackets. This male's plumage was also red, but, unlike the cardinal-birds, it had a trimming of pearl buttons and white lace. The bird's high and conical crest was expressed in the man by a pointed red cap. The bird is nondescript as to the legs, — so also was the man; and the loud and musical note of the Southern songster was reproduced in the fife-like tones of the Acadien, when he presently spoke.

He was an official, and carried in his hand a locked bag containing her Majesty's mail for her Acadien subjects of the Bay. Vesper had seen the mail-carriers along the route, tossing their bags to the passing train, and receiving others in return, but none as gorgeous as this one, and he was wondering why the gentle-faced septuagenarian made himself so peculiar, when he was addressed in a sweet, high voice.

"Sir," said the bird-man, in French, — for was he not Emmanuel Victor De la Rive, lineal descendant of a French marquis who had married a queen's maid of honor, and had subsequently bequeathed his bones and his large family of children to his adored Acadie?— "Sir, is it possible that you are a guest for the inn?"

"It is possible," said Vesper, gravely.

"Alas!" said the old man, turning to the dark-eyed woman, who had left her cradle and spinning-wheel, "is it not always so? When Rose à Charlitte does not send, there are arrivals. When she does, there are not. She will be in despair. Sir, shall I have the honor of taking you over in my road-cart?"

"I have a wheel," said Vesper, pointing to the bicycle, leaning disconsolately against his trunk.

The black-eyed woman immediately put out her hand for his checks.

"Then may I have the honor of showing you the way?" said Monsieur De la Rive, bowing before Vesper as if he were a divinity. "There are sides of the road which it is well to avoid."

"I shall be most happy to avail myself of your offer."

"I will send the trunk over," said the station woman. "There is a constant going that way."

Vesper thanked her, and left the station in the wake of the cardinal-bird, who sat perched on his narrow seat as easily as if it were a branch of a tree, turning his crested head at frequent intervals to look anxiously at the mail-bag which, for reasons best known to himself, he carried slung to a nail in the back of his cart.

At frequent intervals, too, he piped shrill and sweet remarks to Vesper. "Courage; the road will soon improve. It is the ox-teams that cut it up. They load schooners in the Bay. Here at last is a good spot. Monsieur can mount now. Beware of the sharp stones. All the bones of the earth stick up in places. Does monsieur intend to stay long in Sleeping Water? Was it monsieur that Rose à Charlitte expected when she drove through the pouring rain to the station, two days since? What did he say in the letter that he sent yesterday in explanation of his change of plans? Did monsieur come from Halifax, or Boston? Did he know Mrs. de la Rive, laundress, of Cambridge Street? Had he samples of candy or tobacco in that big box of his? How much did he charge a pound for his best peppermints?"

Vesper, fully occupied with keeping his wheel out of the ruts in the road, and in maintaining a safe distance from the cart, which pressed him sore if he went ahead and waited for him if he dallied behind, answered "yes" and "no" at random, until at length he had involved himself in such a maze of contradictions that Monsieur de la Rive felt himself forced to pull up his brown pony and remonstrate.

"But it is impossible, monsieur, that you should have seen Mrs. de la Rive, who has been dying for weeks, dancing at the wedding of the daughter of her step-uncle, the baker, and yet you say 'yes' when I remark that she was not there."

The stop and the remonstrance were so birdlike and so quick, that Vesper, taken aback, fell off his wheel and broke his cyclometer.

He picked himself out of the dust, swearing under his breath, and Monsieur de la Rive, being a gentleman, and seeing that this quiet young stranger was disinclined for conversation, suddenly whipped up his pony and sped madly on ahead, the tails of his red coat streaming out behind him, the tip of his pointed cap fluttering and nodding over his thick white locks of hair.

After the lapse of a few minutes, Vesper had recovered his composure, and was looking calmly about him. The road was better now, and they were nearing the Bay, that lay shimmering and shining like a great sea-serpent coiled between purple hills. He did not know what Grand Pré was like, and was therefore unaware of the extent of the Acadiens' loss in being driven from it; but this was by no means a barren country. On either side of him were fairly prosperous farms, each one with a light painted wooden house, around which clustered usually a group of children, presided over by a mother, who, as the mail-driver dashed by, would appear in the doorway, thrusting forth her matronly face, often partly shrouded by a black handkerchief.

These black handkerchiefs, *la cape Normande* of old France, were almost universal on the heads of women and girls. He could see them in the fields and up and down the roads. They and the vivacious sound of the French tongue gave the foreign touch to his surroundings, which he found, but for these reminders, might once again have been those of an out-of-the-way district in some New England State.

He noticed, with regret, that the forest had all been swept away. The Acadiens, in their zeal for farming, had wielded their axes so successfully that scarcely a tree had been left between the station and the Bay. Here and there stood a lonely guardian angel, in the shape of a solitary pine, hovering over some Acadien roof-tree, and turning a melancholy face towards its brothers of the forest, — rugged giants primeval, now prostrate and forlorn, and being trailed slowly along towards the waiting schooners in the Bay.

The most of these fallen giants were loaded on rough carts drawn by pairs of sleek and well-kept oxen who were yoked by the horns. The carts were covered with mud from the bad roads of the forest, and muddy also were the boots of the stalwart Acadien drivers, who walked beside the oxen, whip in hand, and turned frankly curious faces towards the stranger who flashed by their slow-moving teams on his shining wheel.

The road was now better, and Vesper quickly attained to the top of the last hill between the station and the Bay.

Ah! now the fields did not appear bare, the houses naked, the whole country wind-swept and cold, for the wide, regal, magnificent Bay lay spread out before him. It was no longer a thread of light, a sea-serpent shining in the distance, but a great, broad, beautiful basin, on whose placid bosom all the Acadien, New England, and Nova Scotian fleets might float with never a jostle between any of their ships.

A fire of admiration kindled in his calm eyes, and he allowed himself to glide rapidly down the hill towards this brilliant blue sweep of water, along whose nearer shores stretched, as far as his gaze could reach, the curious dotted line of the French village.

The country had become flat, as flat as Holland, and the fields rolled down into the water in the softest, most exquisite shades of green, according to the different kinds of grass or grain flourishing along the shores. The houses were placed among the fields, some close together, some far apart, all, however, but a stone's throw from the water's edge, as if the Acadiens, fearful of another expulsion, held themselves always in readiness to step into the procession of boats and schooners moored almost in their dooryards.

At the point where Vesper found himself threatened with precipitation into the Bay, they struck the village line. Here, at the corner, was the general shop and post-office of Sleeping Water. The cardinal-bird fluttered his mail-bag in among the loafers at the door, saw the shopkeeper catch it, then, swelling out his vermilion breast with importance, he nimbly took the corner with one wheel in the air and pulled up before the largest, whitest house on the street, and flourished a flaming wing in the direction of a swinging sign, — "The Sleeping Water Inn."

Vesper, biting his lip to restrain a smile, rounded the corner after him, and leisurely stepped from his wheel in front of the house.

"Ring, sir, and enter," piped the bird, then, wishing him *bonne chance* (good luck), he flew away.

Vesper pulled the bell, and, as no one answered his summons, he sauntered through the open door into the hall.

So this was an Acadien house,—and he had expected a log hut. He could command a view from where he stood of a staircase, a smoking-room, and a parlor,—all clean, cool, and comfortably furnished, and having easy chairs, muslin curtains, books, and pictures.

He smiled to himself, murmured "I wonder where the dining-room is? These flies will probably know," and followed a prosperous-looking swarm sailing through the hall to a distant doorway.

A table, covered by a snowy cloth and set ready for a meal, stood before him. He walked around it, rapped on a door, behind which he heard a murmur of voices, and was immediately favored with a sight of an Acadien kitchen.

This one happened to be large, lofty, and of a grateful irregularity in shape. The ceiling was as white as snow, and a delicate blue and cream paper adorned the walls. The floor was of hard wood and partly covered with brightly colored mats, made by the skilful fingers of Acadien women. There were several windows and doors, and two pantries, but no fireplace. An enormous Boston cooking range took its place. Every cover on it glistened with blacking, every bit of nickel plating was polished to the last degree, and, as if to show that this model stove could not possibly be malevolent enough to throw out impurities in the way of soot and ashes, there stood beside it a tall clothes-horse full of white ironed clothes hung up to air.

But the most remarkable thing in this exquisitely clean kitchen was the mistress of the inn, — tall, willowy Mrs. Rose à Charlitte, who stood confronting the newcomer with a dish-cover in one hand and a clean napkin in the other, her pretty oval face flushed from some sacrifice she had been offering up on her huge Moloch of a stove.

"Can you give me some lunch?" asked Vesper, and he wondered whether he should find a descendant of the Fiery Frenchman in this placid beauty, whose limpid blue eyes, girlish, innocent gaze, and thick braid of hair, with the little confusion of curls on the forehead, reminded him rather of a Gretchen or a Marguerite of the stage.

"But yes," said Mrs. Rose à Charlitte, in uncertain yet pretty English, and her gentle and demure glance scrutinized him with some shrewdness and accurate guessing as to his attainments and station in life.

"Can you give it to me soon?" he asked.

"I can give it soon," she replied, and as she spoke she made an almost imperceptible motion of her head in the direction of the neat maid-servant behind her, who at once flew out to the garden for fresh vegetables, while, with her foot, which was almost as slender as her hand, Mrs. Rose à Charlitte pulled out a damper in the stove that at once caused a still more urgent draft to animate the glowing wood inside.

"Can you let me have a room?" pursued Vesper.

"Yes, sir," said Mrs. Rose, and she turned to the third occupant of the kitchen, a pale child with a flowerlike face and large, serious eyes, who sat with folded hands in a little chair. "Narcisse," she said, in French, "wilt thou go and show the judge's room?"

The child, without taking his fascinated gaze from Vesper, responded, in a sweet, drawling voice, "*Ou-a-a-y, ma ma-r-re*" (yes, my mother). Then, rising, he trotted slowly through the dining-room and up the staircase to a hall above, where he gravely threw open the door of a good-sized chamber, whose chief ornament was a huge white bed.

"Why do you call this the judge's room?" asked Vesper, in French.

The child answered him in unintelligible childish speech, that made the young man observe him intently. "I believe you look like me, you black lily," he said, at last.

There was, indeed, a resemblance between their two heads. Both had pale, inscrutable faces, dark eyes, and curls like midnight clustering over their white foreheads. Both were serious, grave, and reserved in expression. The child stared up at

Vesper, then, seizing one of his hands, he patted it gently with his tiny fingers. They were friends.

Vesper allowed the child to hold his hand until he plunged his head into a basin of cold water. Then, with water dripping from his face, he paused to examine a towel before he would press it against his sensitive skin. It was fine and perfectly clean, and, with a satisfied air, he murmured: "So far, Doctor Arseneau has not led me astray."

The child waited patiently until the stranger had smoothed down his black curls, then, stretching out a hand, he mutely invited him to descend to the parlor.

Upon arriving there, he modestly withdrew to a corner, after pointing out a collection of photographs on the table. Vesper made a pretence of examining them until the entrance of his landlady with the announcement that his lunch was served.

She shyly set before him a plate of soup, and a dish which she called a little *ragoût*, "not as good as the *ragoûts* of Boston, and yet eatable."

"How do you know that I am from Boston?" asked Vesper.

"I do not know," she murmured, with a quick blush. "Monsieur is from Halifax, I thought. He seems English. I speak of Boston because it was there that I learned to cook."

Vesper said nothing, but his silence seemed to

invite a further explanation, and she went on, modestly: "When I received news that my husband had died of yellow fever in the West Indies, neighbors said, 'What will you do?' My stepmother said, 'Come home;' but I answered, 'No; a child that has left its father's roof does not return. I will keep hotel. My house is of size. I will go to Boston and learn to cook better than I know.' So I went, and stayed one week."

"That was a short time to learn cooking," observed Vesper, politely.

"I did not study. I bought *cuisine* books. I went to grand hotels and regarded the tables and tasted the dishes. If I now had more money, I would do similar," and she anxiously surveyed her modest table and the aristocratic young man seated at it; "but not many people come, and the money lacks. However, our Lord knows that I wish to educate my child. Strangers will come when he is older.

"And," she went on, after a time, with mingled reluctance and honesty, "I must not hide from you that I have already in the bank two hundred dollars. It is not much; not so much as the Gautreaus, who have six hundred, and Agapit, who has four, yet it is a starting."

Vesper slightly wrinkled his forehead, and Mrs. Rose, fearful that her cooking displeased him, for he had scarcely tasted the *ragoût* and had put aside a roast chicken, hastened to exclaim, "That pudding is but overheated, and I did wrong to place it before you. Despise it if you care, and it will please the hens."

"It is a very good pudding," said Vesper, composedly, and he proceeded to finish it.

"Here is a custard which is quite fresh," said his landlady, feverishly, "and bananas, and oranges, and some coffee."

"Thank you. No cream — may I ask why you call that room you put me in the judge's room?"

"Because we have court near by, every year. The judge who comes exists in that room. It is a most stirabout time, for many witnesses and lawyers come. Perhaps monsieur passed the court-house and saw a lady looking through the bars?"

"No, I did not. Who is the lady?"

"A naughty one, who sold liquor. She had no license, she could not pay her fine, therefore she must look through those iron bars," and Mrs. Rose à Charlitte shuddered.

Vesper looked interested, and presently she went on: "But Clothilde Dubois has some mercies, — one rocking-chair, her own feather bed, some dainties to eat, and many friends to visit and talk through the bars."

"Is there much drinking among the Acadiens on this Bay?" asked Vesper.

"They do not drink at all," she said, stoutly.

"Really, — then you never see a drunken man?"

"I never see a drunken man," rejoined his pretty hostess.

"Then I suppose there are no fights."

"There are no fights among Acadiens. They are good people. They go to mass and vespers on Sunday. They listen to their good priests. In the evening one amuses oneself, and on Monday we rise early to work. There are no dances, no fights."

Vesper's meditative glance wandered through the window to a square of grass outside, where some little girls in pink cotton dresses were playing croquet. He was drinking his coffee and watching their graceful behavior, when his attention was recalled to the room by hearing Mrs. Rose à Charlitte say to her child, "There, Narcisse, is a morsel for thy trees."

The little boy had come from the corner where he had sat like a patient mouse, and, with some excitement, was heaping a plate with the food that Vesper had rejected.

"Not so fast, little one," said his mother, with an apologetic glance at the stranger. "Take these plates to the pantry, it will be better."

"Ah, but they will have a good dinner to-day," said the child. "I will give most to the French willows, my mother. In the morning it will all be gone."

"But, my treasure, it is the dogs that get it, not the trees."

"No, my mother," he drawled, "you do not know. In the night the long branches stretch out their arms; they sweep it up," and he clasped his tiny hands in ecstacy.

Vesper's curiosity was aroused, although he had not understood half that the child had said. "Does he like trees?" he asked.

Rose à Charlitte made a puzzled gesture. "Sir, to him the trees, the flowers, the grass, are quite alive. He will not play croquet with those dear little girls lest his shoes hurt the grass. If I would allow, he would take all the food from the house and lay under the trees and the flowers. He often cries at night, for he says the hollyhocks and sunflowers are hungry, because they are tall and lean. He suffers terribly to see the big spruces and pines cut down and dragged to the shore. The doctor says he should go away for awhile, but it is a puzzle, for I cannot endure to have him leave me."

Vesper gave more attention than he yet had done to the perusal of the child's sensitive yet strangely composed face. Then he glanced at the mother. Did she understand him?

She did. In her deep blue eyes he could readily perceive the quick flash of maternal love and sympathy whenever her boy spoke to her. She was young, too, extremely young, to have the care of rearing a child. She must have been married in her cradle, and with that thought in mind he said, "Do Acadien women marry at an early age?"

"Not more so than the English," said Mrs. Rose, with a shrug of her graceful, sloping shoulders, "though I was but young, — but seventeen. But my husband wished it so. He had built this house. He had been long ready for marriage," and she glanced at the wall behind Vesper.

The young man turned around. Just behind him hung the enlarged photograph of a man of middle age, — a man who must have been many years older than his young wife, and whose death had, evidently, not left a permanent blank in her affections.

In a naïve, innocent way she imparted a few more particulars to Vesper with regard to her late husband, and, as he rose from the table, she followed him to the parlor and said, gently, "Perhaps monsieur will register."

Vesper sat down before the visitors' book on the table, and, taking up a pen, wrote, "Vesper L. Nimmo, *The Evening News*, Boston."

After he had pressed the blotting-paper on his words, and pushed the book from him, his landlady stretched out her hand in childlike curiosity. "Vesper," she said, — "that name is beautiful; it is in a hymn to the blessed virgin; but *Evening News*, — surely it means not a journal?"

Vesper assured her that it did.

The young French widow's face fell. She gazed at him with a sudden and inexplicable change of expression, in which there was something of regret, something of reproach. "*Il faut que je m'en aille*" (I must go away), she murmured, reverting to her native language, and she swiftly withdrew.

Vesper lifted his level eyebrows and languidly strolled out to the veranda. "The Acadienne evidently entertains some prejudice against newspaper men. If my dear father were here he would immediately proceed, in his inimitable way, to clear it from her mind. As for me, I am not sufficiently interested," and he listlessly stretched himself out on a veranda settle.

"Monsieur," said a little voice, in deliberate French, "will you tell me a story about a tree?"

Vesper understood Narcisse this time, and, taking him on his knee, he pointed to the wooded hills across the Bay and related a wonderful tale of a city beyond the sun where the trees were not obliged to stand still in the earth from morning till night, but could walk about and visit men and women, who were their brothers and sisters, and sometimes the young trees would stoop down and play with the children.

CHAPTER V.

AGAPIT, THE ACADIEN.

> "The music of our life is keyed
> To moods that sweep athwart the soul;
> The strain will oft in gladness roll,
> Or die in sobs and tears at need;
> But sad or gay, 'tis ever true
> That, e'en as flowers from light take hue,
> The key is of our mood the deed."
> AMINTA. CORNELIUS O'BRIEN,
> *Archbishop of Halifax.*

AFTER Mrs. Rose à Charlitte left Vesper she passed through the kitchen, and, ascending an open stairway leading to regions above, was soon at the door of the highest room in the house.

Away up there, sitting at a large table drawn up to the window which commanded an extensive view of the Bay, sat a sturdy, black-haired young man. As Mrs. Rose entered the room she glanced about approvingly — for she was a model housekeeper — at the neatly arranged books and papers on tables and shelves, and then said, regretfully, and in French, "There is another of them."

"Of them, — of whom?" said the young man, peevishly, and in the same language.

"Of the foolish ones who write," continued Mrs. Rose, with gentle mischief; "who waste much time in scribbling."

"There are people whose brains are continually stewing over cooking-stoves," said the young man, scornfully; "they are incapable of rising higher."

"La, la, Agapit," she said, good-naturedly. "Do not be angry with thy cousin. I came to warn thee lest thou shouldst talk freely to him and afterward be sorry."

The young man threw his pen on the table, pushed back his chair, and, springing to his feet, began to pace excitedly up and down the room, gesticulating eagerly as he talked.

"When fine weather comes," he exclaimed, "strangers flock to the Bay. We are glad to see them, — all but these abominable idiots. Therefore when they arrive let the frost come, let us have hail, wind, and snow to drive them home, that we may enjoy peace."

"But unfortunately in June we have fine weather," said Mrs. Rose.

"I will insult him," said her black-haired cousin, wildly. "I will drive him from the house," and he stood on tiptoe and glared in her face.

"No, no; thou wilt do nothing of the sort, Agapit."

"I will," he said, distractedly. "I will, I will, I will."

"Agapit," said the young woman, firmly, "if it

were not for the strangers I should have only crusts for my child, not good bread and butter, therefore calm thyself. Thou must be civil to this stranger."

"I will not," he said, sullenly.

Mrs. Rose à Charlitte's temper gave way. "Pack up thy clothes," she said, angrily; "there is no living with thee, — thou art so disagreeable. Take thy old trash, thy papers so old and dusty, and leave my house. Thou wilt make me starve, — my child will not be educated. Go, — I cast thee off."

Agapit became calm as he contemplated her wrathful, beautiful face. "Thou art like all women," he said, composedly, "a little excitable at times. I am a man, therefore I understand thee," and pushing back his coat he stuck his thumbs in the armholes and majestically resumed his walk about the room.

"Come now, cease thy crying," he went on, uneasily, after a time, when Rose, who had thrown herself into a chair and had covered her face with her hands, did not look at him. "I shall not leave thee, Rose."

"He is very distinguished," she sobbed, "very polite, and his finger nails are as white as thy bedspread. He is quite a gentleman; why does he write for those wicked journals?"

"Thou hast been talking to him, Rose," said her cousin, suspiciously, stopping short and fixing her with a fiery glance; "with thy usual innocence thou hast told him all that thou dost know and ever wilt know."

Rose shuddered, and withdrew her hands from her eyes. "I told him nothing, not a word."

"Thou didst not tell him of thy wish to educate thy boy, of thy two hundred dollars in the bank, of thy husband, who teased thy stepmother till she married thee to him, nor of me, for example?" and his voice rose excitedly.

His cousin was quite composed now. "I told him nothing," she repeated, firmly.

"If thou didst do so," he continued, threateningly, "it will all come out in a newspaper, — 'Melting Innocence of an Acadien Landlady. She Tells a Reporter in Five Minutes the Story of Her Life.'"

"It will not appear," said Mrs. Rose, hastily. "He is a worthy young man, and handsome, too. There is not on the Bay a handsomer young man. I will ask him to write nothing, and he will listen to me."

"Oh, thou false one," cried the young man, half in vexation, half in perplexity. "I wish that thou wert a child, — I would shake thee till thy teeth chattered!"

Mrs. Rose ran from the room. "He is a pig, an imbecile, and he terrifies me so that I tell what is not true. What will Father Duvair say to me? I will rise at six to-morrow, and go to confession."

Vesper went early to bed that night, and slept soundly until early the next morning, when he opened his eyes to a vision of hazy green fields, a wide sheet of tremulous water, and a quiet, damp road, bordered by silent houses. He sprang from his bed, and went to the open window. The sun was just coming from behind a bank of clouds. He watched the Bay lighting up under its rays, the green fields brightening, the moisture evaporating; then hastily throwing on his clothes, he went down-stairs, unlatched the front door, and hurried across the road into a hay-field, where the newly cut grass, dripping with moisture, wet his slippered but stockingless feet.

Down by the rocks he saw a small bathing-house. He slipped off his clothes, and, clad only in a thin bathing-suit, stood shivering for an instant at the edge of the water. "It will be frightfully cold," he muttered. "Dare I — yes, I do," and he plunged boldly into the deliciously salt waves, and swam to and fro, until he was glowing from head to foot.

As he was hurrying up to the inn, a few minutes later, he saw, coming down the road, a small two-wheeled cart, in which was seated Mrs. Rose à Charlitte. She was driving a white pony, and she sat demure, charming, with an air of penitence about her, and wearing the mourning garb of Acadien women, — a plain black dress, a black shawl, and a black silk handkerchief, drawn hood-wise over her flaxen mop of hair and tied under her chin.

The young man surveyed her approvingly. She seemed to belong naturally to the cool, sweet dampness of the morning, and he guessed correctly that she had been to early mass in the white church whose steeple he could see in the distance. He was amused with the shy, embarrassed "*Bon jour*" (good morning) that she gave him as she passed, and murmuring, "The shadow of *The Evening News* is still upon her," he went to his room, and made his toilet for breakfast.

An hour later, a loud bell rang through the house, and Vesper, in making his way to the dining-room, met a reserved, sulky-faced young man in the hall, who bowed coolly and stepped aside for him to pass.

"H'm, Agapit LeNoir," reflected Vesper, darting a critical glance at him. "The Acadien who was to unbosom himself to me. He does not look as if he would enjoy the process," and he took his seat at the table, where Mrs. Rose à Charlitte, grown strangely quiet, served his breakfast in an almost unbroken silence.

Vesper thoughtfully poured some of the thick yellow cream on his porridge, and enjoyably dallied over it, but when his landlady would have set before him a dish of smoking hot potatoes and beefsteak, he said, "I do not care for anything further."

Rose à Charlitte drew back in undisguised concern. "But you have eaten nothing. Agapit has taken twice as much as this."

"That is the young man I met just now?"

"Yes, he is my cousin; very kind to me. His parents are dead, and he was brought up by my stepmother. He is so clever, so clever! It is truly strange what he knows. His uncle, who was a priest, left him many papers, and all day, when Agapit does not work, he sits and writes or reads. Some day he will be a learned man — "

Rose paused abruptly. In her regret at the stranger's want of appetite she was forgetting that she had resolved to have no further conversation with him, and in sudden confusion she made the excuse that she wished to see her child, and melted away like a snowflake, in the direction of the kitchen, where Vesper had just heard Narcisse's sweet voice asking permission to talk to the Englishman from Boston.

The young American wandered out to the stable. Two Acadiens were there, asking Agapit for the loan of a set of harness. At Vesper's approach they continued their conversation in French, although he had distinctly heard them speaking excellent English before he joined them.

These men were employing an almost new language to him. This was not the French of *L'Évangéline*, of Doctor Arseneau, nor of Rose à Charlitte.

Nor was it *patois* such as he had heard in France, and which would have been unintelligible to him. This must be the true Acadien dialect, and he listened with pleasure to the softening and sweetening of some syllables and the sharpening and ruining of others. They were saying *ung houmme*, for a man. This was not unmusical; neither was *persounne*, for nobody; but the *ang* sound so freely interspersing their sentences was detestable; as was also the reckless introduction of English phrases, such as "all right," "you bet," "how queer," "too proud," "funny," "steam-cars," and many others.

Their conversation for some time left the stable, then it returned along the line of discussion of a glossy black horse that stood in one of the stalls.

"*Ce cheval est de bounne harage*" (this horse is well-bred), said one of the Acadiens, admiringly, and Vesper's thoughts ran back to a word in the Latin grammar of his boyhood. *Hara*, a pen or stable. *De bonne race*, a modern Frenchman would be likely to say. Probably these men were speaking the language brought by their ancestors to Acadie; without doubt they were. On this Bay would be presented to him the curious spectacle of the descendants of a number of people lifted bodily out of France, and preserving in their adopted country the tongue that had been lost to the motherland. In France the language had drifted. Here the Acadiens were using the same syllables that had hung on the lips of kings, courtiers, poets, and wits of three and four hundred years ago.

With keen interest, for he had a passion for the study of languages, he carefully analyzed each sentence that he heard, until, fearing that his attitude might seem impertinent to the Acadiens, he strolled away.

His feet naturally turned in the direction of the corner, the most lively spot in Sleeping Water. In the blacksmith's shop a short, stout young Acadien with light hair, blue eyes, and a dirty face and arms, was striking the red-hot tip of a pickax with ringing blows. He nodded civilly enough to Vesper when he joined the knot of men who stood about the wide door watching him, but no one else spoke to him.

A farmer was waiting to have a pair of cream white oxen shod, a stable-keeper, from another part of *la ville française*, was impatiently chafing and fretting over the amount of time required to mend his sulky wheel, and conversing with him were two well-dressed young men, who appeared to be Acadiens from abroad spending their holidays at home.

Vesper's arrival had the effect of dispersing the little group. The stable-man moved away to his sulky, as if he preferred the vicinity of his roan horse, who gazed at him so benevolently, to that of Vesper, who surveyed him so indifferently. The farmer entered the shop and sat down on a box in a dark corner, while the Acadien young men, after cold glances at the newcomer, moved away to the post-office.

After a time Vesper remembered that he must have some Canadian stamps, and followed them. Outside the shop five or six teams were lined up. They were on their way to the wharf below, and were loaded with more of the enormous trees that he had seen the day before. Probably their sturdy strength, hoarded through long years in Acadien forests, would be devoted to the support of some warehouse or mansion in his native Puritan city, whose founders had called so loudly for the destruction of the French.

Vesper cast a regretful glance in the direction of the trees, and entered the little shop, whose well-stocked shelves were full of rolls of cotton and flannel, and boxes of groceries, confectionery, and stationery. The drivers of the ox-teams were inside, doing their shopping. They were somewhat rougher in appearance than the inhabitants of Sleeping Water, and were louder and noisier in their conversation. Vesper saw a young Acadien whisper a few words to one of them, and the teamster in return scowled fiercely at him, and muttered something about "a goddam Yankee."

The young American stared coolly at him, and,

going up to the counter, purchased his stamps from a fat man in shirt-sleeves, who served him with exquisite and distant courtesy. Then, leaving the shop, he shrugged his shoulders, and went back the way he had come, murmuring, in amused curiosity, "I must solve this mystery of *The Evening News*. My friend Agapit is infecting all who come within the circle of his influence."

He walked on past the inn, staring with interest at the houses bordering the road. A few were very small, a few very old. He could mark the transition of a family in some cases from their larval state in a low, gray, caterpillar-like house of one story to a gay-winged butterfly home of two or three stories. However, on the whole, the dwellings were nearly all of the same size, — there were no sharp distinctions between rich and poor. He saw no peasants, no pampered landlords. These Acadiens all seemed to be small farmers, and all were on an equality.

The creaking of an approaching team caught his attention. It was drawn by a pair of magnificent red oxen, groomed as carefully as if they had been horses, and beside them walked an old man, who was holding an ejaculatory conversation with them in English; for the Acadiens of the Bay Saint-Mary always address their oxen and horses as if they belonged to the English race.

"I wonder whether this worthy man in homespun

has been informed that I am a kind of leper," reflected Vesper, as he uttered a somewhat guarded "*Bon jour.*"

"*Bon jour,*" said the old man, delightedly, and he halted and admonished his companions to do the same.

"*Il fait beau*" (it is a fine day), pursued Vesper, cautiously.

"*Oui, mais je crais qu'il va mouiller*" (yes, but I think it is going to rain), said the Acadien, with gentle affability; then he went on, apologetically, and in English, "I do not speak the good French."

"It is the best of French," said Vesper, "for it is old."

"And you," continued the old man, not to be outdone in courtesy, "you speak like the sisters of St. Joseph who once called at my house. Their words were like round pebbles dropping from their mouths."

Vesper smoothed his mustache, and glanced kindly at his aged companion, who proceeded to ask him whether he was staying at the inn. "Ah, it is a good inn," he went on, "and Rose à Charlitte is *très-smart, très-smart.* Perhaps you do not understand my English," he added, when Vesper did not reply to him.

"On the contrary, I find that you speak admirably."

"You are kind," said the old man, shaking his

head, "but my English langwidge is spiled since my daughter went to Bostons, for I talk to no one. She married an Irish boy; he is a nusser."

"An usher, — in a theatre?"

"No, sir, in a cross-spittal. He nusses sick people, and gets two dollars a day."

"Oh, indeed."

"Do you come from Bostons?" asked the old man.

"Yes, I do."

"And do you know my daughter?"

"What is her name?"

The Acadien reflected for some time, then said it was MacCraw, whereupon Vesper assured him that he had never had the pleasure of meeting her.

"Is your trade an easy one?" asked the old man, wistfully.

"No; very hard."

"You are then a farmer."

"No; I wish I were. My trade is taking care of my health."

The Acadien examined him from head to foot. "Your face is beautifuller than a woman's, but you are poorly built."

Vesper drew up his straight and slender figure. He was not surprised that it did not come up to the Acadien's standard of manly beauty.

"Let us shake hands lest we never meet again,"

said the old man, so gently, so kindly, and with so much benevolence, that Vesper responded, warmly, "I hope to see you some other time."

"Perhaps you will call. We are but poor, yet if it would please you — "

"I shall be most happy. Where do you live?"

"Near the low down brook, way off there. Demand Antoine à Joe Rimbaut," and, smiling and nodding farewell, the old man moved on.

"A good heart," said Vesper, looking after him.

"Caw, caw," said a solemn voice at his elbow.

He turned around. One of the blackest of crows sat on a garden fence that surrounded a neat pink cottage. The cottage was itself smothered in lilacs, whose fragrant blossoms were in their prime, although the Boston lilacs had long since faded and died.

"Do not be afraid, sir," said a woman in the inevitable handkerchief, who jumped up from a flower bed that she was weeding, "he is quite tame."

"*Un corbeau apprivoisé*" (a tame crow), said Vesper, lifting his cap.

"*Un corbeau privé*, we say," she replied, shyly. "You speak the good French, like the priests out of France."

She was not a very young woman, nor was she very pretty, but she was delightfully modest and retiring in her manner, and Vesper, leaning against the fence, assured her that he feared the Acadiens were lacking in a proper appreciation of their ability to speak their own language.

After a time he looked over the fields behind her cottage, and asked the name of a church crowning a hill in the distance.

"It is the Saulnierville church," she replied, "but you must not walk so far. You will stay to dinner?"

While Vesper was politely declining her invitation, a Frenchman with a long, pointed nose, and bright, sharp eyes, came around the corner of the house.

"He is my husband," said the woman. "Edouard, this gentleman speaks the good French."

The Acadien warmly seconded the invitation of his wife that Vesper should stay to dinner, but he escaped from them with smiling thanks and a promise to come another day.

"They never saw me before, and they asked me to stay to dinner. That is true hospitality, — they have not been infected. I will make my way back to the inn, and interview that sulky beggar."

CHAPTER VI.

VESPER SUGGESTS AN EXPLANATION.

"Glad of a quarrel straight I clap the door;
Sir, let me see you and your works no more."
POPE.

AT twelve o'clock Mrs. Rose à Charlitte was standing in her cold pantry deftly putting a cap of icing on a rich rounded loaf of cake, when she heard a question asked, in Vesper's smooth neutral tones, "Where is madame?"

She stepped into the kitchen, and found that he was interrogating her servant Célina.

"I should like to speak to that young man I saw this morning," he said, when he saw her.

"He has gone out, monsieur," she replied, after a moment's hesitation.

"Which is his room?"

"The one by the smoking-room," she answered, with a deep blush.

Vesper's white teeth gleamed through his dark mustache, and, seeing that he was laughing at her, she grew confused, and hung her head.

"Can I get to it by this staircase?" asked Vesper,

exposing her petty deceit. "I think I can by going up to the roof, and dropping down."

Mrs. Rose lifted her head long enough to flash him a scrutinizing glance. Then, becoming sensible of the determination of purpose under his indifference of manner, she said, in scarcely audible tones, "I will show you."

"I have only a simple question to ask him," said Vesper, reassuringly, as he followed her towards the staircase.

"Agapit is quick like lightning," she said, over her shoulder, "but his heart is good. He helps to keep our grandmother, who spends her days in bed."

"That is exemplary. I would be the last one to hurt the feelings of the prop of an aged person," murmured Vesper.

Rose à Charlitte was not satisfied. She unwillingly mounted the stairs, and pointed out the door of her cousin's room, then withdrew to the next one, and listened anxiously in case there might be some disturbance between the young men. There was none; so, after a time, she went down-stairs.

Agapit, at Vesper's entrance, abruptly pushed back his chair from the table and, rising, presented a red and angry face to his visitor.

"I have interrupted you, I fear," said Vesper, smoothly. "I will not detain you long. I merely wish to ask a question."

"Will you sit down?" said Agapit, sulkily, and he forced himself to offer the most comfortable chair in the room to his caller.

Vesper did not seat himself until he saw that Agapit was prepared to follow his example. Then he looked into the black eyes of the Acadien, which were like two of the deep, dark pools in the forest, and said, "A matter of business has brought me to this Bay. I may have some inquiries to make, in which I would find myself hampered by any prejudice among persons I might choose to question. I fancy that some of the people here look on me with suspicion. I am quite unaware of having given offence in any way. Possibly you can explain, — I am not bent on an explanation, you understand. If you choose to offer one, I shall be glad to listen."

He spoke listlessly, tapping on the table with his fingers, and allowing his eyes to wander around the room, rather than to remain fixed on Agapit's face.

The young Acadien could scarcely restrain a torrent of words until Vesper had finished speaking.

"Since you ask, I will explain, — yes, I will not be silent. We are not rude here, — oh, no. We are too kind to strangers. Vipers have crept in among us. They have stolen heat and warmth from our bosoms"— he paused, choking with rage.

"And you have reason to suppose that I may prove a viper?" asked Vesper, indolently.

"Yes, you also are one. You come here, we receive you. You depart, you laugh in your sleeve, — a newspaper comes. We see it all. The meek and patient Acadiens are once more held up to be a laughing-stock."

Vesper wrinkled his level eyebrows. "Perhaps you will characterize this viperish conduct?"

Agapit calmed himself slightly. "Wait but an instant. Control your curiosity, and I will give you something to read," and he went on his knees, and rummaged among some loose papers in an open box. "Look at it," he said, at last, springing up and handing his caller a newspaper; "read, and possibly you will understand."

Vesper's quick eye ran over the sheet that he held up. "This is a New York weekly paper. Yes, I know it well. What is there here that concerns you?"

"Look, look here," said Agapit, tapping a column in the paper with an impatient gesture. "Read the nonsense, the drivel, the insanity of the thing — "

"Ah, — 'Among the Acadiens, Quaintness Unrivalled, Archaic Forms of Speech, A Dance and a Wedding, The Spirit of Evangeline, Humorous Traits, If You Wish a Good Laugh Go Among Them!'"

"She laughed in print, she screamed in black ink!" exclaimed Agapit. "The silly one, — the witch."

"Who was she, — this lady viper?" asked Vesper, briefly.

"She was a woman — a newspaper woman. She spent a summer among us. She gloomed about the beach with a shawl on her shoulders; a small dog followed her. She laid in bed. She read novels, and then," he continued, with rising voice, "she returned home, she wrote this detestability about us."

"Why need you care?" . said Vesper, coolly. "She had to reel off a certain amount of copy. All correspondents have to do so. She only touched up things a little to make lively reading."

"Not touching up, but manufacturing," retorted Agapit, with blazing eyes. "She had nothing to go on, nothing — nothing — nothing. We are just like other people," and he ruffled his coal-black hair with both his hands, and looked at his caller fiercely. "Do you not find us so?"

"Not exactly," said Vesper, so dispassionately and calmly, and with such statuesque repose of manner, that he seemed rather to breathe the words than to form them with his lips.

"And you will express that in your paper. You will not tell the truth. My countrymen will never have justice, — never, never. They are always misrepresented, always."

"What a firebrand!" reflected Vesper, and he surveyed, with some animation, the inflamed, suspicious face of the Frenchman.

"You also will caricature us," pursued Agapit; "others have done so, why should not you?"

Vesper's lips parted. He was on the point of imparting to Agapit the story of his great-grandfather's letter. Then he closed them. Why should he be browbeaten into communicating his private affairs to a stranger?

"Thank you," he said, and he rose to leave the room. "I am obliged for the information you have given me."

Agapit's face darkened; he would dearly love to secure a promise of good behavior from this stranger, who was so non-committal, so reserved, and yet so strangely attractive.

"See," he said, grandly, and flinging his hand in the direction of his books and papers. "To an honest man, really interested in my people, I would be pleased to give information. I have many documents, many books."

"Ah, you take an interest in this sort of thing," said Vesper.

"An interest — I should die without my books and papers; they are my life."

"And yet you were cut out for a farmer," thought Vesper, as he surveyed Agapit's sturdy frame. "I suppose you have the details of the expulsion at your fingers' ends," he said, aloud.

"Ah, the expulsion," muttered Agapit, turning deathly pale, "the abominable, damnable expulsion!"

"Your feelings run high on the subject," murmured Vesper.

"It suffocates me, it chokes me, when I reflect how it was brought about. You know, of course, that in the eighteenth century there flourished a devil, — no, not a devil," contemptuously. "What is that for a word? Devil, devil, — it is so common that there is no badness in it. Even the women say, 'Poor devil, I pity him.' Say, rather, there was a god of infamy, the blackest, the basest, the most infernal of created beings that our Lord ever permitted to pollute this earth — "

For a minute he became incoherent, then he caught his breath. "This demon, this arch-fiend, the misbegotten Lawrence that your historian Parkman sets himself to whitewash — "

"I know of Parkman," said Vesper, coldly, "he was once a neighbor of ours."

"Was he!" exclaimed Agapit, in a paroxysm of excitement. "A fine neighbor, a worthy man! Parkman, — the New England story-teller, the traducer, who was too careless to set himself to the task of investigating records."

Vesper was not prepared to hear any abuse of his

countryman, and, turning on his heel, he left the room, while Agapit, furious to think that, unasked, he had been betrayed into furnishing a newspaper correspondent with some crumbs of information that might possibly be dished up in appetizing form for the delectation of American readers, slammed the door behind him, and went back to his writing.

CHAPTER VII.

A DEADLOCK.

" I found the fullest summer here
Between these sloping meadow-hills and yon;
And came all beauty then, from dawn to dawn,
Whether the tide was veiled or flowing clear."

J. F. H.

THREE days later, Vesper had only two friends in Sleeping Water, — that is, only two open friends. He knew he had a secret one in Mrs. Rose à Charlitte, who waited on him with the air of a sorrowing saint.

The open friends were the child Narcisse, and Emmanuel Victor de la Rive, the mail-driver. Rose could not keep her child away from the handsome stranger. Narcisse had fallen into a passionate adoration for him, and even in his dreams prattled of the Englishman from Boston.

On the third night of Vesper's stay in Sleeping Water a violent thunder-storm arose. Lying in his bed and watching the weird lighting up of the Bay under the vivid discharges of electricity, he heard a fumbling at his door-knob, and, upon unlocking the door, discovered Narcisse, pale and seraphic, in a long white nightgown, and with beads of distress on his forehead.

"Mr. Englishman," he said to Vesper, who now understood his childish lingo, "I come to you, for my mother sleeps soundly, and she cannot tell me when she wakes, — the trees and the flowers, are they not in a terrible fright?" and, holding up his gown with one hand, he went swiftly to the window, and pointed out towards the willows, writhing and twisting in the wind, and the gentle flowers laid low on the earth.

A yellow glare lighted up the room, a terrible peal of thunder shook the house, but the child did not quail, and stood waiting for an answer to his question.

"Come here," said Vesper, calmly, "and I will explain to you that the thunder does not hurt them, and that they have a way of bending before the blast."

Narcisse immediately drew his pink heels up over the side of Vesper's bed. He was unspeakably soothed by the merest word of this stranger, in whose nervous sensitiveness and reserve he found a spirit more congenial to his own than in that of his physically perfect mother.

Vesper talked to him for some time, and the child at last fell asleep, his tiny hand clasping a scapulary on his breast, his pretty lips murmuring to the picture on it, "Good St. Joseph, Mr. Englishman says that only a few of the trees and flowers are hurt by the storm. Watch over the little willows and the small lilies while I sleep, and do not let them be harmed."

Vesper at first patiently and kindly endured the pressure of the curly head laid on his arm. He would like to have a beautiful child like this for his own. Then thoughts of his childhood began to steal over him. He remembered climbing into his father's bed, gazing worshipfully into his face, and stroking his handsome head.

"O God, my father!" he muttered, "I have lost him," and, unable to endure the presence of the child, he softly waked him. "Go back to your mother, Narcisse. She may miss you."

The child sleepily obeyed him, and went to continue his dreams by his mother's side, while Vesper lay awake until the morning, a prey to recollections at once tender and painful.

Vesper's second friend, the mail-driver, never failed to call on him every morning. If one could put a stamp on a letter it was permissible at any point on the route to call, "*Arrête-toi*" (stop), to the crimson flying bird. If one could not stamp a letter, it was illegal to detain him.

Vesper never had, however, to call "*Arrête-toi.*"

Of his own accord Emmanuel Victor de la Rive, upon arriving before the inn, would fling the reins over his pony's back, and spring nimbly out. He was sure to find Vesper lolling on the seat under the willows, or lying in the hammock, with Narcisse somewhere near, whereupon he would seat himself for a few minutes, and in his own courteous and curious way would ask various and sundry questions of this stranger, who had fascinated him almost as completely as he had Narcisse.

On the morning after the thunder-storm he had fallen into an admiration of Vesper's beautiful white teeth. Were they all his own, and not artificial? With such teeth he could marry any woman. He was a bachelor now, was he not? Did he always intend to remain one? How much longer would he stay in Sleeping Water? And Vesper, parrying his questions with his usual skill, sent him away with his ears full of polite sentences that, when he came to analyze them, conveyed not a single item of information to his surprised brain.

However, he felt no resentment towards Vesper. His admiration rose superior to any rebuffs. It even soared above the warning intimations he received from many Acadiens to the effect that he was laying himself open to hostile criticism by his intercourse with the enemy within the camp.

Vesper was amused by him, and on this particular

morning, after he left, he lay back in the hammock, his mind enjoyably dwelling on the characteristics of the volatile Acadien.

Narcisse, who stood beside him in the centre of the bare spot on the lawn, by the hammock, in vain begged for a story, and at last, losing patience, knelt down and put his head to the ground. The Englishman had told him that each grass-blade came up from the earth with a tale on the tip of its quivering tongue, and that all might hear who bent an ear to listen. Narcisse wished to get news of the storm in the night, and really fancied that the grass-blades told him it had prevailed in the bowels of the earth. He sprang up to impart the news to Vesper, and Agapit, who was passing down the lane by the house to the street, scowled, disapprovingly, at the pretty, wagging head and animated gestures.

Vesper gazed after him, and paid no attention to Narcisse. "I wonder," he murmured, languidly, "what spell holds me in the neighborhood of this Acadien demagogue who has turned his following against me. It must be the Bay," and in a trance of pleasure he surveyed its sparkling surface.

Always beautiful, — never the same. Was ever another sheet of water so wholly charming, was ever another occupation so fitted for unstrung nerves as this placid watching of its varying humors and tumults?

This morning it was like crystal. A fleet of small boats was dancing out to the deep sea fishing-grounds, and three brown-sailed schooners were gliding up the Bay to mysterious waters unknown to him. As soon as he grew stronger, he must follow them up to the rolling country and the fertile fields beyond Sleeping Water. Just now the mere thought of leaving the inn filled him with nervous apprehension, and he started painfully and irritably as the sharp clang of the dinner-bell rang out through the open windows of the house.

Followed by Narcisse, he sauntered to the table, where he caused Rose à Charlitte's heart a succession of pangs and anxieties.

"He does not like my cooking; he eats nothing," she said, mournfully, to Agapit, who was taking a substantial dinner at the kitchen table.

"I wish that he would go away," said Agapit, "I hate his insolent face."

"But he is not insolent," said Rose, pleadingly. "It is only that he does not care for us; he is likely rich, and we are but poor."

"Do many millionaires come to thy quiet inn?" asked Agapit, ironically.

Rose reluctantly admitted that, so far, her patrons had not been people of wealth.

"He is probably a beggar," said Agapit. "He has paid thee nothing yet. I dare say he has only old clothes in that trunk of his. Perhaps he was forced to leave his home. He intends to spend the rest of his life here."

"If he would work," said Rose, timidly, "he could earn his board. If thou goest away, I shall need a man for the stable."

"Look at his white hands," said Agapit, "he is lazy, — and dost thou think I would leave thee with that young sprig? His character may be of the worst. What do we know of him?" and he tramped out to the stable, while Mrs. Rose confusedly withdrew to her pantry.

An hour later, while Agapit was grooming Toochune, the thoroughbred black horse that was the wonder of the Bay, Narcisse came and stood in the stable door, and for a long time silently watched him.

Then he heaved a small sigh. He was thinking neither of the horse nor of Agapit, and said, wistfully, "The Englishman from Boston sleeps as well as my mother. I have tried to wake him, but I cannot."

Agapit paid no attention to him, but the matter was weighing on the child's mind, and after a time he continued, "His face is very white, as white as the breast of the ducks."

"His face is always white," growled Agapit.

Narcisse went away, and sat patiently down by the hammock, while Agapit, who kept an eye on him despite himself, took occasion a little later to go to the garden, ostensibly to mend a hole in the fence, in reality to peer through the willows at Vesper.

What he saw caused him to drop his knife, and go to the well, where Célina was drawing a bucket of water.

"The Englishman has fainted," he said, and he took the bucket from her. Célina ran after him, and watched him thrust Narcisse aside and dash a handful of water in Vesper's marble, immobile face.

Narcisse raised one of his tiny fists and struck Agapit a smart blow, and, in spite of their concern for the Englishman, both the grown people turned and stared in surprise at him. For the first time they saw the sweet-tempered child in a rage.

"Go away," he said, in a choking voice, "you shall not hurt him."

"Hush, little rabbit," said the young man. "I try to do him good. Christophe! Christophe!" and he hailed an Acadien who was passing along the road. "Come assist me to carry the Englishman into the house. This is something worse than a faint."

CHAPTER VIII.

ON THE SUDDEN SOMETHING ILL.

" Dull days had hung like curtained mysteries,
And nights were weary with the starless skies.
At once came life, and fire, and joys untold,
And promises for violets to unfold;
And every breeze had shreds of melodies,
So faint and sweet."
J. F. HERBIN.

ONE midnight, three weeks later, when perfect silence and darkness brooded over Sleeping Water, and the only lights burning were the stars up aloft, and two lamps in two windows of the inn, Vesper opened his eyes and looked about him.

He saw for some dreamy moments only a swimming curtain of black, with a few familiar objects picked out against the gloom. He could distinguish his trunk sailing to and fro, a remembered mirror before which he had brushed his hair, a book in a well-known binding, and a lamp with a soft yellow globe, that immediately took him to a certain restaurant in Paris, and made him fancy that he was dining under the yellow lights in its ceiling.

Where was he, — in what country had he been having this long, dreamless sleep? And by dint of much brain racking, which bathed his whole body in a profuse perspiration, he at length retraced his steps back into his life, and decided that he was in the last place that he remembered before he fell into this disembodied-spirit condition of mind, — his room in the Sleeping Water Inn.

There was the open window, through which he had so often listened to the soothing murmur of the sea; there were the easy chairs, the chest of drawers, the little table, that, as he remembered it last, was not covered with medicine-bottles. The child's cot was a wholly new object. Had the landlady's little boy been sharing his quarters? What was his name? Ah, yes, Narcisse, — and what had they called the sulky Acadien who had hung about the house, and who now sat reading in a rocking-chair by the table?

Agapit — that was it ; but why was he here in his room? Some one had been ill. "I am that person," suddenly drifted into his tortured mind. "I have been very ill; perhaps I am going to die." But the thought caused him no uneasiness, no regret; he was conscious only of an indescribably acute and nervous torture as his weary eyes glued themselves to the unconscious face of his watcher.

Agapit would soon lift his head, would stare at him, would utter some exclamation; and, in mute, frantic expectation, Vesper waited for the start and the exclamation. If they did come he felt that they would kill him; if they did not, he felt that nothing less than a sudden and immediate felling to the floor of his companion would satisfy the demands of his insane and frantic agitation.

Fortunately Agapit soon turned his anxious face towards the bed. He did not start, he did not exclaim: he had been too well drilled for that; but a quick, quiet rapture fell upon him that was expressed only by the trembling of his finger tips.

The young American had come out of the death-like unconsciousness of past days and nights; he now had a chance to recover; but while a thanksgiving to the mother of angels was trembling on his lips, his patient surveyed him in an ecstacy of irritation and weakness that found expression in hysterical laughter.

Agapit was alarmed. He had never heard Vesper laugh in health. He had rarely smiled. Possibly he might be calmed by the offer of something to eat, and, picking up a bowl of jelly, he approached the bed.

Vesper made a supreme effort, slightly moved his head from the descending spoon, and uttered the worst expression that he could summon from his limited vocabulary of abuse of former days.

Agapit drew back, and resignedly put the jelly on

the table. "He remembers the past," he reflected, with hanging head.

Vesper did not remember the past; he was conscious of no resentment. He was possessed only of a wild desire to be rid of this man, whose presence inflamed him to the verge of madness.

After sorrowfully surveying him, while retreating further and further from his inarticulate expressions of rage, Agapit stepped into the hall. In a few minutes he returned with Rose, who looked pale and weary, as if she, too, were a watcher by a sick-bed. She glanced quickly at Vesper, suppressed a smile when he made a face at Agapit, and signed to the latter to leave the room.

Vesper became calm. Instead of sitting down beside him, or staring at him, she had gone to the window, and stood with folded hands, looking out into the night. After some time she went to the table, took up a bottle, and, carefully examining it, poured a few drops into a spoon.

Vesper took the liquid from her, with no sense of irritation; then, as she quickly turned away, he felt himself sinking down, down, through his bed, through the floor, through the crust of the earth, into regions of infinite space, from which he had come back to the world for a time.

The next time he waked up, Agapit was again with him. The former pantomime would have been repeated if Agapit had not at once precipitated himself from the room, and sent Rose to take his place.

This time she smiled at Vesper, and made an effort to retain his attention, even going so far as to leave the room and reënter with a wan effigy of Narcisse in her arms, — a pale and puny thing that stared languidly at him, and attempted to kiss his hand.

Vesper tried to speak to the child, lost himself in the attempt, then roused his slumbering fancy once more and breathed a question to Mrs. Rose, — "My mother?"

"Your mother is well, and is here," murmured his landlady. "You shall see her soon."

Vesper's periods of slumber after this were not of so long duration, and one warm and delicious afternoon, when the sunlight was streaming in and flooding his bed, he opened his eyes on a frail, happy figure fluttering about the room. "Ah, mother," he said, calmly, "you are here."

She flew to the bed, she hovered over him, embraced him, turned away, came back to him, and finally, rigidly clasping her hands to ensure self-control, sat down beside him.

At first she would not talk, the doctor would not permit it; but after some days her tongue was allowed to take its course freely and uninterruptedly.

"My dear boy, what a horrible fright you gave me! Your letters came every day for a week, then they stopped. I waited two days, thinking you had gone to some other place, then I telegraphed. You were ill. You can imagine how I hurried here, with Henry to take care of me. And what do you think I found? Such a curious state of affairs. Do you know that these Acadiens hated you at first?"

"Yes, I remember that."

"But when you fell ill, that young man, Agapit, installed himself as your nurse. They spoke of getting a Sister of Charity, but had some scruples, thinking you might not like it, as you are a Protestant. Mrs. de Forêt closed her inn; she would receive no guests, lest they might disturb you. She and her cousin nursed you. They got an English doctor to drive twelve miles every day, — they thought you would prefer him to a French one. Then her little boy fell ill; he said the young man Agapit had hurt you. They thought he would die, for he had brain fever. He called all the time for you, and when he had lucid intervals, they could only convince him you were not dead by bringing him in, and putting him in this cot. Really, it was a most deplorable state of affairs. But the charming part is that they thought you were a pauper. When I arrived, they were thunderstruck. They had not opened your trunk, which you left locked, though they said they would have done so if I had not come, for they feared you might die, and they wanted to get the addresses of your friends, and every morning, my dear boy, for three days after you were taken ill, you started up at nine o'clock, the time that queer, red postman used to come, — and wrote a letter to me."

Mrs. Nimmo paused, hid her face in her hands, and burst into tears. "It almost broke my heart when I heard it, — to think of you rousing yourself every day from your semi-unconsciousness to write to your mother. I cannot forgive myself for letting you go away without me."

"Why did they not write from here to you?" asked Vesper.

"They did not know I was your mother. I don't think they looked at the address of the letters you had sent. They thought you were poor, and an adventurer."

"Why did they not write to *The Evening News?*"

"My dear boy, they were doing everything possible for you, and they would have written in time."

"You have, of course, told them that they shall suffer no loss by all this?"

"Yes, yes; but they seem almost ashamed to take money from me. That charming landlady says,

'If I were rich I would pay all, myself.' Vesper, she is a wonderful woman."

"Is she?" he said, languidly.

"I never saw any one like her. My darling, how do you feel? Mayn't I give you some wine? I feel as if I had got you back from the grave, I can never be sufficiently thankful. The doctor says you may be carried out-of-doors in a week, if you keep on improving, as you are sure to do. The air here seems to suit you perfectly. You would never have been ill if you had not been run down when you came. That young man Agapit is making a stretcher to carry you. He is terribly ashamed of his dislike for you, and he fairly worships you now."

"I suppose you went through my trunk," said Vesper, in faint, indulgent tones.

"Well, yes," said Mrs. Nimmo, reluctantly. "I thought, perhaps, there might be something to be attended to."

"And you read my great-grandfather's letter?"

"Yes, — I will tell you exactly what I did. I found the key the second day I came, and I opened the trunk. When I discovered that old yellow letter, I knew it was something important. I read it, and of course recognized that you had come here in search of the Fiery Frenchman's children. However, I did not think you would like me to tell these Acadiens that, so I merely said, 'How you have misunderstood my son! He came here to do good to some of your people. He is looking for the descendants of a poor unhappy man. My son has money, and would help you.'"

Vesper tried to keep back the little crease of amusement forming itself about his wasted lips. He had rarely seen his mother so happy and so excited. She prattled on, watching him sharply to see the effect of her words, and hovering over him like a kind little mother-bird. In some way she reminded him curiously enough of Emmanuel de la Rive.

"I simply told them how good you are, and how you hate to have a fuss made over you. The young Acadien man actually writhed, and Mrs. de Forêt cried like a baby. Then they said, 'Oh, why did he put the name of a paper after his name?' 'How cruel in you to say that!' I replied to them. 'He does that because it reminds him of his dead father, whom he adored. My husband was editor and proprietor of the paper, and my son owns a part of it.' You should have seen the young Acadien. He put his head down on his arms, then he lifted it, and said, 'But does your son not write?' 'Write!' I exclaimed, indignantly, 'he hates writing. To me, his own mother, he only sends half a dozen lines. He never wrote a newspaper article in his life.' They would have been utterly overcome if I had not praised them for their disinterestedness in taking care of you in spite of their prejudice against you. Vesper, they will do anything for you now; and that exquisite child, — it is just like a romance that he should have fallen ill because you did."

"Is he better?"

"Almost well. They often bring him in when you are asleep. I daresay it would amuse you to have him sit on your bed for awhile."

Vesper was silent, and, after a time, his mother ran on: "This French district is delightfully unique. I never was in such an out-of-the-world place except in Europe. I feel as if I had been moved back into a former century, when I see those women going about in their black handkerchiefs. I sit at the window and watch them going by, — I should never weary of them."

Vesper said nothing, but he reflected affectionately and acutely that in a fortnight his appreciative but fickle mother would be longing for the rustle of silks, the flutter of laces, and the hum of fashionable conversation on a veranda, which was her idea of an enjoyable summer existence.

CHAPTER IX.

A TALK ON THE WHARF.

"Long have I lingered where the marshlands are,
Oft hearing in the murmur of the tide
The past, alive again and at my side,
With unrelenting power and hateful war."

J. F. H.

"THERE goes the priest of the parish in his buggy," said Mrs. Nimmo. "He must have a sick call."

She sat on a garden chair, crocheting a white shawl and watching the passers-by on the road.

"And there are some Sisters of Charity from one of the convents and an old Indian with a load of baskets is begging from them — Don't you want to look at these bicyclists, Vesper? One, two, three, four, five, six. They are from Boston, I know, by the square collars on their jerseys. The Nova Scotians do not dress in that way."

Vesper gave only a partial though pleased attention to his mother, who had picked up an astonishing amount of neighborhood news, and as he lay on a rug at her feet, with his hat pulled over his brows, his mind soared up to the blue sky above him. During his illness he had always seemed to be sinking down into blackness and desolation. With returning health and decreased nervousness his soul mounted upward, and he would lie for hours at a time bathed in a delicious reverie and dreaming of "a nest among the stars."

"And there is the blacksmith from the corner," continued Mrs. Nimmo, "who comes here so often to borrow things that a blacksmith is commonly supposed to have. Yesterday he wanted a hammer. 'Not a hammer,' said Célina to me, 'but a wife.'"

Vesper's brain immediately turned an abrupt somersault in a descent from the sky to earth. "What did you say, mother?"

"Merely that the blacksmith wishes to marry our landlady. It will be an excellent match for her. Don't you think so?"

"In some respects, — yes."

"She is too young, and too handsome, to remain a widow. Célina says that she has had a great many admirers, but she has never seemed to fancy any one but the blacksmith. She went for a drive with him last Sunday evening. You know that is the time young Acadiens call on the girls they admire. You see them walking by, or driving in their buggies. If a girl's *fiancé* did not call on her that evening she would throw him over — There she is now with your beef tea," and Mrs. Nimmo admiringly watched Rose coming from the kitchen and carefully guarding a dainty china cup in her hand.

Vesper got up and took it from her. "Don't you think it is nonsense for me to be drinking this every morning?" he asked.

Rose looked up at him as he stood, tall, keen-eyed, interested, and waiting for her answer. "What does madame, your mother, say?" she asked, indicating Mrs. Nimmo, by a pretty gesture.

"His mother says," remarked Mrs. Nimmo, indulgently, "that her son should take any dose, no matter how disagreeable, if it has for its object the good of his health."

Vesper glanced sharply at her, then poured the last few drops of his tea on the ground.

"Ah," said Mrs. Rose, anxiously, "I feared that I had not put in enough salt. Now I know."

"It was perfect," said Vesper. "I am only offering a libation to those pansies," and he inclined his dark head towards Narcisse, who was seated cross-legged in the hammock.

Rose took the cup, smiled innocently and angelically on her child and the young man and his mother, and returned to the house.

Agapit presently came hurrying by the fence. "Ah, that is good!" he exclaimed, when he saw

Vesper sauntering to and fro; "do you not think you could essay a walk to the wharf?"

"Yes," said Vesper, while his mother anxiously looked up from her work.

"Then come, — let me have the honor of escorting you," and Agapit showed his big white teeth in an ecstatic smile.

Vesper extended a hand to Narcisse, and, lifting his cap to his mother, went slowly down the lane to the road.

Agapit could scarcely contain his delight. He grinned broadly at every one they met, tried to accommodate his pace to Vesper's, kept forgetting and striding ahead, and finally, cramming his hands in his pockets, fell behind and muttered, "I feel as if I had known you a hundred years."

"You didn't feel that way six weeks ago," said Vesper, good-humoredly.

"I blush for it, — I am ashamed, but can you blame me? Since days of long ago, Acadiens have been so much maligned. You do not find that we are worse than others?"

"Well, I think you would have been a pretty ticklish fellow to have handled at the time of the expulsion."

"Our dear Lord knew better than to bring me into the world then," said Agapit, naïvely. "I should have urged the Acadiens to take up arms.

There were enough of them to kill those devilish English."

"Do all the Acadiens hate the English as much as you do?"

"*I* hate the English?" cried Agapit. "How grossly you deceive yourself!"

"What do you mean then by that strong language?"

Agapit threw himself into an excited attitude. "Let you dare — you youthful, proud young republic, — to insult our Canadian flag. You would see where stands Agapit LeNoir! England is the greatest nation in the world," and proudly swelling out his breast, he swept his glance over the majestic Bay before them.

"Yes, barring the United States of America."

"I cannot quarrel with you," said Agapit, and the fire left his glance, and moisture came to his eyes. "Let us each hold to our own opinion."

"And suppose insults not forthcoming, — give me some further explanation meantime."

"My quarrel is not with the great-minded," said Agapit, earnestly, "the eagerly anxious-for-peace Englishmen in years gone by, who reinforced the kings and queens of England. No, — I impeach the low-born upstarts and their colonial accomplices. Do you know, can you imagine, that the diabolical scheme of the expulsion of the Acadiens was conceived by a barber, and carried into decapitation by a house painter?"

"Not possible," murmured Vesper.

"Yes, possible, — let me find you a seat. I shall not forgive myself if I weary you, and those women will kill me."

They had reached the wharf, and Agapit pointed to a pile of boards against the wooden breastwork that kept the waves from dashing over in times of storm.

"That infamous letter is always like a scroll of fire before me," he exclaimed, pacing restlessly to and fro before Vesper and the child. "In it the once barber and footman, Craggs, who was then secretary of state, wrote to the governor of Nova Scotia: 'I see you do not get the better of the Acadiens. It is singular that those people should have preferred to lose their goods rather than be exposed to fight against their brethren. This sentimentality is stupid.' Ah, let it be stupid!" exclaimed Agapit, breaking off. "Let us once more have an expulsion. The Acadiens will go, they will suffer, they will die, before they give up sentimentality."

"Hear, hear!" observed Vesper.

Agapit surveyed him with a glowing eye. "Listen to further words from this solemn official, this barber secretary: 'These people are evidently too much attached to their fellow countrymen and to their religion ever to make true Englishmen.' Of what are true Englishmen made, Mr. Englishman from Boston?"

"Of poor Frenchmen, according to the barber."

"Now hear more courtly language from the honorable Craggs: 'It must be avowed that your position is deucedly critical. It was very difficult to prevent them from departing after having left the bargain to their choice —'"

"What does he mean by that?" asked Vesper.

"Call to your memory the terms of the treaty of Utrecht."

"I don't remember a word of it, — bear in mind, my friend, that I am not an Acadien, and this question does not possess for me the moving interest it does for you. I only know Longfellow's 'Evangeline,' — which, until lately, has always seemed to me to be a pretty myth dressed up to please the public, and make money for the author, — some magazine articles, and Parkman, my favorite historian, whom you, nevertheless, seem to dislike."

Agapit dropped on a block of wood, and rocked himself to and fro, as if in distress. "I will not characterize Parkman, since he is your countryman; but I would dearly love — I would truly admire to say what I think of him. Now as to the treaty of Utrecht; think just a moment, and you will remember that it transferred the Acadiens as the subjects of Louis XIV. of France to the good Queen Anne of England."

Vesper, instead of puzzling his brain with historical reminiscences, immediately began to make preparations for physical comfort, and stretched himself out on the pile of boards, with his arm for a pillow.

"Do not sleep, but conversate," said Agapit, eagerly. "It is cool here, you possibly would get cold if you shut your eyes. I will change this matter of talk, — there is one I would fain introduce."

Vesper, in inward diversion, found that a new solemnity had taken possession of the young Acadien. He looked unutterable things at the Bay, indescribable things at the sky, and mysterious things at the cook of the schooner, who had just thrust his head through a window in his caboose.

At last he gave expression to his emotion. "Would this not be a fitting time to talk of the wonderful letter of which madame, your mother, hinted?"

Vesper, without a word, drew a folded paper from his pocket, and handed it to him.

Agapit took it reverently, swayed back and forth while devouring its contents, then, unable to restrain himself, sprang up, and walked, or rather ran, to and fro while perusing it a second time.

At last he came to a dead halt, and breathing hard, and with eyes aflame, ejaculated, "Thank you, a thousand, thousand time for showing me this precious letter." Then pressing it to his breast, he disappeared entirely from Vesper's range of vision.

After a time he came back. Some of his excitement had gone from his head through his heels, and he sank heavily on a block of wood.

"You do not know, you cannot tell," he said, "what this letter means to us."

"What does it mean?"

"It means — I do not know that I can say the word, but I will try — cor-rob-oration."

"Explain a little further, will you?"

"In the past all was for the English. Now records are being discovered, old documents are coming to light. The guilty colonial authorities suppressed them. Now these records declare for the Acadiens."

"So — this letter, being from one on the opposite side, is valuable."

"It is like a diamond unearthed," said Agapit, turning it over; "but," — in sudden curiosity, — "this is a copy mutilated, for the name of the captain is not here. From whom did you have it, if I am permitted to ask?"

"From the great-grandson of the old fellow mentioned."

"And he does not wish his name known?"

"Well, naturally one does not care to shout the sins of one's ancestors."

"The noble young man, the dear young man," said Agapit, warmly. "He will atone for the sins of his fathers."

"Not particularly noble, only business-like."

"And has he much money, that he wishes to aid this family of Acadiens?"

"No, not much. His father's family never succeeded in making money and keeping it. His mother is rich."

"I should like to see him," exclaimed Agapit, and his black eyes flashed over Vesper's composed features. "I should love him for his sensitive heart."

"There is nothing very interesting about him," said Vesper. "A sick, used-up creature."

"Ah, — he is delicate."

"Yes, and without courage. He is a college man and would have chosen a profession if his health had not broken down."

"I pity him from my heart; I send good wishes to his sick-bed," said Agapit, in a passion of enthusiasm. "I will pray to our Lord to raise him."

"Can you give him any assistance?" asked Vesper, nodding towards the letter.

"I do not know; I cannot tell. There are many LeNoirs. But I will go over my papers; I will sit up at night, as I now do some writing for the post-office. You know I am poor, and obliged to work. I must pay Rose for my board. I will not depend on a woman."

Vesper half lifted his drooping eyelids. " What are you going to make of yourself ? "

" I wish to study law. I save money for a period in a university."

" How old are you ? "

" Twenty-three."

" Your cousin looks about that age."

" She is twenty-four, — a year older ; and you, — may I ask your age? "

" Guess."

Agapit studied his face. " You are twenty-six."

" No."

" I daresay we are both younger than Rose," said Agapit, ingenuously, " and she has less sense than either."

" Did your ancestors come from the south of France ? " asked Vesper, abruptly.

" Not the LeNoirs ; but my mother's family was from Provence. Why do you ask ? "

" You are like a Frenchman of the south."

" I know that I am impetuous," pursued Agapit. " Rose says that I resemble the tea-kettle. I boil and bubble all the time that I am not asleep, and " — uneasily — " she also says that I speak too hastily of women; that I do not esteem them as clever as they are. What do you think?"

Vesper laughed quickly. "Southerners all have a slight contempt for women. However, they are frank about it. Is there one thought agitating your bosom that you do not express?"

"No; most unfortunately. It chagrins me that I speak everything. I feel, and often speak before I feel, but what can one do? It is my nature. Rose also follows her nature. She is beautiful, but she studies nothing, absolutely nothing, but the science of cooking."

"Without which philosophers would go mad from indigestion."

"Yes; she was born to cook and to obey. Let her keep her position, and not say, 'Agapit, thou must do so and so,' as she sometimes will, if I am not rocky with her."

"Rocky?" queried Vesper.

"Firmy, firm," said Agapit, in confusion. "The words twist in my mind, unless my blood is hot, when I speak better. Will you not correct me? Upon going out in the world I do not wish to be laughed."

"To be laughed at," said his new friend. "Don't worry yourself. You speak well enough, and will improve."

Agapit grew pale with emotion. "Ah, but we

shall miss you when you go! There has been no Englishman here that we so liked. I hope that you will be long in finding the descendants of the Fiery Frenchman."

"Perhaps I shall find some of them in you and your cousin," said Vesper.

"Ah, if you could, what joy! what bliss! — but I fear it is not so. Our forthfathers were not of Grand Pré."

Vesper relapsed into silence, only occasionally rousing himself to answer some of Agapit's restless torrent of remarks about the ancient letter. At last he grew tired, and, sitting up, laid a caressing hand on the head of Narcisse, who was playing with some shells beside him. "Come, little one, we must return to the house."

On the way back they met the blacksmith. Agapit snickered gleefully, "All the world supposes that he is making the velvet paw to Rose."

"She drives with him," said Vesper, indifferently.

"Yes, but to obtain news of her sister who flouts him. She is down the Bay, and Rose receives news of her. She will no longer drive with him if she hears this gossip."

"Why should she not?"

"I do not know, but she will not. Possibly because she is no coquette."

"She will probably marry some one."

"She cannot," muttered Agapit, and he fell into a quiet rage, and out of it again in the duration of a few seconds. Then he resumed a light-hearted conversation with Vesper, who averted his curious eyes from him.

CHAPTER X.

BACK TO THE CONCESSION.

> "And Nature hath remembered, for a trace
> Of calm Acadien life yet holds command,
> Where, undisturbed, the rustling willows stand,
> And the curved grass, telling the breeze's pace."
> J. F. H.

MRS. ROSE À CHARLITTE served her dinner in the middle of the day. The six o'clock meal she called supper.

With feminine insight she noticed, at supper, on a day a week later, that her guest was more quiet than usual, and even dull in humor.

Agapit, who was nearly always in high spirits, and always very much absorbed in himself, came bustling in, — sobered down for one minute to cross himself, and reverently repeat a *bénédicité*, then launched into a voluble and enjoyable conversation on the subject of which he never tired, — his beloved countrymen, the Acadiens.

Rose withdrew to the innermost recesses of her pantry. "Do you know these little berries?" she asked, coming back, and setting a glass dish, full of a thick, whitish preserve, before Vesper.

"No," he said, absently, "what are they?"

"They are *poudabre*, or *capillaire*, — waxen berries that grow deep in the woods. They hide their little selves under leaves, yet the children find them. They are expensive, and we do not buy many, yet perhaps you will find them excellent."

"They are delicious," said Vesper, tasting them.

"Give me also some," said Agapit, with pretended jealousy. "It is not often that we are favored with *poudabre.*"

"There are yours beside your plate," said Rose, mischievously; "you have, if anything, more than Mr. Nimmo."

She very seldom mentioned Vesper's name. It sounded foreign on her lips, and he usually liked to hear her. This evening he paid no attention to her, and, with a trace of disappointment in her manner, she went away to the kitchen.

After Vesper left the table she came back. "Agapit, the young man is dull."

"I assure thee," said Agapit, in French, and very dictatorially, "he is as gay as he usually is."

"He is never gay, but this evening he is troubled."

Agapit grew uneasy. "Dost thou think he will again become ill?"

Rose's brilliant face became pale. "I trust not. Ah, that would be terrible!"

"Possibly he thinks of something. Where is his mother?"

"Above, in her room. Some books came from Boston in a box, and she reads. Go to him, Agapit; talk not of the dear dead, but of the living. Seek not to find out in what his dullness consists, and do not say abrupt things, but gentle. Remember all the kind sayings that thou knowest about women. Say that they are constant if they truly love. They do not forget."

Agapit's fingers remained motionless in the bowl of the big pipe that he was filling with tobacco. "*Ma foi*, but thou art eloquent. What has come over thee?"

"Nothing, nothing," she said, hurriedly, "I only wonder whether he thinks of his *fiancée*."

"How dost thou know he has a *fiancée*?"

"I do not know, I guess. Surely, so handsome a young man must belong already to some woman."

"Ah,—probably. Rose, I am glad that thou hast never been a coquette."

"And why should I be one?" she asked, wonderingly.

"Why, thou hast ways,—sly ways, like most women, and thou art meek and gentle, else why do men run after thee, thou little bleating lamb?"

Rose made him no answer beyond a shrug of her shoulders.

"But thou wilt not marry. Is it not so?" he continued, with tremulous eagerness. "It is better for thee to remain single and guard thy child."

She looked up at him wistfully, then, as solemnly as if she were taking a vow, she murmured, "I do not know all things, but I think I shall never marry."

Agapit could scarcely contain his delight. He laid a hand on her shoulder, and exclaimed, "My good little cousin!" Then he lighted his pipe and smoked in ecstatic silence.

Rose occupied herself with clearing the things from the table, until a sudden thought struck Agapit. "Leave all that for Célina. Let us take a drive, you and I and the little one. Thou hast been much in the house lately."

"But Mr. Nimmo — will it be kind to leave him?"

"He can come if he will, but thou must also ask madame. Go then, while I harness Toochune."

"I am not ready," said Rose, shrinking back.

"Ready!" laughed Agapit. "I will make thee ready," and he pulled her shawl and handkerchief from a peg near the kitchen door.

"I had the intention of wearing my hat," faltered Rose.

"Absurdity! keep it for mass, and save thy

money. Go ask the young man, while I am at the stable."

Rose meekly put on the shawl and the handkerchief, and went to the front of the house.

Vesper stood in the doorway, his hands clasped behind his back. She could only see his curly head, a bit of his cheek, and the tip of his mustache. At the sound of her light step he turned around, and his face brightened.

"Look at the sunset," he said, kindly, when she stood in embarrassment before him. "It is remarkable."

It was indeed remarkable. A blood-red sun was shouldering his way in and out of a wide dull mass of gray cloud that was unrelieved by a single fleck of color.

Rose looked at the sky, and Vesper looked at her, and thought of a grieving Madonna. She had been so gay and cheerful lately. What had happened to call that expression of divine tenderness and sympathy to her face? He had never seen her so ethereal and so spiritually beautiful, not even when she was bending over his sick-bed. What a rest and a pleasure to weary eyes she was, in her black artistic garments, and how pure was the oval of her face, how becoming the touch of brownness on the fair skin. The silk handkerchief knotted under her chin and pulled hood-wise over the shock of flaxen hair combed up from the forehead, which two or three little curls caressed daintily, gave the finishing touch of quaintness and out-of-the-worldness to her appearance.

"You are feeling slightly blue this evening, are you not?" he asked.

"Blue, — that means one's thoughts are black?" said Rose, bringing her glance back to him.

"Yes."

"Then I am a very little blue," she said, frankly. "This inn is like the world to me. When those about me are sad, I, too, am sad. Sometimes I grieve when strangers go, — for days in advance I have a weight at heart. When they leave, I shut myself in my room. For others I do not care."

"And are you melancholy this evening because you are thinking that my mother and I must soon leave?"

Her eyes filled with tears. "No; I did not think of that, but I do now."

"Then what was wrong with you?"

"Nothing, since you are again cheerful," she said, in tones so doleful that Vesper burst into one of his rare laughs, and Rose, laughing with him, brushed the tears from her face.

"There was something running in my mind that made me feel gloomy," he said, after a short silence. "It has been haunting me all day."

Her eager glance was a prayer to him to share the cause of his unhappiness with her, and he recited, in a low, penetrating voice, the lines :

> " Mon Dieu, pour fuir la mort n'est-il aucun moyen?
> Quoi ?   Dans un jour peut-être immobile et glacé. . . .
> Aujourd'hui avenir, le monde, la pensée
> Et puis, demain, . . . plus rien."

Rose had never heard anything like this, and she was troubled, and turned her blue eyes to the sky, where a trailing white cloud was soaring above the dark cloud-bank below. " It is like a soul going up to our Lord," she murmured, reverently.

Vesper would not shock her further with his heterodoxy. " Forget what I said," he went on, lightly, "and let me beg you never to put anything on your head but that handkerchief. You Acadien women wear it with such an air."

" But it is because we know how to tie it. Look, — this is how the Italian women in Boston carry those colored ones," and, pulling the piece of silk from her head, she arranged it in severe lines about her face.

" A decided difference," Vesper was saying, when Agapit came around the corner of the house, driving Toochune, who was attached to a shining dog-cart.

" Are you going with us ? " he called out.

" I have not yet been asked."

" Thou naughty Rose," exclaimed Agapit ; but she

had already hurried up-stairs to invite Mrs. Nimmo to accompany them. "Madame, your mother, prefers to read," she said, when she came back, "therefore Narcisse will come."

"Mount beside me," said Agapit to Vesper; "Rose and Narcisse will sit in the background."

"No," said Vesper, and he calmly assisted Rose to the front seat, then extended a hand to swing Narcisse up beside her. The child, however, clung to him, and Vesper was obliged to take him in the back seat, where he sat nodding his head and looking like a big perfumed flower in his drooping hat and picturesque pink trousers.

"You smile," said Agapit, who had suddenly twisted his head around.

"I always do," said Vesper, "for the space of five minutes after getting into this cart"

"But why?"

"Well — an amusing contrast presents itself to my mind."

"And the contrast, what is it?"

"I am driving with a modern Evangeline, who is not the owner of the rough cart that I would have fancied her in, a few weeks ago, but of a trap that would be an ornament to Commonwealth Avenue."

"Am I the modern Evangeline?" said Agapit, in his breakneck fashion.

"To my mind she was embodied in the person of

your cousin," and Vesper bowed in a sidewise fashion towards his landlady.

Rose crimsoned with pleasure. "But do you think I am like Evangeline, — she was so dark, so beautiful?"

"You are passable, Rose, passable," interjected Agapit, "but you lack the passion, the fortitude of the heroine of Mr. Nimmo's immortal countryman, whom all Acadiens venerate. Alas! only the poets and story-tellers have been true to Acadie. It is the historians who lie."

"Why do you think your cousin is lacking in passion and fortitude?" asked Vesper, who had either lost his gloomy thoughts, or had completely subdued them, and had become unusually vivacious.

"She has never loved, — she cannot. Rose, did you love your husband as I did *la belle Marguerite?*"

"My husband was older, — he was as a father," stammered Rose. "Certainly I did not tear my hair, I did not beat my foot on the ground when he died, as you did when *la belle* married the miller."

"Have you ever loved any man?" pursued Agapit, unmercifully.

"Oh, shut up, Agapit," muttered Vesper; "don't bully a woman."

Agapit turned to stare at him, — not angrily, but rather as if he had discovered something new and peculiar in the shape of young manhood. "Hear what she always says when young men, and often old men, drive up and say, 'Rose à Charlitte, will you marry me?' She says, 'Love,—it is all nonsense. You make all that.' Is it not so, Rose?"

"Yes," she replied, almost inaudibly; "I have said it."

"You make all that," repeated Agapit, triumphantly. "They can rave and cry,—they can say, 'My heart is breaking;' and she responds, 'Love,—there is no such thing. You make all that.' And yet you call her an Evangeline, a martyr of love who laid her life on its holy altar."

Rose was goaded into a response, and turned a flushed and puzzled face to her cousin. "Agapit, I will explain that lately I do not care to say 'You make all that.' I comprehend — possibly because the blacksmith talks so much to me of his wish towards my sister — that one does not make love. It is something that grows slowly, in the breast, like a flower. Therefore, do not say that I am of ice or stone."

"But you do not care to marry,—you just come from telling me so."

"Yes; I am not for marriage," she said, modestly, "yet do not say that I understand not. It is a beautiful thing to love."

"It is," said Agapit, "yet do not think of it, since

thou dost not care for a husband. Let thy thoughts run on thy cooking. Thou wert born for that. I think that thou must have arrived in this world with a little stew-pan in thy hand, a tasting fork hanging at thy girdle. Do not wish to be an Evangeline or to read books. Figure to yourself, Mr. Nimmo," — and he turned his head to the back seat, — " that last night she came to my room, she begged me for an English book, — she who says often to Narcisse, ' I will shake thee, my little one, if thou usest English words.' She says now that she wishes to learn, — she finds herself forgetful of many things that she learned in the convent. I said, 'Go to bed, thou silly fool. Thy eyes are burning and have black rings around them the color of thy stove,' and she whimpered like a baby."

" Your cousin is an egotist, Mrs. Rose," said Vesper, over his shoulder. " I will lend you some books."

" Agapit is as a brother," she replied, simply.

" I have been a good brother to thee," he said, " and I will never forget thee; not even when I go out into the world. Some day I will send for thee to live with me and my wife."

" Perhaps thy wife will not let me," she said, demurely.

" Then she may leave me; I detest women who will not obey."

For some time the cousins chattered on and endeavored to snatch a glimpse, in "time's long and dark prospective glass," of Agapit's future wife, while Vesper listened to them with as much indulgence as if they had been two children. He was just endeavoring to fathom the rationale of their curious interchange of *thou* and *you*, when Agapit said, "If it is agreeable to you, we will drive back in the woods to the Concession. We have a cousin who is ill there, — see, here we pass the station," and he pointed his whip at the gabled roof near them.

The wheels of the dog-cart rolled smoothly over the iron rails, and they entered upon a road bordered by sturdy evergreens that emitted a deliciously resinous odor and occasioned Mrs. Rose to murmur, reverently, "It is like mass; for from trees like these the altar boys get the gum for incense."

Wild gooseberry and raspberry bushes lined the roadside, and under their fruit-laden branches grew many wild flowers. A man who stopped Agapit to address a few remarks to him gathered a handful of berries and a few sprays of wild roses and tossed them in Narcisse's lap.

The child uttered a polite, "*Merci, monsieur*" (thank you, sir), then silently spread the flowers and berries on the lap rug and allowed tears from his beautiful eyes to drop on them.

Vesper took some of the berries in his hand, and

carefully explained to the sorrowing Narcisse that the sensitive shrubs did not shiver when their clothes were stripped from them and their hats pulled off. They were rather shaking their sides in laughter that they could give pleasure to so good and gentle a boy. And the flowers that bowed so meekly when one wished to behead them, were trembling with delight to think that they should be carried, for even a short time, by one who loved them so well.

Narcisse at last was comforted, and, drying his tears, he soberly ate the berries, and presented the roses to his mother in a brilliant nosegay, keeping only one that he lovingly fastened in his neck, where it could brush against his cheek.

Soon they were among the clearings in the forest. Back of every farm stood grim trees in serried rows, like soldiers about to close in on the gaps made in their ranks by the diligent hands of the Acadien farmers. The trees looked inexorable, but the farmers were more so. Here in the backwoods so quiet and still, so favorable for farming, the forest must go as it had gone near the shore.

About every farmhouse, men and women were engaged in driving in cows, tying up horses, shutting up poultry, feeding pigs, and performing the hundred and one duties that fall to the lot of a farmer's family. Everywhere were children. Each farmer seemed to have a quiver full of these quiet, well-behaved little creatures, who gazed shyly and curiously at the dog-cart as it went driving by.

When they came to a brawling, noisy river, having on its banks a saw-mill deserted for the night, Agapit exclaimed, "We are at last arrived!"

Close to the mill was a low, old-fashioned house, situated in the midst of an extensive apple orchard in which the fruit was already taking on size and color.

"They picked four hundred barrels from it last year," said Agapit, "our cousins, the Kessys, who live here. They are rich, but very simple," and springing out, he tied Toochune's head to the gatepost. "Now let us enter," he said, and he ushered Vesper into a small, dull room where an old woman of gigantic stature sat smoking by an open fireplace.

Another tall woman, with soft black eyes, and wearing on her breast a medal of the congregation of St. Anne, took Rose away to the sick-room, while Agapit led Vesper and Narcisse to the fireplace. "Cousin grandmother, will you not tell this gentleman of the commencement of the Bay?"

The old woman, who was nearly sightless, took her pipe from her mouth, and turned her white head. "Does he speak French?"

"Yes, yes," said Agapit, joyfully.

A light came into her face, — a light that Vesper noticed always came into the faces of Acadiens, no matter how fluent their English, if he addressed them in their mother tongue.

"I was born *en haut de la Baie*" (up the Bay), she began, softly.

"Further than Sleeping Water, — towards Digby," said Agapit, in an undertone.

"Near Bleury," she continued, "where there were only eight families. In the morning my mother would look out at the neighbors' chimneys; where she saw smoke she would send me, saying, 'Go, child, and borrow fire.' Ah! those were hard days. We had no roads. We walked over the beach fifteen miles to Pointe à l'Eglise to hear mass sung by the good Abbé.

"There were plenty of fish, plenty of moose, but not so many boats in those days. The hardships were great, so great that the weak died. Now when my daughter sits and plays on the organ, I think of it. David Kessy, my father, was very big. Once our wagon, loaded with twenty bushels of potatoes, stuck in the mud. He put his shoulder against it and lifted it. Nowadays we would rig a jack, but my father was strong, so strong that he took insults, though he trembled, for he knew a blow from his hand would kill a man."

The Acadienne paused, and fell into a gentle reverie, from which Agapit, who was stepping nimbly in and out of the room with jelly and other delicacies that he had brought for the invalid, soon roused her.

"Tell him about the derangement, cousin grandmother," he vociferated in her ear, "and the march from Annapolis."

CHAPTER XI.

NEWS OF THE FIERY FRENCHMAN.

" Below me winds the river to the sea,
    On whose brown slope stood wailing, homeless maids;
    Stood exiled sons; unsheltered hoary heads;
And sires and mothers dumb in agony.
The awful glare of burning homes, where free
    And happy late they dwelt, breaks on the shades,
    Encompassing the sailing fleet; then fades,
With tumbling roof, upon the night-bound sea.
How deep is hope in sorrow sunk! How harsh
    The stranger voice; and loud the hopeless wail!
    Then silence came to dwell; the tide fell low;
The embers died. On the deserted marsh,
    Where grain and grass stirred only to the gale,
    The moose unchased dare cross the Gaspereau."
                              J. F. HERBIN.

AN extraordinary change came over the aged woman at Agapit's words. Some color crept to her withered cheeks. She straightened herself, and, no longer leaning on her cane, said, in a loud, firm voice, to Vesper, "The Acadiens were not all stolen from Annapolis at the derangement. Did you think they were?"

"I don't know that I ever thought about it, madame," he said, courteously; "but I should like to know."

"About fifty families ran to the wood," she said, with mournful vivacity; "they spent the winter there; I have heard the old people talk of it when I was young. They would sit by the fire and cry. I would try not to cry, but the tears would come. They said their good homes were burnt. Only at night could they revisit them, lest soldiers would catch them. They dug their vegetables from the ground. They also got one cow and carried her back. Ah, she was a treasure! There was one man among them who was only half French, and they feared him, so they watched. One day he went out of the woods, — the men took their guns and followed. Soon he returned, fifty soldiers marching behind him. 'Halt!' cried the Acadiens. They fired, they killed, and the rest of the soldiers ran. 'Discharge me! discharge me!' cried the man, whom they had caught. 'Yes, we will discharge you,' they said, and they put his back against a tree, and once more they fired, but very sadly. At the end of the winter some families went away in ships, but the Comeaus, Thibaudeaus, and Melançons said, 'We cannot leave Acadie; we will find a quiet place.' So they began a march, and one could trace them by the graves they dug. I will not tell you all, for why should you be sad? I will say that the Indians were good, but sometimes the food went, and they had to boil their moccasins. One woman, who had a young baby, got very weak. They lifted her up, they shook the pea-straw stuffing from the sack she lay on, and found her a handful of peas, which they boiled, and she got better.

"They went on and on, they crossed streams, and carried the little ones, until they came here to the Bay, — to Grosses Coques, — where they found big clams, and the tired women said, 'Here is food; let us stay.'

"The men cut a big pine and hollowed a boat, in which they went to the head of the Bay for the cow they had left there. They threw her down, tied her legs, and brought her to Grosses Coques. Little by little they carried also other things to the Bay, and made themselves homes.

"Then the families grew, and now they cover all the Bay. Do you understand now about the march from Annapolis?"

"Thank you, yes," said Vesper, much moved by the sight of tears trickling down her faded face.

"What reason did the old people give for this expulsion from their homes?"

"Always the same, always, always," said Madame Kessy, with energy. "They would not take the oath, because the English would not put in it that they need not fight against the French."

"But now you are happy under English rule?"

"Yes, now, — but the past? What can make up for the weeping of the old people?"

Nothing could, and Vesper hastened to introduce a new subject of conversation. "I have heard much about the good Abbé that you speak of. Did you ever see him?"

"See him, — ah, sir, he was an angel of God, on this Bay, and he a gentleman out of France. We were all his children, even the poor Indians, whom he gathered around him and taught our holy religion, till their fine voices would ring over the Bay, in hymns to the ever blessed Virgin. He denied himself, he paid our doctors' bills, even to twenty pounds at a time, — ah, there was mourning when he died. When my bans were published in church the good Abbé rode no more on horseback along the Bay. He lay a corpse, and I could scarcely hold up my head to be married."

"In speaking of those old days," said Vesper, "can you call to mind ever hearing of a LeNoir of Grand Pré called the Fiery Frenchman?"

"Of Etex LeNoir," cried the old woman, in trumpet tones, "of the martyr who shamed an Englishman, and was murdered by him?"

"Yes, that is the man."

"I have heard of him often, often. The old ones spoke of it to me. His heart was broken, — the captain, who was more cruel than Winslow, called him a papist dog, and struck him down, and the sailors threw him into the sea. He laid a curse on the wicked captain, but I cannot remember his name."

"Did you ever hear anything of the wife and child of Etex LeNoir?"

"No," she said, absently, "there was only the husband Etex that I had heard of. Would not his wife come back to the Bay? I do not know," and she relapsed into the dullness from which her temporary excitement had roused her.

"He was called the Fiery Frenchman," she muttered, presently, but so low that Vesper had to lean forward to hear her. "The old ones said that there was a mark like flame on his forehead, and he was like fire himself."

"Agapit, is it not time that we embark?" said Rose, gliding from an inner room. "It will soon be dark."

Agapit sprang up. Vesper shook hands with Madame Kessy and her daughter, and politely assured them, in answer to their urgent request, that he would be sure to call again, then took his seat in the dog-cart, where in company with his new friends he was soon bowling quickly over a bit of smooth and newly repaired road.

Away ahead, under the trees, they soon heard snatches of a lively song, and presently two young men staggered into view supporting each other, and having much difficulty in keeping to their side of the road.

Agapit, with angry mutterings, drove furiously by the young men, with his head well in the air, although they saluted him as their dear cousin from the Bay.

Rose did not speak, but she hung her head, and Vesper knew that she was blushing to the tips of the white ears inside her black handkerchief.

No one ventured a remark until they reached a place where four roads met, when Agapit ejaculated, desperately, "The devil is also here!"

Vesper turned around. The sun had gone down, the twilight was nearly over, but he possessed keen sight and could plainly discover against the dull blue evening sky the figures of a number of men and boys, some of whom were balancing themselves on the top of a zigzag fence, while others stood with hands in their pockets, — all vociferously laughing and jeering at a man who staggered to and fro in their midst with clenched fists, and light shirt-sleeves spotted with red.

"This is abominable," said Agapit, in a rage, and he was about to lay his whip on Toochune's back when Vesper suggested mildly that he was in danger of running down some of his countrymen.

Agapit pulled up the horse with a jerk, and Rose immediately sprang to the road and ran up to the young man, who had plainly been fighting and was about to fight again.

Vesper slipped from his seat and stood by the wheel.

"Do not follow her," exclaimed Agapit; "they will not hurt her. They would beat you."

"I know it."

"She is my cousin, thou impatient one," pursued Agapit, irritably. "I would not allow her to be insulted."

"I know that, too," said Vesper, calmly, and he watched the young men springing off the fences and hurrying up to Rose, who had taken the pugilist by the hand.

"Isidore," she said, sorrowfully, and as unaffectedly as if they had been alone, "hast thou been fighting again?"

"It is her second cousin," growled Agapit; "that is why she interferes."

"*Écoute-moi, écoute-moi,* Rose" (listen to me), stammered the young man in the blood-stained shirt. "They all set upon me. I was about to be massacred. I struck out but a little, and I got some taps here and there. I was drunk at first, but I am not very drunk now."

"Poor Isidore, I will take thee home; come with me."

The crowd of men and boys set up a roar. They were quarrelsome and mischievous, and had not yet got their fill of rowdyism.

" *Va-t'ang, va-t'ang* " (go away), " Rose à Charlitte. We want no women here. Go home about thy business. If Big Fists wishes to fight, we will fight."

Among all the noisy, discordant voices this was the only insulting one, and Rose turned and fixed her mild gaze on the offender, who was one of the oldest men present, and the chief mischief-maker of the neighborhood. " But it is not well for all to fight one man," she said, gently.

" We fight one by one. Isidore is big, — he has never enough. Go away, or there will yet be a bigger row," and he added a sentence of gross abuse.

Vesper made a step forward, but Isidore, the young bully, who was of immense height and breadth, and a son of the old Acadienne that they had just quitted, was before him.

" You wish to fight, my friends," he said, jocularly ; " here, take this," and, lifting his big foot, he quickly upset the offender, and kicked him towards some men in the crowd who were also relatives of Rose.

One of them sprang forward, and, with his dark face alight with glee at the chance to avenge the affront offered to his kinswoman, at once proceeded to beat the offender calmly and systematically, and to roll him under the fence.

Rose, in great distress, attempted to go to his rescue, but the young giant threw his arm around her. "This is only fun, my cousin. Thou must not spoil everything. Come, I will return with thee."

"*Nâni*" (no), cried Agapit, furiously, "thou wilt not. Fit company art thou for strangers!"

Isidore stared confusedly at him, while Vesper settled the question by inviting him in the back seat and installing Rose beside him. Then he held out his arms to Narcisse, who had been watching the disturbance with drowsy interest, fearful only that the Englishman from Boston might leave him to take a hand in it.

As soon as Vesper mounted the seat beside him, Agapit jerked the reins, and set off at a rapid pace; so rapid that Vesper at first caught only snatches of the dialogue carried on behind him, that was tearful on the part of Rose, and meek on that of Isidore.

Soon Agapit sobered down, and Rose's words could be distinguished. "My cousin, how canst thou? Think only of thy mother and thy wife; and the good priest, — suppose he had come!"

"Then thou wouldst have seen running like that of foxes," replied Isidore, in good-natured, semi-interested tones.

"Thou wast not born a drunkard. When sober

thou art good, but there could not be a worse man when drunk. Such a pile of cursing words to go up to the sky, — and such a volley of fisting. Ah, how thou wast wounding Christ!"

Isidore held on tightly, for Agapit was still driving fast, and uttered an inaudible reply.

"Tell me where thou didst get that liquor," said Rose.

"It was a stolen cask, my cousin."

"Isidore!"

"But I did not steal it. It came from thy charming Bay. Thou didst not know that, shortly ago, a captain sailed to Sleeping Water with five casks of rum. He hired a man from the Concession to help him hide them, but the man stole one cask. Imagine the rage of the captain, but he could not prosecute, for it was smuggled. Since then we have fun occasionally."

"Who is that bad man? If I knew where was his cask, I would take a little nail and make a hole in it."

"Rose, couldst thou expect me to tell thee?"

"Yes," she said, warmly. Then, remembering that she had been talking English to his French, she suddenly relapsed into low, swift sentences in her own tongue, which Vesper could not understand. He caught their import, however. She was still inveighing against the sin of drunkenness and was begging him to reform, and her voice did not flag until they reached his home, where his wife — a young woman with magnificent eyes and a straight, queenly figure — stood by the gate.

"*Bon soir* (good evening), Claudine," called out Agapit. "We have brought home Isidore, who, hearing that a distinguished stranger was about to pass through the Concession, thoughtfully put himself on exhibition at the four roads. You had better keep him at home until *La Guerrière* goes back to Saint Pierre."

"It was *La Guerrière* that brought the liquor," said Rose, suddenly, to Isidore.

He did not contradict her, and she said, firmly, "Never shall that captain darken my doors again."

The young Acadien beauty gave Vesper a fleeting glance, then she said, bitterly, "It should rather be Saint Judas, for from there the evil one sends stuff to torture us women — Here enter," and half scornfully, half affectionately, she extended a hand to her huge husband, who was making a wavering effort to reach the gateway.

He clung to her as if she had been an anchor, and when she asked him what had happened to his shirt he stuttered, regretfully, "Torn, Claudine, — torn again."

"How many times should one mend a shirt?" she asked, turning her big blazing eyes on Rose.

"Charlitte never became drunk," said Rose, in a plaintive voice, "but I have mended the shirts of my brothers at least a hundred times."

"Then I have but one more time," said the youthful Madame Kessy. "After that I shall throw it in the fire. Go into the house, my husband. I was a fool to have married thee," she added, under her breath.

Isidore stood tottering on his feet, and regarded her with tipsy gravity. "And thou shalt come with me, my pretty one, and make me a hot supper and sing me a song."

"I will not do that. Thou canst eat cold bread, and I will sing thee a song with my tongue that will not please thee."

"The priest married us," said Isidore, doggedly, and in momentary sobriety he stalked to the place where she stood, picked her up, and, putting her under his arm, carried her into the house, she meanwhile protesting and laughing hysterically while she shrieked out something to Rose about the loan of a sleeve pattern.

"Yes, yes, I understand," called Rose, "the big sleeve, with many folds; I will send it. Make thy husband his supper and come soon to see me."

"Rose," said Agapit, severely, as they drove away, "is it a good thing to make light of that curse of curses?"

"To make light of it! *Mon Dieu,* you do not understand. It is men who make women laugh even when their hearts are breaking."

Agapit did not reply, and, as they were about to enter a thick wood, he passed the reins to Vesper and got out to light the lamps.

While he was fidgeting with them, Rose moved around so that she could look into the front seat.

"Your child is all right," said Vesper, gazing down at the head laid confidingly against his arm. "He is sound asleep, — not a bit alarmed by that fuss."

"It does not frighten him when human beings cry out. He only sorrows for things that have no voices, and he is always right when with you. It is not that; I wish to ask you — to ask you to forgive me."

"For what?"

"But you know — I told you what was not true."

"Do not speak of it. It was a mere bagatelle."

"It is not a bagatelle to make untruths," she said, wearily, "but I often do it, — most readily when I am frightened. But you did not frighten me."

Vesper did not reply except by a reassuring glance, which in her preoccupation she lost, and, catching her breath, she went on, "I think so often of a sentence from an Englishman that the sisters of a convent used to say to us, — it is about the little lies as well as the big ones that come from the pit."

"Do you mean Ruskin?" said Vesper, curiously,

"when he speaks of 'one falsity as harmless, and another as slight, and another as unintended, — cast them all aside; they may be light and accidental, but they are ugly soot from the smoke of the pit for all that?'"

"Yes, yes, it is that, — will you write it for me? — and remember," she continued, hurriedly, as she saw Agapit preparing to reënter the cart, "that I did not say what I did to make a fine tale, but for my people whom I love. You were a stranger, and I supposed you would linger but a day and then proceed, and it is hard for me to say that the Acadiens are no better than the English, — that they will get drunk and fight. I did not imagine that you would see them, yet I should not have told the story," and with her flaxen head drooping on her breast she turned away from him.

"When is lying justifiable?" asked Vesper of Agapit.

The young Acadien plunged into a long argument that lasted until they reached the top of the hill overlooking Sleeping Water. Then he paused, and as he once more saw above him the wide expanse of sky to which he was accustomed, and knew that before him lay the Bay, wide, open, and free, he drew a long breath.

"Ah, but I am glad to arrive home. When I go to the woods it is as if a large window through which

I had been taking in the whole world had been closed."

No one replied to him, and he soon swung them around the corner and up to the inn door. Rose led her sleepy boy into the kitchen, where bright lights were burning, and where the maid Célina seemed to be entertaining callers. Vesper took the lantern and followed Agapit to the stable.

"Is it a habit of yours to give your hotel guests drives?" he asked, hanging the lantern on a hook and assisting Agapit in unbuckling straps.

"Yes, whenever it pleases us. Many, also, hire our horse and pony. You see that we have no common horse in Toochune."

"Yes, I know he is a thoroughbred."

"Rose, of course, could not buy such an animal. He was a gift from her uncle in Louisiana. He also sent her this dog-cart and her organ. He is rich, very rich. He went South as a boy, and was adopted by an old farmer; Rose is the daughter of his favorite sister, and I tell her that she will inherit from him, for his wife is dead and he is alone, but she says not to count on what one does not know."

Vesper had already been favored with these items of information by his mother, so he said nothing, and assisted Agapit in his task of making long-legged Toochune comfortable for the night. Having finished, and being rewarded by a grateful glance from the animal's lustrous eyes, they both went to the pump outside and washed their hands.

"It is too fine for the house," said Agapit. "Are you too fatigued to walk? If agreeable I will take you to Sleeping Water River, where you have not yet been, and tell you how it accumulated its name. There is no one inside," he continued, as Vesper cast a glance at the kitchen windows, "but the miller and his wife, in whom I no longer take pleasure, and the mail-driver who tells so long stories."

"So long that you have no chance."

"Exactly," said Agapit, fumbling in his pocket. "See what I bought to-day of a travelling merchant. Four cigars for ten cents. Two for you, and two for me. Shall we smoke them?"

Vesper took the cigars, slipped them in his pocket, and brought out one of his own, then with Agapit took the road leading back from the village to the river.

CHAPTER XII.

AN UNHAPPY RIVER.

> " Pools and shadows merge
> Beneath the branches, where the rushes lean
>   And stumble prone; and sad along the verge
> The marsh-hen totters. Strange the branches play
>   Above the snake-roots in the dark and wet,
> Adown the hueless trunks, this summer day.
>   Strange things the willows whisper."
>
> J. F. H.

"THERE is a story among the old people," said Agapit, "that a band of Acadiens, who evaded the English at the time of the expulsion, sailed into this Bay in a schooner. They anchored opposite Sleeping Water, and some of the men came ashore in a boat. Not knowing that an English ship lay up yonder, hidden by a point of land, they pressed back into the woods towards Sleeping Water Lake. Some of the English, also, were on their way to this lake, for it is historic. The Acadiens found traces of them and turned towards the shore, but the English pursued over the marshes by the river, which at last the Acadiens must cross. They threw aside their guns and jumped in, and, as one head rose after another, the English, standing on the bank, shot until all but one were killed. This one was a Le Blanc, a descendant of René Le Blanc, that one reads of in 'Evangeline.' Rising up on the bank, he found himself alone. Figure the anguish of his heart, — his brothers and friends were dead. He would never see them again, and he turned and stretched out a hand in a supreme adieu. The English, who would not trouble to swim, fired at him, and called, 'Go to sleep with your comrades in the river.'

"'They sleep,' he cried, 'but they will rise again in their children,' and, quite untouched by their fire, he ran to his boat, and, reaching the ship, set sail to New Brunswick; and in later years his children and the children of the murdered ones came back to the Bay, and began to call the river Sleeping Water, and, in time, the lake, which was Queen Anne's Lake, was also changed to Sleeping Water Lake."

"And the soldiers?"

"Ah! you look for vengeance, but does vengeance always come? Remember the Persian distich:

"'They came, conquered, and burned,
Pillaged, murdered, and went.'"

"I do not understand this question thoroughly," said Vesper, with irritation, "yet from your conversation it seems not so barbarous a thing that the Acadiens should have been transported as that those who remained should have been so persecuted."

"Now is your time to read 'Richard.' I have long been waiting for your health to be restored, for it is exciting."

"That is the Acadien historian you have spoken of?"

"Yes; and when you read him you will understand my joy at the venerable letter you showed me. You will see why we blame the guilty Lawrence and his colleagues, and not England herself, for the wickedness wrought her French children."

Vesper smoked out his cigar in silence. They had left the village street some distance behind them, and were now walking along a flat, narrow road, having a thick, hedge-like border of tangled bushes and wild flowers that were agitated by a gentle breeze, and waved out a sweet, faint perfume on the night air. On either side of them were low, grassy marshes, screened by clumps of green.

"We are arrived at last," said Agapit, pausing on a rustic bridge that spanned the road; "and down there," he went on, in a choking voice, "is where the bones of my countrymen lie."

Vesper leaned over the railing. What a sluggish, silent, stealthy river! He could perceive no flow in its reluctant waters. A few willows, natives, not French ones, swayed above it, and close to its edge grew the tall grasses, rustling and whispering together as if imparting guilty secrets concerning the waters below.

"Which way does it go?" murmured Vesper; but Agapit did not hear him, for he was eagerly muttering: "A hateful river, — I never see a bird drink from it, there are no fishes in it, the lilies will not grow here, and the children fall in and are drowned; and, though it has often been sounded, they can find no bottom to it."

Vesper stared below in silence, only making an involuntary movement when his companion's cap fell off and struck the face of the dull black mirror presented to them.

"Let it go," exclaimed Agapit, with a shudder. "Poor as I am, I would not wear it now. It is tainted," and flinging back the dark locks from his forehead, he turned his face towards the shore.

"No, I will talk no more about the Acadiens," he said, when Vesper tried to get him to enter upon his favorite theme, "for, though you are polite, I fear I shall weary you; we will speak of other things."

The night was a perfect one, and for an hour the two young men walked up and down the quiet road before the inn, talking at first of the fishing that was over, and the hunting that would in a few weeks begin.

Vesper would have enjoyed seeking big game in

the backwoods, if his health had permitted, and he listened with suppressed eagerness to Agapit's account of a moose hunt. The world of sport disposed of, their conversation drifted to literature, to science and art in general, — to women and love affairs, and Agapit rambled on excitedly and delightedly, while Vesper, contenting himself with the briefest of rejoinders, extracted an acute and amused interest from the entirely novel and out-of-the-way opinions presented to him.

"Ah! but I enjoy this," said Agapit, at last; "it is the fault of my countrymen that they do not read enough and study, — their sole fault. I meet with so few who will discuss, yet I must not detain you. Come in, come in, and I will give you my 'Richard.' Begin not to read him to-night, for you could not sleep. I believe," and he raised his brown, flushed face to the stars above, "that he has done justice to the Acadien people; but remember, we do not complain now. We are faithful to our sovereign and to our country, — as faithful as you are to your Union. The smart of the past is over. We ask only that the world may believe that the Acadiens were loyal and consistent, and that we do not wish for reparation from England except, perhaps — " and he hesitated and looked down at the shabby sleeve of his coat, while tears filled his eyes. "*Mon Dieu!* I will not speak of the pitiful economies that I am obliged to practise to educate myself. And there are other young men more poor. If the colonial government would give us some help, I would go to college; for now I hesitate lest I should save my money for my family. If the good lands that were taken from us were now ours, we should be rich —"

Vesper liked the young Acadien best in his quiet moods. "Don't worry," he said, consolingly; "something will turn up. Get me that book, will you?"

Vesper paused for an instant when he entered his room. On a table by his bed was placed a tray, covered by a napkin. Lifting the napkin, he discovered a wing of cold chicken with jelly, thin slices of bread and butter, and a covered pitcher of chocolate.

He poured himself out a cup of the chocolate, and murmuring, "Here's to the Lady of the Sleeping Water Inn," seized one of the two volumes that Agapit had given him, and, throwing himself into an easy chair, began to read.

One by one the hours slipped away, but he did not move in his chair, except to put out a hand at regular intervals and turn a leaf. Shortly before daybreak a chill wind blew up the Bay, and came floating in the window. He threw down the book, rose slowly to his feet, and looked about him in a dreamy way. He had been transported to a previous century and to another atmosphere than this peaceful one.

He shivered sensitively, and, going to the window, closed it, and stood gazing at the faint flush in the sky. "O God! it is true," he muttered, drearily, "we are sent into this world to enact hell. Goethe understood that. And what a hell of long years was enacted on these shores!"

"The devils," he went on, in youthful, generous indignation; "they had no pity, not even after years of suffering on the part of their victims."

His eyes smarted, his head ached. He put his hand to his eyes, and, when it came away wet, he curled his lip. He had not shed tears since he was a boy.

Then he threw himself on his bed, and thoughts of his father mingled with those of the Acadiens. An invincible melancholy took possession of him, and burying his face in his arms, he lay for a long time with his whole frame quivering in emotion.

CHAPTER XIII.

AN ILLUMINATION.

"Sait-on où l'on va?"

"WHAT a sleeper, what a lover of his bed!" exclaimed Agapit, the next morning, as he rapped vigorously on Vesper's door. "Is he never going to rise?"

"What do you want?" said a voice from within.

"I, Agapit, latest and warmest of your friends, apologize for disturbing you, but am forced to ask a question."

"Come in; the door is not locked."

Agapit thrust his head in. "Did you sit late reading my books?"

Vesper lifted his closely cropped curly head from the pillow. "Yes."

"And did not your heart stir with pity for the unfortunate Acadiens?"

"I found the history interesting."

"I wept over it at my first reading, — I gnashed my teeth; but come, — will you not go to the picnic with us? All the Bay is going, as the two former days of it were dull."

"I had forgotten it. Does my mother wish to go?"

"Madame, your mother, is already prepared. See from your window, she talks to the mail-driver, who never tires of her adorable French. Do you know, this morning he came herding down the road three shy children, who were triplets. She was charmed, having never seen more than twins."

Vesper raised himself on his elbow and glanced through the window at Monsieur de la Rive, who, with his bright wings folded close to his sides, was cheeping voluble remarks to Mrs. Nimmo.

"All right, I will go," he said.

Agapit hurried down-stairs, and Vesper began to dress himself in a leisurely way, stopping frequently to go to the window and gaze dreamily out at the Bay.

Soon Rose came to the kitchen door to feed her hens. She looked so lovely, as she stood with her resplendent head in a blaze of sunlight, that Vesper's fingers paused in the act of fastening his necktie, and he stood still to watch her.

Presently the mail-driver went streaking down the road in fiery flight, and Mrs. Nimmo, seeing Rose alone, came tripping towards her. To her son, who understood her perfectly, there were visible in Mrs. Nimmo's manner some sure and certain signs of an inward disturbance. Rose, however, perceived nothing, and continued feeding her hens with her usual grace and composure.

"Are you not going to the picnic?" asked Mrs. Nimmo, and her eye ran over the simple cotton gown that Rose always wore in the morning.

"Yes, madame, but first I do my work."

"You will be glad to see your friends there, — and your family?"

"Ah, yes, madame, — it is such a pleasure."

"I should like see your sister, Perside."

"I will present her, madame; she will be honored."

"And it is she that the blacksmith is going to marry? Do you know," and Mrs. Nimmo laughed tremulously, "I have been thinking all the time that it was you."

"Now I get at the cause of your discontent," soliloquized Vesper, above, "my poor little mother."

Rose surveyed her companion in astonishment: "I thought all the Bay knew."

"But I am not the Bay," said Mrs. Nimmo, with attempted playfulness; "I am Boston."

A shadow crossed Rose's face. "Yes, madame, I know. I might have told you, but I did not think; and you are delicate, — you would not ask."

"No, I am not delicate," said Mrs. Nimmo, honestly. "I am inclined to be curious, or interested in other people, we will say, — I think you are very kind to be making matrimonial plans for other young women, and not to think of yourself."

" Madame ? "

" You do not know that long word. It means pertaining to marriage."

" Ah! marriage, I understand that. But, lately, I resolve not to marry," and Rose turned her deep blue eyes, in which there was not a trace of craft or deceit, on her nervously apprehensive interlocutor, while Vesper murmured in the window above, " She is absolutely guileless, my mother; cast out of your mind that vague and formless suspicion."

Mrs. Nimmo, however, preferred to keep the suspicion, and not only to keep it, but to foster the stealthy creeping thing until it had taken on the rudiments of organized reflection.

" Some young people do not care for marriage," she said, after a long pause. " My son never has."

" May the Lord forgive you for that," ejaculated her son, piously. Then he listened for Rose's response, which was given with deep respect and humility. " He is devoted to you, madame. It is pleasant to see a son thus."

" He is a dear boy, and it would kill me if he were to leave me. I am glad that you appreciate him, and that he has found this place so interesting. We shall hate to leave here."

" Must you go soon, madame ? "

"Pretty soon, I think; as soon as my son finishes this quest of his. You know it is very quiet here. You like it because it is your home, but we, of course, are accustomed to a different life."

"I know that, madame," said Rose, sadly, "and it will seem yet more quiet when we do not see you. I dread the long days."

"I daresay we may come back sometime. My son likes to revisit favorite spots, and the strong air of the Bay certainly agrees wonderfully with him. He is sleeping like a baby this morning. I must go now and see if he is up. Thank you for speaking so frankly to me about yourself. Do you know, I believe you agree with me," — and Mrs. Nimmo leaned confidentially towards her, — "that it is a perfectly wicked thing for a widow to marry again," and she tripped away, folding about her the white shawl she always wore.

Rose gazed after her retreating form with a face that was, for a time, wholly mystified.

By degrees, her expression became clearer. "Good heavens! she understands," muttered Vesper; "now let us see if there will be any resentment."

There was none. A vivid, agonized blush overspread Rose's cheeks. She let the last remnant of food slip to the expectant hens from her two hands, that suddenly went out in a gesture of acute distress; but the glance that she bestowed on Mrs. Nimmo, who was just vanishing around the corner of the house, was one of saintly magnanimity, with not a trace of pride or rebellion in it.

Vesper shrugged his shoulders and left the window. "Strange that the best of women will worry each other," and philosophically proceeding with his toilet, he shortly after went down-stairs.

After a breakfast that was not scanty, as his breakfasts had been before his illness, but one that was comprehensive and eaten with good appetite, he made his way to the parlor, where his mother was sitting among a number of vivacious Acadiens.

Rose, slim and elegant in a new black gown, and having on her head a small straw hat, with a dotted veil drawn neatly over her pink cheeks and mass of light hair, was receiving other young men and women who were arriving, while Agapit, burly, and almost handsome in his Sunday suit of black serge, was bustling about, and, immediately pouncing upon Vesper, introduced him to each member of the party.

The young American did not care to talk. He returned to the doorway, and, loitering there, amused himself by comparing the Acadiens who had remained at home with those who had gone out into the world.

The latter were dressed more gaily; they had

more assurance, and, in nearly every case, less charm of manner than the former. There was Rose's aunt, — white-haired Madame Pitre. She was like a sweet and demure little owl in her hood-like handkerchief and plain gown. Amandine, her daughter who had never left the Bay, was a second little owl; but the sisters Diane and Lucie, factory girls from Worcester, were overdressed birds of paradise, in their rustling silk blouses, big plumed hats, and self-conscious manners.

"Here, at last, is the wagon," cried Agapit, running to the door, as a huge, six-seated vehicle, drawn by four horses, appeared. He made haste to assist his friends and relatives into it, then, darting to Vesper, who stood on the veranda, exclaimed, "The most honorable seat beside me is for madame, your mother."

"Do you care to go?" asked Vesper, addressing her."

"I should like to go to the picnic, but could you not drive me?"

"But certainly he can," exclaimed Agapit. "Toochune is in the stable. Possibly this big wagon would be noisy for madame. I will go and harness."

"You will do nothing of the kind," said Vesper, laying a detaining hand on his shoulder. "You go on. We will follow."

Agapit nodded gaily, and sprang to the box, while Rose bent her flushed face over Narcisse, who set up a sudden wail of despair. "He is coming, my child. Thou knowest he does not break his promises."

Narcisse raised his fist as if to strike her; he was in a fury at being restrained, and, although ordinarily a shy child, he was at present utterly regardless of the strangers about him.

"Stop, stop, Agapit!" cried Diane; "he will cast himself over the wheel!"

Agapit pulled up the horses, and Vesper, hearing the disturbance, and knowing the cause, came sauntering after the wagon, with a broad smile on his face.

He became grave, however, when he saw Rose's pained expression. "I think it better not to yield," she said, in a low voice. "Calm thyself, Narcisse, thou shalt not get out."

"I will," gasped the child. "You are a bad mother. The Englishman may run away if I leave him. You know he is going."

"Let me have him for a minute," said Vesper. "I will talk to him," and, reaching out his arms, he took the child from the blacksmith, who swung him over the side of the wagon.

"Come get a drink of water," said the young American, good-humoredly. "Your little face is as red as a turkey-cock's."

Narcisse pressed his hot forehead to Vesper's

cheek, and meekly allowed himself to be carried into the house.

"Now don't be a baby," said Vesper, putting him on the kitchen sink, and holding a glass of water to his lips; "I am coming after you in half an hour."

"Will you not run away?"

"No," said Vesper, "I will not."

Narcisse gave him a searching look. "I believe you; but my mother once said to me that I should have a ball, and she did not give it."

"What is it that the Englishman has done to the child?" whispered Madame Pitre to her neighbor, when Vesper brought back the quiet and composed Narcisse and handed him to his mother. "It is like magic."

"It is rather that the child needs a father," replied the young Acadienne addressed. "Rose should marry."

"I wish the Englishman was poor," muttered Madame Pitre, "and also Acadien; but he does not think of Rose, and Acadiens do not marry out of their race."

Vesper watched them out of sight, and then he found that Agapit had spoken truly when he said that all the Bay was going to the picnic. Célina's mother, a brown-faced, vigorous old woman who was to take charge of the inn for the day, was the only person to be seen, and he therefore went himself to the stable and harnessed Toochune to the dog-cart.

Célina's mother admiringly watched the dog-cart joining the procession of bicycles, buggies, two-wheeled carts, and big family wagons going down the Bay, and fancied that its occupants must be extremely happy.

Mrs. Nimmo, however, was not happy, and nothing distracted her attention from her own teasing thoughts. She listened abstractedly to the merry chatter of French in the air, and gazed disconsolately at the gloriously sunny Bay, where a few distant schooner sails stood up sharp against the sky like the white wings of birds.

At last she sighed heavily, and said, in a plaintive voice, "Vesper, are you not getting tired of Sleeping Water?"

He flicked his whip at a fly that was torturing Toochune, then said, calmly, "No, I am not."

"I never saw you so interested in a place," she observed, with a fretful side glance. "The travelling agents and loquacious peasants never seem to bore you."

"But I do not talk to the agents, and I do not find the others loquacious; neither would I call them peasants."

"It doesn't matter what you call them. They are all beneath you."

Vesper looked meditatively across the Bay at a zigzag, woolly trail of smoke made by a steamer that was going back and forth in a distressed way, as if unable to find the narrow passage that led to the Bay of Fundy.

"The Checkertons have gone to the White Mountains," said Mrs. Nimmo, in a vexed tone, as if the thought gave her no pleasure. "I should like to join them there."

"Very well, we can leave here to-morrow."

Her face brightened. "But your business?"

"I can send some one to look after it, or Agapit would attend to it."

"And you would not need to come back?"

"Not necessarily. I might do so, however."

"In the event of some of the LeNoirs being found?"

"In the event of my not being able to exist without — the Bay."

"Give me the Charles River," said Mrs. Nimmo, hastily. "It is worth fifty Bays."

"To me also," said Vesper; "but there is one family here that I should like to transplant to the banks of the Charles."

Mrs. Nimmo did not speak until they had passed through long Comeauville and longer Saulnierville, and were entering peaceful Meteghan River with its quietly flowing stream and grassy meadows. Then having partly subdued the first shock of having a horror of such magnitude presented to her, she murmured, "Are you sure that you know your own mind?"

"Quite sure, mother," he said, earnestly and affectionately; "but now, as always, my first duty is to you."

Tears sprang to her eyes, and ran quietly down her cheeks. "When you lay ill," she said, in a repressed voice, "I sat by you. I prayed to God to spare your life. I vowed that I would do anything to please you, yet, now that you are well, I cannot bear the idea of giving you up to another woman."

Vesper looked over his shoulder, then guided Toochune up by one of the gay gardens before the never-ending row of houses in order to allow a hay-wagon to pass them. When they were again in the middle of the road, he said, "I, too, had serious thoughts when I was ill, but you know how difficult it is for me to speak of the things nearest my heart."

"I know that you are a good son," she said, passionately. "You would give up the woman of your choice for my sake, but I would not allow it, for it would make you hate me, — I have seen so much trouble in families where mothers have opposed their sons' marriages. It does no good, and then — I do not want you to be a lonely old man when I'm gone."

"Mother," he said, protestingly.

"How did it happen?" she asked, suddenly composing herself, and dabbing at her face with her handkerchief.

Vesper's face grew pale, and, after a short hesitation, he said, dreamily, "I scarcely know. She has become mixed up with my life in an imperceptible way, and there is an inexpressible something about her that I have never found in any other woman."

Mrs. Nimmo struggled with a dozen conflicting thoughts. Then she sighed, miserably, "Have you asked her to marry you?"

"No."

"But you will?"

"I do not know," he said, reluctantly. "I have nothing planned. I wish to tell you, to save misunderstandings."

"She has some crotchet against marriage, — she told me so this morning. Do you know what it is?"

"I can guess."

Mrs. Nimmo pondered a minute. "She has fallen in love with you," she said at last, "and because she thinks you will not marry her, she will have no other man."

"I think you scarcely understand her. She does not understand herself."

Mrs. Nimmo uttered a soft, "Nonsense!" under her breath.

"Suppose we drop the matter for a time," said Vesper, in acute sensitiveness. "It is in an incipient state as yet."

"I know you better than to suppose that it will remain incipient," said his mother, despairingly. "You never give anything up. But, as you say, we had better not talk any more about it. It has given me a terrible shock, and I will need time to get over it, — I thank you for telling me, however," and she silently directed her attention to the distant red cathedral spire, and the white houses of Meteghan, — the place where the picnic was being held.

They caught up with the big wagon just before it reached a large brown building, surrounded by a garden and pleasure-grounds, and situated some distance from the road. This was the convent, and Vesper knew that, within its quiet walls, Rose had received the education that had added to her native grace the gentle *savoir faire* that reminded him of convent-bred girls that he had met abroad, and that made her seem more like the denizen of a city than the mistress of a little country inn.

In front of the convent the road was almost blocked by vehicles. Rows of horses stood with their heads tied to its garden fence, and bicycles by the dozen were ranged in the shadow of its big trees. Across the road from it a green field had been surrounded by a hedge of young spruce trees, and from this enclosure sounds of music and merrymaking could be heard. A continual stream of people kept pouring in at the entrance-gate, without, however, making much diminution in the crowd outside.

Agapit requested his passengers to alight, then, accompanied by one of the young men of his party, who took charge of Vesper's horse, he drove to a near stable. Five minutes later he returned, and found his companions drawn up together watching Acadien boys and girls flock into the saloon of a travelling photographer.

"There is now no time for picture-taking," he vociferated; "come, let us enter. See, I have tickets," and he proudly marshalled his small army up to the gate, and entered the picnic grounds at their head.

They found Vesper and his mother inside. This ecclesiastical fair going on under the convent walls, and almost in the shadow of the red cathedral, reminded them of the fairs of history. Here, as there, no policemen were needed among the throngs of buyers and sellers, who strolled around and around the grassy enclosure, and examined the wares exhibited in verdant booths. Good order was ensured by the presence of several priests, who were greeted with courtesy and reverence by all. Agapit, who was a devout Catholic, stood with his hat in his hand until his own parish priest had passed; then his eyes fell on the essentially modern and central object in the fair grounds, — a huge merry-go-round from Boston, with brightly painted blue seats, to which a load of Acadien children clung in an ecstacy of delight, as they felt themselves being madly whirled through the air.

"Let us all ride!" he exclaimed. "Come, showman, give us the next turn."

The wheezing, panting engine stopped, and they all mounted, even Madame Pitre, who shivered with delicious apprehension, and Mrs. Nimmo, who whispered in her son's ear, "I never did such a thing before, but in Acadie one must do as the Acadiens do."

Vesper sat down beside her, and took the slightly dubious Narcisse on his knee, holding him closely when an expression of fear flitted over his delicate features, and encouraging him to sit upright when at last he became more bold.

"Another turn," shouted Agapit, when the music ceased, and they were again stationary. The whistle blew, and they all set out again; but no one wished to attempt a third round, and, giddily stumbling over each other, they dismounted and with laughing remarks wandered to another part of the grounds, where dancing was going on in two spruce arbors.

"It is necessary for all to join," he proclaimed, at the top of his voice, but his best persuasions failed to induce either Rose or Vesper to step into the arbors, where two young Acadiens sat perched up in two corners, and gleefully tuned their fiddles.

"She will not dance, because she wishes to make herself singular," reflected Mrs. Nimmo, bitterly, and Vesper, who felt the unspoken thought as keenly as if it had been uttered, moved a step nearer Rose, who modestly stood apart from them.

Agapit flung down his money,— ten cents apiece for each dance, — and, ordering his associates to choose their partners, signed to the fiddlers to begin.

Mrs. Nimmo forgot Rose for a time, as she watched the dancers. The girls were shy and demure; the young men danced lustily, and with great spirit, emphasizing the first note of each bar by a stamp on the floor, and beating a kind of tattoo with one foot, when not taking part in the quadrille.

"Do you have only square dances?" she asked Madame Pitre, when a second and a third quadrille were succeeded by a fourth.

"Yes," said the Acadienne, gravely. "There is no sin in a quadrille. There is in a waltz."

"Come seek the lunch-tables," said Agapit, presently bursting out on them, and mopping his perspiring face with his handkerchief. "Most ambrosial dainties are known to the cooks of this parish."

CHAPTER XIV.

WITH THE OLD ONES.

" The fresh salt breezes mingle with the smell
Of clover fields and ripened hay beside;
And Nature, musing, happy and serene,
Hath here for willing man her sweetest spell."

J. F. H.

AFTER lunch, the Sleeping Water party separated. The Pitres found some old friends from up the Bay. Agapit wandered away with some young men, and Vesper, lazily declining to saunter with them, stood leaning against a tree behind a bench on which his mother and Rose were seated.

The latter received and exchanged numerous greetings with her acquaintances who passed by, sometimes detaining them for an introduction to Mrs. Nimmo, who was making a supreme effort to be gracious and agreeable to the woman that the fates had apparently destined to be her daughter-in-law.

Vesper looked on, well pleased. " Why do you not introduce me?" he said, mischievously, while his mother's attention was occupied with two Acadien girls.

Rose gave him a troubled glance. She took no pleasure in his presence now, — his mother had spoiled all that, and, although naturally simple and unaffected, she was now tortured by self-consciousness.

"I think that you do not care," she said, in a low voice.

Vesper did not pursue the subject. "Have all Acadien women gentle manners?" he asked, with a glance at the pair of shy, retiring ones talking to his mother.

A far-away look came into Rose's eyes, and she replied, with more composure: "The Abbé Casgrain says — he who wrote 'A Pilgrimage to the Land of Evangeline' — that over all Acadiens hangs a quietness and melancholy that come from the troubles of long ago; but Agapit does not find it so."

"What does Agapit say?"

"He finds," and Rose drew her slight figure up proudly, "that we are born to good manners. It was the best blood of France that settled Acadie. Did our forefathers come here poor? No, they brought much money. They built fine houses of stone, not wood; Grand Pré was a very fine village. They also built châteaux. Then, after scatteration, we became poor; but can we not keep our good manners?"

Vesper was much diverted by the glance with which his mother, having bowed farewell to her new acquaintances, suddenly favored Rose. There was pride in it, — pride in the beauty and distinction of the woman beside her who was scarcely more than a girl; yet there was also in her glance a jealousy and aversion that could not yet be overcome. Time alone could effect this; and smothering a sigh, Vesper lifted his head towards Narcisse, who had crawled from his shoulder to a most uncomfortable seat on the lower limb of a pine-tree, where, however, he professed to be most comfortable, and sat with his head against the rough bark as delightedly as if it were the softest of cushions.

"I am quite right," said Narcisse, in English, which language he was learning with astonishing rapidity, and Vesper again turned his attention to the picturesque, constantly changing groups of people. He liked best the brown and wrinkled old faces belonging to farmers and their wives who were enjoying a well-earned holiday. The young men in gray suits, he heard Rose telling his mother, were sailors from up the Bay, whose schooners had arrived just in time for them to throw themselves on their wheels and come to the picnic. The smooth-faced girls in blue, with pink handkerchiefs on their heads, were from a settlement back in the woods. The dark-eyed maidens in sailor hats, who looked like a troop of young Evangelines, were the six demoiselles Aucoin, the daughters of a lawyer in Meteghan, and the tall lady in blue was an Acadienne from New York, who brought her family every summer to her old home on the Bay.

"And that tall priest in the distance," said Rose, "is the father in whose parish we are. Once he was a colonel in the army of France."

"There is something military in his figure," murmured Mrs. Nimmo.

"He was born among the Acadiens in France. They did not need him to ministrate, so when he became a priest he journeyed here," continued Rose, hurriedly, for the piercing eyes of the kindly-faced ecclesiastic had sought out Vesper and his mother, and he was approaching them with an uplifted hat.

Rose got up and said, in a fluttering voice, "May I present you, Father La Croix, to Mrs. Nimmo, and also her son?"

The priest bowed gracefully, and begged to assure madame and her son that their fame had already preceded them, and that he was deeply grateful to them for honoring his picnic with their presence.

"I suppose there are not many English people here to-day," said Mrs. Nimmo, smiling amiably, while Vesper contented himself with a silent bow.

Father La Croix gazed about the crowd, now greatly augmented. "As far as I can see, madame, you and your son are the only English that we have the pleasure of entertaining. You are now in the heart of the French district of Clare."

"And yet I hear a good deal of English spoken."

Father La Croix smiled. "We all understand it, and you see here a good many young people employed in the States, who are home for their holidays."

"And I suppose we are the only Protestants here," continued Mrs. Nimmo.

"The only ones, — you are also alone in the parish of Sleeping Water. If at any time a sense of isolation should prey upon madame and her son —"

He did not finish his sentence except by another smile of infinite amusement, and a slight withdrawal of his firm lips from his set of remarkably white teeth.

Rose was disturbed. Vesper noticed that the mention of the word Protestant at any time sent her into a transport of uneasiness. She was terrified lest a word might be said to wound his feelings or those of his mother.

"*Monsieur le curé* is jesting, Madame de Forêt," he said, reassuringly. "He is quite willing that we should remain heretics."

Rose's face cleared, and Vesper said to the priest, "Are there any old people here to-day who would be inclined to talk about the early settlers?"

"Yes, and they would be flattered, — up behind

the lunch-tables is a knot of old men exchanging reminiscences of early days. May I have the pleasure of introducing you to them?"

"I shall be gratified if you will do so," and both men lifted their hats to Mrs. Nimmo and Rose, and then disappeared among the crowd.

Narcisse immediately demanded to be taken from the tree, and, upon reaching the ground, burst into tears. "Look, my mother,—I did not see before."

Rose followed the direction of his pointing finger. He pretended to have just discovered that under the feet of this changeful assemblage were millions of crushed and suffering grass-blades.

Rose exchanged a glance with Mrs. Nimmo. This was a stroke of childish diplomacy. He wished to follow Vesper.

"Show him something to distract his attention," whispered the elder woman. "I will go talk to Madame Pitre."

"See, Narcisse, this little revolver," said Rose, leading him up to a big wheel of fortune, before which a dozen men sat holding numbered sticks in their hands. "When the wheel stops, some men lose, others gain."

"I see only the grass-blades," wailed Narcisse. "My mother, does it hurt them to be trampled on?"

"No, my child; see, they fly back again. I have even heard that it made them grow."

"Let us walk where there is no grass," said Narcisse, passionately, and, drawing her along with him, he went obliviously past the fruit and candy booths, and the spread tables, to a little knoll where sat three old men on rugs.

Vesper lay stretched on the grass before them, and, catching sight of Narcisse, who was approaching so boldly, and his mother, who was holding back so shyly, he craved permission from the old men to seat them on one of the rugs.

The permission was gladly given, and Rose shook hands with the three old men, whom she knew well. Two of them were brothers, from Meteghan, the other was a cousin, from up the Bay, whom they rarely saw. The brothers were slim, well-made, dapper old men; the cousin was a fat, jolly farmer, dressed in homespun.

"I can tell you one of olden times," said this latter, in a thick, syrupy voice, "better dan dat last."

"Suppose we have it then," said Vesper.

"Dere was Pierre Belliveau, — Pierre aged dwenty-one and a half at de drama of 1755. His fadder was made prisoner. Pierre, he run to de fores' wid four, — firs' Cyprian Gautreau and de tree brudders, Joseph *dit* Coudgeau, Charlitte *dit* Le Fort —"

"Is that where the husband of Madame de Forêt got his name?" interrupted Vesper, indicating his landlady by a gesture.

"Yes," said the old man, "it is a name of long ago, — besides Charlitte was Bonaventure, an' dese five men suffered horrible, mos' horrible, for winter came on, an' dey was all de time hungry w'en dey wasn't eatin', an' dey had to roam by night like dogs, to pick up w'at dey could. But dey live till de spring, an' dey wander like de wile beasties roun' de fores' of Beauséjour, an' dey was well watched by de English. If dey had been shot, dis man would not be talkin' to you, for Bonaventure was my ancessor on my modder's side. On a day w'en dey come to Tintamarre — you know de great ma'sh of Tintamarre?"

"No; I never heard of it."

"Well, it big ma'sh in Westmoreland County. One day dey come dere, an' dey perceive not far from dem a *goêlette*, — a schooner. De sea was low, an' all de men in de schooner atten' de return of de tide, for dey was high an' dry. Dose five Acadiens look at dat schooner, den dey w'isper, — den dey wander, as perchance, near dat schooner. De cap'en look at dem like a happy wile beas', 'cause he was sent from Port Royal to catch the runawoods. He call out, he invite dose Acadiens, he say, 'Come on, we make you no harm,' an' dey go, meek like sheep; soon de sea mount, de cap'en shout, 'Raise de anchor,' but Pierre said, 'We mus' go ashore.' 'Trow dose Romans in *la cale*,' say dat bad man. *La cale c'est* —"

"In the hold," supplied the two other eager old men, in a breath.

"Yes, in de hole, — but tink you dey went? No; Charlitte he was big, he had de force of five men, he look at Pierre. Pierre he shout, '*Fesse*, Charlitte,' and Charlitte he snatch a bar from de deck, he bang it on de head of de Englishman an' massacre him. 'Debarrass us of anoder,' cried Pierre. Charlitte he raise his bar again, — an' still anoder, an' tree Englishmen lay on de deck. Only de cap'en remain, an' a sailor very big, — mos' as big as Charlitte. De cap'en was consternate, yet he made a sign of de han'. De sailor jump on Pierre an' try to pitch him in de hole. Tink you Charlitte let him go? No; he runs, he chucks dat sailor in de sea. Den de cap'en falls on his knees. 'Spare me de life an' I will spare you de lives.' 'Spare us de lives!' said Pierre, 'did you spare de lives of dose unhappy ones of Port Royal whom you sen' to exile? No; an' you would carry us to Halifax to de cruel English. Dat is how you spare. Where are our mudders an' fadders, our brudders an' sisters? You carry dem to a way-off shore w'ere dey cry mos' all de time. We shall see dem never. Recommen' your soul to God.' Den after a little he say very low, 'Charlitte *fesse*,' again. An' Charlitte he *fesse*, an' dey brush de han' over de eyes an' lower dat cap'en in de sea.

"Den Pierre, who was fine sailor, run de schooner

up to Petitcodiac. Later on, de son of Bonaventure come to dis Bay, an' his daughter was my mudder."

When the old man finished speaking, a shudder ran over the little group, and Vesper gazed thoughtfully at the lively scene beyond them. This was a dearly bought picnic. These quiet old men, gentle Mrs. Rose, the prattling children, the vivacious young men and women, were all descendants of ancestors who had with tears and blood sought a resting-place for their children. He longed to hear more of their exploits, and he was just about to prefer a request when little Narcisse, who had been listening with parted lips, leaned forward and patted the old man's boot. "Tell Narcisse yet another story with trees in it."

The fat old man nodded his head. "I know anodder of a Belliveau, dis one Charles. He was a carpenter an' he made ships from trees. At de great derangement de English hole him prisoner at Port Royal. One of de ships to take away de Acadiens had broke her mas' in a tempes'. Charles he make anodder, and w'en he finish dat mas' he ask his pay. One refuse him dat. Den de mas' will fall,' he say. 'I done someting to it.' De cap'en hurry to give him de price, an' Charlie he say, 'It all right.' W'en dey embark de prisoners dey put Charles on dat schooner. Dey soon leave de war-ship dat go wid dem, but de cap'en of de war-ship he say to de cap'en of de schooner, 'Take care, my fren', you got some good sailors 'mong dose Acadiens.' De cap'en of de schooner laugh. He was like dose trees, Narcisse, dat is rooted so strong dey tink dat no ting can never upset dem. He still let dose Acadiens come on deck, — six, seven at a times, cause de hole pretty foul, an' dey might die. One day, w'en de order was given, 'Go down, you Acadiens, an' come up seven odder,' de firs' lot dey open de hatch, den spring on de bridge. Dey garrotte de cap'en and crew, an' Charles go to turn de schooner. De cap'en call, 'Dat gran' mas' is weak, — you go for to break it.' 'Liar,' shouted Charles, 'dis is I dat make it.' Dose Acadiens mount de River St. John, — I don' know what dey did wid dose English. I hope dey kill 'em," he added, mildly.

"Père Baudouin," said Rose, bending forward, "this is an Englishman from Boston."

"I know," said the old man; "he is good English, dose were bad."

Vesper smiled, and asked him whether he had ever heard of the Fiery Frenchman of Grand Pré.

The old man considered carefully and consulted with his cousins. Neither of them had ever heard of such a person. There were so many Acadiens, they said, in an explanatory way, so many different bands, so many scattering groups journeying homeward. But they would inquire.

"Here comes Father La Croix," said Rose, softly; "will you not ask him to help you?"

"You are very kind to be so much interested in this search of mine," said Vesper, in a low voice.

Rose's lip trembled, and avoiding his glance, she kept her eyes fixed steadily on the ex-colonel and present priest, who was expressing a courteous hope that Vesper had obtained the information he wished.

"Not yet," said Vesper, "though I am greatly indebted to these gentlemen," and he turned to thank the old men.

"I know of your mission," said Father La Croix, "and if you will favor me with some details, perhaps I can help you."

Vesper walked to and fro on the grass with him for some minutes, and then watched him threading his way in and out among the groups of his parishioners and their guests until at last he mounted the band-stand, and extended his hand over the crowd.

He did not utter a word, yet there was almost instantaneous silence. The merry-go-round stopped, the dancers paused, and a hush fell on all present.

"My dear people," he said, "it rejoices me to see so many of you here to-day, and to know that you are enjoying yourselves. Let us be thankful to God for the fine weather. I am here to request you to do me a favor. You all have old people in your homes, — you hear them talking of the great expulsion. I wish you to ask these old ones whether they remember a certain Etex LeNoir, called the Fiery Frenchman of Grand Pré. He, too, was carried away, but never reached his destination, having died on the ship *Confidence*, but his wife and child probably arrived in Philadelphia. Find out, if you can, the fate of this widow and her child, — whether they died in a foreign land, or whether she succeeded in coming back to Acadie, — and bring the information to me."

He descended the steps, and Vesper hastened to thank him warmly for his interest.

"It may result in nothing," said the priest, "yet there is an immense amount of information stored up among the Acadiens on this Bay; I do not at all despair of finding this family," and he took a kindly leave of Vesper, after directing him where to find his mother.

"But this is terrible," said Rose, trying to restrain the ardent Narcisse, who was dragging her towards his beloved Englishman. "My child, thy mother will be forced to whip thee."

Vesper at that moment turned around, and his keen glance sought her out. "Why do you struggle with him?" he asked, coming to meet them.

"But I cannot have him tease you."

"He does not tease me," and in quiet sympathy Vesper endeavored to restore peace to her troubled mind. She, most beautiful flower of all this show, and most deserving of joy and comfort, had been unhappy and ill at ease ever since they entered the gates. The lingering, furtive glances of several young Acadiens were unheeded by her. Her only thought was to reach her home and be away from this bustle and excitement, and it was his mother who had wrought this change in her; and in sharp regret, Vesper surveyed the little lady, who, apparently in the most amiable of moods, was sitting chatting to an Acadien matron to whom Father La Croix had introduced her.

A slight scuffle in a clump of green bushes beside them distracted his attention from her. A pleading exclamation from a manly voice was followed by an eloquent silence, a brisk sound like a slap, or a box on the ears, and a laugh from a girl, with a threatening, "*Tu me paieras ça*" (Thou shalt pay me for that).

Vesper laughed too. There was something so irresistibly comical in the man's second exclamation of dismayed surprise.

"It is Perside," said Rose, wearily. "How can she be so gay, in so public a place?"

"Serves the blacksmith right, for trying to kiss her," said Vesper.

"Perside," said Rose, rebukingly, and thrusting her head through the verdant screen, "come and be presented to Mrs. Nimmo."

Perside came forward. She was a laughing, piquant beauty, smaller and more self-conscious than Rose.

With admirable composure she dismissed her blacksmith-*fiancé*, and followed her sister.

Mrs. Nimmo had been receiving a flattering amount of attention, and was holding quite a small court of Acadien women about her. Among them was Rose's stepmother. Vesper had not met her before, and he gazed at her calm, statuesque, almost severe profile, under the dark handkerchief. Her hands, worn by honest toil, and folded in her lap, were unmistakable signs of a long and hard struggle with poverty. Yet her smile was gentleness and sweetness itself, when she returned Vesper's salutation. A poor farm, many cares, many children, — he knew her history, for Rose had told him of her mother's death during Perside's infancy, and the great kindness of the young woman who had married their father and had brought up not only his children, but also the motherless Agapit.

With a filial courtesy that won the admiration of the Acadiens, among whom respect for parents is earnestly inculcated, Vesper asked his mother if she wished him to take her home.

"If you are quite ready to leave," she replied, getting up and drawing her wrap about her.

The Acadien women uttered their regrets that madame should leave so soon. But would she not come to visit them in their own homes?

"You are very kind," she said, graciously, "but we

leave soon, — possibly in two days," and her inquiring eyes rested on her son, who gravely inclined his head in assent.

There was a chorus of farewells and requests that madame would, at some future time, visit the Bay, and Mrs. Nimmo, bowing her acknowledgments, and singling out Perside for a specially approving glance, took her son's arm and was about to move away when he said, "If you do not object, we will take the child with us. He is tired, and is wearing out his mother."

Mrs. Nimmo could afford to be magnanimous, as they were so soon to go away, and might possibly shake off all connection with this place. Therefore she favored the pale and suffering Rose with a compassionate glance, and extended an inviting hand to the impetuous boy, who, however, disdained it and ran to Vesper.

"But why are they going?" cried Agapit, hurrying up to Rose, as she stood gazing after the retreating Nimmos. "Did you tell them of the fireworks, and the concert, and the French play; also that there would be a moon to return by?"

"Madame was weary."

"Come thou then with me. I enjoy myself so much. My shirt is wet on my back from the dancing. It is hot like a hay field — what, thou wilt not? Rose, why art thou so dull to-day?"

She tried to compose herself, to banish the heartrending look of sorrow from her face, but she was not skilled in the art of concealing her emotions, and the effort was a vain one.

"Rose!" said her cousin, in sudden dismay. "Rose — Rose!"

"What is the matter with thee?" she asked, alarmed in her turn by his strange agitation.

"Hush, — walk aside with me. Now tell me, what is this?"

"Narcisse has been a trouble," began Rose, hurriedly; then she calmed herself. "I will not deceive thee, — it is not Narcisse, though he has worried me. Agapit, I wish to go home."

"I will send thee; but be quiet, speak not above thy breath. Tell me, has this Englishman —"

"The Englishman has done nothing," said Rose, brokenly, "except that in two days he goes back to the world."

"And dost thou care? Stop, let me see thy face. Rose, thou art like a sister to me. My poor one, my dear cousin, do not cry. Come, where is thy dignity, thy pride? Remember that Acadien women do not give their hearts; they must be begged."

"I remember," she said, resolutely. "I will be strong. Fear not, Agapit, and let us return. The women will be staring."

She brushed her hand over her face, then by a determined effort of will summoned back her lost composure, and with a firm, light step rejoined the group that they had just left.

"*Mon Dieu!*" muttered Agapit, "my pleasure is gone, and I was lately so happy. I thought of this nightmare, and yet I did not imagine it would come. I might have known, — he is so calm, so cool, so handsome. That kind charms women and men too, for I also love him, yet I must give him up. Rose, my sister, thou must not go home early. I must keep thee here and suffer with thee, for, until the Englishman leaves, thou must be kept from him as a little bunch of tow from a slow fire. Does he already love thee? May the holy saints forbid — yes — no, I cannot tell. He is inscrutable. If he does, I think it not. If he does not, I think it so."

CHAPTER XV.

THE CAVE OF THE BEARS.

> " I had found out a sweet green spot,
>   Where a lily was blooming fair;
> The din of the city disturbed it not;
> But the spirit that shades the quiet cot
>   With its wings of love was there.
>
> " I found that lily's bloom
>   When the day was dark and chill;
> It smiled like a star in a misty gloom,
> And it sent abroad a sweet perfume,
>   Which is floating around me still."
>
> PERCIVAL.

MORE than twenty miles beyond Sleeping Water is a curious church built of cobblestones.

Many years ago, the devoted priest of this parish resolved that his flock must have a new church, and yet how were they to obtain one without money? He pondered over the problem for some time, and at last he arrived at a satisfactory solution. Would his parishioners give time and labor, if he supplied the material for construction?

They would, — and he pointed to the stones on the beach. The Bay already supplied them with meat and drink, they were now to obtain a place of worship from it. They worked with a will, and in a short time their church went up like the temple of old, without the aid of alien labor.

Vesper, on the day after the picnic, had announced his intention of visiting this church, and Agapit, in unconcealed disapproval and slight vexation, stood watching him clean his wheel, preparatory to setting out on the road down the Bay.

He would be sure to overtake Rose, who had shortly before left the inn with Narcisse. She had had a terrible scene with the child relative to the approaching departure of the American, and Agapit himself had advised her to take him to her stepmother. He wished now that he had not done so, he wished that he could prevent Vesper from going after her, — he almost wished that this quiet, imperturbable young man had never come to the Bay.

"And yet, why should I do that?" he reflected, penitently. "Does not good come when one works from honest motives, though bad only is at first apparent? Though we suffer now, we may yet be happy," and, casting a long, reluctant look at the taciturn young American, he rose from his comfortable seat and went up-stairs. He was tired, out of sorts, and irresistibly sleepy, having been up all night examining the old documents left by his uncle, the priest, in the hope of finding something relating to the Fiery Frenchman, for he was now as anxious to conclude Vesper's mission to the Bay as he had formerly been to prolong it.

With a quiet step he crept past the darkened room where Mrs. Nimmo, after worrying her son by her insistence on doing her own packing, had been obliged to retire, in a high state of irritation, and with a raging headache.

He hoped that the poor lady would be able to travel by the morrow; her son would be, there was no doubt of that. How well and strong he seemed now, how immeasurably he had gained in physical well-being since coming to the Bay.

"For that we should be thankful," said Agapit, in sincere admiration and regard, as he stood by his window and watched Vesper spinning down the road.

"He goes so cool, so careless, like those soldiers who went to battle with a rose between their lips, and I do not dare to warn, to question, lest I bring on what I would keep back. But do thou, my cousin Rose, not linger on the way. It would be better for thee to bite a piece from thy little tongue than to have words with this handsome stranger whom I fear thou lovest. Now to work again, and then, if there is time, half an hour's sleep before supper, for my eyelids flag strangely."

Agapit sat down before the table bestrewn with papers, while Vesper went swiftly over the road until he reached the picnic ground of the day before, now restored to its former quietness as a grazing place for cows. Of all the cheerful show there was left only the big merry-go-round, that was being packed in an enormous wagon drawn by four pairs of oxen.

"What are you going to do with it?" asked Vesper, springing off his wheel, and addressing the Acadiens at work.

"We take it to a parish farther down the Bay, where there is to be yet another picnic," said one of them.

"How much did they make yesterday?" pursued Vesper.

"Six hundred dollars, and only four hundred the day before, and three the first, for you remember those days were partly rainy."

"And some people say that you Acadiens are poor."

The man grinned. "There were many people here, many things. This wooden darling," and he pointed to the dismembered merry-go-round, "earned one dollar and twenty cents every five minutes. We need much for our churches," and he jerked his thumb towards the red cathedral. "The plaster falls, it must be restored. Do you go far, sir?"

Vesper mentioned his destination.

All the Acadiens on the Bay knew him and took a

friendly interest in his movements, and the man advised him to take in the Cave of the Bears, that was also a show-place for strangers. "It is three miles farther, where there is a bite in the shore, and the bluff is high. You will know it by two yellow houses, like twins. Descend there, and you will see a troop of ugly bears quite still about a cave. The Indians of this coast say that their great man, Glooscap, in days before the French came, once sat in the cave to rest. Some hungry bears came to eat him, but he stretched out a pine-tree that he carried and they were turned to stone."

Vesper thanked him, and went on. When he reached the sudden and picturesque cove in the Bay, his attention was caught, not so much by its beauty, as by the presence of the inn pony, who neighed a joyful welcome, and impatiently jerked back and forth the road-cart to which he was attached.

Vesper glanced sharply at the yellow houses. Perhaps Rose was making a call in one of them. Then he stroked the pony, who playfully nipped his coat sleeve, and, after propping his wheel against a stump, ran nimbly down a grassy road, where a goat was soberly feeding among lobster-traps and drawn-up boats.

He crossed the strip of sand in the semicircular inlet, and there before him were the bears, — ugly brown rocks with coats of slippery seaweed, their grinning heads turned towards the mouth of a black cavern in the lower part of the bluff, their staring eye-sockets fixed on the dainty woman's figure inside, as if they would fain devour her.

Rose sat with her face to the sea, her head against the damp rock wall, — her whole attitude one of abandonment and mournful despair.

Vesper began to hurry towards her, but, catching sight of Narcisse, he stopped.

The child, with a face convulsed and tear-stained, was angrily seizing stones from the beach to fling them against the most lifelike bear of all, — a grotesque, hideous creature, that appeared to be shouldering his way from the water in order to plunge into the cave.

"Dost thou mock me?" exclaimed Narcisse, furiously. "I will strike thee yet again, thou hateful thing. Thou shalt not come on shore to eat my mother and the Englishman," and he dashed a yet larger stone against it.

"Narcisse," said Vesper.

The child turned quickly. Then his trouble was forgotten, and stumbling and slipping over the seaweed, but at last attaining his goal, he flung his small unhappy self against Vesper's breast. "I love you, I love you, — *gros comme la grange à Pinot*" (as much as Pinot's barn), — "yet my mother carried me away. Take me with you, Mr. Englishman. Narcisse is very sick without you."

In maternal alarm Rose sprang up at her child's first shriek. Then she sank back, pale and confused, for Vesper's eye was upon her, although apparently he was engaged only in fondling the little curly head, and in allowing the child to stroke his face and dive into his pockets, to pull out his watch, and indulge in the fond and foolish familiarities permitted to a child by a loving father.

"Go to her, Narcisse," said Vesper, presently, and the small boy ran into the cave. "My mother, my mother!" he cried, in an ecstacy; and he wagged his curly head as if he would shake it from his body. "The Englishman returns to you and to me, — he will stay away only a short time. Come, get up, get up. Let us go back to the inn. I am to go no more to my grandmother. Is it not so?" and he anxiously gazed at Vesper, who was slowly approaching.

Vesper did not speak, neither did Rose. What was the matter with these grown people that they stared so stupidly at each other?

"Have you a headache, Mr. Englishman?" he asked, with abrupt childish anxiety, as he noticed a sudden and unusual wave of color sweeping over his friend's face. "And you, my mother, — why do you hang your head? Give only the Englishman your hand and he will lift you from the rock. He is strong, very strong, — he carries me over the rough places."

"Will you give me your hand, Rose?"

She started back, with a heart-broken gesture.

"But you are imbecile, my darling mother!" cried Narcisse, throwing himself on her in terror. "The Englishman will become angry, — he will leave us. Give him your hand, and let us go from this place," and, resolutely seizing her fluttering fingers in his own soft ones, he directed them to Vesper's strong, true clasp.

"Go stone the bears again, Narcisse," said the young man, with a strange quiver in his voice. "I will talk to your mother about going back to the inn. See, she is not well;" for Rose had bowed her weary head on her arm.

"Yes, talk to her," said the child, "that is good, and, above all, do not let her hand go. She runs from me sometimes, the little naughty mother," and, with affected roguishness that, however, concealed a certain anxiety, he put his head on one side, and stared affectionately at her as he left the cave.

He had gone some distance, and Vesper had already whispered a few words in Rose's ear, when he returned and stared again at them. "Will you tell me only one little story, Mr. Englishman?"

"About what, you small bother?"

"About bears, big brown bears, not gentle trees."

"There was once a sick bear," said the young man, "and he went all about the world, but could not get well until he found a quiet spot, where a gentle lady cured him."

"And then — "

"The lady had a cub," said Vesper, suddenly catching him in his arms and taking him out to the strip of sand, "a fascinating cub that the bear — I mean the man — adored."

Narcisse laughed gleefully, snatched Vesper's cap and set off with it, fell into a pool of water and was rescued, and set to the task of taking off his shoes and stockings and drying them in the sun, while Vesper went back to Rose, who still sat like a person in acute distress of body and mind.

"I was sudden, — I startled you," he murmured.

She made a dissenting gesture, but did not speak.

"Will you look at me, Rose?" he said, softly; "just once."

"But I am afraid," fluttered from her pale lips. "When I gaze into your eyes it is hard — "

He stood over her in such quiet, breathless sympathy that presently she looked up, thinking he was gone.

His glance caught and held hers. She got up, allowed him to take her hands and press them to his lips, and to place on her head the hat that had fallen to the ground.

"I will say nothing more now," he murmured,

"you are shocked and upset. We had better go home."

"Come and be presented to Mrs. Nimmo," suddenly said a saucy, laughing voice.

Rose started nervously. Her sister Perside had caught sight of them, — teasing, yet considerate Perside, since she had bestowed only one glance on the lovers, and had then gone sauntering past the mouth of the cave, out to the wide array of black rocks beyond them. She carried a hooked stick over her shoulder, and a tin pail in her hand, and sometimes she looked back at a second girl, similarly equipped, who was running down the grassy road after her.

Nothing could have made Rose more quickly recover herself. "It is not the time of perigee, — you will find nothing," she called after Perside; then she added to Vesper, in a low, shy voice, "She seeks lobsters. She danced so much at the picnic that she was too tired to go home, and had to stay here with cousins."

"Times and seasons do not matter for some things," returned Perside, gaily, over her shoulder; "one has the fun."

Narcisse stopped digging his bare toes in the sand and shrieked, delightedly, "Aunt Perside, aunt Perside, do you know the Englishman returns to my mother and me? He will never leave us, and I am not to go to my grandmother." Then, fearful that his assertions had been too strong, he averted his gaze from the two approaching people, and fixed it on the blazing sun.

"Will you promise not to make a scene when I leave to-morrow?" said Vesper.

Narcisse blinked at him, his eyes full of spots and wheels and revolving lights. He was silly with joy, and gurgled deep down in his little throat. "Let me kiss your hand, as you kissed my mother's. It is a pretty sight."

"Will you be a good boy when I leave to-morrow," said Vesper again.

"But why should I cry if you return?" cried the child, excitedly flinging a handful of sand at his boots. "Narcisse will never again be bad," and rolling over and over, and kicking his pink heels in glee, he forced Vesper and Rose to retire to a respectful distance.

They stood watching him for some time, and, as they watched, Rose's tortured face grew calm, and a spark of the divine passion animating her lover's face came into her deep blue eyes. She had no right to break the tender, sensitive little heart given so strangely to this stranger. She would forget Agapit and his warnings; she would forget the proud women of her race, who would not wed a stranger, and one of another creed; she would also forget the nervous, jealous mother who would keep her son from all women.

"You have asked me for myself," she said, impulsively stretching out her hands to him, "for myself and my child. We are yours."

Vesper bent down, and pressed her cool fingers against his burning cheeks. She smiled at him, even laughed gleefully, and passed her hands over his head in a playful caress; then, with her former expression of exaltation and virginal modesty and shyness, she ran up the grassy road, and paused at the top to look back at him, as he toiled up with Narcisse.

She was vivacious and merry now, — he had never seen her just so before. In an instant, — a breath, — with her surrender to him, she had seemed to drop her load of care, that usually made her youthful face so grave and sweet beyond her years. He would like to see her cheerful and laughing — thoughtless even; and murmuring endearing epithets under his breath, he assisted her into the cart, placed the reins in her hands, tucked Narcisse in by her side, and, surreptitiously lifting a fold of her dress to his face, murmured, "*Au revoir*, my sweet saint."

Then, stroking his mustache to conceal from the yellow houses his proud smile of ownership, he watched the upright pose of the light head, and the contorted appearance of the dark one that was twisted over a little shoulder as long as the cart was in sight.

He forgot all about the church, and, going back to the beach, he lay for a long time sunning himself on the sand, and plunged in a delicious reverie. Then, mounting his wheel, he returned to the inn.

Agapit was running excitedly to and fro on the veranda. "Come, make haste," he cried, as he caught sight of him in the distance. "Extremely strange things have happened — Let me assist you with that wheel, — a malediction on it, these bicycles go always where one does not expect. There is news of the Fiery Frenchman. I found something, also Father La Croix."

"This is interesting," said Vesper, good-naturedly, as he folded his arms, and lounged against one of the veranda posts.

"I was delving among my uncle's papers. I had precipitately come on the name of LeNoir, — Etex, the son of Raphael, who was a wealthy *bourgeois* of Calais, and emigrated to Grand Pré. He was dead when the expulsion came, and of his two sons one, Gabriel LeNoir, escaped up the St. John River, and that Gabriel was my ancestor, and that of Rose; therefore, most astonishingly to me, we are related to this family whom you have sought," and Agapit wound up with a flourish of his hands and his heels.

"I am glad of this," said Vesper, in a deeply gratified voice.

"But more remains. I was shouting over my discovery, when Father La Croix came. I ran, I descended, — the good man presented his compliments to madame and you. Several of his people went to him this morning. They had questioned the old ones. He wrote what they said, and here it is. See — the son of the murdered Etex was Samson. His mother landed in Philadelphia. In griping poverty the boy grew up. He went to Boston. He joined the Acadiens who marched the five hundred miles through the woods to Acadie. He arrived at the Baie Chaleur, where he married a Comeau. He had many children, but his eldest, Jean, is he in whom you will interest yourself, as in the direct line."

"And what of Jean?" asked Vesper, when Agapit stopped to catch his breath.

Agapit pointed to the Bay. "He lies over Digby Neck, in the Bay of Fundy, but his only child is on this Bay."

"A boy or a girl?"

"A devil," cried Agapit, in a burst of grief, "a little devil."

CHAPTER XVI.

FOR THE HONOR OF THEIR RACE.

> " Love is the perfect sum
> Of all delight!
> I have no other choice
> Either for pen or voice
> To sing or write."

"Why is the descendant of the Fiery Frenchman a devil?" asked Vesper.

"Because she has no heart. They have taken from her her race, her religion. Her mother, who had some Indian blood, was also wild. She would not sweep her kitchen floor. She went to sea with her husband, and when she was drowned with him, her sister, who is also gay, took the child."

"What do you mean by gay?"

"I mean like hawks. They go here and there, — they love the woods. They do not keep neat houses, and yet they are full of strange ambitions. They change their names. They are not so much like the English as we are, yet they pretend to have no French blood. Sometimes I visit them, for the uncle of the child — Claude à Sucre — is worthy, but his wife I detestate. She has no bones of purpose; she is like a flabby sunfish."

"Where do they live?"

"Up the Bay, — near Bleury."

"And do you think there is nothing I can do for this little renegade?"

"Nothing?" cried Agapit. "You can do everything. It is the opportunity of your life. You so wise, so generous, so understanding the Acadiens. You have in your power to make born again the whole family through the child. They are superstitious. They will respect the claim of the dead. Come to the garden to talk, for there are strangers approaching."

Vesper shivered. He was not altogether happy over the discovery of the lost link connecting him with the far-back tragedy in which his great-grandfather had been involved. However, he suppressed all signs of emotion, and, following Agapit to the lawn, he walked to and fro, listening attentively to the explanations and information showered upon him. When Rose came to the door to ring the supper-bell, both young men paused. She thought they had been speaking of her, and blushed divinely.

Agapit, with an alarmed expression, turned to his companion, who smiled quietly, and was just about to address him, when a lad came running up to them.

"Agapit, come quickly, — old miser Lefroy is dying, and would make his will. He calls for thee."

"Return, — say that I will come," exclaimed Agapit, waving his hand; then he looked at Vesper. "One word only, why does Rose look so strangely?"

"Rose has promised to be my wife."

Agapit groaned, flung himself away a few steps, then came back. "Say no more to her till you see me. How could you — and yet you do her honor. I cannot blame you," and with a farewell glance, in which there was a curious blending of despair and gratified pride, he ran after the boy.

Vesper went up-stairs to his mother, who announced herself no better, and begged only that she might not be disturbed. He accordingly descended to the dining-room and took his place at the table.

Rose was quietly moving to and fro with a heightened color. She was glad that Agapit was away, — it was more agreeable to her to have only one lord and master present; yet, sensitively alive to the idiosyncrasies of this new one, she feared that he was disapproving of her unusual number of guests.

He, however, nobly suppressed his disapproval, and even talked pleasantly of recent political happenings in his own country with some travelling agents who happened to be some of his own fellow citizens.

"Ah, it is a wonderful thing, this love," she said to herself, as she went to the kitchen for a fresh supply of coffee; "it makes one more anxious to please, and to think less of oneself. Mr. Nimmo wishes to aid me, — and yet, though he is so kind, he slightly wrinkles his beautiful eyebrows when I place dishes on the table. He does not like me to serve. He would have me sit by him; some day I shall do so;" and, overcome by the confused bliss of the thought, she retired behind the pantry door, where the curious Célina found her with her face buried in her hands, and in quick, feminine intuition at once guessed her secret.

There were many dishes to wash after supper, and Vesper, who was keeping an eye on the kitchen, inwardly applauded Célina, who, instead of running to the door as she usually did to exchange pleasantries with waiting friends and admirers, accomplished her tasks with surprising celerity. In the brief space of three-quarters of an hour she was ready to go out, and after donning a fresh blouse and a clean apron, and coquettishly tying a handkerchief on her head, she went to the lawn, where she would play croquet and gossip with her friends until the stars came out.

Vesper left the smokers on the veranda and the chattering women in the parlor, and sauntered through the quiet dining-room and kitchen. Rose was nowhere in sight, but her pet kitten, that followed her from morning till night, was mewing at the door of a small room used as a laundry.

Vesper cautiously looked in. The supple young back of his sweetheart was bent over a wash-tub. "Rose," he exclaimed, "what are you doing?"

She turned a blushing face over her shoulder. "Only a little washing — a very little. The washer-woman forgot."

Vesper walked around the tub.

"It was such a pleasure," she stammered. "I did not know that you would wish to talk to me till perhaps later on."

Her slender hands gripped a white garment affectionately, and partly lifted it from the soap-suds. Vesper, peering in the tub, discovered that it was one of the white jerseys that he wore bicycling, and, gently taking it from her, he dropped it out of sight in the foam.

"But it is of wool, — it will shrink," she said, anxiously.

He laughed, dried her white arms on his handkerchief, and begged her to sit down on a bench beside him.

She shyly drew back and, pulling down her sleeves, seated herself on a stool opposite.

"Rose," he said, seriously, "do you know how to flirt?"

Her beautiful lips parted, and she laughed in a gleeful, wholehearted way that reminded him of Narcisse. "I think that it would be possible to learn," she said, demurely.

Vesper did not offer to teach her. He fell into an intoxicated silence, and sat musing on this, the purest and sweetest passion of his life. What had she done — this simple Acadien woman — to fill his heart with such profound happiness? A light from the window behind her shone around her flaxen head, and reminded him of the luminous halos surrounding the heads of her favorite saints. Since the ecstatic dreams of boyhood he had experienced nothing like this, — and yet this dream was more extended, more spiritual and less earthly than those, for infinite worlds of happiness now unfolded themselves to his vision, and endless possibilities and responsibilities stretched out before him. This woman's life would be given fearlessly into his hands, and also the life of her child. He, Vesper Nimmo, almost a broken link in humanity's chain, would become once more a part in the glorious whole.

Rose, enraptured with this intellectual love-making, sat watching every varying emotion playing over her lover's face. How different he was from Charlitte, — ah, poor Charlitte! — and she shuddered. He was so rough, so careless. He had been like a good-natured bear that wished a plaything. He had not loved her as gently, as tenderly as this man did.

"Rose," asked Vesper, suddenly, "what is the matter with Agapit?"

"I do not know," she said, and her face grew

troubled. "Perhaps he is angry that I have told a story, for I said I would not marry."

"Why should he not wish you to marry?"

Again she said that she did not know.

"Will you marry me in six weeks?"

"I will marry when you wish," she replied, with dignity, "yet I beg you to think well of it. My little boy is in his bed, and when I no longer see him, I doubt. There are so few things that I know. If I go to your dear country, that you love so much, you may drop your head in shame, — notwithstanding what you have said, I give you up if you wish."

"Womanlike, you must inject a drop of bitterness into the only full cup of happiness ever lifted to your lips. Let us suppose, however, that you are right. My people are certainly not as your people. Shall we part now, — shall I go away to-morrow, and never see you again?"

Rose stared blindly at him.

"Are you willing for me to go?" he asked, quietly.

His motive in suggesting the parting was the not unworthy one of a lover who longs for an open expression of affection from one dear to him, yet he was shocked at the signs of Rose's suppressed passion and inarticulate terror. She did not start from her seat, she did not throw herself in his inviting arms, and beg him to stay with her. No; the terrified blue eyes were lowered meekly to the floor, and, in scarcely audible accents, she murmured, "What seems right to you must be done."

"Rose, — I shall never leave you."

"I feel that I have reached up to heaven, and plucked out a very bright star," she stammered, with white lips, "and yet here it is," and trying to conceal her agony, she opened her clenched and quivering hand, as if to restore something to him.

He went down on his knees before her. "You are a princess among your people, Rose. Keep the star, — it is but a poor ornament for you," and seizing her suffering hands, he clasped them to his breast. "Listen, till I tell you my reasons for not leaving the woman who has given me my life and inspired me with hope for the future."

Rose listened, and grew pale at his eloquent words, and still more eloquent pauses.

After some time, a gentle, melancholy smile came creeping to her face; a smile that seemed to reflect past suffering rather than present joy. "It is like pain," she said, and she timidly laid a finger on his dark head, "this great joy. I have had so many terrors, — I have loved you so long, I find, and I thought you would die."

Vesper felt that his veins had been filled with some glowing elixir of earthly and heavenly delight. How adorable she was, — how unique, with her modesty, her shyness, her restrained eagerness. Surely he had found the one peerless woman in the world.

"Talk to me more about yourself and your feelings," he entreated.

"I have longed to tell you," she murmured, "that you have taught me what it is, — this love; and also that one does not make it, for it is life or death, and therefore can only come from the Lord. When you speak, your words are so agreeable that they are like rain on dusty ground. I feel that you are quite admirable," and, interrupting herself, she bent over to gently kiss his cheek as he still knelt before her.

"Continue, Rose," he said, shutting his eyes in an ecstasy.

"I speak freely," she said, "because I feel that I can trust you without fear, and always, always love and serve you till you are quite, quite old. I also understand you. Formerly I did not. You say that I am like a princess. Ah, not so much as you. You are altogether like a prince. You had the air of being contented; I did not know your thoughts. Now I can look into your beautiful white soul. You hide nothing from me. No, do not put your face down. You are a very, very good man. I do not think that there can be any one so good."

Vesper looked up, and laid a finger across the sweet, praising mouth.

"Let us talk of your mother," said Rose. "Since I love you, I love her more; but she does not like me equally."

"But she will, my ingenuous darling. I have talked to her twice. She is quite reconciled, but it will take time for her to act a mother's part. You will have patience?"

Rose wrinkled her delicate brows. "I put myself in her place, — ah, how hard for her! Let me fancy you my son. How could I give you up? And yet it would be wrong for her to take you from one who can make you more happy; is it not so?"

Vesper sprang to his feet. "Yes, Rose; it is you and I against the world, — one heart, one soul; it is wonderful, and a great mystery," and clasping his hands behind him, he walked to and fro along the narrow room.

Rose, with a transfigured face, watched him, and hung on every word falling from his lips, as he spoke of his plans for the future, his disappointed hopes and broken aspirations of the past. It did not occur to either of them, so absorbed were they with each other, to glance at the small window overlooking the dooryard, where an eager face came and went at intervals.

Sometimes the face was angry; sometimes sorrowful. Sometimes a clenched fist was raised between it and the glass as if at an imaginary enemy. The unfortunate watcher, in great perplexity of mind, was going through every gesture in the pantomine of distress.

The lovers, unmindful of him, continued their conversation, and the suffering Agapit continued to suffer.

Vesper talked and walked on, occasionally stopping to listen to a remark from Rose, or to bend over her in an adoring, respectful attitude while he bestowed a caress or received a shy and affectionate one from her.

"It is sinful, — I should interrupt," groaned Agapit, "yet it would be cruel. They are in paradise. Ah, dear blessed Virgin, — mother of suffering hearts, — have pity on them, for they are both noble, both good;" and he dashed his hand across his eyes to hide the sight of the beautiful head held as tenderly between the hands of the handsome stranger as if it were indeed a fragile, full-blown rose.

"They take leave," he muttered; "I will look no more, — it is a sacrilege," and he rushed into the house by another door.

The croquet players called to him from the lawn. He could hear the click of the balls and the merry voices as he passed, but he paid no heed to them. Only in the dining-room did he stay his hasty steps. There, in front of the picture of Rose's husband, he paused with uplifted arm.

"Scoundrel!" he muttered, furiously; then striking his fist through the glass, he shattered the portrait, from the small twinkling eyes to its good-natured, sensuous mouth.

CHAPTER XVII.

THE SUBLIMEST THING IN THE WORLD.

"Ah, tragedy of lusty life! How oft
  Some high emprise a soul divinely grips,
  But as it crests, fate's undertow despoils!"
                       THEODORE H. RAND.

MRS. NIMMO was better the next morning, and, rising betimes, gave her son an early audience in her room.

"You need not tell me anything," she said, with a searching glance at him. "It is all arranged between you and the Acadien woman. I know, — you cannot stave off these things. I will be good, Vesper, only give me time, — give me time, and let us have no explanations. You can tell her that you have not spoken to me, and she will not expect me to gush."

Her voice died away in a pitiful quaver, and Vesper quietly, but with intense affection, kissed the cold cheek she offered him.

"Go away," she said, pushing him from her, "or I shall break down, and I want my strength for the journey."

Vesper went down-stairs, his eyes running before him for the sweet presence of Rose. She was not in the dining-room, and with suppressed disappointment he looked curiously at Célina, who was red-eyed and doleful, and requested her to take his mother's breakfast up-stairs. Then, with a disagreeable premonition of trouble, he turned his attention to Agapit, whose face had turned a sickly yellow and who was toying abstractedly with his food. He appeared to be ill, and, refusing to talk, waited silently for Vesper to finish his breakfast.

"Will you come to the smoking-room?" he then said; and being answered by a silent nod, he preceded Vesper to that room and carefully closed the door.

"Now give me your hand," he said, tragically, "for I am going to make you angry, and perhaps you will never again clasp mine in friendship."

"Get out," said Vesper, peevishly. "I detest melodrama, — and say quickly what you have to say. We have only an hour before the train leaves."

"My speech can be made in a short time," said Agapit, solemnly. "Your farewell of Sleeping Water to-day must be eternal."

"Don't be a fool, Agapit, but go look for a rope for my mother's trunk; she has lost the straps."

"If I found a rope it would be to hang myself," said Agapit, desperately. "Never was I so unhappy, never, never."

"What is wrong with you?"

"I am desolated over your engagement to my cousin. We thank you for the honor, but we decline it."

"Indeed! as the engagement does not include you, I must own that I will take my dismissal only from your cousin."

"Look at me, — do I seem like one in play? God knows I do not wish to torment you. All night I walked my floor, and Rose, — unhappy Rose! I shudder when I think how she passed the black hours after my cruel revealings."

"What have you said to Rose?" asked Vesper, in a fury. "You forget that she now belongs to me."

"She belongs to no one but our Lord," said Agapit, in an agony. "You cannot have her, though the thought makes my heart bleed for you."

Vesper's face flushed. "If you will let it stop bleeding long enough to be coherent, I shall be obliged to you."

"Oh, do not be angry with me, — let me tell you now that I love you for your kindness to my people. You came among us, — you, an Englishman. You did not despise us. You offer my cousin your hand, and it breaks our hearts to refuse it, but she cannot marry you. She sends you that message, — 'You must go away and forget me. Marry another woman if you so care. I must give you up.' These are her words as she stood pale and cold."

Vesper seated himself on the edge of the big table in the centre of the room. Very deliberately he took out his watch and laid it beside him. So intense was the stillness of the room, so nervously sensitive and unstrung was Agapit by his night's vigil, that he started at the rattling of the chain on the polished surface.

"I give you five minutes," said Vesper, "to explain your attitude towards your cousin, on the subject of her marriage. As I understand the matter, you were an orphan brought up by her father. Of late years you arrogate the place of a brother. Your decisions are supreme. You announce now that she is not to marry. You have some little knowledge of me. Do you fancy that I will be put off by any of your trumpery fancies?"

"No, no," said Agapit, wildly. "I know you better,— you have a will of steel. But can you not trust me? I say an impediment exists. It is like a mountain. You cannot get over it, you cannot get around it; it would pain you to know, and I cannot tell it. Go quietly away therefore."

Vesper was excessively angry. With his love for Rose had grown a certain jealousy of Agapit, whose influence over her had been unbounded. Yet he controlled himself, and said, coldly, "There are other ways of getting past a mountain."

"By flying?" said Agapit, eagerly.

"No, — tunnelling. Tell me now how long this obstacle has existed?"

"It would be more agreeable to me not to answer questions."

"I daresay, but I shall stay here until you do."

"Then, it is one year," said Agapit, reluctantly.

"It has, therefore, not arisen since I came?"

"Oh, no, a thousand times no."

"It is a question of religion?"

"No, it is not," said Agapit, indignantly; "we are not in the Middle Ages."

"It seems to me that we are; does Rose's priest know?"

"Yes, but not through her."

"Through you, — at confession?"

"Yes, but he would die rather than break the seal of confession."

"Of course. Does any one here but you know?"

"Oh, no, no; only myself, and Rose's uncle, and one other."

"It has something to do with her first marriage," said Vesper, sharply. "Did she promise her husband not to marry again?"

Agapit would not answer him.

"You are putting me off with some silly bugbear," said Vesper, contemptuously.

"A bugbear! holy mother of angels, it is a question of the honor of our race. But for that, I would tell you."

"You do not wish her to marry me because I am an American."

"I would be proud to have her marry an American," said Agapit, vehemently.

"I shall not waste more time on you," said Vesper, disdainfully. "Rose will explain."

"You must not go to her," said Agapit, blocking his way. "She is in a strange state. I fear for her reason."

"You do," muttered Vesper, "and you try to keep me from her?"

Agapit stood obstinately pressing his back against the door.

"You want her for yourself," said Vesper, suddenly striking him a smart blow across the face.

The Acadien sprang forward, his burly frame trembled, his hot breath enveloped Vesper's face as he stood angrily regarding him. Then he turned on his heel, and pressed his handkerchief to his bleeding lips.

"I will not strike you," he mumbled, "for you do not understand. I, too, have loved and been unhappy."

The glance that he threw over his shoulder was so humble, so forgiving, that Vesper's heart was touched.

"I ask your pardon, Agapit, — you have worried me out of my senses," and he warmly clasped the hand that the Acadien extended to him.

"Come," said Agapit, with an adorable smile. "Follow me. You have a generous heart. You shall see your Rose."

Agapit knocked softly at his cousin's door, then, on receiving permission, entered with a reverent step.

Vesper had never been in this little white chamber before. One comprehensive glance he bestowed on it, then his eyes came back to Rose, who had, he knew without being told, spent the whole night on her knees before the niche in the wall, where stood a pale statuette of the Virgin.

This was a Rose he did not know, and one whose frozen beauty struck a deadly chill to his heart. He had lost her, — he knew it before she opened her lips. She seemed not older, but younger. The look on her face he had seen on the faces of dead children; the blood had been frightened from her very lips. What was it that had given her this deadly shock? He was more than ever determined to know, and, subduing every emotion but that of stern curiosity, he stood expectant.

"You insisted on an adieu," she murmured, painfully.

"I am coming back in a week," said Vesper, stubbornly.

The hand that held her prayer-book trembled. "You have told him that he must not return?" and she turned to Agapit, and lifted her flaxen eyebrows, that seemed almost dark against the unearthly pallor of her skin.

"Yes," he said, with a gusty sigh. "I have told him, but he does not heed me."

"It is for the honor of our race," she said to Vesper.

"Rose," he said, keenly, "do you think I will give you up?"

Her white lips quivered. "You must go; it is wrong for me even to see you."

Vesper stared at Agapit, and seeing that he was determined not to leave the room, he turned his back squarely on him. "Rose," he said, in a low voice, "Rose."

The saint died in her, the woman awoke. Little by little the color crept back to her face. Her ears, her lips, her cheeks, and brow were suffused with the faint, delicate hue of the flower whose name she bore.

A passionate light sprang into her blue eyes. "Agapit," she murmured, "Agapit," yet her glance did not leave Vesper's face, "can we not tell him?"

"Shall we be unfaithful to our race?" said her cousin, inexorably.

"What is our race?" she asked, wildly. "There are the Acadiens, there are also the Americans, — the one Lord makes all. Agapit, permit that we tell him."

"Think of your oath, Rose."

"My oath — my oath — and did I not also swear to love him? I told him only yesterday, and now I must give him up forever, and cause him pain. Agapit, you shall tell him. He must not go away angry. Ah, my cousin, my cousin," and, evading Vesper, she stretched out the prayer-book, "by our holy religion, I beg that you have pity. Tell him, tell him, — I shall never see him again. It will kill me if he goes angry from me."

There were tears of agony in her eyes, and Agapit faltered as he surveyed her.

"We are to be alone here all the years," she said, "you and I. It will be a sin even to think of the past. Let us have no thought to start with as sad as this, that we let one so dear go out in the world blaming us."

"Well, then," said Agapit, sullenly, "I surrender. Tell you this stranger; let him have part in an unusual shame of our people."

"I tell him!" and she drew back, hurt and startled. "No, Agapit, that confession comes better from thee. Adieu, adieu," and she turned, in a paroxysm of tenderness, to Vesper, and in her anguish burst into her native language. "After this minute, I must put thee far from my thoughts, — thou, so good, so kind, that I had hoped to walk with through life. But purgatory does not last forever; the blessed saints also suffered. After we die, perhaps —" and she buried her face in her hands, and wept violently.

"But do not thou remember," she said at last, checking her tears. "Go out into the world and find another, better wife. I release thee, go, go —"

Vesper said nothing, but he gave Agapit a terrible glance, and that young man, although biting his lip and scowling fiercely, discreetly stepped into the hall.

For half a minute Rose lay unresistingly in Vesper's arms, then she gently forced him from the room, and with a low and bitter cry, "For this I must atone," she opened her prayer-book, and again dropped on her knees.

Once more the two young men found themselves in the smoking-room.

"Now, what is it?" asked Vesper, sternly.

Agapit hung his head. In accents of deepest shame he murmured, "Charlitte yet lives."

"Charlitte — what, Rose's husband?"

A miserable nod from Agapit answered his question.

"It is rumor," stammered Vesper; "it cannot be. You said that he was dead."

"He has been seen, — the miserable man lives with another woman."

Vesper had received the worst blow of his life, yet his black eyes fixed themselves steadily on Agapit's face. "What proof have you?"

Agapit stumbled through some brief sentences. "An Acadien — Michel Amireau — came home to die. He was a sailor. He had seen Charlitte in New Orleans. He had changed his name, yet Michel knew him, and went to the uncle of Rose, on the Bayou Vermillon. The uncle promised to watch him. That is why he is so kind to Rose, this good uncle, and sends her so much. But Charlitte goes no more to sea, but lives with this woman. He is happy; such a devil should die."

Vesper was stunned and bewildered, yet his mind had never worked more clearly. "Does any other person know?" he asked, sharply.

"No one; Michel would not tell, and he is dead."

Vesper leaned on a chair-back, and convulsively clasped his fingers until every drop of blood seemed to have left them. "Why did he leave Rose?"

"Who can tell?" said Agapit, drearily. "Rose is beautiful; this other woman unbeautiful and older, much older. But Charlitte was always gross like a pig, — but good-natured. Rose was too fine, too spiritual. She smiled at him, she did not drink, nor dance, nor laugh loudly. These are the women he likes."

"How old is he?"

"Not old, — fifty, perhaps. If our Lord would only let him die! But those men live forever. He is strong, very strong."

"Would Rose consent to a divorce?"

"A divorce! *Mon Dieu,* she is a good Catholic."

Vesper sank into a chair and dropped his head on his hand. Hot, rebellious thoughts leaped into his heart. Yesterday he had been so happy; to-day —

"My friend," said Agapit, softly, "do not give way."

His words stung Vesper as if they had been an insult.

"I am not giving way," he said, fiercely. "I am trying to find a way out of this diabolical scrape."

"But surely there is only one road to follow."

Vesper said nothing, but his eyes were blazing, and Agapit recoiled from him with a look of terror.

"You surely would not influence one who loves you to do anything wrong?"

"Rose is mine," said Vesper, grimly.

"But she is married to Charlitte."

"To a dastardly villain, — she must separate from him."

"But she cannot."

"She will if I ask her," and Vesper started up, as if he were about to seek her.

"Stop but an instant," and Agapit pressed both hands to his forehead with a gesture of bewilderment.

"Let me say over some things first to you. Think of what you have done here, — you, so quiet, so strong, — so pretending not to be good, and yet very good. You have led Rose as a grown one leads a child. Before you came I did not revere her as I do at present. She is now so careful, she will not speak even the least of untruths; she wishes to improve herself, — to be more fitted for the company of the blessed in heaven."

Vesper made some inarticulate sound in his throat, and Agapit went on hurriedly. "Women are weak, men are imperious; she may, perhaps, do anything you say, but is it not well to think over exactly what one would tell her? She is in trouble now, but soon she will recover and look about her. She will see all the world equally so. There are good priests with sore hearts, also holy women, but they serve God. All the world cannot marry. Marriage, what is it? — a little living together, — a separation. There is also a holy union of hearts. We can live for God, you, and I, and Rose, but for a time is it not best that we do not see each other?"

Again Vesper did not reply except by a convulsive movement of his shoulders, and an impatient drumming on the table with his fingers.

"Dear young man, whom I so much admire," said Agapit, leaning across towards him, "I have confidence in you. You, who think so much of the honor of your race, — you who shielded the name of your ancestor lest dishonor should come on it, I trust you fully. You will, some day when it seems good to you, find out this child who has cast off her race ; and now go, — the door is open, seek Rose if you will. You will say nothing unworthy to her. You know love, the greatest of things, but you also know duty, the sublimest."

His voice died away, and Vesper still preserved a dogged silence. At last, however, his struggle with himself was over, and in a harsh, rough voice, utterly unlike his usual one, he looked up and said, " Have we time to catch the train ? "

" By driving fast," said Agapit, mildly, " we may. Possibly the train is late also."

" Make haste then," said Vesper, and he hurried to his mother, whose voice he heard in the hall.

Agapit fairly ran to the stable, and as he ran he muttered, " We are all very young, — the old ones say that trouble cuts into the hearts of youth. Let us pray our Lord for old age."

CHAPTER XVIII.

NARCISSE GOES IN SEARCH OF THE ENGLISHMAN.

"L'homme s'agite, Dieu le mène."

MRS. NIMMO was a very unhappy woman. She had never before had a trouble equal to this trouble, and, as she sat at the long window in the bedroom of her absent son, she drearily felt that it was eating the heart and spirit out of her.

Vesper was away, and she had refused to share his unhappy wanderings, for she knew that he did not wish her to do so. Very calmly and coldly he had told her that his engagement to Rose à Charlitte was over. He assigned no cause for it, and Mrs. Nimmo, in her desperation, earnestly wished that he had never heard of the Acadiens, that Rose à Charlitte had never been born, and that the little peninsula of Nova Scotia had never been traced on the surface of the globe.

It was a lovely evening of late summer. The square in which she lived was cool and quiet, for very few of its inhabitants had come back from their summer excursions. Away in the distance, beyond the leafy common, she could hear the subdued roar of the city, but on the brick pavements about her there was scarcely a footfall.

The window at which she sat faced the south. In winter her son's room was flooded with sunlight, but in summer the branching elm outside put forth a kindly screen of leaves to shield it from the too oppressive heat. Her glance wandered between the delicate lace curtains, swaying to and fro, to this old elm that seemed a member of her family. How much her son loved it, — and with an indulgent thought of Vesper's passion for the natives of the outdoor world, a disagreeable recollection of the Acadien woman's child leaped into her mind.

How absurdly fond of trees and flowers he had been, and what a fanciful, unnatural child he was, altogether. She had never liked him, and he had never liked her, and she wrinkled her brows at the distasteful remembrance of him.

A knock at the half-open door distracted her attention, and, languidly turning her head, she said, "What is it, Henry?"

"It's a young woman, Mis' Nimmo," replied that ever alert and demure colored boy, "what sometimes brings you photographs. She come in a hack with a girl."

"Let her come up. She may leave the girl below."

"I guess that girl ain't a girl, Mis' Nimmo, — she looks mighty like a boy. She's the symbol of the little feller in the French place I took you to."

Mrs. Nimmo gave him a rebuking glance. "Let the girl remain down-stairs."

"Madame," said a sudden voice, "this is now Boston, — where is the Englishman?"

Mrs. Nimmo started from her chair. Here was the French child himself, standing calmly before her in the twilight, his small body habited in ridiculous and disfiguring girl's clothes, his cropped curly head and white face appearing above an absurd kind of grayish yellow cloak.

"Narcisse!" she ejaculated.

"Madame," said the faint yet determined little voice, "is the Englishman in his house?"

Mrs. Nimmo's glance fell upon Henry, who was standing open-mouthed and grotesque, and with a gesture she sent him from the room.

Narcisse, exhausted yet eager, had started on a tour of investigation about the room, holding up with one hand the girl's trappings, which considerably hampered his movements, and clutching something to his breast with the other. He had found the house of the Englishman and his mother, and by sure tokens he recognized his recent presence in this very room. Here were his books, his gloves, his cap, and, best of all, another picture of him; and, with a cry of delight, he dropped on a footstool before a full-length portrait of the man he adored. Here he would rest: his search was ended; and meekly surveying Mrs. Nimmo, he murmured, " Could Narcisse have a glass of milk?"

Mrs. Nimmo's emotions at present all seemed to belong to the order of the intense. She had never before been so troubled; she had never before been so bewildered. What did the presence of this child under her roof mean? Was his mother anywhere near? Surely not, — Rose would never clothe her comely child in those shabby garments of the other sex.

She turned her puzzled face to the doorway, and found an answer to her questions in the presence of an anxious-faced young woman there, who said, apologetically, " He got away from me; he's been like a wild thing to get here. Do you know him?"

"Know him? Yes, I have seen him before."

The anxious-faced young woman breathed a sigh of relief. " I thought, maybe, I'd been taken in. I was just closing up the studio, an hour ago, when two men came up the stairs with this little fellow wrapped in an old coat. They said they were from a schooner called the *Nancy Jane*, down at one of the wharves, and they picked up this boy in a drifting boat on the Bay Saint-Mary two days ago. They said he was frightened half out of his senses, and was holding on to that photo in his hand, — show the lady, dear."

Narcisse, whose tired head was nodding sleepily on his breast, paid no attention to her request, so she gently withdrew one of his hands from under his cloak and exhibited in it a torn and stained photograph of Vesper.

Mrs. Nimmo caught her breath, and attempted to take it from him, but he quickly roused himself, and, placing it beneath him, rolled over on the floor, and, with a farewell glance at the portrait above, fell sound asleep.

"He's beat out," said the anxious-faced young woman. "I'm glad I've got him to friends. The sailors were awful glad to get rid of him. They kind of thought he was a French child from Nova Scotia, but they hadn't time to run back with him, for they had to hurry here with their cargo, and then he held on to the photo and said he wanted to be taken to that young man. The sailors saw our address on it, but they sort of misdoubted we wouldn't keep him. However, I thought I'd take him off their hands, for he was frightened to death they would carry him back to their vessel, though I guess they was kind enough to him. I gave them back their coat, and borrowed some things from the woman who takes care of our studio. I forgot to say the boy had only a night-dress on when they found him."

Mrs. Nimmo mechanically felt in her pocket for her purse. "They didn't say anything about a woman being with him?"

"No, ma'am; he wouldn't talk to them much, but they said it was likely a child's trick of getting in a boat and setting himself loose."

"Would you — would you care to keep him until he is sent for?" faltered Mrs. Nimmo.

"I — oh, no, I couldn't. I've only a room in a lodging-house. I'd be afraid of something happening to him, for I'm out all day. I offered him something to eat, but he wouldn't take it — oh, thank you, ma'am, I didn't spend all that. I guess I'll have to go. Does he come from down East?"

"Yes, he is French. My son visited his house this summer, and used to pet him a good deal."

The young woman cast a glance of veiled admiration at the portrait. "And the little one ran away to find him. Quite a story. He's cute, too," and, airily patting Narcisse's curly head, she took her leave of Mrs. Nimmo, and made her way down-stairs. A good many strange happenings came into her daily life in this large city, and this was not one of the strangest.

Mrs. Nimmo sat still and stared at Narcisse. Rose had probably not been in the boat with him, — had probably not been drowned. He had apparently run away from home, and the first thing to do was to communicate with his mother, who would be frantic with anxiety about him. She therefore wrote out a telegram to Rose, " Your boy is with me, and safe and well," and ringing for Henry, she bade him send it as quickly as possible.

Then she sank again into profound meditation. The child had come to see Vesper. Had she better not let him know about it? If she applied the principles of sound reasoning to the case, she certainly should do so. It might also be politic. Perhaps it would bring him home to her, and, sighing heavily, she wrote another telegram.

In the meantime Narcisse did not awake. He lay still, enjoying the heavy slumber of exhaustion and content. He was in the house of his beloved Englishman; all would now be well.

He did not know that, after a time, his trustful confidence awoke the mother spirit in the woman watching him. The child for a time was wholly in her care. No other person in this vast city was interested in him. No one cared for him. A strange, long-unknown feeling fluttered about her breast, and memories of her past youth awoke. She had also once been a child. She had been lonely and terrified, and suffered childish agonies not to be revealed until years of maturity. They were mostly agonies about trifles, — still, she had suffered. She pictured to herself the despair and anger of the boy upon finding that Vesper did not return to Sleeping Water as he had promised to do. With his little white face in a snarl, he would enter the boat and set himself adrift, to face sufferings of fright and loneliness of which in his petted childhood he could have had no conception. And yet what courage. She could see that he was exhausted, yet there had been no whining, no complaining; he had attained his object and he was satisfied. He was really like her own boy, and, with a proud, motherly smile, she gazed alternately from the curly head on the carpet to the curly one in the portrait.

· The external resemblance, too, was indeed remarkable, and now the thought did not displease her, although it had invariably done so in Sleeping Water, when she had heard it frequently and naïvely commented on by the Acadiens.

Well, the child had thrown himself on her protection, — he should not repent it; and, summoning a housemaid, she sent her in search of some of Vesper's long-unused clothing, and then together they slipped the disfiguring girl's dress from Narcisse's shapely body, and put on him a long white night-robe.

He drowsily opened his eyes as they were lifting him into Vesper's bed, saw that the photograph was still in his possession, and that a familiar face was bending over him, then, sweetly murmuring "*Bon soir*" (good night), he again slipped into the land of dreams.

Several times during the night Mrs. Nimmo stole into her son's room, and drew the white sheet from the black head half buried in the pillow. Once she kissed him, and this time she went back to her bed with a lighter heart, and was soon asleep herself.

She was having a prolonged nap the next morning when something caused her suddenly to open her eyes. Just for an instant she fancied herself a happy young wife again, her husband by her side, their adored child paying them an early morning call. Then the dream was over. This was the little foreign boy who was sitting curled up on the foot of her bed, nibbling hungrily at a handful of biscuits.

"I came, madame, because those others I do not know," and he pointed towards the floor, to indicate her servants. "Has your son, the Englishman, yet arrived?"

"No," she said, gently.

"Your skin is white," said Narcisse, approvingly; "that is good; I do not like that man."

"But you have seen colored people on the Bay, — you must not dislike Henry. My husband brought him here as a boy to wait on my son. I can never give him up."

"He is amiable," said Narcisse, diplomatically. "He gave me these," and he extended his biscuits.

They were carrying on their conversation in French, for only with Vesper did Narcisse care to speak English. Perfectly aware, in his acute childish intelligence, that he was, for a time, entirely dependent on "madame," whom, up to this, he had been jealous of, and had positively disliked, he was keeping on her a watchful and roguish eye. Mrs. Nimmo, meanwhile, was interested and amused, but would make no overtures to him.

"Is your bed as soft as mine, madame?" he said, politely.

"I do not know; I never slept in that one."

Narcisse drew a corner of her silk coverlet over his feet. "Narcisse was very sick yesterday."

"I do not wonder," said his hostess.

"Your son said that he would return, but he did not."

"My son has other things to think of, little boy."

Mrs. Nimmo's manner was one that would have checked confidences in an ordinary child. It made Narcisse more eager to justify himself. "Why does my mother cry every night?" he asked, suddenly.

"How can I tell?" answered Mrs. Nimmo, peevishly.

"I hear a noise in the night, like trees in a storm," said Narcisse, tragically, and, drawing himself up, he fetched a tremendous sigh from the pit of his little stomach; "then I put up my hand so,"—and leaning over, he placed three fingers on Mrs. Nimmo's eyelids, — "and my mother's face is quite wet, like leaves in the rain."

Mrs. Nimmo did not reply, and he went on with alarming abruptness. "She cries for the Englishman. I also cried, and one night I got out of bed. It was very fine; there was the night sun in the sky, — you know, madame, there is a night sun and a day sun —"

"Yes, I know."

"I went creeping, creeping to the wharf like a fly on a tree. I was not afraid, for I carried your son in my hand, and he says only babies cry when they are alone."

"And then, —" said Mrs. Nimmo.

"Oh, the beautiful stone!" cried Narcisse, his volatile fancy attracted by a sparkling ring on Mrs. Nimmo's finger.

She sighed, and allowed him to handle it for a moment. "I have just put it on again, little boy. I have been in mourning for the last two years. Tell me about your going to the boat."

"There is nothing to tell," said Narcisse; "it was a very little boat."

"Whose boat was it?"

"The blacksmith's."

"How did you get it off from the wharf?"

"Like this," and bending over, he began to

fumble with the strings of her nightcap, tying and untying until he tickled her throat and made her laugh irresistibly and push him away. "There was no knife," he said, "or I would have cut it."

"But you did wrong to take the blacksmith's boat."

Narcisse's face flushed, yet he was too happy to become annoyed with her. "When the Englishman is there, I am good, and my mother does not cry. Let him go back with me."

"And what shall I do?"

Narcisse was plainly embarrassed. At last he said, earnestly, "Remain, madame, with the black man, who will take care of you. When does the Englishman arrive?"

"I do not know; run away now, I want to dress."

"You have here a fine bathroom," said Narcisse, sauntering across the room to an open door. "When am I to have my bath?"

"Does your mother give you one every day?"

"Yes, madame, at night, before I go to bed. Do you not know the screen in our room, and the little tub, and the dish with the soap that smells so nice? I must scour myself hard in order to be clean."

"I am glad to hear that. I will send a tub to your room."

"But I like this, madame."

"Come, come," she said, peremptorily, "run away. No one bathes in my tub but myself."

Narcisse had a passion for dabbling in water, and he found this dainty bathroom irresistible. "I hate you, madame," he said, flushing angrily, and stamping his foot at her. "I hate you."

Mrs. Nimmo looked admiringly past the child at his reflection in her cheval glass. What a beauty he was, as he stood furiously regarding her, his sweet, proud face convulsed, his little body trembling inside his white gown! In his recklessness he had forgotten to be polite to her, and she liked him the better for it.

"You are a naughty boy," she said, indulgently. "I cannot have you in my room if you talk like that."

Without a word Narcisse went to her dressing-table, picked up his precious photograph that he had left propped against a silver-backed brush, and turned to leave her, when she said, curiously, "Why did you tear that picture if you think so much of it?"

Narcisse immediately fell into a state of pitiable confusion, and, hanging his head, remained speechless.

"If you will say you are sorry for being rude, I will give you another one," she said, and in a luxury of delight at playing with this little soul, she raised herself on her arm and held out a hand to him.

Narcisse drew back his lips at her as if he had

been a small dog. "Madame," he faltered, tapping his teeth, "these did it, but I stopped them."

"What do you mean?" said Mrs. Nimmo, and a horrible suspicion entered her mind.

"Narcisse was hungry — in the boat —" stammered the boy. "He nibbled but a little of the picture. He could not bite the Englishman long."

Mrs. Nimmo shuddered. She had never been hungry in her life. "Come here, you poor child. You shall have a bath in my room as soon as I finish. Give me a kiss."

Narcisse's sensitive spirit immediately became bathed with light. "Shall I kiss you as your son the Englishman kissed my mother?"

"Yes," said Mrs. Nimmo, bravely, and she held out her arms.

"But you must not do so," said Narcisse, drawing back. "You must now cry, and hide your face like this," — and his slender, supple fingers guided her head into a distressed position, — "and when I approach, you must wave your hands."

"Did your mother do that?" asked Mrs. Nimmo, eagerly.

"Yes, — and your son lifted her hand like this," and Narcisse bent a graceful knee before her.

"Did she not throw her arms around his neck and cling to him?" inquired the lady, in an excess of jealous curiosity.

"No, she ran from us up the bank."

"Your mother is a wicked woman to cause my son pain," said Mrs. Nimmo, in indignant and rapid French.

"My mother is not wicked" said Narcisse, vehemently. "I wish to see her. I do not like you."

They were on the verge of another disagreement, and Mrs. Nimmo, with a soothing caress, hurried him from the room. What a curious boy he was! And as she dressed herself she sometimes smiled and sometimes frowned at her reflection in the glass, but the light in her eyes was always a happy one, and there was an unusual color in her cheeks.

CHAPTER XIX.

AN INTERRUPTED MASS.

"Here is our dearest theme where skies are blue and brightest,
To sing a single song in places that love it best;
Freighting the happy breeze when snowy clouds are lightest;
Making a song to cease not when the singer is dumb in rest."

J. F. H.

AWAY up the Bay, past Sleeping Water and Church Point, past historic Piau's Isle and Belliveau's Cove and the lovely Sissiboo River, past Weymouth and the Barrens, and other villages stretched out along this highroad, between Yarmouth and Digby, is Bleury, — beautiful Bleury, which is the final outpost in the long-extended line of Acadien villages. Beyond this, the Bay — what there is of it, for it soon ends this side of Digby — is English.

But beautiful Bleury, which rejoices in a high bluff, a richly wooded shore, swelling hills, and an altogether firmer, bolder outlook than flat Sleeping Water, is not wholly French. Some of its inhabitants are English. Here the English tide meets the French tide, and, swelling up the Bay and back in the woods, they overrun the land, and form curious contrasts and results, unknown and unfelt in the purely Acadien districts nearer the sea.

In Bleury there is one schoolhouse common to both races, and on a certain afternoon, three weeks after little Narcisse's adventurous voyage in search of the Englishman, the children were tumultuously pouring out from it. Instinctively they formed themselves into four distinct groups. The groups at last resolved themselves into four processions, two going up the road, two down. The French children took one side of the road, the English the other, and each procession kept severely to its own place.

Heading the rows of English children who went up the Bay was a red-haired girl of some twelve summers, whose fiery head gleamed like a torch, held at the head of the procession. As far as the coloring of her skin was concerned, and the exquisite shading of her velvety brown eyes, and the shape of her slightly upturned nose, she might have been English. But her eager gestures, her vivacity, her swiftness and lightness of manner, marked her as a stranger and an alien among the English children by whom she was surrounded.

This was Bidiane LeNoir, Agapit's little renegade, and just now she was highly indignant over a matter of offended pride. A French girl had taken a place above her in a class, and also, secure in the fortress of the schoolroom, had made a detestable face at her.

"I hate them, — those Frenchies," she cried, casting a glance of defiance at the Acadien children meekly filing along beyond her. "I sha'n't walk beside 'em. Go on, you ———," and she added an offensive epithet.

The dark-faced, shy Acadiens trotted soberly on, swinging their books and lunch-baskets in their hands. They would not go out of their way to seek a quarrel.

"Run," said Bidiane, imperiously.

The little Acadiens would not run, they preferred to walk, and Bidiane furiously called to her adherents, "Let's sing mass."

This was the deepest insult that could be offered to the children across the road. Sometimes in their childish quarrels aprons and jackets were torn, and faces were slapped, but no bodily injury ever equalled in indignity that put upon the Catholic children when their religion was ridiculed.

However, they did not retaliate, but their faces became gloomy, and they immediately quickened their steps.

"Holler louder," Bidiane exhorted her followers, and she broke into a howling "*Pax vobiscum*," while a boy at her elbow groaned, "*Et cum spiritu tuo*," and the remainder of the children screamed in an irreverent chorus, that ran all up and down the scale, "*Gloria tibi Domine.*"

The Acadien children fled now, some of them with fingers in their ears, others casting bewildered looks of horror, as if expecting to see the earth open and swallow up their sacrilegious tormentors, who stood shrieking with delight at the success of their efforts to rid themselves of their undesired companions.

"Shut up," said Bidiane, suddenly, and at once the laughter was stilled. There was a stranger in their midst. He had come gliding among them on one of the bright shining wheels that went up and down the Bay in such large numbers. Before Bidiane had spoken he had dismounted, and his quick eye was surveying them with a glance like lightning.

The children stared silently at him. Ridicule cuts sharply into the heart of a child, and a sound whipping inflicted on every girl and boy present would not have impressed on them the burden of their iniquity as did the fine sarcasm and disdainful amusement with which this handsome stranger regarded them.

One by one they dropped away, and Bidiane only remained rooted to the spot by some magic incomprehensible to her.

"Your name is Bidiane LeNoir," he said, quietly.

"It ain't," she said, doggedly; "it's Biddy Ann Black."

"Really,—and there are no LeNoirs about here, nor Corbineaus?"

"Down the Bay are LeNoirs and Corbineaus," said the little girl, defiantly; then she burst out with a question, "You ain't the Englishman from Boston?"

"I am."

"Gosh!" she said, in profound astonishment; then she lowered her eyes, and traced a serpent in the dust with her great toe. All up and down the Bay had flashed the news of this wonderful stranger who had come to Sleeping Water in quest of an heir or heiress to some vast fortune. The heir had been found in the person of herself,—small, red-haired Biddy Ann Black, and it had been firmly believed among her fellow playmates that at any moment the prince might appear in a golden chariot and whisk her away with him to realms of bliss, where she would live in a gorgeous palace and eat cakes and sweetmeats all day long, sailing at intervals in a boat of her own over a bay of transcendent loveliness, in which she would catch codfish as big as whales. This story had been believed until very recently, when it had somewhat died away by reason of the non-appearance of the prince.

Now he had arrived, and Bidiane's untrained mind and her little wild beast heart were in a tumult. She felt that he did not approve of her, and she loved and hated him in a breath. He was smooth, and dignified, and sleek, like a priest. He was dark, too, like the French people, and she scowled fiercely. He would see that her cotton gown was soiled; why had she not worn a clean one to-day, and also put on her shoes? Would he really want her to go away with him? She would not do so; and a lump arose in her throat, and with a passionate emotion that she did not understand she gazed across the Bay towards the purple hills of Digby Neck.

Vesper, perfectly aware of what was passing in her mind, waited for her to recover herself. "I would like to see your uncle and aunt," he said, at last. "Will you take me to them?"

She responded by a gesture in the affirmative, and, still with eyes bent obstinately on the ground, led the way towards a low brown house situated in a hollow between two hills, and surrounded by a grove of tall French poplars, whose ancestors had been nourished by the sweet waters of the Seine.

Vesper's time was limited, and he was anxious to gain the confidence of the little maid, if possible, but she would not talk to him.

"Do you like cocoanuts?" he said, presently, on seeing in the distance a negro approaching, with a load of this foreign fruit, that he had probably obtained from some schooner.

"You bet," said Bidiane, briefly.

Vesper stopped the negro, and bought as many nuts at five cents apiece as he and Bidiane could carry. Then, trying to make her smile by balancing one on the saddle of his wheel, he walked slowly beside her.

Bidiane solemnly watched him. She would not talk, she would not smile, but she cheerfully dropped her load when one of his cocoanuts rolled in the ditch, and, at the expense of a scratched face from an inquisitive rose-bush that bent over to see what she was doing, she restored it to him.

"Your cheek is bleeding," said Vesper.

"No odds," she remarked, with Indian-like fortitude, and she preceded him into a grassy dooryard, that was pervaded by a powerful smell of frying doughnuts.

Mirabelle Marie, her fat, good-natured young aunt, stood in the kitchen doorway with a fork in her hand, and seeing that the stranger was English, she beamed a joyous, hearty welcome on him.

"Good day, sir; you'll stop to supper? That's right. Shove your wheel ag'in that fence, and come right in. Biddy, git the creamer from the well and give the genl'man a glass of milk. You won't? — All right, sir, walk into the settin'-room. What! you'd rather set under the trees? All right. My man's up in the barn, fussin' with a sick cow that's lost her cud. He's puttin' a rind of bacon on her horns. What d'ye say, Biddy?"—this latter in an undertone to the little girl, who was pulling at her dress. "This is the Englishman from Boston—*sakerjé!*" and, dropping her fork, she wiped her hands on her dress and darted out to offer Vesper still more effusive expressions of hospitality.

He smiled amiably on her, and presently she returned to the kitchen, silly and distracted in appearance, and telling Bidiane that she felt like a hen with her head cut off. The stranger who was to do so much for them had come. She could have prostrated herself in the dust before him. "Scoot, Biddy, scoot," she exclaimed; "borry meat of some kind. Go to the Maxwells or to the Whites. Tell 'em he's come, and we've got nothin' but fish and salt pork, and they know the English hate that like pizen. And git a junk of butter with only a mite of salt in it. Mine's salted heavy for the market. And skip to the store and ask 'em to score us for a pound of cheese and some fancy crackers."

Bidiane ran away, and, as she ran, her ill humor left her, and she felt herself to be a very important personage. Vivaciously and swiftly she exclaimed, "He's come!" to several children whom she met, and with a keen and exquisite sense of pleasure looked back to see them standing open-mouthed in the road, impressed in a most gratifying way by the news communicated.

In the meantime Mirabelle Marie began to make frantic and ludicrous preparations to set a superfine meal before the stranger, who was now entitled to a double share of honor. In her extreme haste everything went wrong. She upset her pot of lard; the cat and dog got at her plate of doughnuts, and stole half of them; the hot biscuits that she hastily mixed burnt to a cinder, and the jar of preserved berries that she opened proved to have been employing their leisure time in the cellar by fermenting most viciously.

However, she did not lose her temper, and, as she was not a woman to be cast down by trifles, she seated herself in a rocking-chair, fanned herself vigorously with her apron, and laughed spasmodically.

Bidiane found her there on her return. The little girl possessed a keener sense of propriety than her careless relative; she was also more moody and variable, and immediately falling into a rage, she conveyed some plain truths to Mirabelle Marie, in inelegant language.

The woman continued to laugh, and to stare through the window at Vesper, who sat motionless under the trees. One arm was thrown over the back of his seat, and his handsome head was turned away from the house.

"Poor calf," said Mirabelle Marie, "he looks down

the Bay; he is a very divil for good looks. Rose à Charlitte is one big fool."

"We shall have only slops for supper," said Bidiane, in a fury, and swearing under her breath at her.

Mirabelle Marie at this bestirred herself, and tried to evolve a meal from the ruin of her hopes, and the fresh supply of food that her niece had obtained.

The little girl meantime found a clean cloth, and spread it on the table. She carefully arranged on it their heavy white dishes and substantial knives and spoons. Then she blew a horn, which made Claude à Sucre, her strapping great uncle, suddenly loom against the horizon, in the direction of the barn.

He came to the house, and was about to ask a question, but closed his mouth when he saw the stranger in the yard.

"Go change," said Bidiane, pouncing upon him.

Claude knew what she meant, and glanced resignedly from his homespun suit to her resolved face. There was no appeal, so he went to his bedroom to don his Sunday garments. He had not without merit gained his nickname of Sugar Claude; for he was, if possible, more easy-going than his wife.

Bidiane next attacked her aunt, whose face was the color of fire, from bending over the stove. "Go put on clean duds; these are dirty."

"Go yourself, you little cat," said Mirabelle Marie, shaking her mountain of flesh with a good-natured laugh.

"I'm going — I ain't as dirty as you, anyway — and take off those sneaks."

Mirabelle Marie stuck out one of the flat feet encased in rubber-soled shoes. "My land! if I do, I'll go barefoot."

Bidiane subsided and went to the door to look for her two boy cousins. Where were they? She shaded her eyes with her two brown hands, and her gaze swept the land and the water. Where were those boys? Were they back in the pasture, or down by the river, or playing in the barn, or out in the boat? A small schooner beating up the Bay caught her eye. That was Johnny Maxwell's schooner. She knew it by the three-cornered patch on the mainsail. And in Captain Johnny's pockets, when he came from Boston, were always candy, nuts, and raisins, — and the young Maxwells were of a generous disposition, and the whole neighborhood knew it. Her cousins would be on the wharf below the house, awaiting his arrival. Well, they should come to supper first; and, like a bird of prey, she swooped down the road upon her victims, and, catching them firmly by the shoulders, marched them up to the house.

CHAPTER XX.

WITH THE WATERCROWS.

"Her mouth was ever agape,
Her ears were ever ajar;
If you wanted to find a sweeter fool,
You shouldn't have come this far."
— *Old Song.*

WHEN the meal was at last prepared, and the whole family were assembled in the sitting-room, where the table had been drawn from the kitchen, they took a united view of Vesper's back; then Claude à Sucre was sent to escort him to the house.

With a rapturous face Mirabelle Marie surveyed the steaming dish of *soupe à la patate* (potato soup), the mound of buttered toast, the wedge of tough fried steak, the strips of raw dried codfish, the pink cake, and fancy biscuits. Surely the stranger would be impressed by the magnificence of this display, and she glanced wonderingly at Bidiane, whose eyes were lowered to the floor. The little girl had enjoyed advantages superior to her own, in that she mingled freely in English society, where she herself — Mirabelle Marie — was strangely shunned. Could it be that she was ashamed of this board? Certainly she could never have seen anything much grander; and, swelling with gratified pride and ambition, the mistress of the household seated herself behind her portly teapot, from which vantage-ground she beamed, huge and silly, like a full-grown moon upon the occupants of the table.

Her guest was not hungry, apparently, for he scarcely touched the dishes that she pressed upon him. However, he responded so gracefully and with such well-bred composure to her exhortations that he should eat his fill, for there was more in the cellar, that she was far from resenting his lack of appetite. He was certainly a "boss young man;" and as she sat, delicious visions swam through her brain of new implements for the farm, a new barn, perhaps, new furniture for the house, with possibly an organ, a spick and span wagon, and a horse, or even a pair, and the eventual establishment of her two sons in Boston, — the El Dorado of her imagination, — where they would become prosperous merchants, and make heaps of gold for their mother to spend.

In her excitement she began to put her food in her mouth with both hands, until reminded that she was flying in the face of English etiquette by a vigorous kick administered under the table by Bidiane.

Vesper, with an effort, called back his painful wandering thoughts, which had indeed gone down the Bay, and concentrated them upon this picturesquely untidy family. This was an entirely different establishment from that of the Sleeping Water Inn. Fortunately there was no grossness, no clownishness of behavior, which would have irreparably offended his fastidious taste. They were simply uncultured, scrambling, and even interesting with the background of this old homestead, which was one of the most ancient that he had seen on the Bay, and which had probably been built by some of the early settlers.

While he was quietly making his observations, the family finished their meal, and seeing that they were waiting for him to give the signal for leaving the table, he politely rose and stepped behind his chair.

Mirabelle Marie scurried to her feet and pushed the table against the wall. Then the whole family sat down in a semicircle facing a large open fireplace heaped high with the accumulated rubbish of the summer, and breathlessly waited for the stranger to tell them of his place of birth, the amount of his fortune, his future expectations and hopes, his intentions with regard to Bidiane, and of various and sundry other matters that might come in during the course of their conversation.

Vesper, with his usual objection to having any course of action mapped out for him, sat gazing imperturbably at them. He was really sorry for Mirabelle Marie, who was plainly bursting with eagerness. Her husband was more reserved, yet he, too, was suffering from suppressed curiosity, and timidly and wistfully handled his pipe, that he longed to and yet did not dare to smoke.

His two small boys sat dangling their legs from seats that were uncomfortably high for them. They were typical Acadien children, — shy, elusive, and retreating within themselves in the presence of strangers; and if, by chance, Vesper caught a stealthy glance from one of them, the little fellow immediately averted his glossy head, as if afraid that the calm eyes of the stranger might lay bare the inmost secrets of his youthful soul.

Bidiane was the most interesting of the group. She was evidently a born manager and the ruling spirit in the household, for he could see that they all stood in awe of her. She must possess some force of will to enable her to subdue her natural eagerness and vivacity, so as to appear sober and reserved. His presence was evidently a constraint to the little red-haired witch, and he could scarcely have understood her character, if Agapit had not supplied him with a key to it.

Young as she was, she acutely appreciated the racial differences about her. There were two worlds in her mind, — French and English. The careless predilections of her aunt had become fierce prejudices with her, and, at present, although she was proud to have an Englishman under their roof, she was at the same time tortured by the contrast that she knew he must find between the humble home of her relatives and the more prosperous surroundings of the English people with whom he was accustomed to mingle.

"She is a clever little imp," Agapit had said, "and wise beyond her years."

Vesper, when his unobtrusive examination of her small resolved face was over, glanced about the low, square room in which they sat. The sun was just leaving it. The family would soon be thinking of going to bed. All around the room were other rooms evidently used as sleeping apartments, for through a half-open door he saw an unmade bed, and he knew, from the construction of the house, that there was no upper story.

After a time the silence became oppressive, and Mirabelle Marie, seeing that the stranger would not entertain her, set herself to the task of entertaining him, and with an ingratiating and insinuating smile informed him that the biggest liar on the Bay lived in Bleury.

"His name's Bill," she said, "Blowin' Bill Duckfoot, an' the boys git 'round him an' say, 'Give us a yarn.' He says, 'Well, give me a chaw of 'baccy,' then he starts off. 'Onct when I went to sea' — he's never bin off the Bay, you know — 'it blowed as hard as it could for ten days. Then it blowed ten times harder. We had to lash the cook to the mast.' 'What did you do when you wanted grub?' says the boys. 'Oh, we unlashed him for awhile,' says Bill. 'One day the schooner cracked from stern to stem. Cap'en and men begun to holler and says we was goin' to the bottom.' 'Cheer up,' says Bill, 'I'll fix a way.' So he got 'em to lash the anchor chains 'roun' the schooner, an' that hold 'em together till they got to Boston, and there was nothin' too good for Bill. It was cousin Duckfoot, an' brother Duckfoot, and good frien' Duckfoot, and lots of treatin'.''

Vesper in suppressed astonishment surveyed Mirabelle Marie, who, at the conclusion of her story, burst into a fit of such hearty laughter that she seemed to be threatened there and then with a fit of apoplexy. Her face grew purple, tears ran down her cheeks, and through eyes that had become mere slits in her face she looked at Claude, who too was convulsed with amusement, at her two small boys, who giggled behind their hands, and at Bidiane, who only smiled sarcastically.

Vesper at once summoned an expression of interest to his face, and Mirabelle Marie, encouraged by it, caught her breath with an explosive sound, wiped the tears from her eyes, and at once continued. " Here's another daisy one. 'Onct,' says Bill, 'all han's was lost 'cept me an' a nigger. I went to the stern as cap'en, and he to the bow as deck-han'. A big wave struck the schooner, and when we righted, wasn't the nigger at stern as cap'en, an' I was at bow as deck-han'!'"

While Vesper was waiting for the conclusion of the story, a burst of joyous cachinnation assured him that it had already come. Mirabelle Marie was again rocking herself to and fro in immoderate delight, her head at each dip forward nearly touching her knees, while her husband was slapping his side vigorously.

Vesper laughed himself. Truly there were many different orders of mind in the universe. He saw nothing amusing in the reported exploits of the liar Duckfoot. They also would not have brought a smile to the face of his beautiful Rose, yet the Corbineaus, or Watercrows, as they translated their name in order to make themselves appear English, found these stories irresistibly comical. It was a blessing for them that they did so, otherwise the whole realm of humor might be lost to them; and he was going off in a dreamy speculation with regard to their other mental proclivities, when he was roused by another story from his hostess.

"Duckfoot is a mason by trade, an' onct he built a chimbley for a woman. 'Make a good draught,' says she. 'You bet,' says he, an' he built his chimbley an' runs away; as he runs he looks back, an' there was the woman's duds that was hangin' by the fire goin' up the chimbley. He had built such a draught that nothin' could stay in the kitchen, so she had to go down on her knees an' beg him to change it."

"To beg him to change it," vociferated Claude, and he soundly smacked his unresisting knee. "Oh, Lord, 'ow funny!" and he roared with laughter so stimulating that he forgot his fear of Vesper and Bidiane, and, boldly lighting his pipe, put it between his lips.

Mirabelle Marie, whose flow of eloquence it was difficult to check, related several other tales of Duckfoot Bill. Many times, before the railway in this township of Clare had been built, he had told them of his uncle, who had, he said, a magnificent residence in Louisiana, with a park full of valuable animals called skunks. These animals he had never fully described, and they were consequently enveloped in a cloud of admiration and mystery, until a horde of them came with the railroad to the Bay, when the credulous Acadiens learned for themselves what they really were.

During the recital of this tale, Bidiane's face went from disapproval to disgust, and at last, diving under the table, she seized a basket and went to work vigorously, as if the occupation of her fingers would ease the perturbation of her mind.

Vesper watched her closely. She was picking out the threads of old cotton and woollen garments that had been cut into small pieces. These threads would be washed, laid out on the grass to dry, and then be carded, and spun, and woven over again, according to a thrifty custom of the Acadiens, and made into bedcovers, stockings, and cloth. The child must possess some industry, for this work — " pickings," as it was called — was usually done by the women. In brooding silence the little girl listened to Mirabelle Marie's final tale of Duckfoot Bill, whose wife called out to him, one day, from the yard, that there was a flock of wild geese passing over the house. Without troubling to go out, he merely discharged his gun up the chimney beside which he sat, and the ramrod, carelessly being left in, killed a certain number of geese.

"How many do you guess that ramrod run through?"

Vesper good-naturedly guessed two.

"No, — seven," she shrieked; "they was strung in a row like dried apples," and she burst into fresh peals of laughter, until suddenly plunged into the calmness of despair by a few words from Bidiane, who leaned over and whispered angrily to her.

Mirabelle Marie trembled, and gazed at the stranger. Was it true, — did he wish to commend her to a less pleasant place than Bleury for teasing him with these entrancing stories?

She could gather nothing from his face; so she entered tremulously into a new subject of conversation, and, pointing to Claude's long legs, assured him that his heavy woollen stockings had been made entirely by Bidiane. "She's smart,—as smart as a steel trap," said the aunt. "She can catch the sheeps, hold 'em down, shear the wool, an' spin it."

Bidiane immediately pushed her basket under the table with so fiery and resentful a glance that the unfortunate Mirabelle Marie relapsed into silence.

"Have you ever gone to sea?" asked Vesper, of the silently smoking Claude.

"Yessir, we mos' all goes to sea when we's young."

"Onct he was wrecked," interrupted his wife.

"Yessir, I was. Off Arichat we got on a ledge. We thump up an' down. We was all on deck but the cook. The cap'en sends me to the galley for 'im. 'E come up, we go ashore, an' the schooner go to pieces."

"Tell him about the mouse," said Bidiane, abruptly.

"The mouse?—oh, yess, when I go for the cook I find 'im in the corner, a big stick in his 'and. I dunno 'ow 'e stan'. 'Is stove was upside down, an' there was an awful wariwarie" (racket). "'E seem not to think of danger. ' 'Ist,' says 'e. 'Don' mek a noise, — I wan' to kill that mouse.'"

Vesper laughed at this, and Mirabelle Marie's face cleared.

"Tell the Englishman who was the cap'en of yous," she said, impulsively, and she resolutely turned her back on Bidiane's terrific frown.

"Well, 'e was smart," said Claude, apologetically. "'E always get on though 'e not know much. One day when 'e fus' wen' to sea 'is wife says, ' All the cap'ens' wives talk about their charts, an' you ain't gut none. I buy one.' So she wen' to Yarmouth, an' buy 'im a chart. She also buy some of that shiny cloth for kitchen table w'at 'as blue scrawly lines like writin' on it. The cap'en leave the nex' mornin' before she was up, an' 'e takes with 'im the oilcloth instid of the chart, an' 'e 'angs it in 'is cabin; 'e didn't know no differ. 'E never could write, — that man. He mek always a pictur of 'is men when 'e wan' to write the fish they ketch. But 'e was smart, very smart. 'E mek also money. Onct 'e was passenger on a schooner that smacks ag'in a steamer in a fog. All 'an's scuttle, 'cause that mek a big scare. They forgit 'im. 'E wake; 'e find 'imself lonely. Was 'e frightful? Oh, no; 'e can't work sails, but 'e steer that schooner to Boston, an' claim salvage."

"Tell also the name of the cap'en," said Mirabelle Marie.

Claude moved uneasily in his chair, and would not speak.

"What was it?" asked Vesper.

"It was Crispin," said Mirabelle Marie, solemnly. "Crispin, the brother of Charlitte."

Vesper calmly took a cigarette from his pocket, and lighted it.

"It is a nice place down the Bay," said Mirabelle Marie, uneasily.

"Very nice," responded her guest.

"Rose à Charlitte has a good name," she continued, "a very good name."

Vesper fingered his cigarette, and gazed blankly at her.

"They speak good French there," she said.

Her husband and Bidiane stared at her. They had never heard such a sentiment from her lips before. However, they were accustomed to her ways, and they soon got over their surprise.

"Do you not speak French?" asked Vesper.

Mrs. Watercrow shrugged her shoulders. "It is no good. We are all English about here. How can one be French? Way back, when we went to mass, the priest was always botherin'—'Talk French to your young ones. Don't let them forgit the way the old people talked.' One day I come home and

says to my biggest boy, '*Va ramasser des écopeaux*'"
(Go pick up some chips). "He snarl at me, 'Do you
mean potatoes?' He didn't like it."

"Did he not understand you?" asked Vesper.

"Naw, naw," said Claude, bitterly. "We 'ave
French nebbors, but our young ones don' play with.
They don' know French. My wife she speak it
w'en we don' want 'em to know w'at we say."

"You always like French," said his wife, contemptuously. "I guess you gut somethin' French inside you."

Claude, for some reason or other, probably because, usually without an advocate, he now knew that he had one in Vesper, was roused to unusual animation. He snatched his pipe from his mouth and said, warmly, "It's me 'art that's French, an' sometimes it's sore. I speak not much, but I think often we are fools. Do the Eenglish like us? No, only a few come with us; they grin 'cause we put off our French speakin' like an ole coat. A man say to me one day, 'You 'ave nothin'. You do not go to mass, you preten' to be Protestan', w'en you not brought up to it. You big fool, you don' know w'at it is. If you was dyin' to-morrer you'd sen' for the priest.'"

Mirabelle Marie opened her eyes wide at her husband's eloquence.

He was not yet through. "An' our children, they

are silly with it. They donno' w'at they are. All day Sunday they play; sometimes they say cuss words. I say, 'Do it not, 'an' they ast me w'y. I cannot tell. They are not French, they are not Eenglish. They 'ave no religion. I donno' w'ere they go w'en they die."

Mirabelle Marie boldly determined to make confidences to the Englishman in her turn.

"The English have loads of money. I wish I could go to Boston. I could make it there, — yes, lots of it."

Claude was not to be put down. "I like our own langwidge, oh, yes," he said, sadly. "W'en I was a leetle boy I wen' to school. All was Eenglish. They put in my 'and an Eenglish book. I'd lef' my mother, I was stoopid. I thought all the children's teeth was broke, 'cause they spoke so strange. Never will I forgit my firs' day in school. W'y do they teach Eenglish to the French? The words was like fish 'ooks in my flesh."

"Would you be willing to send that little girl down the Bay to a French convent?" said Vesper, waving his cigarette towards Bidiane.

"We can't pay that," said Mirabelle Marie, eagerly.

"But I would."

While she was nodding her head complacently over this, the first of the favors to be showered on them, Claude said, slowly, " Down the Bay is like a bad, bad place to my children; they do not wish to go, not even to ride. They go towards Digby. Biddy Ann would not go to the convent, — would she, Biddy ? "

The little girl threw up her head angrily. " I hate Frenchtown, and that black spider, Agapit LeNoir."

Claude's face darkened, and his wife chuckled. Surely now there would be nothing left for the Englishman to do but to transplant them all to Boston.

" Would you not go ? " asked Vesper, addressing Bidiane.

" Not a damn step," said the girl, in a fury, and, violently pushing back her chair, she rushed from the room. If this young man wished to make a French girl of her, he might go on his way. She would have nothing to do with him. And with a rebellious and angry heart at this traitor to his race, as she regarded him, she climbed up a ladder in the kitchen that led to a sure hiding-place under the roof.

Her aunt clutched her head in despair. Bidiane would ruin everything. " She's all eaten up to go to Boston," she gasped.

" I am not a rich man," said Vesper, coldly. " I don't feel able at present to propose anything further for her than to give her a year or two in a convent."

Mirabelle Marie gaped speechlessly at him. In one crashing ruin her new barn, and farming implements, the wagon and horses, and trunks full of fine clothes fell into the abyss of lost hopes. The prince had not the long purse that she supposed he would have. And yet such was her good-nature that, when she recovered from the shock, she regarded him just as kindly and as admiringly as before, and if he had been in the twinkling of an eye reduced to want she would have been the first to relieve him, and give what aid she could. Nothing could destroy her deep-rooted and extravagant admiration for the English race.

Her fascinated glance followed him as he got up and sauntered to the open door.

"You'll stop all night?" she said, hospitably, shuffling after him. "We have one good bed, with many feathers."

He did not hear her, for in a state of extreme boredom, and slight absent-mindedness, he had stepped out under the poplars.

"Better leave 'im alone, I guess," said Claude; then he slipped off his coat. "I'll go milk."

"An' I'll make up the bed," said his wife; and taking the hairpins out of the switch that Bidiane had made her attach to her own thick lump of hair, she laid it on the shelf by the clock, and allowed her own brown wave to stream freely down her back. Then she unfastened her corsets, which she did not dare to take off, as no woman in Bleury who did not wear that article of dress tightly enfolding her chest and waist was considered to have reached the acme of respectability. However, she could for a time allow them to gape slightly apart, and having by this proceeding added much to her comfort, she entered one of the small rooms near by.

Vesper meanwhile walked slowly towards the gate, while Bidiane watched him through a loophole in the roof. His body only was in Bleury; his heart was in Sleeping Water. Step by step he was following Rose about her daily duties. He knew just at what time of day her slender feet carried her to the stable, to the duck-yard, to the hen-house. He knew the exact hour that she entered her kitchen in the morning, and went from it to the pantry. He could see her beautiful face at the cool pantry window, as she stood mixing various dishes, and occasionally glancing at the passers-by on the road. Sometimes she sang gently to herself, "Rose of the cross, thou mystic flower," or "Dear angel ever at my side," or some of the Latin hymns to the Virgin.

At this present moment her tasks would all be done. If there were guests who desired her presence, she might be seated with them in the little parlor. If there were none, she was probably alone in her room. Of what was she thinking? The blood surged to his face, there was a beating in his ears, and he raised his suffering glance to the sky. "O God! now I know why I suffered when my father died. It was to prepare me for this."

Then his mind went back to Rose. Had she succeeded in driving his image from her pure mind and imagination? Alas! he feared not, — he would like to know. He had heard nothing of her since leaving Sleeping Water. Agapit had written once, but he had not mentioned her.

This inaction was horrible, — this place wearied him insufferably. He glanced towards his wheel, and a sentence from one of Agapit's books came into his mind. It contained the advice of an old monk to a penitent, " My son, when in grievous temptation from trouble of the mind, engage violently in some exercise of the body."

He was a swift rider, and there was no need for him to linger longer here. These people were painfully subservient. If at any time anything came into his mind to be done for the little girl, they would readily agree to it; that is, if the small tigress concurred; at present there was nothing to be done for her.

He laid his hand on his bicycle and went towards the house again. There was no one to be seen, so he hurried up to the rickety barn where Claude sat on a milking-stool, trying to keep his long legs out of the way of a frisky cow.

The Frenchman was overcome with stolid dismay when Vesper briefly bade him good-by, and going to the barn door, he stared regretfully after him.

Mirabelle Marie, in blissful unconsciousness of the sudden departure, went on with her bed-making, but Bidiane, through the crack in the roof, saw him go, and in childish contradiction of spirit shed tears of anger and disappointment at the sight.

CHAPTER XXI.

A SUPREME ADIEU.

"How reads the riddle of our life,
That mortals seek immortal joy,
That pleasures here so quickly cloy,
And hearts are e'en with yearnings rife?
That love's bright morn no midday knows,
And darkness comes ere even's close,
And fondest hopes bear seeds of strife.

"Let fools deride; Faith's God-girt breast
Their puny shafts can turn aside,
And mock with these their sin-born pride.
Our souls were made for God the Best;
'Tis He alone can satisfy
Their every want, can still each cry;
In Him alone shall they find rest."

CORNELIUS O'BRIEN, *Archbishop of Halifax.*

THE night was one of velvety softness, and the stars, as if suspecting his mission, blinked delicately and discreetly down upon him, while Vesper, who knew every step of the way, went speeding down the Bay with a wildly beating heart.

Several Acadiens recognized him as he swept past

them on the road, but he did not stop to parley with them, for he wished to reach Yarmouth as soon as possible. His brain was tortured, and it seemed to him that, at every revolution of his wheels, a swift, subtle temptation assaulted him more insidiously and more fiercely. He would pass right by the Sleeping Water Inn. Why should he not pause there for a few minutes and make some arrangement with Rose about Narcisse, who was still in Boston? He certainly had a duty to perform towards the child. Would it not be foolish for him to pass by the mother's door without speaking to her of him? What harm could there be in a conversation of five minutes' duration?

His head throbbed, his muscles contracted. Only this afternoon he had been firm, as firm as a rock. He had sternly resolved not to see her again, not to write to her, not to meet her, not to send her a message, unless he should hear that she had been released from the bond of her marriage. What had come over him now? He was as weak as a child. He had better stop and think the matter over; and he sprang from his wheel and threw himself down on a grassy bank, covered with broad leaves that concealed the dead and withered flowers of the summer.

Somewhere in the darkness behind him was lonely Piau's Isle, where several of the Acadien forefathers of the Bay lay buried. What courage and powers of endurance they had possessed! They had bravely borne their burdens, lived their day, and were now at rest. Some day,—in a few years, perhaps,—he, too, would be a handful of dust, and he, too, would leave a record behind him; what would his record be?

He bit his lip and set his teeth savagely. He was a fool and a coward. He would not go to Sleeping Water, but would immediately turn his back on temptation, and go to Weymouth. He could stay at a hotel there all night, and take the train in the morning.

The soft air caressed his weary head; for a long time he lay staring up at the stars through the interlaced branches of an apple-tree over him, then he slowly rose. His face was towards the head of the Bay; he no longer looked towards Sleeping Water, but for a minute he stood irresolutely, and in that brief space of time his good resolution was irrevocably lost.

Some girls were going to a merrymaking, and, as they went, they laughed gaily and continuously. One of them had clear, silvery tones like those of Rose. The color again surged to his face, the blood flew madly through his veins. He must see her, if only for an instant; and, hesitating no longer, he turned and went careering swiftly through the darkness.

A short time later he had reached the inn. There

was a light in Rose's window. She must have gone to bed. Célina only was in the kitchen, and, with a hasty glance at her, he walked to the stable.

A terrible quacking in the duck-yard advised him who was there, and he was further assured by hearing an irritable voice exclaim, "If fowls were hatched dumb, there would not be this distracting tumult!"

Agapit was after a duck. It fell to his lot to do the killing for the household, and it was so great a trial to his kind heart that, if the other members of the family had due warning, they usually, at such times, shut themselves up to be out of reach of his lamentable outcries when he was confronted by a protesting chicken, an innocent lamb, a tumultuous pig, or a trusting calf.

Just now he emerged from the yard, holding a sleepy drake by the wing.

"*Miséricorde!*" he exclaimed, when he almost ran into Vesper, "who is it? You — you?" and he peered at him through the darkness.

"Yes, it is I."

"Confiding fool," said Agapit, impatiently tossing the drake back among his startled comrades, "I will save thy neck once more."

Vesper marked the emphasis. "I am on my way to Yarmouth," he said, calmly, "and I have stopped to see your cousin about Narcisse."

"Ah! — he is well, I trust."

"He is better than when he was here."

"His mother has gone to bed."

"I will wait, then, until the morning."

"Ah!" said Agapit again; then he laughed recklessly and seized Vesper's hand. "I cannot pretend. You see that I am rejoiced to have you again with us."

"I, too, am glad to be here."

"But you will not stay?"

"Oh, no, Agapit, — you know me better than that."

Vesper's tone was confident, yet Agapit looked anxiously at him through the gathering gloom. "It would be better for Rose not to see you."

"Agapit, — we are not babies."

"No, you are worse, — it is well said that only our Lord loves lovers. No other would have patience."

Vesper held his straight figure a little straighter, and his manner warned the young Acadien to be careful of what he said, but he dashed on, "Words are brave; actions are braver."

"How is Madame de Forêt?" asked Vesper, shortly.

"What do you expect, — joyous, riotous health? Reflect only that she has been completely overthrown about her child. I hope that madame, your mother, is well."

"She has not been in such good health for years.

She is greatly entertained by Narcisse," and Vesper smiled at some reminiscence.

"It is one of the most charming of nights," said Agapit, insinuatingly. "Toochune would be glad to have a harness on his back. We could fly over the road to Yarmouth. It would be more agreeable than travelling by day."

"Thank you, Agapit, — I do not wish to go to-night."

"Oh, you self-willed one, — you Lucifer!" said Agapit, wildly. "You dare-all, you conquer-all! Take care that you are not trapped."

"Come, show me a room," said Vesper, who was secretly gratified with the irrepressible delight of the Acadien in again seeing him, — a delight that could not be conquered by his anxiety.

"This evening the house is again full," said Agapit. "Rose is quite wearied; come softly up-stairs. I can give you but the small apartment next her own, but you must not rise early in the morning, and seek an interview with her."

Two angry red spots immediately appeared in Vesper's cheeks, and he stared haughtily at him.

Agapit snapped his fingers. "I trust you not that much, though if you had not come back, my confidence would have reached to eternity. You are unfortunately too nobly human, — why were you not divine? But I must not reproach. Have I not too been a lover? You are capable of all, even of talking through the wall with your beloved. You should have stayed away, you should have stayed away!" and, grumbling and shaking his head, he ushered his guest up-stairs, and into a tiny and exquisitely clean room, that contained only a bed, a table, a wash-stand, and one chair.

Agapit motioned Vesper to the chair, and sprawled himself half over the foot of the bed, half out the open window, while he talked to his companion, whose manner had a new and caressing charm that attracted him even more irresistibly than his former cool and somewhat careless one had done.

"Ah, why is life so?" he at last exclaimed, springing up, with a sigh. "Under all is such sadness. Your presence gives such joy. Why should it be denied us?"

Vesper stared at his shoes to hide the nervous tears that sprang to his eyes.

Agapit immediately averted his sorrowful glance. "You are not angry with me for my free speech?"

"Good heavens, no!" said Vesper, irritably turning his back on him, "but I would thank you to leave me."

"Good night," said the Acadien, softly. "May the blessed Virgin give you peace. Remember that I love you, for I prophesy that we on the morrow shall quarrel," and with this cheerful assurance he gently closed the door, and went to the next room.

Rose threw open the door to him, and Agapit, though he was prepared for any change in her, yet for an instant could not conceal his astonishment. Where was her pallor, — her weariness? Gone, like the mists of the morning before the glory of the sun. Her face was delicately colored, her blue eyes were flooded with the most exquisite and tender light that he had ever seen in them. She had heard her lover's step, and Agapit dejectedly reflected that he should have even more trouble with her than with Vesper.

"Surely, I am to see him to-night?" she murmured.

"Surely not," growled Agapit. "For what do you wish to see him?"

"Agapit, — should not a mother hear of her little one?"

"Is it for that only you wish to see him?"

"For that, — also for other things. Is he changed, Agapit? Has his face grown more pale?"

Agapit broke into vigorous French. "He is more foolish than ever, that I assure thee. Such a simpleton, and thou lovest him!"

"If he is a fool, then there are no wise men in the world; but thou art only teasing. Ah, Agapit, dear Agapit," and she clasped her hands, and extended them towards him. "Tell me only what he says of Narcisse."

"He is well; he will tell thee in the morning of a plan he has. Go now to bed, — and Rose, to-morrow be sensible, be wise. Thou wert so noteworthy these three weeks ago, what has come to thee now?"

"Agapit, thou dost remember thy mother a very little, is it not so?"

"Yes, yes."

"Thou couldst part from her; but suppose she came back from the dead. Suppose thou couldst hear her voice in the hall, what wouldst thou do?"

"I would run to greet her," he said, rashly. "I would be mad with pleasure."

"That man was as one dead," she said, with an eloquent gesture towards the next room. "I did not think of seeing him again. How can I cease from joy?"

"Give me thy promise," he said, abruptly, "not to see him without me. Otherwise, thou mayst be prowling in the morning, when I oversleep myself, and thou wilt talk about me to this charming stranger."

"Agapit," she said, in amazement, "wouldst thou insult me?"

"No, little rabbit, — I would only prevent thee from insulting me."

"It is like jailorizing. I shall not be a naughty child in a cell."

"But thou wilt," he said, with determination. "Give me thy promise."

Rose became indignant, and Agapit, who was watching her keenly, stepped inside her room, lest he should be overheard. "Rose," he said, swiftly, and with a deep, indrawn breath, "have I not been a brother to thee?"

"Yes, yes, — until now."

"Now, most of all, — some day thou wilt feel it. Would I do anything to injure thee? I tell thee thou art like a weak child now. Have I not been in love? Do not I know that for a time one's blood burns, and one is mad?"

"But what do you fear?" she asked, proudly, drawing back from him.

"I fear nothing, little goose," he exclaimed, catching her by the wrist, "for I take precautions. I have talked to this young man, — do not I also esteem him? I tell thee, as I told him, — he is capable of all, and when thou seest him, a word, a look, and he will insist upon thy leaving thy husband to go with him."

"Agapit, I am furious with thee. Would I do a wrong thing?"

"Not of thyself; but think, Rose, thou art weak and nervous. Thy strength has been tried; when thou seest thy lover thou wilt be like a silly sheep. Trust me, — when thy father, on his dying bed, pointed to thee, I knew his meaning. Did not I say 'Yes, yes, I will take care of her, for she is beautiful, and men are wicked.'"

"But thou didst let me marry Charlitte," she said, with a stifled cry.

Agapit was crushed by her accusation. He made a despairing gesture. "I have expected this, but, Rose, I was younger. I did not know the hearts of women. We thought it well, — your stepmother and I. He begged for thee, and we did not dream — young girls sometimes do well to settle. He seemed a wise man — "

"Forgive me," cried Rose, wildly, and suddenly pushing him towards the door, "and go away. I will not talk to Mr. Nimmo without thee."

"Some day thou wilt thank me," said Agapit. "It is common to reproach those who favor us. Left alone, thou wouldst rise early in the morning, — thy handsome Vesper would whisper in thy ear, and I, rising, might find thee convinced that there is nothing for thee but to submit to the sacrilege of a divorce."

Rose was not touched by his wistful tones. Her pretty fingers even assisted him gently from the room, and, philosophically shrugging his shoulders, he went to bed.

Rose, left alone, pressed her empty arms and palpitating heart against the bare walls of the next room. "You are good and noble,— you would do nothing wrong. That wicked Agapit, he thinks evil of thee —" and, with other fond and foolish words, she stood mutely caressing the wall until fatigue overpowered her, when she undressed and crept into her lonely bed.

Agapit, who possessed a warm heart, an ardent imagination, and a lively regard for the other sex, was at present without a love-affair of his own, and his mind was therefore free to dwell on the troubles of Rose and Vesper. All night long he dreamed of lovers. They haunted him, tortured him with their griefs, misunderstandings, and afflictions, and, rather glad than sorry to awake from his disturbed sleep, he lifted his shaggy head from the pillow early in the morning and, vehemently shaking it, muttered, "The devil himself is in those who make love."

Then, with his protective instinct keenly alive, he sprang up and went to the window, where he saw something that made him again mutter a reference to the evil one. His window was directly over that of his cousin, and although it was but daybreak, she was up and dressed, and leaning from it to look at Vesper, who stood on the grass below. They were not carrying on a conversation; she was true to the letter of her promise, but this mute, unspoken dialogue was infinitely more dangerous.

Agapit groaned, and surveyed Vesper's glowing face. Who would dream that he, so dignified, would condescend to this? Was it arranged through the wall, or did he walk under her window and think of her until his influence drew her from her bed? "I also have done such things," he muttered; "possibly I may again, therefore I must be merciful."

Vesper at this instant caught sight of his dishevelled head. Rose also looked up, and Agapit retreated in dismay at the sound of their stifled but irresistible laughter.

"Ah, you do not cry all the time," he ejaculated, in confusion; then he made haste to attire himself and to call for Rose, who demurely went down-stairs with him and greeted Vesper with quiet and loving reserve.

The two young men went with her to the kitchen, where she touched a match to the fire. While it was burning she sat down and talked to them, or, rather, they talked to her. The question was what to do with Narcisse.

"Madame de Forêt," said Vesper, softly, "I will tell you what I have already told your cousin. I returned home unexpectedly a fortnight ago, having in the interval missed a telegram from my mother, telling me that your boy was in Boston. When I reached my own door, I saw to my surprise the child of — of —"

"Of the woman you love," thought Agapit, grimly.

"Your child," continued Vesper, in some confusion, "who was kneeling on the pavement before our house. He had dug a hole in the narrow circle of earth left around the tree, and he was thrusting porridge and cream down it, while the sparrows on the branches above watched him with interest. Here in Sleeping Water we had about stopped that feeding of the trees ; but my mother, I found, indulged him in everything. He was glad to see me, and I — I had dreaded the solitude of my home, and I quickly discovered that it had been banished by his presence. He has effected a transformation in my mother, and she wishes me to beg you that we may keep him for a time."

Agapit had never before heard Vesper speak at such length. He himself was silent, and waited for some expression of opinion from Rose.

She turned to him. "You remember what our doctor says when he looks over my little one, — that he is weak, and the air of the Bay is too strong for him ? "

The doctors in Boston also say it," responded Agapit. "Mrs. Nimmo has taken him to them."

Rose flashed a glance of inexpressible gratitude at Vesper.

"You wish him to remain in Boston ? " said Agapit.

"Yes, yes, — if they will be so kind, and if it is right that we allow that they keep him for a time."

Agapit reflected a minute. Could Rose endure the double blow of a separation from her child and from her lover? Yes, he knew her well enough to understand that, although her mother heart and her woman's heart would be torn, she would, after the first sharp pang was over, cheerfully endure any torture in order to contribute to the welfare of the two beings that she loved best on earth. Narcisse would be benefited physically by the separation, Vesper would be benefited mentally. He knew, in addition, that a haunting dread of Charlitte possessed her. Although he was a fickle, unfaithful man, the paternal instinct might some day awake in him, and he would return and demand his child. Agapit would not himself be surprised to see him reappear at any time in Sleeping Water, therefore he said, shortly, "It is a good plan."

"We can at least try it," said Vesper. "I will report how it works."

"And while he is with you, you will have some instruction in his own religion given him?" said Rose, timidly.

"You need not mention that," said Vesper; "it goes without saying."

Rose took a crucifix from her breast and handed

it to him. "You will give him that from his mother," she said, with trembling lips.

Vesper held it in his hand for a minute, then he silently put it in his pocket.

There was a long pause, broken at last by Agapit, who said, "Will you get the breakfast, Rose? Mr. Nimmo assured me that he wished to start at once. Is it not so?"

"Yes," said Vesper, shortly.

Rose got up and went to the pantry.

"Will you put the things on this table?" said Vesper. "And will not you and Agapit have breakfast with me?"

Rose nodded her head, and, with a breaking heart, she went to and fro, her feet touching the hardwood floor and the rugs as noiselessly as if there had been a death in the house.

The two young men sat and stared at the stove or out the windows. Agapit was anathematizing Vesper for returning to settle a matter that could have been arranged by writing, and Vesper was alternately in a dumb fury with Agapit for not leaving him alone with Rose, or in a state of extravagant laudation because he did not do so. What a watch-dog he was,—what a sure guardian to leave over his beautiful sweetheart!

Dispirited and without appetite, the three at last assembled around the table. Rose choked over every morsel that she ate, until, unable longer to endure the trial, she left the table, and contented herself with waiting upon them.

Vesper was famished, having eaten so little the evening before, yet he turned away from the toast and coffee and chops that Rose set before him.

"I will go now; Agapit, come to the gate with me. I want to speak to you."

Rose started violently. It seemed to her that her whole agitated, overwrought soul had gone out to her lover in a shriek of despair, yet she had not uttered a sound.

Vesper could not endure the agony of her eyes. "Rose," he said, stretching out his hands to her, "will you do as I wish?"

"No," said Agapit, stepping between them.

"Rose," said Vesper, caressingly, "shall I go to see Charlitte?"

"Yes, yes," she moaned, desperately, and sinking to a chair, she dropped her swimming head on the table.

"No," said Agapit, again, "you shall not break God's laws. Rose is married to Charlitte."

Vesper tried to pass him, to assist Rose, who was half fainting, but Agapit's burly form was immovable, and the furious young American lifted his arm to strike him.

"*Nâni*," said Agapit, tossing his arm in the air,

"two blows from no man for me," and he promptly knocked Vesper down.

Rose, shocked and terrified, instantly recovered. She ran to her fallen hero, bent over him with fond and distracted words, and when he struggled to his feet, and with a red and furious face would have flown at Agapit, she restrained him, by clinging to his arm.

"Dear fools," said Agapit, "I would have saved you this humbling, but you would not listen. It is now time to part. The doctor comes up the road."

Vesper made a superhuman effort at self-control, and passed his hand over his eyes, to clear away the mists of passion. Then he looked through the kitchen window. The doctor was indeed driving up to the inn.

"Good-by, Rose," he exclaimed, "and do you, Agapit," and he surveyed the Acadien in bitter resentment, "treat Charlitte as you have treated me, if he comes for her."

Even in her despair Rose reflected that they were parting in anger.

"Vesper, Vesper, — most darling of men," she cried, wildly, detaining him, "shake hands, at least."

"I will not," he muttered, then he gently put her from him, and flung himself from the room.

"One does not forget those things," said Agapit, gloomily, and he followed her out-of-doors.

Vesper, staggering so that he could hardly mount his wheel, was just about to leave the yard. Rose clung to the doorpost, and watched him; then she ran to the gate.

Down, down the Bay he went; farther, farther, always from her. First the two shining wheels disappeared, then his straight blue back, then the curly head with the little cap. She had lost him, — perhaps forever; and this time she fainted in earnest, and Agapit carried her to the kitchen, where the English doctor, who had been the one to attend Vesper, stood, with a shrewd and pitying look on his weather-beaten face.

BOOK II.

BIDIANE

CHAPTER I.

A NEW ARRIVAL AT SLEEPING WATER.

> " But swift or slow the days will pass,
> The longest night will have a morn,
> And to each day is duly born
> A night from Time's inverted glass."
> — *Aminta.*

FIVE years have passed away, — five long years. Five times the Acadien farmers have sown their seeds. Five times they have gathered their crops. Five times summer suns have smiled upon the Bay, and five times winter winds have chilled it. And five times five changes have there been in Sleeping Water, though it is a place that changes little.

Some old people have died, some new ones have been born, but chief among all changes has been the one effected by the sometime presence, and now always absence, of the young Englishman from Boston, who had come so quietly among the Acadiens, and had gone so quietly, and yet whose influence had lingered, and would always linger among them.

In the first place, Rose à Charlitte had given up

the inn. Shortly after the Englishman had gone away, her uncle had died, and had left her, not a great fortune, but a very snug little sum of money- and with a part of it she had built herself a cottage on the banks of Sleeping Water River, where she now lived with Célina, her former servant, who had, in her devotion to her mistress, taken a vow never to marry unless Rose herself should choose a husband. This there seemed little likelihood of her doing. She had apparently forsworn marriage when she rejected the Englishman. All the Bay knew that he had been violently in love with her, all the Bay knew that she had sent him away, but none knew the reason for it. She had apparently loved him, — she had certainly never loved any other man. It was suspected that Agapit LeNoir was in the secret, but he would not discuss the Englishman with any one, and, gentle and sweet as Rose was, there were very few who cared to broach the subject to her.

Another change had been the coming to Sleeping Water of a family from up the Bay. They kept the inn now, and they were *protégés* of the Englishman, and relatives of a young girl that he and his mother had taken away — away across the ocean to France some four years before — because she was a badly brought up child, who did not love her native tongue nor her father's people.

It had been a wonderful thing that had happened

to these Watercrows in the coming of the Englishman to the Bay. His mission had been to search for the heirs of Etex LeNoir, who had been murdered by his great-grandfather at the time of the terrible expulsion, and he had found a direct one in the person of this naughty little Bidiane.

She had been a great trouble to him at first, it was said, but, under his wise government, she had soon sobered down; and she had also brought him luck, as much luck as a pot of gold, for, directly after he had discovered her he — who had not been a rich young man, but one largely dependent on his mother — had fallen heir to a large fortune, left to him by a distant relative. This relative had been a great-aunt, who had heard of his romantic and dutiful journey to Acadie, and, being touched by it, and feeling assured that he was a worthy young man, she had immediately made a will, leaving him all that she possessed, and had then died.

He had sought to atone for the sins of his forefathers, and had reaped a rich reward.

A good deal of the Englishman's money had been bestowed on these Watercrows. With kindly tolerance, he had indulged a whim of theirs to go to Boston when they were obliged to leave their heavily mortgaged farm. It was said that they had expected to make vast sums of money there. The Englishman knew that they could not do so, but that they might cease the repinings and see for themselves what a great city really was for poor people, he had allowed them to make a short stay in one.

The result had been that they were horrified; yes, absolutely horrified, — this family transported from the wide, beautiful Bay, — at the narrowness of the streets in the large city of Boston, at the rush of people, the race for work, the general crowding and pushing, the oppression of the poor, the tiny rooms in which they were obliged to live, and the foul air which fairly suffocated them.

They had begged the Englishman to let them come back to the Bay, even if they lived only in a shanty. They could not endure that terrible city.

He generously had given them the Sleeping Water Inn that he had bought when Rose à Charlitte had left it, and there they had tried to keep a hotel, with but indifferent success, until Claudine, the widow of Isidore Kessy, had come to assist them.

The Acadiens in Sleeping Water, with their keen social instincts, and sympathetically curious habit of looking over, and under, and into, and across every subject of interest to them, were never tired of discussing Vesper Nimmo and his affairs. He had still with him the little Narcisse who had run from the Bay five years before, and, although the Englishman himself never wrote to Rose à Charlitte, there came every week to the Bay a letter addressed to her in the handwriting of the young Bidiane LeNoir, who, according to the instructions of the Englishman, gave Rose a full and minute account of every occurrence in her child's life. In this way she was kept from feeling lonely.

These letters were said to be delectable, yes, quite delectable. Célina said so, and she ought to know.

The white-headed, red-coated mail-driver, who never flagged in his admiration for Vesper, was just now talking about him. Twice a day during the long five years had Emmanuel de la Rive flashed over the long road to the station. Twice a day had this descendant of the old French nobleman courteously taken off his hat to the woman who kept the station, and then, placing it on his knee, had sat down to discuss calmly and impartially the news of the day with her, in the ten minutes that he allowed himself before the train arrived. He in the village, she at the station, could most agreeably keep the ball of gossip rolling, so that on its way up and down the Bay it might not make too long a tarrying at Sleeping Water.

On this particular July morning he was on his favorite subject. "Has it happened to come to your ears," he said in his shrill, musical voice to Madame Thériault, who, as of old, was rocking a cradle with her foot, and spinning with her hands, "that there is talk of a great scheme that the Englishman has in mind for having cars that will run along the shores of the Bay, without a locomotive?"

"Yes, I have heard."

"It would be a great thing for the Bay, as we are far from these stations in the woods."

"It is my belief that he will some day return, and Rose will then marry him," said the woman, who, true to the traditions of her sex, took a more lively interest in the affairs of the heart than in those connected with means of transportation.

"It is evident that she does not wish to marry now," he said, modestly.

"She lives like a nun. It is incredible; she is young, yet she thinks only of good works."

"At least, her heart is not broken."

"Hearts do not break when one has plenty of money," said Madame Thériault, wisely.

"If it were not for the child, I daresay that she would become a holy woman. Did you hear that the family with typhoid fever can at last leave her house?"

"Yes, long ago, — ages."

"I heard only this morning," he said, dejectedly, then he brightened, "but it was told to me that it is suspected that the young Bidiane LeNoir will come back to the Bay this summer."

"Indeed, — can that be so?"

"It is quite true, I think. I had it from the blacksmith, whose wife Perside heard it from Célina."

"Who had it from Rose — *eh bonn! eh bonn! eh bonn!*" (*Eh bien!* — well, well, well). "The young girl is now old enough to marry. Possibly the Englishman will marry her."

Emmanuel's fine face flushed, and his delicate voice rose high in defence of his adored Englishman. "No, no; he does not change, that one, — not more so than the hills. He waits like Gabriel for Evangeline. This is also the opinion of the Bay. You are quite alone — but hark! is that the train?" and clutching his mail-bag by its long neck, he slipped to the kitchen door, which opened on the platform of the station.

Yes; it was indeed the Flying Bluenose, coming down the straight track from Pointe à l'Eglise, with a shrill note of warning.

Emmanuel hurried to the edge of the platform, and extended his mail-bag to the clerk in shirt-sleeves, who leaned from the postal-car to take it, and to hand him one in return. Then, his duty over, he felt himself free to take observations of any passengers that there might be for Sleeping Water.

There was just one, and — could it be possible — could he believe the evidence of his eyesight — had the little wild, red-haired apostate from up the Bay at last come back, clothed and in her right mind? He made a mute, joyous signal to the station woman who stood in the doorway, then he drew a little nearer to the very composed and graceful girl who had just been assisted from the train, with great deference, by a youthful conductor.

"Are my trunks all out?" she said to him, in a tone of voice that assured the mail-man that, without being bold or immodest, she was quite well able to take care of herself.

The conductor pointed to the brakemen, who were tumbling out some luggage to the platform.

"I hope that they will be careful of my wheel," said the girl.

"It's all right," replied the conductor, and he raised his arm as a signal for the train to move on. "If anything goes wrong with it, send it to this station, and I will take it to Yarmouth and have it mended for you."

"Thank you," said the girl, graciously; then she turned to Emmanuel, and looked steadfastly at his red jacket.

He, meanwhile, politely tried to avert his eyes from her, but he could not do so. She was fresh from the home of the Englishman in Paris, and he could not conceal his tremulous eager interest in her. She was not beautiful, like flaxen-haired Rose à Charlitte, nor dark and statuesque, like the stately Claudine; but she was *distinguée*, yes, *très-distinguée*, and her manner was just what he had imagined that of a true Parisienne would be like. She was small and dainty, and possessed a back as straight as a soldier's, and a magnificent bust. Her round face was slightly freckled, her nose was a little up-turned, but the hazy, fine mass of hair that surrounded her head was most beauteous, — it was like the sun shining through the reddish meadow grass.

He was her servant, her devoted slave, and Emmanuel, who had never dreamed that he possessed patrician instincts, bowed low before her, " Mademoiselle, I am at your service."

"*Merci, monsieur*" (thank you, sir), she said, with conventional politeness ; then in rapid and exquisite French, that charmed him almost to tears, she asked, mischievously, " But I have never been here before, how do you know me ? "

He bowed again. " The name of Mademoiselle Bidiane LeNoir is often on our lips. Mademoiselle, I salute your return."

"You are very kind, Monsieur de la Rive," she said, with a frank smile ; then she precipitated herself on a bed of yellow marigolds growing beside the station house. " Oh, the delightful flowers ! "

" Is she not charming? " murmured Emmanuel, in a blissful undertone, to Madame Thériault. " What grace, what courtesy ! — and it is due to the Englishman."

Madame Thériault's black eyes were critically running over Bidiane's tailor-made gown. " The Englishman will marry her," she said, sententiously. Then she asked, abruptly, " Have you ever seen her before?"

" Yes, once, years ago; she was a little hawk, I assure you."

" She will do now," and the woman approached her. " Mademoiselle, may I ask for your checks."

Bidiane sprang up from the flower bed and caught her by both hands. " You are Madame Thériault — I know of you from Mr. Nimmo. Ah, it is pleasant to be among friends. For days and days it has been strangers — strangers — only strangers. Now I am with my own people," and she proudly held up her red head.

The woman blushed in deep gratification. " Mademoiselle, I am more than glad to see you. How is the young Englishman who left many friends on the Bay ?"

" Do you call him young ? He is at least thirty."

" But he was young when here."

" True, I forgot that. He is well, very well. He is never ill now. He is always busy, and such a good man — oh, so good!" and Bidiane clasped her hands, and rolled her lustrous, tawny eyes to the sky.

"And the child of Rose à Charlitte?" said Emmanuel, eagerly.

" A little angel, — so calm, so gentle, so polite. If

you could see him bow to the ladies, — it is ravishing, I assure you. And he is always spoiled by Mrs. Nimmo, who adores him."

"Will he come back to the Bay?"

"I do not know," and Bidiane's vivacious face grew puzzled. "I do not ask questions — alas! have I offended you? — I assure you I was thinking only of myself. I am curious. I talk too much, but you have seen Mr. Nimmo. You know that beyond a certain point he will not go. I am ignorant of his intentions with regard to the child. I am ignorant of his mother's intentions; all I know is that Mr. Nimmo wishes him to be a forester."

"A forester!" ejaculated Madame Thériault, "and what is that trade?"

Bidiane laughed gaily. "But, my dear madame, it is not a trade. It is a profession. Here on the Bay we do not have it, but abroad one hears often of it. Young men study it constantly. It is to take care of trees. Do you know that if they are cut down, water courses dry up? In Clare we do not think of that, but in other countries trees are thought useful and beautiful, and they keep them."

"Hold — but that is wonderful," said Emmanuel.

Bidiane turned to him with a winning smile. "Monsieur, how am I to get to the shore? I am eaten up with impatience to see Madame de Forêt and my aunt."

"But there is my cart, mademoiselle," and he pointed to the shed beyond them. "I shall feel honored to conduct you."

"I gladly accept your offer, monsieur. *Au revoir*, madame."

Madame Thériault reluctantly watched them depart. She would like to keep this gay, charming creature with her for an hour longer.

"It is wonderful that they did not come to meet you," said Emmanuel, "but they did not expect you naturally."

"I sent a telegram from Halifax," said Bidiane, "but can you believe it?— I was so stupid as to say Wednesday instead of Tuesday. Therefore Madame de Forêt expects me to-morrow."

"You advised her rather than Mirabelle Marie, but wherefore?"

Bidiane shook her shining head. "I do not know. I did not ask; I did simply as Mr. Nimmo told me. He arranges all. I was with friends until this morning. Only that one thing did I do alone on the journey,— that is to telegraph,— and I did it wrong," and a joyous, subdued peal of laughter rang out on the warm morning air.

Emmanuel reverently assisted her into his cart, and got in beside her. His blood had been quickened in his veins by this unexpected occurrence. He tried not to look too often at this charming girl beside him, but, in spite of his best efforts, his eyes irresistibly and involuntarily kept seeking her face. She was so eloquent, so well-mannered; her clothes were smooth and sleek like satin; there was a faint perfume of lovely flowers about her,— she had come from the very heart and centre of the great world into which he had never ventured. She was charged with magic. What an acquisition to the Bay she would be!

He carefully avoided the ruts and stones of the road. He would not for the world give her an unnecessary shock, and he ardently wished that this highway from the woods to the Bay might be as smooth as his desire would have it.

"And this is Sleeping Water," she said, dreamily.

Emmanuel assured her that it was, and she immediately began to ply him with questions about the occupants of the various farms that they were passing, until a sudden thought flashed into her mind and made her laughter again break out like music.

"I am thinking — ah, me! it is really too absurd for anything — of the astonishment of Madame de Forêt when I walk in upon her. Tell me, I beg you, some particulars about her. She wrote not very much about herself."

Emmanuel had a great liking for Rose, and he joyfully imparted to Bidiane the most minute particulars concerning her dress, appearance, conduct, daily life, her friends and surroundings. He talked steadily for a mile, and Bidiane, whose curiosity seemed insatiable on the subject of Rose, urged him on until he was forced to pause for breath.

Bidiane turned her head to look at him, and immediately had her attention attracted to a new subject. "That red jacket is charming, monsieur," she said, with flattering interest. "If it is quite agreeable, I should like to know where you got it."

"Mademoiselle, you know that in Halifax there are many soldiers."

"Yes, — English ones. There were French ones in Paris. Oh, I adore the short blue capes of the military men."

"The English soldiers wear red coats."

"Yes, monsieur."

"Sometimes they are sold when their bright surface is soiled. Men buy them, and, after cleaning, sell them in the country. It is cheerful to see a farmer working in a field clad in red."

"Ah! this is one that a soldier used to wear."

"No, mademoiselle, — not so fast. I had seen these red coats, — Acadiens have always loved that color above others. I wished to have one; therefore, when asked to sing at a concert many years ago, I said to my sister, 'Buy red cloth and make me a red coat. Put trimmings on it.'"

"And you sang in this?"

"No, mademoiselle, — you are too fast again," and he laughed delightedly at her precipitancy. "I sang in one long years ago, when I was young. Afterwards, to save, — for we Acadiens do not waste, you know, — I wore it to drive in. In time it fell to pieces."

"And you liked it so much that you had another made?"

"Exactly, mademoiselle. You have guessed it now," and his tones were triumphant.

Her curiosity on the subject of the coat being satisfied, she returned to Rose, and finally asked a series of questions with regard to her aunt.

Her chatter ceased, however, when they reached the Bay, and, overcome with admiration, she gazed silently at the place where

> From shore to shore the shining waters lay,
> Beneath the sun, as placid as a cheek.

Emmanuel, discovering that her eyes were full of tears, delicately refrained from further conversation until they reached the corner, when he asked, softly, "To the inn, or to Madame de Forêt's?"

Bidiane started. "To Madame de Forêt's — no, no, to the inn, otherwise my aunt might be offended."

He drew up before the veranda, where Mirabelle Marie and Claude both happened to be standing. There were at first incredulous glances, then a great burst of noise from the woman and an amazed grunt from the man.

Bidiane flew up the steps and embraced them, and Emmanuel lingered on in a trance of ecstasy. He could not tear himself away, and did not attempt to do so until the trio vanished into the house.

CHAPTER II.

BIDIANE GOES TO CALL ON ROSE À CHARLITTE.

"Love duty, ease your neighbor's load,
Learn life is but an episode,
And grateful peace will fill your mind."
AMINTA. ARCHBISHOP O'BRIEN.

MIRABELLE MARIE and her husband seated themselves in the parlor with Bidiane close beside them.

"You're only a mite of a thing yet," shrieked Mrs. Watercrow, "though you've growed up; but *sakerjé!* how fine, how fine, — and what a shiny cloth in your coat! How much did that cost?"

"Do not scream at me," said Bidiane, good-humoredly. "I still hear well."

Claude à Sucre roared in a stentorian voice, and clapped his knee. "She comes home Eenglish, — quite Eenglish."

"And the Englishman, — he is still rich," said Mirabelle Marie, greedily, and feeling not at all snubbed. "Does he wear all the time a collar with white wings and a split coat?"

"But you took much money from him," said Bidiane, reproachfully.

"Oh, that Boston, — that divil's hole!" vociferated Mirabelle Marie. "We did not come back some first-class Yankees *whitewashés.* No, no, we are French now, — you bet! When I was a young one my old mother used to ketch flies between her thumb and finger. She'd say, '*Je te squeezerai*'" (I will squeeze you). "Well, we were the flies, Boston was my old mother. But you've been in cities, Biddy Ann, you know 'em."

"Ah! but I was not poor. We lived in a beautiful quarter in Paris, — and do not call me Biddy Ann; my name is Bidiane."

"Lord help us, — ain't she stylish!" squealed her delighted aunt. "Go on, Biddy, tell us about the fine ladies, and the elegant frocks, and the dimens; everythin' shines, ain't that so? Did the Englishman shove a dollar bill in yer hand every day?"

"No, he did not," said Bidiane, with dignity. "I was only a little girl to him. He gave me scarcely any money to spend."

"Is he goin' to marry yer, — say now, Biddy, ain't that so?"

Bidiane's quick temper asserted itself. "If you don't stop being so vulgar, I sha'n't say another word to you."

"Aw, shut up, now," said Claude, remonstratingly, to his wife.

Mrs. Watercrow was slightly abashed. "I don't go for to make yeh mad," she said, humbly.

"No, no, of course you did not," said the girl, in quick compunction, and she laid one of her slim white hands on Mirabelle Marie's fat brown ones. "I should not have spoken so hastily."

"Look at that, — she's as meek as a cat," said the woman, in surprise, while her husband softly caressed Bidiane's shoulder.

"The Englishman, as you call him, does not care much for women," Bidiane went on, gently. "Now that he has money he is much occupied, and he always has men coming to see him. He often went out with his mother, but rarely with me or with any ladies. He travels, too, and takes Narcisse with him; and now, tell me, do you like being down the Bay?"

Her aunt shrugged her shoulders. "A long sight more'n Boston."

"Why did you give up the farm?" said the girl to Claude; "the old farm that belonged to your grandfather."

"I be a fool, an' I don' know it teel long after," said Claude, slowly.

"And you speak French here, — the boys, have they learned it?"

"You bet, — they learned in Boston from *Acajens*. Biddy, what makes yeh come back? Yer a big goose not to stay with the Englishman."

Bidiane surveyed her aunt disapprovingly. "Could I live always depending on him? No, I wish to work hard, to earn some money, — and you, are you not going to pay him for this fine house?"

"God knows, he has money enough."

"But we mus' pay back," said Claude, smiting the table with his fist. "I ain't got much larnin', but I've got a leetle idee, an' I tell you, maw, — don' you spen' the money in that stockin'."

His wife's fat shoulders shook in a hearty laugh.

His face darkened. "You give that to Biddy."

"Yes," said his niece, "give it to me. Come now, and get it, and show me the house."

Mrs. Watercrow rose resignedly, and preceded the girl to the kitchen. "Let's find Claudine. She's a boss cook, mos' as good as Rose à Charlitte. Biddy, be you goin' to stay along of us?"

"I don't know," said the girl, gaily. "Will you have me?"

"You bet! Biddy," — and she lowered her voice, — "you know 'bout Isidore?"

The girl shuddered. "Yes."

"It was drink, drink, drink, like a fool. One day, when he works back in the woods with some of those Frenchmen out of France, he go for to do like them, an' roast a frog on the biler in the mill ingine. His brain overswelled, overfoamed, an' he fell agin the biler. Then he was dead."

"Hush,— don't talk about him; Claudine may hear you."

"How,— you know her?"

"I know everybody. Mr. Nimmo and his mother talked so often of the Bay. They do not wish Narcisse to forget."

"That's good. Does the Englishman's maw like the little one?"

"Yes, she does."

"Claudine ain't here," and Mirabelle Marie waddled through the kitchen, and directed her sneaks to the back stairway. "We'll skip up to her room."

Bidiane followed her, but when Mrs. Watercrow would have pushed open the door confronting them, she caught her hand.

"The divil," said her surprised relative, "do you want to scare the life out of me?"

"Knock," said Bidiane, "always, always at the door of a bedroom or a private room, but not at that of a public one such as a parlor."

"Am I English?" exclaimed Mirabelle Marie, drawing back and regarding her in profound astonishment.

"No, but you are going to be,— or rather you are going to be a polite Frenchwoman," said Bidiane, firmly.

Mirabelle Marie laughed till the tears ran down her cheeks. She had just had presented to her, in the person of Bidiane, a delicious and first-class joke.

Claudine came out of her room, and silently stared at them until Bidiane took her hand, when her handsome, rather sullen face brightened perceptibly.

Bidiane liked her, and some swift and keen perception told her that in the young widow she would find a more apt pupil and a more congenial associate than in her aunt. She went into the room, and, sitting down by the window, talked at length to her of Narcisse and the Englishman.

At last she said, "Can you see Madame de Forêt's house from here?"

Mirabelle Marie, who had squatted comfortably on the bed, like an enormous toad, got up and toddled to the window. "It's there ag'in those pines back of the river. There's no other sim'lar."

Bidiane glanced at the cool white cottage against its green background. "Why, it is like a tiny Grand Trianon!"

"An' what's that?"

"It is a villa near Paris, a very fine one, built in the form of a horseshoe."

"Yes, — that's what we call it," interrupted her aunt. "We ain't blind. We say the horseshoe cottage."

"One of the kings of France had the Grand Trianon built for a woman he loved," said Bidiane, reverently. "I think Mr. Nimmo must have sent the plan for this from Paris, — but he never spoke to me about it."

"He is not a man who tells all," said Claudine, in French.

Bidiane and Mirabelle Marie had been speaking English, but they now reverted to their own language.

"When do you have lunch?" asked Bidiane.

"Lunch, — what's that?" asked her aunt. "We have dinner soon."

"And I must descend," said Claudine, hurrying down-stairs. "I smell something burning."

Bidiane was about to follow her, when there was a clattering heard on the stairway.

"It's the young ones," cried Mirabelle Marie, joyfully. "Some fool has told 'em. They'll wring your neck like the blowpipe of a chicken."

The next minute two noisy, rough, yet slightly shy boys had taken possession of their returned cousin and were leading her about the inn in triumph.

Mirabelle Marie tried to keep up with them, but could not succeed in doing so. She was too excited to keep still, too happy to work, so she kept on waddling from one room to another, to the stable, the garden, and even to the corner, — to every spot where she could catch a glimpse of the tail of Bidiane's gown, or the heels of her twinkling shoes. The girl was indefatigable; she wished to see everything at once. She would wear herself out.

Two hours after lunch she announced her determination to call on Rose.

"I'll skip along, too," said her aunt, promptly.

"I wish to be quite alone when I first see this wonderful woman," said Bidiane.

"But why is she wonderful?" asked Mirabelle Marie.

Bidiane did not hear her. She had flitted out to the veranda, wrapping a scarf around her shoulders as she went. While her aunt stood gazing longingly after her, she tripped up the village street, enjoying immensely the impression she created among the women and children, who ran to the doorways and windows to see her pass.

There were no houses along the cutting in the hill through which the road led to the sullen stream of Sleeping Water. Rose's house stood quite alone, and at some distance from the street, its gleaming, freshly painted front towards the river, its curved back against a row of pine-trees.

It was very quiet. There was not a creature stirring, and the warm July sunshine lay languidly on some deserted chairs about a table on the lawn.

Bidiane went slowly up to the hall door and rang the bell.

Rosy-cheeked Célina soon stood before her; and

smiling a welcome, for she knew very well who the visitor was, she gently opened the door of a long, narrow blue and white room on the right side of the hall.

Bidiane paused on the threshold. This dainty, exquisite apartment, furnished so simply, and yet so elegantly, had not been planned by an architect or furnished by a decorator of the Bay. This bric-à-brac, too, was not Acadien, but Parisian. Ah, how much Mr. Nimmo loved Rose à Charlitte! and she drew a long breath and gazed with girlish and fascinated awe at the tall, beautiful woman who rose from a low seat, and slowly approached her.

Rose was about to address her, but Bidiane put up a protesting hand. "Don't speak to me for a minute," she said, breathlessly. "I want to look at you."

Rose smiled indulgently, and Bidiane gazed on. She felt herself to be a dove, a messenger sent from a faithful lover to the woman he worshipped. What a high and holy mission was hers! She trembled blissfully, then, one by one, she examined the features of this Acadien beauty, whose quiet life had kept her from fading or withering in the slightest degree. She was, indeed, "a rose of dawn."

These were the words written below the large painting of her that hung in Mr. Nimmo's room. She must tell Rose about it, although of course the picture and the inscription must be perfectly familiar to her, through Mr. Nimmo's descriptions.

"Madame de Forêt," she said at last, "it is really you. Oh, how I have longed to see you! I could scarcely wait."

"Won't you sit down?" said her hostess, just a trifle shyly.

Bidiane dropped into a chair. "I have teased Mrs. Nimmo with questions. I have said again and again, 'What is she like?'— but I never could tell from what she said. I had only the picture to go by."

"The picture?" said Rose, slightly raising her eyebrows.

"Your painting, you know, that is over Mr. Nimmo's writing-table."

"Does he have one of me?" asked Rose, quietly.

"Yes, yes,— an immense one. As broad as that,"— and she stretched out her arms. "It was enlarged from a photograph."

"Ah! when he was here I missed a photograph one day from my album, but I did not know that he had taken it. However, I suspected."

"But does he not write you everything?"

"You only are my kind little correspondent,— with, of course, Narcisse."

"Really, I thought that he wrote everything to you. Dear Madame de Forêt, may I speak freely to you?"

"As freely as you wish, my dear child."

Bidiane burst into a flood of conversation. "I think it is so romantic, — his devotion to you. He does not talk of it, but I can't help knowing, because Mrs. Nimmo talks to me about it when she gets too worked up to keep still. She really loves you, Madame de Forêt. She wishes that you would allow her son to marry you. If you only knew how much she admires you, I am sure you would put aside your objection to her son."

Rose for a few minutes seemed lost in thought, then she said, "Does Mrs. Nimmo think that I do not care for her son?"

"No, she says she thinks you care for him, but there is some objection in your mind that you cannot get over, and she cannot imagine what it is."

"Dear little mademoiselle, I will also speak freely to you, for it is well for you to understand, and I feel that you are a good friend, because I have received so many letters from you. It is impossible that I should marry Mr. Nimmo, therefore we will not speak of it, if you please. There is an obstacle, — he knows and agrees to it. Years ago, I thought some day this obstacle might be taken away. Now, I think it is the will of our Lord that it remain, and I am content."

"Oh, oh!" said Bidiane, wrinkling her face as if

she were about to cry, "I cannot bear to hear you say this."

Rose smiled gently. "When you are older, as old as I am, you will understand that marriage is not the chief thing in life. It is good, yet one can be happy without. One can be pushed quietly further and further apart from another soul. At first, one cries out, one thinks that the parting will kill, but it is often the best thing for the two souls. I tell you this because I love you, and because I know Mr. Nimmo has taken much care in your training, and wishes me to be an elder sister. Do not seek sorrow, little one, but do not try to run from it. This dear, dear man that you speak of, was a divine being, a saint to me. I did wrong to worship him. To separate from me was a good thing for him. He is now more what I then thought him, than he was at the time. Do you understand?"

"Yes, yes," said Bidiane, breaking into tears, and impulsively throwing herself on her knees beside her, "but you dash my pet scheme to pieces. I wish to see you two united. I thought perhaps if I told you that, although no one knows it but his mother, he just wor — wor — ships you — "

Rose stroked her head. "Warm-hearted child, — and also loyal. Our Lord rewards such devotion. Nothing is lost. Your precious tears remind me of those I once shed."

Bidiane did not recover herself. She was tired, excited, profoundly touched by Rose's beauty and "sweet gravity of soul," and her perfect resignation to her lot. "But you are not happy," she exclaimed at last, dashing away her tears; "you cannot be. It is not right. I love to read in novels, when Mr. Nimmo allows me, of the divine right of passion. I asked him one day what it meant, and he explained. I did not know that it gave him pain, — that his heart must be aching. He is so quiet, — no one would dream that he is unhappy; yet his mother knows that he is, and when she gets too worried, she talks to me, although she is not one-half as fond of me as she is of Narcisse."

A great wave of color came over Rose's face at the mention of her child. She would like to speak of him at once, yet she restrained herself.

"Dear little girl," she said, in her low, soothing voice, "you are so young, so delightfully young. See, I have just been explaining to you, yet you do not listen. You will have to learn for yourself. The experience of one woman does not help another. Yet let me read to you, who think it so painful a thing to be denied anything that one wants, a few sentences from our good archbishop."

Bidiane sprang lightly to her feet, and Rose went to a bookcase, and, taking out a small volume bound in green and gold, read to her: "'Marriage is a high and holy state, and intended for the vast majority of mankind, but those who expand and merge human love in the divine, espousing their souls to God in a life of celibacy, tread a higher and holier path, and are better fitted to do nobler service for God in the cause of suffering humanity.'"

"Those are good words," said Bidiane, with twitching lips.

"It is of course a Catholic view," said Rose; "you are a Protestant, and you may not agree perfectly with it, yet I wish only to convince you that if one is denied the companionship of one that is beloved, it is not well to say, 'Everything is at an end. I am of no use in the world.'"

"I think you are the best and the sweetest woman that I ever saw," said Bidiane, impulsively.

"No, no; not the best," said Rose, in accents of painful humility. "Do not say it, — I feel myself the greatest of sinners. I read my books of devotion, I feel myself guilty of all, — even the blackest of crimes. It seems that there is nothing I have not sinned in my thoughts. I have been blameless in nothing, except that I have not neglected the baptism of children in infancy."

"You — a sinner!" said Bidiane, in profound scepticism. "I do not believe it."

"None are pure in the sight of our spotless Lord," said Rose, in agitation; "none, none. We can only try to be so. Let me repeat to you one more line from our archbishop. It is a poem telling of the struggle of souls, of the search for happiness that is not to be found in the world. This short line is always with me. I cannot reach up to it, I can only admire it. Listen, dear child, and remember it is this only that is important, and both Protestant and Catholic can accept it — ' Walking on earth, but living with God.' "

Bidiane flung her arms about her neck. " Teach me to be good like you and Mr. Nimmo. I assure you I am very bad and impatient."

" My dear girl, my sister," murmured Rose, tenderly, " you are a gift and I accept you. Now will you not tell me something of your life in Paris ? Many things were not related in your letters."

CHAPTER III.

TAKEN UNAWARES.

"Who can speak
The mingled passions that surprised his heart?"
THOMSON.

BIDIANE nothing loath, broke into a vivacious narrative. "Ah, that Mr. Nimmo, I just idolize him. How much he has done for me! Just figure to yourself what a spectacle I must have been when he first saw me. I was ignorant, — as ignorant as a little pig. I knew nothing. He asked me if I would go down the Bay to a convent. I said, quite violently, 'No, I will not.' Then he went home to Boston, but he did not give me up. I soon received a message. Would I go to France with him and his mother, for it had been decided that a voyage would be good for the little Narcisse? That dazzled me, and I said 'yes.' I left the Bay, but just fancy how utterly stupid, how frightfully from out of the woods I was. I will give one instance: When my uncle put me on the steamer at Yarmouth it was late, he had to hurry ashore. He did not show me the stateroom prepared for me, and

I, dazed owl, sat on the deck shivering and drawing my cloak about me. I thought I had paid for that one tiny piece of the steamer and I must not move from it. Then a kind woman came and took me below."

"But you were young, you had never travelled, mademoiselle."

"Don't say mademoiselle, say Bidiane, — please do, I would love it."

"Very well, Bidiane, — dear little Bidiane."

The girl leaned forward, and was again about to embrace her hostess with fervent arms, but suddenly paused to exclaim, "I think I hear wheels!"

She ran to one of the open windows. "Who drives a black buggy, — no, a white horse with a long tail?"

"Agapit LeNoir," said Rose, coming to stand beside her.

"Oh, how is he? I hate to see him. I used to be so rude, but I suppose he has forgiven me. Mrs. Nimmo says he is very good, still I do not think Mr. Nimmo cares much for him."

Rose sighed. That was the one stain on the character of the otherwise perfect Vesper. He had never forgiven Agapit for striking him.

"Why he looks quite smart," Bidiane rattled on. "Does he get on well with his law practice?"

"Very well; but he works hard — too hard. This horse is his only luxury."

"I detest white horses. Why didn't he get a dark one?"

"I think this one was cheaper."

"Is he poor?"

"Not now, but he is economical. He saves his money."

"Oh, he is a screw, a miser."

"No, not that, — he gives away a good deal. He has had a hard life, has my poor cousin, and now he understands the trials of others."

"Poverty is tiresome, but it is sometimes good for one," said Bidiane, wisely.

Rose's white teeth gleamed in sudden amusement. "Ah, the dear little parrot, she has been well trained."

Bidiane leaned out the window. There was Agapit, peering eagerly forward from the hood of his carriage, and staring up with some of the old apprehensiveness with which he used to approach her.

"What a dreadful child I was," reflected Bidiane, with a blush of shame. "He is yet afraid of me."

Agapit, with difficulty averting his eyes from her round, childish face and its tangle of reddish hair, sprang from his seat and fastened his horse to the post sunk in the grass at the edge of the lawn, while Rose, followed by Bidiane, went out to meet him.

"How do you do, Rose," he murmured, taking her

hand in his own, while his eyes ran behind to the waiting Bidiane.

The girl, ladylike and modest, and full of contrition for her former misdeeds, was yet possessed by a mischievous impulse to find out whether her power over the burly, youthful, excitable Agapit extended to this thinner, more serious-looking man, with the big black mustache and the shining eye-glasses.

"Ah, fanatic, Acadien imbecile," she said, coolly extending her fingers, "I am glad to see you again."

Though her tone was reassuring, Agapit still seemed to be overcome by some emotion, and for a few seconds did not recover himself. Then he smiled, looked relieved, and, taking a step nearer her, bowed profoundly. "When did you arrive, mademoiselle?"

"But you knew I was here," she said, gaily, "I saw it in your face when you first appeared."

Agapit dropped his eyes nervously. "He is certainly terribly afraid of me," reflected Bidiane again; then she listened to what he was saying.

"The Bay whispers and chatters, mademoiselle; the little waves that kiss the shores of Sleeping Water take her secrets from her and carry them up to the mouth of the Weymouth River —"

"You have a telephone, I suppose," said Bidiane, in an eminently practical tone of voice.

"Yes, I have," and he relapsed into silence.

"Here we are together, we three," said Bidiane, impulsively. "How I wish that Mr. Nimmo could see us."

Rose lost some of her beautiful color. These continual references to her lover were very trying. "I will leave you two to amuse each other for a few minutes, while I go and ask Célina to make us some tea *à l'anglaise.*"

"I should not have said that," exclaimed Bidiane, gazing after her; "how easy it is to talk too much. Each night, when I go to bed, I lie awake thinking of all the foolish things I have said during the day, and I con over sensible speeches that I might have uttered. I suppose you never do that?"

"Why not, mademoiselle?"

"Oh, because you are older, and because you are so clever. Really, I am quite afraid of you," and she demurely glanced at him from under her curly eyelashes.

"Once you were not afraid," he remarked, cautiously.

"No; but now you must be very learned."

"I always was fond of study."

"Mr. Nimmo says that some day you will be a judge, and then probably you will write a book. Will you?"

"Some day, perhaps. At present, I only write short articles for magazines and newspapers."

"How charming! What are they about?"

"They are mostly Acadien and historical."

"Do you ever write stories — love stories?"

"Sometimes, mademoiselle."

"Delicious! May I read them?"

"I do not know," and he smiled. "You would probably be too much amused. You would think they were true."

"And are they not?"

"Oh, no, although some have a slight foundation of fact."

Bidiane stared curiously at him, opened her lips, closed them again, set her small white teeth firmly, as if bidding them stand guard over some audacious thought, then at last burst out with it, for she was still excited and animated by her journey, and was bubbling over with delight at being released from the espionage of strangers to whom she could not talk freely. "You have been in love, of course?"

Agapit modestly looked at his boots.

"You find me unconventional," cried Bidiane, in alarm. "Mrs. Nimmo says I will never get over it. I do not know what I shall do, — but here, at least, on the Bay, I thought it would not so much matter. Really, it was a consolation in leaving Paris."

"Mademoiselle, it is not that," he said, hesitatingly. "I assure you, the question has been asked before, with not so much delicacy — But with whom should I fall in love?"

"With any one. It must be a horrible sensation. I have never felt it, but I cry very often over tales of lovers. Possibly you are like Madame de Forêt, you do not care to marry."

"Perhaps I am waiting until she does, mademoiselle."

"I suppose you could not tell me," she said, in the dainty, coaxing tones of a child, "what it is that separates your cousin from Mr. Nimmo?"

"No, mademoiselle, I regret to say that I cannot."

"Is it something she can ever get over?"

"Possibly."

"You don't want to be teased about it. I will talk of something else; people don't marry very often after they are thirty. That is the dividing line."

Agapit dragged at his mustache with restless fingers.

"You are laughing at me, you find me amusing," she said, with a sharp look at him. "I assure you I don't mind being laughed at. I hate dull people — oh, I must ask you if you know that I am quite Acadien now?"

"Rose has told me something of it."

"Yes, I know. She says that you read my letters, and I think it is perfectly sweet in you. I know what you have done for me. I know, you need not try to conceal it. It was you that urged Mr. Nimmo not to give me up, it is to you that I am indebted for my glimpse of the world. I assure you I am grateful. That is why I speak so freely to you. You are a friend and also a relative. May we not call ourselves cousins?"

"Certainly, mademoiselle, — I am honored," said Agapit, in a stumbling voice.

"You are not used to me yet. I overcome you, but wait a little, you will not mind my peculiarities, and let me tell you that if there is anything I can do for you, I shall be so glad. I could copy papers or write letters. I am only a mouse and you are a lion, yet perhaps I could bite your net a little."

Agapit straightened himself, and stepped out rather more boldly as they went to and fro over the grass.

"I seem only like a prattling, silly girl to you," she said, humbly, "yet I have a little sense, and I can write a good hand — a good round hand. I often used to assist Mr. Nimmo in copying passages from books."

Agapit felt like a hero. "Some day, mademoiselle, I may apply to you for assistance. In the meantime, I thank you."

They continued their slow walk to and fro. Sometimes they looked across the river to the village, but mostly they looked at each other, and Agapit, with acute pleasure, basked in the light of Bidiane's admiring glances.

"You have always stayed here," she exclaimed; "you did not desert your dear Bay as I did."

"But for a short time only. You remember that I was at Laval University in Quebec."

"Oh, yes, I forgot that. Madame de Forêt wrote me. Do you know, I thought that perhaps you would not come back. However, Mr. Nimmo was not surprised that you did."

"There are a great many young men out in the world, mademoiselle. I found few people who were interested in me. This is my home, and is not one's home the best place to earn one's living?"

"Yes; and also you did not wish to go too far away from your cousin. I know your devotion, it is quite romantic. She adores you, I easily saw that in her letters. Do you know, I imagined" — and she lowered her voice, and glanced over her shoulder — "that Mr. Nimmo wrote to her, because he never seemed curious about my letters from her."

"That is Mr. Nimmo's way, mademoiselle."

"It is a pity that they do not write. It would be such a pleasure to them both. I know that. They cannot deceive me."

"But she is not engaged to him."

"If you reject a man, you reject him," said Bidiane, with animation, "but you know there is a kind of lingering correspondence that decides nothing. If the affair were all broken off, Mr. Nimmo would not keep Narcisse."

Agapit wrinkled his forehead. "True; yet I assure you they have had no communication except through you and the childish scrawls of Narcisse."

Bidiane was surprised. "Does he not send her things?"

"No, mademoiselle."

"But her furniture is French."

"There are French stores in the States, and Rose travels occasionally, you know."

"Hush, — she is coming back. Ah! the adorable woman."

Agapit threw his advancing cousin a glance of affectionate admiration, and went to assist her with the tea things.

Bidiane watched him putting the tray on the table, and going to meet Célina, who was bringing out a teapot and cups and saucers. "Next to Mr. Nimmo, he is the kindest man I ever saw," she murmured, curling herself up in a rattan chair. "But we are not talking," she said, a few minutes later.

Rose and Agapit both smiled indulgently at her. Neither of them talked as much as in former days. They were quieter, more subdued.

"Let me think of some questions," said the girl. "Are you, Mr. LeNoir, as furious an Acadien as you used to be?"

Agapit fixed his big black eyes on her, and began to twist the ends of his long mustache. "Mademoiselle, since I have travelled a little, and mingled with other men, I do not talk so loudly and vehemently, but my heart is still the same. It is Acadie forever with me."

"Ah, that is right," she said, enthusiastically. "Not noisy talk, but service for our countrymen."

"Will you not have a cup of tea, and also tell us how you became an Acadien?" said Agapit, who seemed to divine her secret thought.

"Thank you, thank you, — yes, I will do both," and Bidiane's round face immediately became transfigured, — the freckles almost disappeared. One saw only "the tiger dusk and gold" of her eyes, and her reddish crown of hair. "I will tell you of that noblest of men, that angel, who swept down upon the Bay, and bore away a little owl in his pinions, — or talons, is it? — to the marvellous city of Paris, just because he wished to inspire the stupid owl with love for its country."

"But the great-grandfather of the eagle, or, rather, the angel, killed the great-grandfather of the owl," said Agapit; "do not forget that, mademoiselle. Will you have a biscuit?"

"Thank you, — suppose he did, that does not alter the delightfulness of his conduct. Who takes account of naughty grandfathers in this prosaic age?

No one but Mr. Nimmo. And do we not put away from us — that is, society people do — all those who are rough and have not good manners? Did Mr. Nimmo do this? No, he would train his little Acadien owl. The first night we arrived in Paris he took me with Narcisse for a fifteen minutes' stroll along the Arcades of the Rue de Rivoli. I was overcome. We had just arrived, we had driven through lighted streets to a magnificent hotel. The bridges across the river gleamed with lights. I thought I must be in heaven. You have read the descriptions of it?"

"Of Paris, — yes," said Agapit, dreamily.

"Every one was speaking French, — the language that I detested. I was dumb. Here was a great country, a great people, and they were French. I had thought that all the world outside the Bay was English, even though I had been taught differently at school. But I did not believe my teachers. I told stories, I thought that they also did. But to return to the Rue de Rivoli, — there were the shops, there were the merchants. Now that I have seen so much they do not seem great things to me, but then — ah! then they were palaces, the merchants were kings and princes offering their plate and jewels and gorgeous robes for sale.

"'Choose,' said Mr. Nimmo to Narcisse and to me, 'choose some souvenir to the value of three francs.' I stammered, I hesitated, I wished everything, I selected nothing. Little Narcisse laid his finger on a sparkling napkin-ring. I could not decide. I was intoxicated, and Mr. Nimmo calmly conducted us home. I got nothing, because I could not control myself. The next day, and for many days, Mr. Nimmo took us about that wonderful city. It was all so ravishing, so spotless, so immense. We did not visit the ugly parts. I had neat and suitable clothes. I was instructed to be quiet, and not to talk loudly or cry out, and in time I learned, — though at first I very much annoyed Mrs. Nimmo. Never, never, did her son lose patience. Madame de Forêt, it is charming to live in a peaceful, splendid home, where there are no loud voices, no unseemly noises, — to have servants everywhere, even to push the chair behind you at the table."

"Yes, if one is born to it," said Rose, quietly.

"But one gets born to it, dear madame. In a short time, I assure you, I put on airs. I straightened my back, I no longer joked with the servants. I said, quietly, 'Give me this. Give me that,' — and I disliked to walk. I wished always to step in a carriage. Then Mr. Nimmo talked to me."

"What did he say?" asked Agapit, jealously and unexpectedly.

"My dear sir," said Bidiane, drawing herself up, and speaking in her grandest manner, "I beg permission to withhold from you that information. You, I see, do not worship my hero as wildly as I do. I address my remarks to your cousin," and she turned her head towards Rose.

They both laughed, and she herself laughed merrily and excitedly. Then she hurried on: "I had a governess for a time, then afterwards I was sent every day to a boarding-school near by the hotel where we lived. I was taught many things about this glorious country of France, this land from which my forefathers had gone to Acadie. Soon I began to be less ashamed of my nation. Later on I began to be proud. Very often I would be sent for to go to the *salon* (drawing-room). There would be strangers, — gentlemen and ladies to whom Mrs. Nimmo would introduce me, and her son would say, 'This is a little girl from Acadie.' Immediately I would be smiled on, and made much of, and the fine people would say, 'Ah, the Acadiens were courageous, — they were a brave race,' and they would address me in French, and I could only hang my head and listen to Mr. Nimmo, who would remark, quietly, 'Bidiane has lived among the English, — she is just learning her own language.'

"Ah, then I would study. I took my French grammar to bed, and one day came the grand revelation. I of course had always attended school here on the Bay, but you know, dear Madame de Forêt, how little Acadien history is taught us. Mr. Nimmo had given me a history of our own people to read. Some histories are dull, but this one I liked. It was late one afternoon; I sat by my window and read, and I came to a story. You, I daresay, know it," and she turned eagerly to Agapit.

"I daresay, mademoiselle, if I were to hear it —"

"It is of those three hundred Acadiens, who were taken from Prince Edward Island by Captain Nichols. I read of what he said to the government, ' My ship is leaking, I cannot get it to England.' Yet he was forced to go, you know, — yet let me have the sad pleasure of telling you that I read of their arrival to within a hundred leagues of the coast of England. The ship had given out, it was going down, and the captain sent for the priest on board, — at this point I ran to the fire, for daylight faded. With eyes blinded by tears I finished the story, — the priest addressed his people. He said that the captain had told him that all could not be saved, that if the Acadiens would consent to remain quiet, he and his sailors would seize the boats, and have a chance for their lives. ' You will be quiet, my dear people,' said the priest. ' You have suffered much, — you will suffer more,' and he gave them absolution. I shrieked with pain when I read that they were quiet, very quiet, — that one Acadien, who ventured in a boat, was rebuked by his wife so that he stepped contentedly back to her side. Then the captain and sailors embarked, they set out for the shore, and finally reached it; and the Acadiens remained calmly on board. They went calmly to the bottom of the sea, and I flung the book far from me, and rushed down-stairs, — I must see Mr. Nimmo. He was in the *salon* with a gentleman who was to dine with him, but I saw only my friend. I precipitated myself on a chair beside him. 'Ah, tell me, tell me!' I entreated, 'is it all true? Were they martyrs, — these countrymen of mine? Were they patient and afflicted? Is it their children that I have despised, — their religion that I have mocked?'

"'Yes, yes,' he said, gently, 'but you did not understand.'

"'I understand,' I cried, 'and I hate the English. I will no longer be a Protestant. They murdered my forefathers and mothers.'

"He did not reason with me then, — he sent me to bed, and for six days I went every morning to mass in the Madeleine. Then I grew tired, because I had not been brought up to it, and it seemed strange to me. That was the time Mr. Nimmo explained many things to me. I learned that, though one must hate evil, there is a duty of forgiveness — but I weary you," and she sprang up from her chair. "I must also go home; my aunt will wonder where I am. I shall soon see you both again, I hope," and waving her hand, she ran lightly towards the gate.

"An abrupt departure," said Agapit, as he watched her out of sight.

"She is nervous, and also homesick for the Nimmos," said Rose; "but what a dear child. Her letters have made her seem like a friend of years' standing. Perhaps we should have kept her from lingering on those stories of the old time."

"Do not reproach yourself," said Agapit, as he took another piece of cake, "we could not have kept her from it. She was just about to cry, — she is probably crying now," and there was a curious satisfaction in his voice.

"Are you not well to-day, Agapit?" asked Rose, anxiously.

"*Mon Dieu*, yes, — what makes you think otherwise?"

"You seem subdued, almost dull."

Agapit immediately endeavored to take on a more sprightly air. "It is that child, — she is overcoming. I was not prepared for such life, such animation. She cannot write as she speaks."

"No; her letters were stiff."

"Without doubt, Mr. Nimmo has sent her here to be an amiable distraction for you," said Agapit. "He is afraid that you are getting too holy, too far beyond him. He sends this Parisian butterfly to amuse you. He has plenty of money, he can indulge his whims."

His tone was bitter, and Rose forbore to answer him. He was so good, this cousin of hers, and yet his poverty and his long-continued struggle to obtain an education had somewhat soured him, and he had not quite fulfilled the promise of his earlier years. He was also a little jealous of Vesper.

If Vesper had been as generous towards him as he was towards other people, Agapit would have kept up his old admiration for him. As it was, they both possessed indomitable pride along different lines, and all through these years not a line of friendly correspondence had passed between them, — they had kept severely apart.

But for this pride, Rose would have been allowed to share all that she had with her adopted brother, and would not have been obliged to stand aside and, with a heart wrung with compassion, see him suffer for the lack of things that she might easily have provided.

However, he was getting on better now. He had a large number of clients, and was in a fair way to make a good living for himself.

They talked a little more of Bidiane's arrival, that had made an unusual commotion in their quiet lives, then Agapit, having lingered longer than usual, hurried back to his office and his home, in the town of

Weymouth, that was some miles distant from Sleeping Water.

A few hours later, Bidiane laid her tired, agitated head on her pillow, after putting up a very fervent and Protestant petition that something might enable her to look into the heart of her Catholic friend, Rose à Charlitte, and discover what the mysterious obstacle was that prevented her from enjoying a happy union with Mr. Nimmo.

CHAPTER IV.

AN UNKNOWN IRRITANT.

"Il est de ces longs jours d'indicible malaise
Où l'on voudrait dormir du lourd sommeil des morts,
De ces heures d'angoisse où l'existence pèse
Sur l'âme et sur le corps."

Two or three weeks went by, and, although Bidiane's headquarters were nominally at the inn, she visited the horseshoe cottage morning, noon, and night.

Rose always smiled when she heard the rustling of her silk-lined skirts, and often murmured:

"Sa robe fait froufrou, froufrou,
Ses petits pieds font toc, toc, toc."

"I wonder how long she is going to stay here?" said Agapit, one day, to his cousin.

"She does not know, — she obeys Mr. Nimmo blindly, although sometimes she chatters of earning her own living."

"I do not think he would permit that," said Agapit, hastily.

"Nor I, but he does not tell her so."

"He is a kind of *Grand Monarque* among you women. He speaks, and you listen; and now that Bidiane has broken the ice and we talk more freely of him, I may say that I do not approve of his keeping your boy any longer, although it is a foolish thing for me to mention, since you have never asked my advice on the subject."

"My dear brother," said Rose, softly, "in this one thing I have not agreed with you, because you are not a mother, and cannot understand. I feared to bring back my boy when he was delicate, lest he should die of the separation from Mr. Nimmo. It was better for me to cry myself to sleep for many nights than for me to have him for a few weeks, and then, perhaps, lay his little body in the cold ground. Where would then be my satisfaction? And now that he is strong, I console myself with the thought of the fine schools that he attends, I follow him every hour of the day, through the letters that Mr. Nimmo sends to Bidiane. As I dust my room in the morning, I hold conversations with him.

"I say, 'How goes the Latin, little one, and the Greek? They are hard, but do not give up. Some day thou wilt be a clever man.' All the time I talk to him. I tell him of every happening on the Bay. Naturally I cannot put all this in my letters to him, that are few and short on account of — well you know why I do not write too much. Agapit, I do not dare to bring him back. He gives that dear young man an object in life; he also interests his mother, who now loves me, through my child. I speak of the schools, and yet it is not altogether for that, for have we not a good college for boys here on the Bay? It is something higher. It is for the good of souls that he stays away. Not yet, not yet, can I recall him. It would not seem right, and I cannot do what is wrong; also there is his father."

Agapit, with a resigned gesture, drew on his gloves. He had been making a short call and was just about to return home.

"Are you going to the inn?" asked Rose.

"Why should I call there?" he said, a trifle irritably. "I have not the time to dance attendance on young girls."

Rose was lost in gentle amazement at Agapit's recent attitude towards Bidiane. Her mind ran back to the long winter and summer evenings when he had come to her house, and had sat for hours reading the letters from Paris. He had taken a profound interest in the little renegade. Step by step he had followed her career. He had felt himself in a measure responsible for the successful issue of the venture in taking her abroad. And had he not often spoken delightedly of her return, and her probable dissemination among the young people of the stock of new ideas that she would be sure to bring with her?

This was just what she had done. She had enlarged the circle of her acquaintance, and every one liked her, every one admired her. Day after day she flashed up and down the Bay, on the bicycle that she had brought with her from Paris, and, as she flew by the houses, even the old women left their windows and hobbled to the door to catch a gay salutation from her.

Only Agapit was dissatisfied, only Agapit did not praise her, and Rose on this day, as she stood wistfully looking into his face, carried on an internal soliloquy. It must be because she represents Mr. Nimmo. She has been educated by him, she reveres him. He has only lent her to the Bay, and will some day take her away, and Agapit, who feels this, is jealous because he is rich, and because he will not forgive. It is strange that the best of men and women are so human; but our dear Lord will some day melt their hearts; and Rose, who had never disliked any one and had not an enemy in the world, checked a sigh and endeavored to turn her thoughts to some more agreeable subject.

Agapit, however, still stood before her, and while he was there it was difficult to think of anything else. Then he presently asked a distracting question, and one that completely upset her again, although it was put in a would-be careless tone of voice.

"Does the Poirier boy go much to the inn?"

Rose tried to conceal her emotion, but it was hard for her to do so, as she felt that she had just been afforded a painful lightning glance into Agapit's mind. He felt that he was growing old. Bidiane was associating with the girls and young men who had been mere children five years before. The Poirier boy, in particular, had grown up with amazing rapidity and precociousness. He was handsomer, far handsomer than Agapit had ever been, he was also very clever, and very much made of on account of his being the most distinguished pupil in the college of Sainte-Anne, that was presided over by the Eudist fathers from France.

"Agapit," she said, suddenly, and in sweet, patient alarm, "are we getting old, you and I?"

"We shall soon be thirty," he said, gruffly, and he turned away.

Rose had never before thought much on the subject of her age. Whatever traces the slow, painful years had left on her inner soul, there were no revealing marks on the outer countenance of her body. Her glass showed her still an unruffled, peaceful face, a delicate skin, an eye undimmed, and the same beautiful abundance of shining hair.

"But, Agapit," she said, earnestly, "this is absurd. We are in our prime. Only you are obliged to wear glasses. And even if we were old, it would not be a terrible thing — there is too much praise of youth. It is a charming time, and yet it is a time of follies.

As for me, I love the old ones. Only as we grow older do we find rest."

"The follies of youth," repeated Agapit, sarcastically, "yes, such follies as we have had, — the racking anxiety to find food to put in one's mouth, to find sticks for the fire, books for the shelf. Yes, that is fine folly. I do not wonder that you sigh for age."

Rose followed him to the front door, where he stood on the threshold and looked down at the river.

"Some days I wish I were there," he said, wearily.

Rose had come to the end of her philosophy, and in real alarm she examined his irritated, disheartened face. "I believe that you are hungry," she said at last.

"No, I am not, — I have a headache. I was up all last night reading a book on Commercial Law. I could not eat to-day, but I am not hungry."

"You are starving — come, take off your gloves," she said, peremptorily. "You shall have such a fine little dinner. I know what Célina is preparing, and I will assist her so that you may have it soon. Go lie down there in the sitting-room."

"I do not wish to stay," said Agapit, disagreeably; "I am like a bear."

"The first true word that you have spoken," she said, shaking a finger at him. "You are not like my good Agapit to-day. See, I will leave you for a time — Jovite, Jovite," and she went to the back door and waved her hand in the direction of the stable. "Go take out Monsieur LeNoir's horse. He stays to dinner."

After dinner she persuaded him to go down to the inn with her. Bidiane was in the parlor, sitting before a piano that Vesper had had sent from Boston for her. Two young Acadien girls were beside her, and when they were not laughing and exchanging jokes, they sang French songs, the favorite one being "*Un Canadien Errant*," to which they returned over and over again.

Several shy young captains from schooners in the Bay were sitting tilted back on chairs on the veranda, each one with a straw held between his teeth to give him countenance. Agapit joined them, while Rose went in the parlor and assisted the girls with their singing. She did not feel much older than they did. It was curious how this question of age oppressed some people; and she glanced through the window at Agapit's now reasonably contented face.

"I am glad you came with him," whispered Bidiane, mischievously. "He avoids me now, and I am quite afraid of him. The poor man, he thought to find me a blue-stocking, discussing dictionaries and encyclopædias; he finds me empty-headed and silly, so he abandons me to the younger set, although I admire him so deeply. You, at least, will never give me up," and she sighed and laughed at the same time, and affectionately squeezed Rose's hand.

Rose laughed too. She was becoming more lighthearted under Bidiane's half-nonsensical, half-sensible influence, and the two young Acadien girls politely averted their surprised eyes from the saint who would condescend to lay aside for a minute her crown of martyrdom. All the Bay knew that she had had some trouble, although they did not know what it was.

CHAPTER V.

BIDIANE PLAYS AN OVERTURE.

" I've tried the force of every reason on him,
Soothed and caressed, been angry, soothed again."
ADDISON.

A FEW days later, Bidiane happened to be caught in a predicament, when none of her new friends were near, and she was forced to avail herself of Agapit's assistance.

She had been on her wheel nearly to Weymouth to make a call on one of her numerous and newly acquired girl friends. Merrily she was gliding homeward, and being on a short stretch of road bounded by hay-fields that contained no houses, and fancying that no one was near her, she lifted up her voice in a saucy refrain, "*L'homme qui m'aura, il n'aura pas tout ce qu'il voudra*" (The man that gets me, will not get all he wants).

"*La femme qui m'aura, elle n'aura pas tout ce qu'elle voudra*" (The woman that gets me, she'll not get all she wants), chanted Agapit, who was coming behind in his buggy.

Suddenly the girl's voice ceased; in the twinkling of an eye there had been a rip, a sudden evacuation of air from one of the rubber tubes on her wheel, and she had sprung to the road.

"Good afternoon," said Agapit, driving up, "you have punctured a tire."

"Yes," she replied, in dismay, "the wretched thing! If I knew which wicked stone it was that did it, I would throw it into the Bay."

"What will you do?"

"Oh, I do not know. I wish I had leather tires."

"I will take you to Sleeping Water, mademoiselle, if you wish."

"But I do not care to cause you that trouble," and she gazed mischievously and longingly up and down the road.

"It will not be a trouble," he said, gravely.

"Anything is a trouble that one does not enjoy."

"But there is duty, mademoiselle."

"Ah, yes, duty, dear duty," she said, making a face. "I have been instructed to love it, therefore I accept your offer. How fortunate for me that you happened to be driving by! Almost every one is haying. What shall we do with the wheel?"

"We can perhaps lash it on behind. I have some rope. No, it is too large. Well, we can at least wheel it to the post-office in Belliveau's Cove, — or stay, give me your wrench. I will take off the wheel, carry it to Meteghan River, and have it mended. I am going to Chéticamp to-night. To-morrow I will call for it and bring it to you."

"Oh, you are good, — I did not know that there is a repair shop at Meteghan River."

"There is, — they even make wheels."

"But the outside world does not know that. The train conductor told that if anything went wrong with my bicycle, I would have to send it to Yarmouth."

"The outside world does not know of many things that exist in Clare. Will you get into the buggy, mademoiselle? I will attend to this."

Bidiane meekly ensconced herself under the hood, and took the reins in her hands. "What are you going to do with the remains?" she asked, when Agapit put the injured wheel in beside her.

"We might leave them at Madame LeBlanc's," and he pointed to a white house in the distance. "She will send them to you by some passing cart."

"That is a good plan, — she is quite a friend of mine."

"I will go on foot, if you will drive my horse."

They at once set out, Bidiane driving, and Agapit walking silently along the grassy path at the side of the road.

The day was tranquil, charming, and a perfect specimen of "the divine weather" that Saint-Mary's Bay is said to enjoy in summer. Earlier in the afternoon there had been a soft roll of pearl gray fog on the Bay, in and out of which the schooners had been slipping like phantom ships. Now it had cleared away, and the long blue sweep of water was open to them. They could plainly see the opposite shores of long Digby Neck, — each fisherman's cottage, each comfortable farmhouse, each bit of forest sloping to the water's edge. Over these hills hung the sun, hot and glowing, as a sun should be in haying time. On Digby Neck the people were probably making hay. Here about them there had been a general desertion of the houses for work in the fields. Men, women, and children were up on the slopes on their left, and down on the banks on their right, the women's cotton dresses shining in gay spots of color against the green foliage of the evergreen and hardwood trees that grew singly or in groups about the extensive fields of grass.

Madame LeBlanc was not at home, so Agapit pinned a note to the bicycle, and left it standing outside her front gate with the comfortable assurance that, although it might be the object of curious glances, no one would touch it until the return of the mistress of the house.

Then he entered the buggy, and, with one glance into Bidiane's eyes, which were dancing with merriment, he took the reins from her and drove on briskly.

She stared at the magnificent panorama of purple hills and shining water spread out before them, and, remembering the company that she was in, tried to concentrate her attention on the tragic history of her countrymen. Her most earnest effort was in vain; she could not do so, and she endeavored to get further back, and con over the romantic exploits of Champlain and De Monts, whose oddly shaped ships had ploughed these waters; but here again she failed. Her mind came back, always irresistibly back, from the ancient past to the man of modern times seated beside her.

She was sorry that he did not like her; she had tried hard to please him. He really was wiser than any one she knew; could she not bring about a better understanding with him? If he only knew how ignorant she felt, how anxious she was to learn, perhaps he would not be so hard on her.

It was most unfortunate that she should have had on her bicycling dress. She had never heard him speak against the wheel as a means of exercise, yet she felt intuitively that he did not like it. He adored modest women, and in bicycling they were absolutely forced to occasionally show their ankles. Gradually and imperceptibly she drew her trim-gaitered feet under her blue skirt; then she put up a cautious hand to feel that her jaunty sailor hat was set straight on her coils of hair. Had he heard, she wondered, that six other Acadien girls, inspired by her example, were to have wheels? He would think that she had set the Bay crazy. Perhaps he regarded it as a misfortune that she had ever come back to it.

If he were any other man she would be furiously angry with him. She would not speak to him again. And, with an abrupt shrug of her shoulders, she watched the squawking progress of a gull from the Bay back to the woods, and then said, impulsively, " It is going to rain."

Agapit came out of his reverie and murmured an assent. Then he looked again into her yellowish brown, certainly charming eyes when full of sunlight, as they were at present from their unwinking stare at the bright sky.

" Up the Bay, Digby Neck was our barometer," she said, thoughtfully. " When it grew purple, we were to have rain. Here one observes the gulls, and the sign never fails, — a noisy flight is rain within twenty-four hours. The old gull is telling the young ones to stay back by the lake in the forest, I suppose."

Agapit tried to shake off his dreaminess and to carry on a conversation with her, but failed dismally, until he discovered that she was choking with suppressed laughter.

" Oh, pardon, pardon, monsieur ; I was thinking —

ah! how delicious is one's surprise at some things — I am thinking how absurd. You that I fancied would be a brother — you almost as angelic as Mr. Nimmo — you do not care for me at all. You try so hard, but I plague you, I annoy. But what will you? I cannot make myself over. I talk all the Acadienism that I can, but one cannot forever linger on the old times. You yourself say that one should not."

"So you think, mademoiselle, that I dislike you?"

"Think it, my dear sir, — I know it. All the Bay knows it."

"Then all the Bay is mistaken; I esteem you highly."

"Actions speak louder than words," and her teasing glance played about his shining glasses. "In order to be polite you perjure yourself."

"Mademoiselle!"

"I am sorry to be so terribly plain-spoken," she said, nodding her head shrewdly, yet childishly. "But I understand perfectly that you think I have a feather for a brain. You really cannot stoop to converse with me. You say, 'Oh, that deceived Mr. Nimmo! He thinks he has accomplished a wonderful thing. He says, "Come now, see what I have done for a child of the Bay; I will send her back to you. Fall down and worship her."'"

Agapit smiled despite himself. "Mademoiselle, you must not make fun of yourself."

"But why not? It is my chief amusement. I am the most ridiculous mortal that ever lived, and I know how foolish I am; but why do you not exercise your charity? You are, I hear, kind and forbearing with the worst specimens of humanity on the Bay. Why should you be severe with me?"

Agapit winced as if she had pinched him. "What do you wish me to do?"

"Already it is known that you avoid me," she continued, airily; "you who are so much respected. I should like to have your good opinion, and, ridiculous as I am, you know that I am less so than I used to be."

She spoke with a certain dignity, and Agapit was profoundly touched. "Mademoiselle," he said, in a low voice, "I am ashamed of myself. You do not understand me, and I assert again that I do not dislike you."

"Then why don't you come to see me?" she asked, pointedly.

"I cannot tell you," he said, and his eyes blazed excitedly. "Do not urge the question. However, I will come — yes, I will. You shall not complain of me in future."

Bidiane felt slightly subdued, and listened in silence to his energetic remarks suddenly addressed to the horse, who had taken advantage of his master's wandering attention by endeavoring to draw the buggy into a ditch where grew some luscious bunches of grass.

"There comes Pius Poirier," she said, after a time.

The young Acadien was on horseback. His stolid, fine-featured face was as immovable as marble, as he jogged by, but there was some play between his violet eyes and Bidiane's tawny ones that Agapit did not catch, but strongly suspected.

"Do you wish to speak to him?" he inquired, coldly, when Bidiane stretched her neck outside the buggy to gaze after him.

"No," she said, composedly, "I only want to see how he sits his horse. He is my first admirer," she added, demurely, but with irrepressible glee.

"Indeed, — I should fancy that mademoiselle might have had several."

"What, — and I am only seventeen? You are crazy, my dear sir, — I am only beginning that sort of thing. It is very amusing to have young men come to see you; although, of course," she interpolated, modestly, "I shall not make a choice for some years yet."

"I should hope not," said her companion, stiffly.

"I say I have never had an admirer; yet sometimes gay young men would stare at me in the street, — I suppose on account of this red hair, — and Mr. Nimmo would be very much annoyed with them."

"A city is a wicked place; it is well that you have come home."

"With that I console myself when I am sometimes lonely for Paris," said Bidiane, wistfully. "I long to see those entrancing streets and parks, and to mingle with the lively crowds of people; but I say to myself what Mr. Nimmo often told me, that one can be as happy in one place as in another, and home is the best of all to keep the heart fresh. 'Bidiane,' he said, one day, when I was extolling the beauties of Paris, 'I would give it all for one glimpse of the wind-swept shores of your native Bay.'"

"Ah, he still thinks that!"

"Yes, yes; though I never after heard him say anything like it. I only know his feelings through his mother."

Agapit turned the conversation to other subjects. He never cared to discuss Vesper Nimmo for any length of time.

When they reached the Sleeping Water Inn, Bidiane hospitably invited him to stay to supper.

"No, thank you, — I must hurry on to Chéticamp."

"Good-by, then; you were kind to bring me home. Shall we not be better friends in future?"

"Yes, yes," said Agapit, hurriedly. "I apologize, mademoiselle," and jumping into his buggy, he drove quickly away.

Bidiane's gay face clouded. "You are not very polite to me, sir. Sometimes you smile like a sunbeam, and sometimes you glower like a rain-cloud, but I'll find out what is the matter with you, if it takes me a year. It is very discomposing to be treated so."

CHAPTER VI.

A SNAKE IN THE GRASS INTERFERES WITH THE EDUCATION OF MIRABELLE MARIE.

" Fair is the earth and fair is the sky;
God of the tempest, God of the calm,
What must be heaven when here is such balm?"
—*Aminta.*

BIDIANE, being of a practical turn of mind, and having a tremendous fund of energy to bestow upon the world in some way or other, was doing her best to follow the hint given her by Vesper Nimmo, that she should, as a means of furthering her education, spend some time at the Sleeping Water Inn, with the object of imparting to Mirabelle Marie a few ideas hitherto outside her narrow range of thought.

Sometimes the girl became provoked with her aunt, sometimes she had to check herself severely, and rapidly mutter Vesper's incantation, " Do not despise any one; if you do, it will be at a great loss to yourself."

At other times Bidiane had no need to think of the incantation. Her aunt was so good-natured, so forgiving, she was so full of pride in her young niece, that it seemed as if only the most intense provocation could justify any impatience with her.

Mirabelle Marie loved Bidiane almost as well as she loved her own children, and it was only some radical measure, such as the changing of her sneaks at sundown for a pair of slippers, or the sitting in the parlor instead of the kitchen, that excited her rebellion. However, she readily yielded, — these skirmishes were not the occurrences that vexed Bidiane's soul. The renewed battles were the things that discouraged her. No victory was sustained. Each day she must contend for what had been conceded the day before, and she was tortured by the knowledge that so little hold had she on Mirabelle Marie's slippery soul that, if she were to leave Sleeping Water on any certain day, by the next one matters would at once slip back to their former condition.

"Do not be discouraged," Vesper wrote her. "The Bay was not built in a day. Some of your ancestors lived in camps in the woods."

This was an allusion on his part to the grandmother of Mrs. Watercrow, who had actually been a squaw, and Bidiane, as a highly civilized being, winced slightly at it. Very little of the Indian strain had entered her veins, except a few drops that were exhibited in a passion for rambling in the woods. She was more like her French ancestors, but her aunt had the lazy, careless blood, as had also her children.

One of the chief difficulties that Bidiane had to contend with, in her aunt, was her irreligion. Mirabelle Marie had weak religious instincts. She had as a child, and as a very young woman, been an adherent of the Roman Catholic Church, and had obtained some grasp of its doctrines. When, in order to become "stylish," she had forsaken this church, she found herself in the position of a forlorn dog who, having dropped his substantial bone, finds himself groping for a shadow. Protestantism was an empty word to her. She could not comprehend it; and Bidiane, although a Protestant herself, shrewdly made up her mind that there was no hope for her aunt save in the church of her forefathers. However, in what way to get her back to it, — that was the question. She scolded, entreated, reasoned, but all in vain. Mirabelle Marie lounged about the house all day Sunday, very often, strange to say, amusing herself with declamations against the irreligion of the people of Boston.

Bidiane's opportunity to change this state of affairs at last came, and all unthinkingly she embraced it.

The opportunity began on a hot and windy afternoon, a few days after her drive with Agapit. She sat on the veranda reading, until struck by a sudden thought which made her close her book, and glance up and down the long road, to see if the flying clouds of dust were escorting any approaching traveller to the inn. No one was coming, so she hastily left the house and ran across the road to the narrow green field that lay between the inn and the Bay.

The field was bounded by straggling rows of raspberry bushes, and over the bushes hung a few apple-trees, — meek, patient trees, their backs bent from stooping before the strong westerly winds, their short, stubby foliage blown all over their surprised heads.

There was a sheep-pen in the corner of the field next the road, and near it was a barred gate, opening on a winding path that led down to the flat shore. Bidiane went through the gate, frowned slightly at a mowing-machine left out-of-doors for many days by the careless Claude, then laughed at the handle of its uplifted brake, that looked like a disconsolate and protesting arm raised to the sky.

All the family were in the hay field. Two white oxen drew the hay wagon slowly to and fro, while Claudine and the two boys circled about it, raking together scattered wisps left from the big cocks that Claude threw up to Mirabelle Marie.

The mistress of the house was in her element. She gloried in haying, which was the only form of exercise that appealed in the least to her. Her face was overspread by a grin of delight, her red dress fluttered in the strong breeze, and she gleefully jumped up and down on top of the load, and superimposed her fat jolly weight on the masses of hay.

Bidiane ran towards them, dilating her small nostrils as she ran to catch the many delicious odors of the summer air. The strong perfume of the hay overpowered them all, and, in an intoxication of delight, she dropped on a heap of it, and raised an armful to her face.

A squeal from Claudine roused her. Her rake had uncovered a mouse's nest, and she was busily engaged in killing every one of the tiny velvety creatures.

"But why do you do it?" asked Bidiane, running up to her.

Claudine stared at her. She was a magnificent specimen of womanhood as she stood in the blazing light of the sun, and Bidiane, even in the midst of her subdued indignation, thought of some lines in the Shakespeare that she had just laid down:

> "'Tis not your inky brows, your black silk hair,
> Your bugle eyeballs, nor your cheek of cream,
> That can entame my spirits to your worship."

Claudine was carrying on a vigorous line of reasoning. She admired Bidiane intensely, and she quietly listened with pleasure to what she called her *rocamboles* of the olden times, which were Bidiane's tales of Acadien exploits and sufferings. She was a more apt pupil than the dense and silly Mirabelle Marie.

"If I was a mouse I wouldn't like to be killed," she said, presently, going on with her raking; and Bidiane, having made her think, was satisfied.

"Now, Claudine," she said, "you must be tired. Give me your rake, and do you go up to the house and rest."

"Yes, go, Claudine," said Mirabelle Marie, from her height, "you look drug out."

"I am not tired," said Claudine, in French, "and I shall not give my rake to you, Bidiane. You are not used to work."

Bidiane bubbled over into low, rippling laughter. "I delicate, — ah, that is good! Give me your rake, Claude. You go up to the barn now, do you not?"

Claude nodded, and extended a strong hand to assist his wife in sliding to the ground. Then, accompanied by his boys, he jogged slowly after the wagon to the barn, where the oxen would be unyoked, and the grasping pitcher would lift the load in two or three mouthfuls to the mows.

Bidiane threw down her rake and ran to the fence for some raspberries, and while her hands were busy with the red fruit, her bright eyes kept scanning the road. She watched a foot-passenger coming slowly from the station, pausing at the corner, drifting in a leisurely way towards the inn, and finally, after a glance at Mirabelle Marie's conspicuous gown, climbing the fence, and moving deliberately towards her.

"H'm — a snake in the grass," murmured Bidiane, keeping an eye on the new arrival, and presently she, too, made her way towards her aunt and Claudine, who had ceased work and were seated on the hay.

"This is Nannichette," said Mirabelle Marie, somewhat apprehensively, when Bidiane reached them.

"Yes, I know," said the girl, and she nodded stiffly to the woman, who was almost as fat and as easy-going as Mirabelle Marie herself.

Nannichette was half Acadien and half English, and she had married a pure Indian who lived back in the woods near the Sleeping Water Lake. She was not a very desirable acquaintance for Mirabelle Marie, but she was not a positively bad woman, and no one would think of shutting a door against her, although her acquaintance was not positively sought after by the scrupulous Acadiens.

"We was gabbin' about diggin' for gold one day, Nannichette and I," said Mirabelle Marie, insinuatingly. "She knows a heap about good places, and the good time to dig. You tell us, Biddy, — I mean Bidiane, — some of yer yarns about the lake. Mebbe there's some talk of gold in 'em."

Bidiane sat down on the hay. If she talked, it would at least prevent Nannichette from pouring her nonsense into her aunt's ear, so she began. "I have not yet seen this lake of *L'Eau Dormante*, but I have read of it. Long, long ago, before the English came to this province, and even before the French came, there was an Indian encampment on the shores of this deep, smooth, dark lake. Many canoes shot gaily across its glassy surface, many camp-fires sent up their smoke from among the trees to the clear, blue sky. The encampment was an old, old one. The Indians had occupied it for many winters; they planned to occupy it for many more, but one sweet spring night, when they were dreaming of summer roamings, a band of hostile Indians came slipping behind the tree-trunks. A bright blaze shot up to the clear sky, and the bosom of Sleeping Water looked as if some one had drawn a bloody finger across it. Following this were shrieks and savage yells, and afterward a profound silence. The Indians left, and the shuddering trees grew closer together to hide the traces of the savage invaders — no, the marks of devastation," she said, stopping suddenly and correcting herself, for she had a good memory, and at times was apt to repeat verbatim the words of some of her favorite historians or story-tellers.

"The green running vines, also," she continued, "made haste to spread over the blackened ground, and the leaves fell quietly over the dead bodies and warmly covered them. Years went by, the leaf-mould had gathered thick over the graves of the Indians, and then, on a memorable day, the feast of Sainte-Anne's, the French discovered the lovely, silent Sleeping Water, the gem of the forest, and erected a fort on its banks. The royal flag floated over the trees, a small space of ground was cleared for the planting of corn, and a garden was laid out, where seeds from old France grew and flourished, for no disturbing gales from the Bay ever reached this sanctuary of the wildwood.

"All went merrily as a marriage bell until one winter night, when the bosom of the lake was frosted with ice, and the snow-laden branches of the trees hung heavily earthward. Then, in the hush before morning, a small detachment of men on snowshoes, arrayed in a foreign uniform, and carrying hatchets in their hands —"

"More Injuns!" gasped Mirabelle Marie, clapping her hand to her mouth in lively distress at Bidiane's tragic manner.

"No, no! I didn't say tomahawks," said Bidiane, who started nervously at the interruption; "the hatchets weren't for killing, — they were to cut the branches. These soldiers crept stealthily and painfully through the underbrush, where broken limbs and prickly shrubs stretched out detaining arms to hold them back; but they would not be held, for the lust of murder was in their hearts. When they reached the broad and open lake — "

"You jist said it was frozen," interrupted the irrepressible Mirabelle Marie.

"I beg your pardon, — the ice-sealed sheet of water, — the soldiers threw away their hatchets and unslung their guns, and again a shout of horror went up to the clear vault of heaven. White men slew white men, for the invaders were not Indians, but English soldiers, and there were streaks of crimson on the snow where the French soldiers laid themselves down to die.

"There seemed to be a curse on the lake, and it was deserted for many years, until a band of sorrowing Acadien exiles was forced to take refuge in the half-ruined fort. They summered and wintered there, until they all died of a strange sickness and were buried by one man who, only, survived. He vowed that the lake was haunted, and would never be an abode for human beings; so he came to the shore and built himself a log cabin, that he occupied in fear and trembling until at last the time came when the French were no longer persecuted."

"Agapit LeNoir also says that the lake is haunted," exclaimed Claudine, in excited French. "He hates the little river that comes stealing from it. He likes the Bay, the open Bay. There is no one here that loves the river but Rose à Charlitte."

"But dere is gold dere, — heaps," said the visitor, in English, and her eyes glistened.

"Only foolish people say that," remarked Claudine, decidedly, "and even if there should be gold there, it would be cursed."

"You not think that," said Nannichette, shrinking back.

"Oh, how stupid all this is!" said Bidiane. "Up the Bay I used to hear this talk of gold. You remember, my aunt?"

Mirabelle Marie's shoulders shook with amusement. "*Mon jheu*, yes, on the stony Dead Man's Point, where there ain't enough earth to *fricasser les cailloux*" (fricassee the pebbles); "it's all dug up like graveyards. Come on, Nannichette, tell us ag'in of yer fantome."

Nannichette became suddenly shy, and Mirabelle Marie took it upon herself to be spokeswoman. "She was rockin' her baby, when she heard a divil of a noise. The ceiling gapped at her, jist like you open yer mouth, and a fantome voice says —"

"'Dere is gole in Sleepin' Water Lake,'" interrupted Nannichette, hastily. "'Only women shall dig, — men cannot fine.'"

"An' Nannichette was squshed, — she fell ag'in the floor with her baby."

"And then she ran about to see if she could find

some women foolish enough to believe this," said Bidiane, with fine youthful disdain.

A slow color crept into Nannichette's brown cheek. "Dere is gole dere," she said, obstinately. "De speerit tell me where to look."

"That was Satan who spoke to you, Nannichette," said Claudine, seriously; "or maybe you had had a little rum. Come now, hadn't you?"

Nannichette scowled, while Mirabelle Marie murmured, with reverent admiration, "I dessay the divil knows where there is lots of gold."

"It drives me frantic to hear you discuss this subject," said Bidiane, suddenly springing to her feet. "Oh, if you knew how ignorant it sounds, how way back in the olden times! What would the people in Paris say if they could hear you? Oh, please, let us talk of something else; let us mention art."

"What's dat?" asked Nannichette, pricking up her ears.

"It is all about music, and writing poetry, and making lovely pictures, and all kinds of elegant things, — it elevates your mind and soul. Don't talk about hateful things. What do you want to live back in the woods for? Why don't you come out to the shore?"

"Dat's why I wan' de gole," said Nannichette, triumphantly. "Of'en I use to hunt for some of Cap'en Kidd's pots."

"Good gracious!" said Bidiane, with an impatient gesture, "how much money do you suppose that man had? They are searching for his treasure all along the coast. I don't believe he ever had a bit. He was a wicked old pirate, — I wouldn't spend his money if I found it — "

Mirabelle Marie and Nannichette surveyed each other's faces with cunning, glittering eyes. There was a secret understanding between them; no speech was necessary, and they contemplated Bidiane as two benevolent wild beasts might survey an innocent and highly cultured lamb who attempted to reason with them.

Bidiane dimly felt her powerlessness, and, accompanied by Claudine, went back to her raking, and left the two sitting on the hay.

While the girl was undressing that night, Claudine tapped at her door. "It is all arranged, Bidiane. They are going to dig."

Bidiane impatiently shook her hanging mass of hair, and stamped her foot on the floor. "They shall not."

"Nannichette did not go away," continued Claudine. "She hung about the stable, and Mirabelle Marie took her up some food. I was feeding the pig, and I overheard whispering. They are to get some women together, and Nannichette will lead them to the place the spirit told her of."

"Oh, the simpleton! She shall not come here again, and my aunt shall not accompany her — but where do they wish to go?"

"To the Sleeping Water Lake."

"Claudine, you know there is no gold there. The Indians had none, the French had none, — where would the poor exiles get it?"

"All this is reasonable, but there are people who are foolish, — always foolish. I tell you, this seeking for gold is like a fever. One catches it from another. I had an uncle who thought there was a treasure hid on his farm; he dug it all over, then he went crazy."

Bidiane's head, that, in the light of her lamp, had turned to a dull red-gold, sank on her breast. "I have it," she said at last, flinging it up, and choking with irrepressible laughter. "Let them go, — we will play them a trick. Nothing else will cure my aunt. Listen, — " and she laid a hand on the shoulder of the young woman confronting her, and earnestly unfolded a primitive plan.

Claudine at once fell in with it. She had never yet disapproved of a suggestion of Bidiane, and after a time she went chuckling to bed.

CHAPTER VII.

GHOSTS BY SLEEPING WATER.

"Which apparition, it seems, was you."
— *Tatler.*

THE next day Claudine's left eyelid trembled in Bidiane's direction.

The girl followed her to the pantry, where she heard, murmured over a pan of milk, "They go to-night, as soon as it is dark, — Mirabelle Marie, Suretta, and Mosée-Délice."

"Very well," said Bidiane, curling her lip, "we will go too."

Accordingly, that evening, when Mirabelle Marie clapped her rakish hat on her head, — for nothing would induce her to wear a handkerchief, — and said that she was going to visit a sick neighbor, Bidiane demurely commended her thoughtfulness, and sent an affecting message to the invalid.

However, the mistress of the inn had no sooner disappeared than her younger helpmeets tied black handkerchiefs on their heads, and slipped out to the yard, each carrying a rolled-up sheet and a paper of pins. With much suppressed laughter they glided up behind the barn, and struck across the fields to the station road. When half-way there, Bidiane felt something damp and cold touch her hand, and, with a start and a slight scream, discovered that her uncle's dog, Bastarache, in that way signified his wish to join the expedition.

"Come, then, good dog," she said, in French, for he was a late acquisition and, having been brought up in the woods, understood no English, "thou, too, shalt be a ghost."

It was a dark, furiously windy night, for the hot gale that had been blowing over the Bay for three days was just about dying away with a fiercer display of energy than before.

The stars were out, but they did not give much light, and Bidiane and Claudine had only to stand a little aside from the road, under a group of spruces, in order to be completely hidden from the three women as they went tugging by. They had met at the corner, and, in no fear of discovery, for the night was most unpleasant and there were few people stirring, they trudged boldly on, screaming neighborhood news at the top of their voices, in order to be heard above the noise of the wind.

Bidiane and Claudine followed them at a safe distance. "*Mon Dieu*, but Mirabelle Marie's fat legs will ache to-morrow," said Claudine, "she that walks so little."

"If it were an honest errand that she was going on, she would have asked for the horse. As it is, she was ashamed to do so."

The three women fairly galloped over the road to the station, for, at first, both tongues and heels were excited, and even Mirabelle Marie, although she was the only fat one of the party, managed to keep up with the others.

To Claudine, Bidiane, and the dog, the few miles to the station were a mere bagatelle. However, after crossing the railway track, they were obliged to go more slowly, for the three in front had begun to flag. They also had stopped gossiping, and when an occasional wagon approached, they stepped into the bushes beside the road until it had passed by.

The dog, in great wonderment of mind, chafed at the string that Bidiane took from her pocket and fastened around his neck. He scented his mistress on ahead, and did not understand why the two parties might not be amicably united.

A mile beyond the station, the three gold-seekers left the main road and plunged into a rough wood-track that led to the lake. Here the darkness was intense; the trees formed a thick screen overhead, through which only occasional glimpses of a narrow lane of stars could be obtained.

"This is terrible," gasped Bidiane, as her foot struck a root; "lift your feet high, Claudine."

Claudine gave her a hand. She was almost hysterical from listening to the groaning on ahead. "Since the day of my husband's death, I have not laughed so much," she said, winking away the nervous tears in her eyes. "I do not love fun as much as some people, but when I laugh, I laugh hard."

"My aunt will be in bed to-morrow," sighed Bidiane; "what a pity that she is such a goose."

"She is tough," giggled Claudine, "do not disturb yourself. It is you that I fear for."

At last, the black, damp, dark road emerged on a clearing. There stood the Indian's dwelling, — small and yellow, with a fertile garden before it, and a tiny, prosperous orchard at the back.

"You must enter this house some day," whispered Claudine. "Everything shines there, and they are well fixed. Nannichette has a sewing-machine, and a fine cook-stove, and when she does not help her husband make baskets, she sews and bakes."

"Will her husband approve of this expedition?"

"No, no, he must have gone to the shore, or Nannichette would not undertake it, — listen to what Mirabelle Marie says."

The fat woman had sunk exhausted on the doorstep of the yellow house. "Nannichette, I be *dèche* if I go a step furder, till you gimme *checque chouse pour mouiller la langue*" (give me something to wet my tongue).

"All right," said Nannichette, in the soft, drawling tones that she had caught from the Indians, and she brought her out a pitcher of milk.

Mirabelle Marie put the pitcher to her lips, and gurgled over the milk a joyful thanksgiving that she had got away from the rough road, and the rougher wind, that raged like a bull; then she said, "Your husband is away?"

"No," said Nannichette, in some embarrassment, "he ain't, but come in."

Mirabelle Marie rose, and with her companions went into the house, while Bidiane and Claudine crept to the windows.

"Dear me, this is the best Indian house that I ever saw," said Bidiane, taking a survey, through the cheap lace curtains, of the sewing-machine, the cupboard of dishes, and the neat tables and chairs inside. Then she glided on in a voyage of discovery around the house, skirting the diminutive bedrooms, where half a dozen children lay snoring in comfortable beds, and finally arriving outside a shed, where a tall, slight Indian was on his knees, planing staves for a tub by the light of a lamp on a bracket above him.

His wife's work lay on the floor. When not suffering from the gold fever, she twisted together the dried strips of maple wood and scented grasses, and made baskets that she sold at a good price.

The Indian did not move an eyelid, but he plainly saw Bidiane and Claudine, and wondered why they were not with the other women, who, in some uneasiness of mind, stood in the doorway, looking at him over each other's shoulders.

After his brief nod and taciturn "Hullo, ladies," his wife said, "We go for walk in woods."

"What for you lie?" he said, in English, for the Micmacs of the Bay are accomplished linguists, and make use of three languages. "You go to dig gold," and he grunted contemptuously.

No one replied to him, and he continued, "Ladies, all religions is good. I cannot say, you go hell 'cause you Catholic, an' I go heaven 'cause I Protestant. All same with God, if you believe your religion. But your priesties not say to dig gold."

He took up the stave that he had laid down, and went on with his work of smoothing it, while the four "ladies," Mirabelle Marie, Suretta, Mosée-Délice, and his wife, appeared to be somewhat ashamed of themselves.

"'Pon my soul an' body, there ain't no harm in diggin' gold," said Mirabelle Marie. "That gives us fun."

"How many you be?" he asked.

"Four," said Nannichette, who was regarding her lord and master with some shyness; for stupid as she was, she recognized the fact that he was the more civilized being, and that the prosperity of their family was largely due to him.

The Indian's liquid eyes glistened for an instant towards the window, where stood Bidiane and Claudine. "Take care, ladies, there be ghosties in the woods."

The four women laughed loudly, but in a shaky manner; then taking each a handful of raspberries, from a huge basketful that Nannichette offered them, and that was destined for the preserve pot on the morrow, they once more plunged into the dark woods.

Bidiane and Claudine restrained the leaping dog, and quietly followed them. The former could not conceal her delight when they came suddenly upon the lake. It lay like a huge, dusky mirror, turned up to the sky with a myriad stars piercing its glassy bosom.

"Stop," murmured Claudine.

The four women had paused ahead of them. They were talking and gesticulating violently, for all conversation was forbidden while digging. One word spoken aloud, and the charm would be broken, the spirit would rush angrily from the spot.

Therefore they were finishing up their ends of talk, and Nannichette was assuring them that she would take them to the exact spot revealed to her in the vision.

Presently they set off in Indian file, Nannichette in front, as the one led by the spirit, and carrying with her a washed and polished spade, that she had brought from her home.

Claudine and Bidiane were careful not to speak, for there was not a word uttered now by the women in front, and the pursuers needed to follow them with extreme caution. On they went, climbing silently over the grassy mounds that were now the only reminders of the old French fort, or stumbling unexpectedly and noisily into the great heap of clam shells, whose contents had been eaten by the hungry exiles of long ago.

At last they stopped. Nannichette stared up at the sky, down at the ground, across the lake on her right, and into the woods on her left, and then pointed to a spot in the grass, and with a magical flourish of the spade began to dig.

Having an Indian husband, she was accustomed to work out-of-doors, and was therefore able to dig for a long time before she became sensible of fatigue, and was obliged mutely to extend the spade to Suretta.

Not so enduring were the other women. Their ancestors had ploughed and reaped, but Acadiennes of the present day rarely work on the farms, unless it is during the haying season. Suretta soon gave out. Mosée-Délice took her place, and Mirabelle Marie hung back until the last.

Bidiane and Claudine withdrew among the trees, stifling their laughter and trying to calm the dog, who had finally reached a state of frenzy at this mysterious separation.

"My unfortunate aunt!" murmured Bidiane; "do let us put an end to this."

Claudine was snickering convulsively. She had begun to array herself in one of the sheets, and was transported with amusement and anticipation.

Meanwhile, doubt and discord had reared their disturbing heads among the members of the digging party. Mirabelle Marie persisted in throwing up the spade too soon, and the other women, regarding her with glowing, eloquent looks, quietly arranged that the honorable agricultural implement, now perverted to so unbecoming a use, should return to her hands with disquieting frequency.

The earth was soft here by the lake, yet it was heavy to lift out, for the hole had how become quite deep. Suddenly, to the horror and anger of Nannichette and the other two women, both of whom were beginning to have mysterious warnings and impressions that they were now on the brink of discovery of one pot of gold, and perhaps two, there was an impatient exclamation from Mirabelle Marie.

"The divil!" she cried, and her voice broke out shrilly in the deathly silence; "Bidiane was right. It ain't no speerit you saw. I'm goin'," and she scrambled out of the hole.

With angry reproaches for her precipitancy and laziness, the other women fell upon her with their tongues. She had given them this long walk to the lake, she had spoiled everything, and, as their furious voices smote the still air, Bidiane, Claudine, and the dog emerged slowly and decently from the heavy gloom behind them like ghosts rising from the lake.

"I will give you a bit of my sheet," Bidiane had said to Bastarache; consequently he stalked beside them like a diminutive bogey in a graceful mantle of white.

"*Ah, mon jheu! chesque j'vois?*" (what do I see), screamed Suretta, who was the first to catch sight of them. "Ten candles to the Virgin if I get out of this!" and she ran like a startled deer.

With various expressions of terror, the others followed her. They carried with them the appearance of the white ethereal figures, standing against the awful black background of the trees, and as they ran, their shrieks and yells of horror, particularly those from Mirabelle Marie, were so heartrending that Bidiane, in sudden compunction, screamed to her, "Don't you know me, my aunt? It is Bidiane, your niece. Don't be afraid!"

Mirabelle Marie was making so much noise herself that she could scarcely have heard a trumpet sounding in her ears, and fear lent her wings of such extraordinary vigor in flight that she was almost immediately out of sight.

Bidiane turned to the dog, who was tripping and stumbling inside his snowy drapery, and to Claudine, who was shrieking with delight at him.

"Go then, good dog, console your mistress," she said. "Follow those piercing screams that float backward," and she was just about to release him when she was obliged to go to the assistance of Claudine, who had caught her foot, and had fallen to the ground, where she lay overcome by hysterical laughter.

Bidiane had to get water from the lake to dash on her face, and when at last they were ready to proceed on their way, the forest was as still as when they had entered it.

"Bah, I am tired of this joke," said Bidiane. "We have accomplished our object. Let us throw these things in the lake. I am ashamed of them;" and she put a stone inside their white trappings, and hurled them into Sleeping Water, which mutely received and swallowed them.

"Now," she said, impatiently, "let us overtake them. I am afraid lest Mirabelle Marie stumble, she is so heavy."

Claudine, leaning against a tree and mopping her eyes, vowed that it was the best joke that she had ever heard of; then she joined Bidiane, and they hurriedly made their way to the yellow cottage.

It was deserted now, except for the presence of the six children of mixed blood, who were still sleeping like six little dark logs, laid three on a bed.

"We shall overtake them," said Bidiane; "let us hurry."

However, they did not catch up to them on the forest path, nor even on the main road, for when the terrified women had rushed into the presence of the Indian and had besought him to escort them away from the spirit-haunted lake, that amused man, with a cheerful grunt, had taken them back to the shore by a short cut known only to himself.

Therefore, when Bidiane and Claudine arrived breathlessly home, they found Mirabelle Marie there before them. She sat in a rocking-chair in the middle of the kitchen, surrounded by a group of sympathizers, who listened breathlessly to her tale of woe, that she related with chattering teeth.

Bidiane ran to her and threw her arms about her neck.

"*Mon jheu*, Biddy, I've got such a fright. I'm mos' dead. Three ghosties came out of Sleepin' Water, and chased us, — we were back for gold. Suretta an' Mosée-Délice have run home. They're mos' scairt to pieces. Oh, I'll never sin again. I wisht I'd made my Easter duties. I'll go to confession to-morrer."

"It was I, my aunt," cried Bidiane, in distress.

"It was awful," moaned Mirabelle Marie. "I see the speerit of me mother, I see the speerit of me sister, I see the speerit of me leetle lame child."

"It was the dog," exclaimed Bidiane, and, gazing around the kitchen for him, she discovered Agapit sitting quietly in a corner.

"Oh, how do you do?" she said, in some embarrassment; then she again gave her attention to her distressed aunt.

"The dogue, — Biddy, you ain't crazy?"

"Yes, yes, the dog and Claudine and I. See how she is laughing. We heard your plans, we followed you, we dressed in sheets."

"The dogue," reiterated Mirabelle Marie, in blank astonishment, and pointing to Bastarache, who lay under the sofa solemnly winking at her. "Ain't he ben plumped down there ever since supper, Claude?"

"Yes, he's ben there."

"But Claude sleeps in the evenings," urged Bidiane. "I assure you that Bastarache was with us."

"Oh, the dear leetle liar," said Mirabelle Marie, affectionately embracing her. "But I'm glad to git back again to yeh."

"I'm telling the truth," said Bidiane, desperately. "Can't you speak, Claudine?"

"We did go," said Claudine, who was still possessed by a demon of laughter. "We followed you."

"Followed us to Sleepin' Water! You're lyin', too. *Sakerjé*, it was awful to see me mother and me sister and the leetle dead child," and she trotted both feet wildly on the floor, while her rolling eye sought comfort from Bidiane.

"What shall I do?" said Bidiane. "Mr. LeNoir, you will believe me. I wanted to cure my aunt of her foolishness. We took sheets —"

"Sheets?" repeated Mirabelle. "Whose sheets?"

"Yours, my aunt, — oh, it was very bad in us, but they were old ones; they had holes."

"What did you do with 'em?"

"We threw them in the lake."

"Come, now, look at that, ha, ha," and Mirabelle Marie laughed in a quavering voice. "I can see Claudine throwing sheets in the lake. She would make pickin's of 'em. Don't lie, Bidiane, me girl, or you'll see ghosties. You want to help your poor aunt, — you've made up a nice leetle lie, but don't tell it. See, Jude and Edouard are heatin' some soup. Give some to Agapit LeNoir and take a cup yourself."

Bidiane, with a gesture of utter helplessness, gave up the discussion and sat down beside Agapit.

"You believe me, do you not?" she asked, under

cover of the joyful bustle that arose when the two boys began to pass around the soup.

"Yes," he replied, making a wry face over his steaming cup.

"And what do you think of me?" she asked, anxiously.

Agapit, although an ardent Acadien, and one bent on advancing the interests of his countrymen in every way, had yet little patience with the class to which Mirabelle Marie belonged. Apparently kind and forbearing with them, he yet left them severely alone. His was the party of progress, and he had been half amused, half scornful of the efforts that Bidiane had put forth to educate her deficient relative.

"On general principles," he said, coolly, "it is better not to chase a fat aunt through dark woods; yet, in this case, I would say it has done good."

"I did not wish to be heartless," said Bidiane, with tears in her eyes. "I wished to teach her a lesson."

"Well, you have done so. Hear her swear that she will go to mass, — she will, too. The only way to work upon such a nature is through fear."

"I am glad to have her go to mass, but I did not wish her to go in this way."

"Be thankful that you have attained your object," he said, dryly. "Now I must go. I hoped to spend the evening with you, and hear you sing."

"You will come again, soon?" said Bidiane, following him to the door.

"It is a good many miles to come, and a good many to go back, mademoiselle. I have not always the time — and, besides that, I have soon to go to Halifax on business."

"Well, I thank you for keeping your promise to come," said Bidiane, humbly, and with gratitude. She was completely unnerved by the events of the evening, and was in no humor to find fault.

Agapit clapped his hat firmly on his head as a gust of wind whirled across the yard and tried to take it from him.

"We are always glad to see you here," said Bidiane, wistfully, as she watched him step across to the picket fence, where his white horse shone through the darkness; "though I suppose you have pleasant company in Weymouth. I have been introduced to some nice English girls from there."

"Yes, there are nice ones," he said. "I should like to see more of them, but I am usually busy in the afternoons and evenings."

"Do not work too hard, — that is a mistake. One must enjoy life a little."

He gathered up the reins in his hands and paused a minute before he stepped into the buggy. "I suppose I seem very old to you."

She hesitated for an instant, and the wind dying

down a little seemed to take the words from her lips and softly breathe them against his dark, quiet face. "Not so very old, — not as old as you did at first. If I were as old as you, I should not do such silly things."

He stared solemnly at her wind-blown figure swaying lightly to and fro on the gravel, and at the little hands put up to keep her dishevelled hair from her eyes and cheeks, which were both glowing from her hurried scamper home. "Are you really worried because you played this trick on your aunt?"

"Yes, terribly, she has been like a mother to me. I would be ashamed for Mr. Nimmo to know."

"And will you lie awake to-night and vex yourself about it?"

"Oh, yes, yes, — how can you tell? Perhaps you also have troubles."

Agapit laughed in sudden and genuine amusement. "Mademoiselle, my cousin, let me say something to you that you may perhaps remember when you are older. It is this: you have at present about as much comprehension and appreciation of real heart trouble, and of mental struggles that tear one first this way, then that way, — you have about as much understanding of them as has that kitten sheltering itself behind you."

Bidiane quietly stowed away this remark among the somewhat heterogeneous furniture of her mind;

then she said, "I feel quite old when I talk to my aunt and to Claudine."

"You are certainly ahead of them in some mental experiences, but you are not yet up to some other people."

"I am not up to Madame de Forêt," she said, gently, "nor to you. I feel sure now that you have some troubles."

"And what do you imagine they are?"

"I imagine that they are things that you will get over," she said, with spirit. "You are not a coward."

He smiled, and softly bade her good night.

"Good night, *mon cousin*," she said, gravely, and taking the crying kitten in her arms, she put her head on one side and listened until the sound of the carriage wheels grew faint in the distance.

CHAPTER VIII.

FAIRE BOMBANCE.

" Could but our ancestors retrieve their fate,
And see their offspring thus degenerate,
How we contend for birth and names unknown ;
And build on their past acts, and not our own ;
They'd cancel records and their tombs deface,
And then disown the vile, degenerate race ;
For families is all a cheat,
'Tis personal virtue only, makes us great."
THE TRUE BORN ENGLISHMAN. DEFOE.

BIDIANE was late for supper, and Claudine was regretfully remarking that the croquettes and the hot potatoes in the oven would all be burnt to cinders, when the young person herself walked into the kitchen, her face a fiery crimson, a row of tiny beads of perspiration at the conjunction of her smooth forehead with her red hair.

"I have had a glorious ride," she said, opening the door of the big oven and taking out the hot dishes.

Claudine laid aside the towel with which she was wiping the cups and saucers that Mirabelle Marie washed. " Go sit down at the table, Bidiane; you must be weary."

The girl, nothing loath, went to the dining-room, while Claudine brought her in hot coffee, buttered toast, and preserved peaches and cream, and then returning to the kitchen watched her through the open door, as she satisfied the demands of a certainly prosperous appetite.

" And yet, it is not food I want, as much as drink," said Bidiane, gaily, as she poured herself out a second glass of milk. " Ah, the bicycle, Claudine. If you rode, you would know how one's mouth feels like a dry bone."

" I think I would like a wheel," said Claudine, modestly. " I have enough money saved."

" Have you ? Then you must get one, and I will teach you to ride."

" How would one go about it ? "

" We will do it in this way," said Bidiane, in a businesslike manner, for she loved to arrange the affairs of other people. " How much money have you ? "

" I have one hundred dollars."

" ' Pon me soul an' body, I'd have borrered some if I'd known that," interrupted Mirabelle Marie, with a chuckle.

" Good gracious," observed Bidiane, " you don't want more than half that. We will give fifty to one of the men on the schooners. Isn't *La Sauterelle* going to Boston, to-morrow?"

"Yes; the cook was just in for yeast."

"Has he a head for business?"

"Pretty fair."

"Does he know anything about machines?"

"He once sold sewing-machines, and he also would show how to work them."

"The very man, — we will give him the fifty dollars and tell him to pick you out a good wheel and bring it back in the schooner."

"Then there will be no duty to pay," said Claudine, joyfully.

"H'm, — well, perhaps we had better pay the duty," said Bidiane; "it won't be so very much. It is a great temptation to smuggle things from the States, but I know we shouldn't. By the way, I must tell Mirabelle Marie a good joke I just heard up the Bay. My aunt, — where are you?"

Mirabelle Marie came into the room and seated herself near Claudine.

"Marc à Jaddus à Dominique's little girl gave him away," said Bidiane, laughingly. "She ran over to the custom-house in Belliveau's Cove and told the man what lovely things her papa had brought from Boston, in his schooner, and the customs man hurried over, and Marc had to pay — I must tell you, too, that I bought some white ribbon for Alzélie Gauterot, while

I was in the Cove," and Bidiane pulled a little parcel from her pocket.

Mirabelle Marie was intensely interested. Ever since the affair of the ghosts, which Bidiane had given up trying to persuade her was not ghostly, but very material, she had become deeply religious, and took her whole family to mass and vespers every Sunday.

Just now the children of the parish were in training for their first communion. She watched the little creatures daily trotting up the road towards the church to receive instruction, and she hoped that her boys would soon be among them. In the small daughter of her next-door neighbor, who was to make her first communion with the others, she took a special interest, and in her zeal had offered to make the dress, which kind office had devolved upon Bidiane and Claudine.

"Also, I have been thinking of a scheme to save money," said Bidiane. "For a veil we can just take off this fly screen," and she pointed to white netting on the table. "No one but you and Claudine will know. It is fine and soft, and can be freshly done up."

"*Mon jheu!* but you are smart, and a real Acadien brat," said her aunt. "Claudine, will you go to the door? Some divil rings, — that is, some lady or gentleman," she added, as she caught a menacing glance from Bidiane.

"If you keep a hotel you must always be glad to see strangers," said Bidiane, severely. "It is money in your pocket."

"But such a trouble, and I am sleepy."

"If you are not careful you will have to give up this inn, — however, I must not scold, for you do far better than when I first came."

"It is the political gentleman," said Claudine, entering, and noiselessly closing the door behind her. "He who has been going up and down the Bay for a day or two. He wishes supper and a bed."

"*Sakerjé!*" muttered Mirabelle Marie, rising with an effort. "If I was a man I guess I'd let pollyticks alone, and stay to hum. I s'ppose he's got a nest with some feathers in it. I guess you'd better ask him out, though. There's enough to start him, ain't there?" and she waddled out to the kitchen.

"Ah, the political gentleman," said Bidiane. "It was he for whom I helped Maggie Guilbaut pick blackberries, yesterday. They expected him to call, and were going to offer him berries and cream."

Mirabelle Marie, on going to the kitchen, had left her niece sitting composedly at the table, only lifting an eyelid to glance at the door by which the stranger would enter; but when she returned, as she almost immediately did, to ask the gentleman whether he would prefer tea to coffee, a curious spectacle met her gaze.

Bidiane, with a face that was absolutely furious, had sprung to her feet and was grasping the sides of her bicycle skirt with clenched hands, while the stranger, who was a lean, dark man, with a pale, rather pleasing face, when not disfigured by a sarcastic smile, stood staring at her as if he remembered seeing her before, but had some difficulty in locating her among his acquaintances.

Upon her aunt's appearance, Bidiane found her voice. "Either I or that man must leave this house," she said, pointing a scornful finger at him.

Mirabelle Marie, who was not easily shocked, was plainly so on the present occasion. "Whist, Bidiane," she said, trying to pull her down on her chair; "this is the pollytickle genl'man, — county member they call 'im."

"I do not care if he is member for fifty counties," said Bidiane, in concentrated scorn. "He is a libeller, a slanderer, and I will not stay under the same roof with him, — and to think it was for him I picked the blackberries, — we cannot entertain you here, sir."

The expression of disagreeable surprise with which the man with the unpleasant smile had regarded her gave way to one of cool disdain. "This is your house, I think?" he said, appealing to Mirabelle Marie.

"Yessir," she said, putting down her tea-caddy, and arranging both her hands on her hips, in which position she would hold them until the dispute was finished.

"And you do not refuse me entertainment?" he went on, with the same unpleasant smile. "You cannot, I think, as this is a public house, and you have no just reason for excluding me from it."

"My aunt," said Bidiane, flashing around to her in a towering passion, "if you do not immediately turn this man out-of-doors, I shall never speak to you again."

"I be *dèche*," sputtered the confused landlady, "if I see into this hash. Look at 'em, Claudine. This genl'man 'll be mad if I do one thing, an' Biddy 'll take my head off if I do another. *Sakerjé!* You've got to fit it out yourselves."

"Listen, my aunt," said Bidiane, excitedly, and yet with an effort to control herself. "I will tell you what happened. On my way here I was in a hotel in Halifax. I had gone there with some people from the steamer who were taking charge of me. We were on our way to our rooms. We were all speaking English. No one would think that there was a French person in the party. We passed a gentleman, this gentleman, who stood outside his door; he was speaking to a servant. 'Bring me quickly,' he said, 'some water, — some hot water.

I have been down among the evil-smelling French of Clare. I must go again, and I want a good wash first.'"

Mirabelle Marie was by no means overcome with horror at the recitation of this trespass on the part of her would-be guest; but Claudine's eyes blazed and flashed on the stranger's back until he moved slightly, and shrugged his shoulders as if he felt their power.

"Imagine," cried Bidiane, "he called us 'evil-smelling,' — we, the best housekeepers in the world, whose stoves shine, whose kitchen floors are as white as the beach! I choked with wrath. I ran up to him and said, '*Moi, je suis Acadienne*'" (I am an Acadienne). "Did I not, sir?"

The stranger lifted his eyebrows indulgently and satirically, but did not speak.

"And he was astonished," continued Bidiane. "*Ma foi*, but he was astonished! He started, and stared at me, and I said, 'I will tell you what you are, sir, unless you apologize.'"

"I guess yeh apologized, didn't yeh?" said Mirabelle Marie, mildly.

"The young lady is dreaming," said the stranger, coolly, and he seated himself at the table. "Can you let me have something to eat at once, madame? I have a brother who resembles me; perhaps she saw him."

Bidiane grew so pale with wrath, and trembled so violently that Claudine ran to support her, and cried, "Tell us, Bidiane, what did you say to this bad man?"

Bidiane slightly recovered herself. "I said to him, 'Sir, I regret to tell you that you are lying.'"

The man at the table surveyed her in intense irritation. "I do not know where you come from, young woman," he said, hastily, "but you look Irish."

"And if I were not Acadien I would be Irish," she said, in a low voice, "for they also suffer for their country. Good-by, my aunt, I am going to Rose à Charlitte. I see you wish to keep this story-teller."

"Hole on, hole on," ejaculated Mirabelle Marie in distress. "Look here, sir, you've gut me in a fix, and you've gut to git me out of it."

"I shall not leave your house unless you tell me to do so," he said, in cool, quiet anger.

Bidiane stretched out her hands to him, and with tears in her eyes exclaimed, pleadingly, "Say only that you regret having slandered the Acadiens. I will forget that you put my people to shame before the English, for they all knew that I was coming to Clare. We will overlook it. Acadiens are not ungenerous, sir."

"As I said before, you are dreaming," responded the stranger, in a restrained fury. "I never was so put upon in my life. I never saw you before."

Bidiane drew herself up like an inspired prophetess. "Beware, sir, of the wrath of God. You lied before, — you are lying now."

The man fell into such a repressed rage that Mirabelle Marie, who was the only unembarrassed spectator, inasmuch as she was weak in racial loves and hatreds, felt called upon to decide the case. The gentleman, she saw, was the story-teller. Bidiane, who had not been particularly truthful as a child, had yet never told her a falsehood since her return from France.

"I'm awful sorry, sir, but you've gut to go. I brought up this leetle girl, an' her mother's dead."

The gentleman rose, — a gentleman no longer, but a plain, common, very ugly-tempered man. These Acadiens were actually turning him, an Englishman, out of the inn. And he had thought the whole people so meek, so spiritless. He was doing them such an honor to personally canvass them for votes for the approaching election. His astonishment almost overmastered his rage, and in a choking voice he said to Mirabelle Marie, "Your house will suffer for this, — you will regret it to the end of your life."

"I know some business," exclaimed Claudine, in sudden and irrepressible zeal. "I know that you wish to make laws, but will our men send you when they know what you say?"

He snatched his hat from the seat behind him.

His election was threatened. Unless he chained these women's tongues, what he had said would run up and down the Bay like wildfire, — and yet a word now would stop it. Should he apologize? A devil rose in his heart. He would not.

"Do your worst," he said, in a low, sneering voice. "You are a pack of liars yourselves," and while Bidiane and Claudine stiffened themselves with rage, and Mirabelle Marie contemptuously muttered, "Get out, ole beast," he cast a final malevolent glance on them, and left the house.

For a time the three remained speechless; then Bidiane sank into her chair, pushed back her half-eaten supper, propped her red head on her hand, and burst into passionate weeping.

Claudine stood gloomily watching her, while Mirabelle Marie sat down, and shifting her hands from her hips, laid them on her trembling knees. "I guess he'll drive us out of this, Biddy, — an' I like Sleepin' Water."

Bidiane lifted her face to the ceiling, just as if she were "taking a vowel," her aunt reflected, in her far from perfect English. "He shall not ruin us, my aunt, — we will ruin him."

"What'll you do, sissy?"

"I will tell you something about politics," said Bidiane, immediately becoming calm. "Mr. Nimmo has explained to me something about them, and if you listen, you will understand. In the first place, do you know what politics are?" and hastily wiping her eyes, she intently surveyed the two women who were hanging on her words.

"Yes, I know," said her aunt, joyfully. "It's when men quit work, an' gab, an' git red in the face, an' pass the bottle, an' pick rows, to fine out which shall go up to the city of Boston to make laws an' sit in a big room with lots of other men."

Bidiane, with an impatient gesture, turned to Claudine. "You know better than that?"

"Well, yes, — a little," said the black-eyed beauty, contemptuously.

"My aunt," said Bidiane, solemnly, "you have been out in the world, and yet you have many things to learn. Politics is a science, and deep, very deep."

"Is it?" said her aunt, humbly. "An' what's a science?"

"A science is — well, a science is something wonderfully clever — when one knows a great deal. Now this Dominion of Canada in which we live is large, very large, and there are two parties of politicians in it. You know them, Claudine?"

"Yes, I do," said the young woman, promptly; "they are Liberals and Conservatives."

"That is right; and just now the Premier of the Dominion is a Frenchman, my aunt, — I don't believe you knew that, — and we are proud of him."

"An' what's the Premier?"

"He is the chief one, — the one who stands over the others, when they make the laws."

"Oh, the boss! — you will tell him about this bad man."

"No, it would grieve him too much, for the Premier is always a good man, who never does anything wrong. This bad man will impose on him, and try to get him to promise to let him go to Ottawa — oh, by the way, Claudine, we must explain about that. My aunt, you know that there are two cities to which politicians go to make the laws. One is the capital."

"Yes, I know, — in Boston city."

"Nonsense, — Boston is in the United States. We are in Canada. Halifax is the capital of Nova Scotia."

"But all our folks go to Boston when they travels," said Mirabelle Marie, in a slightly injured tone.

"Yes, yes, I know, — the foolish people; they should go to Halifax. Well, that is where the big house is in which they make the laws. I saw it when I was there, and it has pictures of kings and queens in it. Now, when a man becomes too clever for this house, they send him to Ottawa, where the Premier is."

"Yes, I remember, — the good Frenchman."

"Well, this bad man now wishes to go to Halifax; then if he is ambitious, — and he is bad enough to be anything, — he may wish to go to Ottawa. But we must stop him right away before he does more mischief, for all men think he is good. Mr. Guilbaut was praising him yesterday."

"He didn't say he is bad?"

"No, no, he thinks him very good, and says he will be elected; but we know him to be a liar, and should a liar make laws for his country?"

"A liar should stay to hum, where he is known," was the decisive response.

"Very good, — now should we not try to drive this man out of Clare?"

"But what can we do?" asked Mirabelle Marie. "He is already out an' lying like the divil about us — that is, like a man out of the woods."

"We can talk," said her niece, seriously. "There are women's rights, you know."

"Women's rights," repeated her aunt, thoughtfully. "It is not in the prayer-book."

"No, of course not."

"Come now, Biddy, tell us what it is."

"It is a long subject, my aunt. It would take too many words to explain, though Mr. Nimmo has often told me about it. Women who believe that — can do as men. Why should we not vote, — you, and I, and Claudine?"

"I dunno. I guess the men won't let us."

"I should like to vote," said Bidiane, stoutly, "but

even though we cannot, we can tell the men on the Bay of this monster, and they will send him home."

"All right," said her aunt; while Claudine, who had been sitting with knitted brows during the last few minutes, exclaimed, "I have it, Bidiane; let us make *bombance*" (feasting). "Do you know what it means?"

No, Bidiane did not, but Mirabelle Marie did, and immediately began to make a gurgling noise in her throat. "Once I helped to make it in the house of an aunt. Glory! that was fun. But the tin, Claudine, where'll you git that?"

"My one hundred dollars," cried the black-eyed assistant. "I will give them to my country, for I hate that man. I will do without the wheel."

"But what is this?" asked Bidiane, reproachfully. "What are you agreeing to? I do not understand."

"Tell her, Claudine," said Mirabelle Marie, with a proud wave of her hand. "She's English, yeh know."

Claudine explained the phrase, and for the next hour the three, with chairs drawn close together, nodded, talked, and gesticulated, while laying out a feminine electioneering campaign.

CHAPTER IX.

LOVE AND POLITICS.

"Calm with the truth of life, deep with the love of loving,
New, yet never unknown, my heart takes up the tune.
Singing that needs no words, joy that needs no proving,
Sinking in one long dream as summer bides with June."

ONE morning, three weeks later, Rose, on getting up and going out to the sunny yard where she kept her fancy breed of fowls, found them all overcome by some strange disorder. The morning was bright and inspiring, yet they were all sleeping heavily and stupidly under, instead of upon, their usual roosting-place.

She waked up one or two, ran her fingers through their showy plumage, and, after receiving remonstrating glances from reproachful and recognizing eyes, softly laid them down again, and turned her attention to a resplendent red and gold cock, who alone had not succumbed to the mysterious malady, and was staggering to and fro, eyeing her with a doubtful, yet knowing look.

"Come, Fiddéding," she said, gently, "tell me what has happened to these poor hens?"

Fiddéding, instead of enlightening her, swaggered towards the fence, and, after many failures, succeeded in climbing to it and in propping his tail against a post.

Then he flapped his gorgeous wings, and opened his beak to crow, but in the endeavor lost his balance, and with a dismal squawk fell to the ground. Sheepishly resigning himself to his fate, he tried to gain the ranks of the somniferous hens, but, not succeeding, fell down where he was, and hid his head under his wing.

A slight noise caught Rose's attention, and looking up, she found Jovite leaning against the fence, and grinning from ear to ear.

"Do you know what is the matter with the hens?" she asked.

"Yes, madame; if you come to the stable, I will show you what they have been taking."

Rose, with a grave face, visited the stable, and then instructed him to harness her pony to the cart and bring him around to the front of the house.

Half an hour later she was driving towards Weymouth. As it happened to be Saturday, it was market-day, and the general shopping-time for the farmers and the fishermen all along the Bay, and even from back in the woods. Many of them, with wives and daughters in their big wagons, were on their way to sell butter, eggs, and farm produce, and obtain, in exchange, groceries and dry goods, that they would find in larger quantities and in greater varieties in Weymouth than in the smaller villages along the shore.

Upon reaching Weymouth, she stopped on the principal street, that runs across a bridge over the lovely Sissiboo River, and leaving the staid and sober pony to brush the flies from himself without the assistance of her whip, she knocked at the door of her cousin's office.

"Come in," said a voice, and she was speedily confronted by Agapit, who sat at a table facing the door.

He dropped his book and sprang up, when he saw her. "Oh! *ma chère*, I am glad to see you. I was just feeling dull."

She gently received and retained both his hands in hers. "One often does feel dull after a journey. Ah! but I have missed you."

"It has only been two weeks —"

"And you have come back with that same weary look on your face," she said, anxiously. "Agapit, I try to put that look in the back of my mind, but it will not stay."

He lightly kissed her fingers, and drew a chair beside his own for her. "It amuses you to worry."

"My cousin!"

"I apologize, — you are the soul of angelic

concern for the minds and bodies of your fellow mortals. And how goes everything in Sleeping Water? I have been quite homesick for the good old place."

Rose, in spite of the distressed expression that still lingered about her face, began to smile, and said, impulsively, " Once or twice I have almost recalled you, but I did not like to interrupt. Yours was a case at the supreme court, was it not, if that is the way to word it?"

"Yes, Rose; but has anything gone wrong? You mentioned nothing in your letters," and, as he spoke, he took off his glasses and began to polish them with his handkerchief.

"Not wrong, exactly, yet—" and she laughed. "It is Bidiane."

The hand with which Agapit was manipulating his glasses trembled slightly, and hurriedly putting them on, he pushed back the papers on the table before him, and gave her an acute and undivided attention. "Some one wants to marry her, I suppose," he said, hastily. "She is quite a flirt."

"No, no, not yet,— Pius Poirier may, by and by, but do not be too severe with her, Agapit. She has no time to think of lovers now. She is— but have you not heard? Surely you must have— every one is laughing about it."

"I have heard nothing. I returned late last night.

I came directly here this morning. I intended to go to see you to-morrow."

"I thought you would, but I could not wait. Little Bidiane should be stopped at once, or she will become notorious and get into the papers, — I was afraid it might already be known in Halifax."

"My dear Rose, there are people in Halifax who never heard of Clare, and who do not know that there are even a score of Acadiens left in the country; but what is she doing?" and he masked his impatience under an admirable coolness.

"She says she is making *bombance*," said Rose, and she struggled to repress a second laugh; "but I will begin from the first, as you know nothing. The very day you left, that Mr. Greening, who has been canvassing the county for votes, went to our inn, and Bidiane recognized him as a man who had spoken ill of the Acadiens in her presence in Halifax."

"What had he said?"

"He said that they were 'evil-smelling,'" said Rose, with reluctance.

"Oh, indeed, — he did," and Agapit's lip curled. "I would not have believed it of Greening. He is rather a decent fellow. Sarcastic, you know, but not a fool, by any means. Bidiane, I suppose, cut him."

"No, she did not cut him; he had not been introduced. She asked him to apologize, and he would not. Then she told Mirabelle Marie to request him to leave the house. He did so."

"Was he angry?"

"Yes, and insulting; and you can figure to yourself into what kind of a state our quick-tempered Bidiane became. She talked to Claudine and her aunt, and they agreed to pass Mr. Greening's remark up and down the Bay."

Agapit began to laugh. Something in his cousin's strangely excited manner, in the expression of her face, usually so delicately colored, now so deeply flushed and bewildered over Bidiane's irrepressibility, amused him intensely, but most of all he laughed from sheer gladness of heart, that the question to be dealt with was not one of a lover for their distant and youthful cousin.

Rose was delighted to see him in such good spirits. "But there is more to come, Agapit. The thing grew. At first, Bidiane contented herself with flying about on her wheel and telling all the Acadien girls what a bad man Mr. Greening was to say such a thing, and they must not let their fathers vote for him. Following this, Claudine, who is very excited in her calm way, began to drive Mirabelle Marie about. They stayed at home only long enough to prepare meals, then they went. It is all up and down the Bay, — that wretched epithet of the unfortunate Mr. Greening, — and while the men laugh, the women are furious. They cannot recover from it."

"Well, 'evil-smelling' is not a pretty adjective," said Agapit, with his lips still stretched back from his white teeth. "At Bidiane's age, what a rage I should have been in!"

"But you are in the affair now," said Rose, helplessly, "and you must not be angry."

"I!" he ejaculated, suddenly letting fall a ruler that he had been balancing on his finger.

"Yes, — at first there was no talk of another candidate. It was only, 'Let the slanderous Mr. Greening be driven away;' but, as I said, the affair grew. You know our people are mostly Liberals. Mr. Greening is the new one; you, too, are one. Of course there is old Mr. Gray, who has been elected for some years. One afternoon the blacksmith in Sleeping Water said, jokingly, to Bidiane, 'You are taking away one of our candidates; you must give us another.' He was mending her wheel at the time, and I was present to ask him to send a hoe to Jovite. Bidiane hesitated a little time. She looked down the Bay, she looked up here towards Weymouth, then she shot a quick glance at me from her curious yellow eyes, and said, 'There is my far-removed cousin, Agapit LeNoir. He is a good Acadien; he is also clever. What do you want of an Englishman?'

'By Jove!' said the blacksmith, and he slapped his leather apron, — you know he has been much in the States, Agapit, and he is very wide in his opinions, — 'By Jove!' he said, 'we couldn't have a better. I never thought of him. He is so quiet nowadays, though he used to be a firebrand, that one forgets him. I guess he'd go in by acclamation.' Agapit, what is acclamation? I searched in my dictionary, and it said, 'a clapping of hands.'"

Agapit was thunderstruck. He stared at her confusedly for a few seconds, then he exclaimed, "The dear little diablette!"

"Perhaps I should have told you before," said Rose, eagerly, "but I hated to write anything against Bidiane, she is so charming, though so self-willed. But yesterday I began to think that people may suppose you have allowed her to make use of your name. She chatters of you all the time, and I believe that you will be asked to become one of the members for this county. Though the talk has been mostly among the women, they are influencing the men, and last evening Mr. Greening had a quarrel with the Comeaus, and went away."

"I must go see her, — this must be stopped," said Agapit, rising hastily.

Rose got up, too. "But stay a minute, — hear all. The naughty thing that Bidiane has done is about money, but I will not tell you that. You must question her. This only I can say: my hens are all quite drunk this morning."

"Quite drunk!" said Agapit, and he paused with his arms half in a dust coat that he had taken from a hook on the wall. "What do you mean?"

Rose suffocated a laugh in her throat, and said, seriously, "When Jovite got up this morning, he found them quite weak in their legs. They took no breakfast, they wished only to drink. He had to watch to keep them from falling in the river. Afterwards they went to sleep, and he searched the stable, and found some burnt out matches, where some one had been smoking and sleeping in the barn, also two bottles of whiskey hidden in a barrel where one had broken on some oats that the hens had eaten. So you see the affair becomes serious when men prowl about at night, and open hen-house doors, and are in danger of setting fire to stables."

Agapit made a grimace. He had a lively imagination, and had readily supplied all these details. "I suppose you do not wish to take me back to Sleeping Water?"

Rose hesitated, then said, meekly, "Perhaps it would be better for me not to do it, nor for you to say that I have talked to you. Bidiane speaks plainly, and, though I know she likes me, she is most extremely animated just now. Claudine, you know, spoils her. Also, she avoids me lately, — you will not be too severe with her. It is so loving that she should work for you. I think she hopes to break down some of your prejudice that she says still exists against her."

Rose could not see her cousin's face, for he had abruptly turned his back on her, and was staring out the window.

"You will remember, Agapit," she went on, with gentle persistence; "do not be irritable with her; she cannot endure it just at present."

"And why should I be irritable?" he demanded, suddenly wheeling around. "Is she not doing me a great honor?"

Rose fell back a few steps, and clasped her amazed hands. This transfigured face was a revelation to her. "You, too, Agapit!" she managed to utter.

"Yes, I, too," he said, bravely, while a dull, heavy crimson mantled his cheeks. "I, too, as well as the Poirier boy, and half a dozen others; and why not?"

"You love her, Agapit?"

"Does it seem like hatred?"

"Yes — that is, no — but certainly you have treated her strangely, but I am glad, glad. I don't know when anything has so rejoiced me, — it takes me back through long years," and, sitting down, she covered her face with her nervous hands.

"I did not intend to tell you," said her cousin, hurriedly, and he laid a consoling finger on the back of her drooping head. "I wish now I had kept it from you."

"Ah, but I am selfish," she cried, immediately lifting her tearful face to him. "Forgive me, — I wish to know everything that concerns you. Is it this that has made you unhappy lately?"

With some reluctance he acknowledged that it was.

"But now you will be happy, my dear cousin. You must tell her at once. Although she is young, she will understand. It will make her more steady. It is the best thing that could happen to her."

Agapit surveyed her in quiet, intense affection. "Softly, my dear girl. You and I are too absorbed in each other. There is the omnipotent Mr. Nimmo to consult."

"He will not oppose. Oh, he will be pleased, enraptured, — I know that he will. I have never thought of it before, because of late years you have seemed not to give your thoughts to marriage, but now it comes to me that, in sending her here, one object might have been that she would please you; that you would please her. I am sure of it now. He is sorry for the past, he wishes to atone, yet he is still proud, and cannot say, 'Forgive me.' This young girl is the peace-offering."

Agapit smiled uneasily. "Pardon me for the

thought, but you dispose somewhat summarily of the young girl."

Rose threw out her hands to him. "Your happiness is perhaps too much to me, yet I would also make her happy in giving her to you. She is so restless, so wayward, — she does not know her own mind yet."

"She seems to be leading a pretty consistent course at present."

Rose's face was like an exquisitely tinted sky at sunrise. "Ah! this is wonderful, it overcomes me; and to think that I should not have suspected it! You adore this little Bidiane. She is everything to you, more than I am, — more than I am."

"I love you for that spice of jealousy," said Agapit, with animation. "Go home now, dear girl, and I will follow; or do you stay here, and I will start first."

"Yes, yes, go; I will remain a time. I will be glad to think this over."

"You will not cry," he said, anxiously, pausing with his hand on the door-knob.

"I will try not to do so."

"Probably I will have to give her up," he said, doggedly. "She is a creature of whims, and I must not speak to her yet; but I do not wish you to suffer."

Rose was deeply moved. This was no boyish

passion, but the unspeakably bitter, weary longing of a man. "If I could not suffer with others I would be dead," she said, simply. "My dear cousin, I will pray for success in this, your touching love-affair."

"Some day I will tell you all about it," he said, abruptly. "I will describe the strange influence that she has always had over me, — an influence that made me tremble before her even when she was a tiny girl, and that overpowered me when she lately returned to us. However, this is not the occasion to talk; my acknowledgment of all this has been quite unpremeditated. Another day it will be more easy — "

"Ah, Agapit, how thou art changed," she said, gliding easily into French; "how I admire thee for thy reserve. That gives thee more power than thou hadst when young. Thou wilt win Bidiane, — do not despair."

"In the meantime there are other, younger men," he responded, in the same language. "I seem old, I know that I do to her."

"Old, and thou art not yet thirty! I assure thee, Agapit, she respects thee for thy age. She laughs at thee, perhaps, to thy face, but she praises thee behind thy back."

"She is not beautiful," said Agapit, irrelevantly, "yet every one likes her."

"And dost thou not find her beautiful? It seems

to me that, when I love, the dear one cannot be ugly."

"Understand me, Rose," said her cousin, earnestly; "once when I loved a woman she instantly became an angel, but one gets over that. Bidiane is even plain-looking to me. It is her soul, her spirit, that charms me, — that little restless, loving heart. If I could only put my hand on it, and say, 'Thou art mine,' I should be the happiest man in the world. She charms me because she changes. She is never the same; a man would never weary of her."

Rose's face became as pale as death. "Agapit, would a man weary of me?"

He did not reply to her. Choked by some emotion, he had again turned to the door.

"I thank the blessed Virgin that I have been spared that sorrow," she murmured, closing her eyes, and allowing her flaxen lashes to softly brush her cheeks. "Once I could only grieve, — now I say perhaps it was well for me not to marry. If I had lost the love of a husband, — a true husband, — it would have killed me very quickly, and it would also have made him say that all women are stupid."

"Rose, thou art incomparable," said Agapit, half laughing, half frowning, and flinging himself back to the table. "No man would tire of thee. Cease thy foolishness, and promise me not to cry when I am gone."

She opened her eyes, looked as startled as if she had been asleep, but submissively gave the required promise.

"Think of something cheerful," he went on.

She saw that he was really distressed, and, disengaging her thoughts from herself by a quiet, intense effort, she roguishly murmured, "I will let my mind run to the conversation that you will have with this fair one — no, this plain one — when you announce your love."

Agapit blushed furiously, and hurried from the room, while Rose, as an earnest of her obedience to him, showed him, at the window, until he was out of sight, a countenance alight with gentle mischief and entire contentment of mind.

CHAPTER X.

A CAMPAIGN BEGUN IN BRIBERY.

"After madness acted, question asked."
TENNYSON.

BEFORE the day was many hours older, Agapit was driving his white horse into the inn yard.

There seemed to be more people about the house then there usually were, and Bidiane, who stood at the side door, was handing a long paper parcel to a man. "Take it away," Agapit heard her say, in peremptory tones; "don't you open it here."

The Acadien to whom she was talking happened to be, Agapit knew, a ne'er-do-weel. He shuffled away, when he caught sight of the young lawyer, but Bidiane ran delightedly towards him. "Oh, Mr. LeNoir, you are as welcome as Mayflowers in April!"

Her face was flushed, there were faint dark circles around the light brown eyes that harmonized so much better with her red hair than blue ones would have done. The sun shone down into these eyes, emphasizing this harmony between them and the hair, and

Agapit, looking deeply into them, forgot immediately the mentor's part that he was to act, and clasped her warmly and approvingly by the hand.

"Come in," she said; but Agapit, who would never sit in the house if it were possible to stay out-of-doors, conducted her to one of the rustic seats by the croquet lawn. He sat down, and she perched in the hammock, sitting on one foot, swinging the other, and overwhelming him with questions about his visit to Halifax.

"And what have you been doing with yourself since I have been away?" he asked, with a hypocritical assumption of ignorance.

"You know very well what I have been doing," she said, rapidly. "Did not I see Rose driving in to call on you this morning? And you have come down to scold me. I understand you perfectly; you cannot deceive me."

Agapit was silent, quite overcome by this mark of feminine insight.

"I will never do it again," she went on, "but I am going to see this through. It is such fun — 'Claude,' said my aunt to her husband, when we first decided to make *bombance*, 'what politics do you belong to?' 'I am a Conservative,' he said; because, you know, my aunt has always told him to vote as the English people about him did. She has known nothing of politics. 'No, you are not,' she replied, 'you are a Liberal;' and Claudine and I nearly exploded with laughter to hear her trying to convince him that he must be a Liberal like our good French Premier, and that he must endeavor to drive the Conservative candidate out. Claude said, 'But we have always been Conservatives, and our house is to be their meeting-place on the day of election.' 'It is the meeting-place for the Liberals,' said my aunt. But Claude would not give in, so he and his party will have the laundry, while we will have the parlor; but I can tell you a secret," and she leaned forward and whispered, " Claude will vote for the Liberal man. Mirabelle Marie will see to that."

"You say Liberal man, — there are two —"

"But one is going to retire."

"And who will take his place?"

"Never mind," she said, smiling provokingly. "The Liberals are going to have a convention tomorrow evening in the Comeauville schoolhouse, and women are going. Then you will see — why there is Father Duvair. What does he wish?"

She sprang lightly from the hammock, and while she watched the priest, Agapit watched her, and saw that she grew first as pale as a lily, then red as a rose.

The parish priest was walking slowly towards the inn. He was a young man of tall, commanding presence, and being a priest "out of France," he had on a *soutane* (cassock) and a three-cornered hat. On the

Bay are Irish priests, Nova Scotian priests, Acadien priests, and French-Canadian priests, but only the priests "out of France" hold to the strictly French customs of dress. The others dress as do the Halifax ecclesiastics, in tall silk or shovel hats and black broadcloth garments like those worn by clergymen of Protestant denominations.

"*Bon jour, mademoiselle*," he said to Bidiane.

"*Bon jour, monsieur le curé*," she replied, with deep respect.

"Is Madame Corbineau within?" he went on, after warmly greeting Agapit, who was an old favorite of his.

"Yes, *monsieur le curé*, — I will take you to her," and she led the way to the house.

In a few minutes she came dejectedly back. "You are in trouble," said Agapit, tenderly; "what is it?"

She glanced miserably at him from under her curling eyelashes. "When Mirabelle Marie went into the parlor, Father Duvair said politely, so politely, 'I wish to buy a little rum, madame; can you sell me some?' My aunt looked at me, and I said, 'Yes, *monsieur le curé*,' for I knew if we set the priest against us we should have trouble, — and then we have not been quite right, I know that."

"Where did you get the rum?" asked Agapit, kindly.

"From a schooner, — two weeks ago, — there were

four casks. It is necessary, you know, to make *bombance*. Some men will not vote without."

"And you have been bribing."

"Not bribing," she said, and she dropped her head; "just coaxing."

"Where did you get the money to buy it?"

For some reason or other she evaded a direct answer to this question, and after much deliberation murmured, in the lowest of voices, that Claudine had had some money.

"Bidiane, she is a poor woman."

"She loves her country," said the girl, flashing out suddenly at him, "and she is not ashamed of it. However, Claude bought the rum and found the bottles, and we always say, 'Take it home, — do not drink it here.' We know that the priests are against drinking, so we had to make haste, for Claudine said they would get after us. Therefore, just now, I at once gave in. Father Duvair said, 'I would like to buy all you have; how much is it worth?' I said fifty dollars, and he pulled the money out of his pocket and Mirabelle Marie took it, and then he borrowed a nail and a hammer and went down in the cellar, and Claudine whispered loudly as he went through the kitchen, 'I wonder whether he will find the cask under the coal?' and he heard her, for she said it on purpose, and he turned and gave her a quick look as he passed."

"I don't understand perfectly," said Agapit, with patient gravity. "This seems to be a house divided against itself. Claudine spends her money for something she hates, and then informs on herself."

Bidiane would not answer him, and he continued, "Is Father Duvair at present engaged in the work of destruction in the cellar?"

"I just told you that he is."

"How much rum will he find there?"

"Two casks," she said, mournfully. "It is what we were keeping for the election."

"And you think it wise to give men that poison to drink?" asked Agapit, in an impartial and judicial manner.

"A little does not hurt; why, some of the women say that it makes their husbands good-natured."

"If you were married, would you like your husband to be a drunkard?"

"No," she said, defiantly; "but I would not mind his getting drunk occasionally, if he would be gentlemanly about it."

Her tone was sharp and irritated, and Agapit, seeing that her nerves were all unstrung, smiled indulgently instead of chiding her.

She smiled, too, rather uncertainly; then she said, "Hush, here is Father Duvair coming back."

That muscular young priest was sauntering towards them, his stout walking-stick under his arm, while he slowly rubbed his damp hands with his white handkerchief.

Agapit stood up when he saw him, and went to meet him, but Bidiane sat still in her old seat in the hammock.

Agapit drew a cheque-book from his pocket, and, resting it on the picket fence, wrote something quickly on it, tore out the leaf, and extended it towards the priest.

"This is for you, father; will you be good enough to hand it to some priest who is unexpectedly called upon to make certain outlays for the good of his parishioners?"

Father Duvair bowed slightly, and, without offering to take it, went on wiping his hands.

"How are you getting on with your business, Agapit?"

"I am fully occupied. My income supports me, and I am even able to lay up a little."

"Are you able to marry?"

"Yes, father, whenever I wish."

A gleam of humor appeared in Father Duvair's eyes, and he glanced towards the apparently careless girl seated in the hammock.

"You will take the cheque, father," said Agapit, "otherwise it will cause me great pain."

The priest reluctantly took the slip of paper from him, then, lifting his hat, he said to Bidiane, "I have the honor to wish you good morning, mademoiselle."

"*Monsieur le curé*," she said, disconsolately, rising and coming towards him, "you must not think me too wicked."

"Mademoiselle, you do not do yourself justice," he said, gravely.

Bidiane's eyes wandered to the spots of moisture on his cassock. "I wish that rum had been in the Bay," she said; "yet, *monsieur le curé*, Mr. Greening is a very bad man."

"Charity, charity, mademoiselle. We all speak hastily at times. Shall I tell you what I think of you?"

"Yes, yes, *monsieur le curé*, if you please."

"I think that you have a good heart, but a hasty judgment. You will, like many others, grow wise as you grow older, yet, mademoiselle, we do not wish you to lose that good heart. Do you not think that Mr. Greening has had his lesson?"

"Yes, I do."

"Then, mademoiselle, you will cease wearying yourself with — with —"

"With unwomanly exertions against him," said Bidiane, with a quivering lip and a laughing eye.

"Hardly that, — but you are vexing yourself unnecessarily."

"Don't you think that my good cousin here ought to go to Parliament?" she asked, wistfully.

Father Duvair laughed outright, refused to commit himself, and went slowly away.

"I like him," said Bidiane, as she watched him out of sight, "he is so even-tempered, and he never scolds his flock as some clergymen do. Just to think of his going down into that cellar and letting all that liquor run out. His boots were quite wet, and did you notice the splashes on his nice black cassock?"

"Yes; who will get the fifty dollars?"

"Dear me, I forgot all about it. I have known a good deal of money to go into my aunt's big pocket, but very little comes out. Just excuse me for a minute, — I may get it if I pounce upon her at once."

Bidiane ran to the house, from whence issued immediately after a lively sound of squealing. In a few minutes she appeared in the doorway, cramming something in her pocket and looking over her shoulder at her aunt, who stood slapping her sides and vowing that she had been robbed.

"I have it all but five dollars," said the girl, breathlessly. "The dear old thing was stuffing it into her stocking for Mr. Nimmo. 'You sha'n't rob Peter to pay Paul,' I said, and I snatched it away from her. Then she squealed like a pig, and ran after me."

"You will give this to Claudine?"

"I don't know. I think I'll have to divide it.

We had to give that maledicted Jean Drague three dollars for his vote. That was my money."

"Where did you see Jean Drague?"

"I went to his house. Some one told me that the Conservative candidate had called, and had laid seven dollars on the mantelpiece. I also called, and there were the seven dollars, so I took them up, and laid down ten instead."

Agapit did not speak, but contented himself with twisting the ends of his mustache in a vigorous manner.

"And the worst of it is that we are not sure of him now," she said, drearily. "I wonder what Mr. Nimmo would say if he knew how I have been acting?"

"I have been wondering, myself."

"Some of you will be kind enough to tell him, I suppose," she said. "Oh, dear, I'm tired," and leaning her head against the hammock supports, she began to cry wearily and dejectedly.

Agapit was nearly frantic. He got up, walked to and fro about her, half stretched out his hand to touch her burnished head, drew it back upon reflecting that the eyes of the street, the neighbors, and the inn might be upon him, and at last said, desperately, "You ought to have a husband, Bidiane. You are a very torrent of energy; you will always be getting into scrapes."

"Why don't you get married yourself?" and she turned an irritated eye upon him.

"I cannot," said Agapit, in sudden calm, and with an inspiration; "the woman that I love does not love me."

"Are you in love?" asked Bidiane, immediately drying her eyes. "Who is she?"

"I cannot tell you."

"Oh, some English girl, I imagine," she said, disdainfully.

"Suppose Mr. Greening could hear you?"

"I am not talking against the English," she retorted, snappishly, "but I should think that you, of all men, would want to marry a woman of your own nation, — the dear little Acadien nation, — the only thing that I love," and she wound up with a despairing sob.

"The girl that I love is an Acadien," said Agapit, in a lower voice, for two men had just driven into the yard.

"Is it Claudine?"

"Claudine has a good education," he said, coldly, "yet she is hardly fitted to be my wife."

"I daresay it is Rose."

"It is not Rose," said Agapit; and rendered desperate by the knowledge that he must not raise his voice, must not seem excited, must not stand too close to her, lest he attract the attention of some of the people at a little distance from them, and yet that he must snatch this, the golden moment, to press his suit upon her, he crammed both hands in his coat pockets, and roamed distractedly around the square of grass.

"Do I know her?" asked Bidiane when, after a time, he came back to the hammock.

"A little, — not thoroughly. You do not appreciate her at her full value."

"Well," said Bidiane, resignedly, "I give it up. I daresay I will find out in time. I can't go over the names of all the girls on the Bay — I wish I knew what it is that keeps our darling Rose and Mr. Nimmo apart."

"I wish I could tell you."

"Is it something that can be got over?"

"Yes."

She swung herself more vigorously in her delight. "If they could only marry, I would be willing to die an old maid."

"But I thought you had already made up your mind to do that," said Agapit, striking an attitude of pretended unconcern.

"Oh, yes, I forgot, — I have made up my mind that I am not suited to matrimony. Just fancy having to ask a man every time you wanted a little money, — and having to be meek and patient all the time. No, indeed, I wish to have my own way rather more than most women do," and, in a gay and heartless derision of the other sex, she hummed a little tune.

"Just wait till you fall in love," said Agapit, threateningly.

"A silly boy asked me to marry him, the other evening. Just as if I would! Why, he is only a baby."

"That was Pius Poirier," said Agapit, delightedly and ungenerously.

"I shall not tell you. I did wrong to mention him," said Bidiane, calmly.

"He is a diligent student; he will get on in the world," said Agapit, more thoughtfully.

"But without me, — I shall never marry."

"I know a man who loves you," said Agapit, cautiously.

"Do you? — well, don't tell me. Tell him, if you have his confidence, that he is a goose for his pains," and Bidiane reclined against her hammock cushions in supreme indifference.

"But he is very fond of you," said Agapit, with exquisite gentleness, "and very unhappy to think that you do not care for him."

Bidiane held her breath and favored him with a sharp glance. Then she sat up very straight. "What makes you so pale?"

"I am sympathizing with that poor man."

"But you are trembling, too."

"Am I?" and with the pretence of a laugh he turned away.

"*Mon cousin*," she said, sweetly, "tell that poor man that I am hoping soon to leave Sleeping Water, and to go out in the world again."

"No, no, Bidiane, you must not," he said, turning restlessly on his heel, and coming back to her.

"Yes, I am. I have become very unhappy here. Every one is against me, and I am losing my health. When I came, I was intoxicated with life. I could run for hours. I was never tired. It was a delight to live. Now I feel weary, and like a consumptive. I think I shall die young. My parents did, you know."

"Yes; they were both drowned. You will pardon me, if I say that I think you have a constitution of iron."

"You are quite mistaken," she said, with dignity. "Time will show that I am right. Unless I leave Sleeping Water at once, I feel that I shall go into a decline."

"May I ask whether you think it a good plan to leave a place immediately upon matters going wrong with one living in it?"

"It would be for me," she said, decidedly.

"Then, mademoiselle, you will never find rest for the sole of your foot."

"I am tired of Sleeping Water," she said, excitedly quitting the hammock, and looking as if she were about to leave him. "I wish to get out in the world to do something. This life is unendurable."

"Bidiane, — dear Bidiane, — you will not leave us?"

"Yes, I will," she said, decidedly; "you are not willing for me to have my own way in one single thing. You are not in the least like Mr. Nimmo," and holding her head well in the air, she walked towards the house.

"Not like Mr. Nimmo," said Agapit, with a darkening brow. "Dear little fool, one would think you had never felt that iron hand in the velvet glove. Because I am more rash and loud-spoken, you misjudge me. You are so young, so foolish, so adorable, so surprised, so intoxicated with what I have said, that you are beside yourself. I am not discouraged, oh, no," and, with a sudden hopeful smile overspreading his face, he was about to spring into his buggy and drive away, when Bidiane came sauntering back to him.

"I am forgetting the duties of hospitality," she said, stiffly. "Will you not come into the house and have something to eat or drink after your long drive?"

"Bidiane," he said, in a low, eager voice, "I am not a harsh man."

"Yes, you are," she said, with a catching of her

breath. " You are against me, and the whole Bay will laugh at me, — and I thought you would be pleased."

" Bidiane," he muttered, casting a desperate glance about him, " I am frantic — oh, for permission to dry those tears! If I could only reveal my heart to you, but you are such a child, you would not understand."

" Will you do as I wish you to ? " she asked, obstinately.

" Yes, yes, anything, my darling one."

" Then you will take Mr. Greening's place ? "

" Oh, the baby, — you do not comprehend this question. I have talked to no one, — I know nothing, — I am not one to put myself forward."

" If you are requested or elected to-night, — or whatever they call it, — will you go up to Halifax to ' make the laws,' as my aunt says ? " inquired Bidiane, smiling slightly, and revealing to him just the tips of her glittering teeth.

" Yes, yes, — anything to please you."

She was again about to leave him, but he detained her. " I, also, have a condition to make in this campaign of bribery. If I am nominated, and run an election, what then, — where is my reward ? "

She hesitated, and he hastened to dissipate the cloud overspreading her face. " Never mind, I bind myself with chains, but I leave you free. Go, little one, I will not detain you, — I exact nothing."

"Thank you," she said, soberly, and, instead of hurrying away, she stood still and watched him leaving the yard.

Just before he reached Weymouth, he put his hand in his pocket to take out his handkerchief. To his surprise there came fluttering out with it a number of bills. He gathered them together, counted them, found that he had just forty-five dollars, and smiling and muttering, "The little sharp-eyes, — I did not think that she took in my transaction with Father Duvair," he went contentedly on his way.

CHAPTER XI.

WHAT ELECTION DAY BROUGHT FORTH.

" Oh, my companions, now should we carouse, now we should strike the ground with a free foot, now is the time to deck the temples of the gods."

ODE 37. HORACE.

IT was election time all through the province of Nova Scotia, and great excitement prevailed, for the Bluenoses are nothing if not keen politicians.

In the French part of the county of Digby there was an unusual amount of interest taken in the election, and considerable amusement prevailed with regard to it.

Mr. Greening had been spirited away. His unwise and untrue remark about the inhabitants of the township Clare had so persistently followed him, and his anger with the three women at the Sleeping Water Inn had at last been so stubbornly and so deeply resented by the Acadiens, who are slow to arouse but difficult to quiet when once aroused, that he had been called upon to make a public apology.

This he had refused to do, and the discomfited

Liberals nad at once relegated him to private life. His prospective political career was ruined. Thenceforward he would lead the life of an unostentatious citizen. He had been chased and whipped out of public affairs, as many another man has been, by an unwise sentence that had risen up against him in his day of judgment.

The surprised Liberals had not far to go to seek his successor. The whole French population had been stirred by the cry of an Acadien for the Acadiens, and Agapit LeNoir, *nolens volens*, but in truth quite *volens*, had been called to become the Liberal nominee. There was absolutely nothing to be said against him. He was a young man, — not too young, — he was of good habits; he was well educated, well bred, and he possessed the respect not only of the population along the Bay, but of many of the English residents of the other parts of the county, who had heard of the diligent young Acadien lawyer of Weymouth.

The wise heads of the Liberal party, in welcoming this new representative to their ranks, had not the slightest doubt of his success.

Without money, without powerful friends, without influence, except that of a blameless career, and without asking for a single vote, he would be swept into public life on a wave of public opinion. However, they did not tell him this, but in secret anxiety they put forth all their efforts towards making sure the calling and election of their other Liberal candidate, who would, from the very fact of Agapit's assured success, be more in danger from the machinations of the one Conservative candidate that the county had returned for years.

One Liberal and one Conservative candidate had been elected almost from time immemorial. This year, if the campaign were skilfully directed in the perilously short time remaining to them, there might be returned, on account of Agapit's sudden and extraordinary popularity, two Liberals and no Conservative at all.

Agapit, in truth, knew very little about elections, although he had always taken a quiet interest in them. He had been too much occupied with his struggle for daily bread for mind and body, to be able to afford much time for outside affairs, and he showed his inexperience immediately after his informal nomination by the convention, and his legal one by the sheriff, by laying strict commands upon Bidiane and her confederates that they should do no more canvassing for him.

Apparently they subsided, but they had gone too far to be wholly repressed, and Mirabelle Marie and Claudine calmly carried on their work of baking enormous batches of pies and cakes, for a whole week before the election took place, and of laying in a stock of confectionery, fruit, and raisins, and of engaging sundry chickens and sides of beef, and also the ovens of neighbors to roast them in.

"For men-folks," said Mirabelle Marie, "is like pigs; if you feed 'em high, they don' squeal."

Agapit did not know what Bidiane was doing. She was shy and elusive, and avoided meeting him, but he strongly suspected that she was the power behind the throne in making these extensive preparations. He was not able to visit the inn except very occasionally, for, according to instructions from headquarters, he was kept travelling from one end of the county to the other, cramming himself with information *en route*, and delivering it, at first stumblingly, but always modestly and honestly, to Acadien audiences, who wagged delighted heads, and vowed that this young fellow should go up to sit in Parliament, where several of his race had already honorably acquitted themselves. What had they been thinking of, the last five years? Formerly they had always had an Acadien representative, but lately they had dropped into an easy-going habit of allowing some Englishman to represent them. The English race were well enough, but why not have a man of your own race? They would take up that old habit again, and this time they would stick to it.

At last the time of canvassing and lecturing was over, and the day of the election came. The Sleeping Water Inn had been scrubbed from the attic to the cellar, every article of furniture was resplendent, and two long tables spread with every variety of dainties known to the Bay had been put up in the two large front rooms of the house.

In these two rooms, the smoking-room and the parlor, men were expected to come and go, eating and drinking at will,—Liberal men, be it understood. The Conservatives were restricted to the laundry, and Claude ruefully surveyed the cold stove, the empty table, and the hard benches set apart for him and his fellow politicians.

He was exceedingly confused in his mind. Mirabelle Marie had explained to him again and again the reason for the sudden change in her hazy beliefs with regard to the conduct of state affairs, but Claude was one Acadien who found it inconsistent to turn a man out of public life on account of one unfortunate word, while so many people in private life could grow, and thrive, and utter scores of unfortunate words without rebuke.

However, his wife had stood over him until he had promised to vote for Agapit, and in great dejection of spirit he smoked his pipe and tried not to meet the eyes of his handful of associates, who did not know that he was to withhold his small support from them.

From early morn till dewy eve the contest went

on between the two parties. All along the shore, and back in the settlements in the woods, men left their work, and, driving to the different polling-places, registered their votes, and then loitered about to watch others do likewise.

It was a general holiday, and not an Acadien and not a Nova Scotian would settle down to work again until the result of the election was known.

Bidiane early retreated to one of the upper rooms of the house, and from the windows looked down upon the crowd about the polling-booth at the corner, or crept to the staircase to listen to jubilant sounds below, for Mirabelle Marie and Claudine were darting about, filling the orders of those who came to buy, but in general insisting on "treating" the Liberal tongues and palates weary from much talking.

Bidiane did not see Agapit, although she had heard some one say that he had gone down the Bay early in the morning. She saw the Conservative candidate, Mr. Folsom, drive swiftly by, waving his hat and shouting a hopeful response to the cheering that greeted him from some of the men at the corner, and her heart died within her at the sound.

Shortly before noon she descended from her watch-tower, and betook herself to the pantry, where she soberly spent the afternoon in washing dishes, only turning her head occasionally as Mirabelle Marie or

Claudine darted in with an armful of soiled cups and saucers and hurried ejaculations such as "They vow Agapit'll go in. There's an awful strong party for him down the Bay. Every one's grinning over that story about old Greening. They say we'll not know till some time in the night — Bidiane, you look pale as a ghost. Go lie down, — we'll manage. I never did see such a time, — and the way they drink! Such thirsty throats! More lemonade glasses, Biddy. It's lucky Father Duvair got that rum, or we'd have 'em all as drunk as goats." And the girl washed on, and looked down the road from the little pantry window, and in a fierce, silent excitement wished that the thing might soon be over, so that her throbbing head would be still.

Soon after five o'clock, when the legal hour for closing the polling-places arrived, they learned the majority for Agapit, for he it was that obtained it in all the villages in the vicinity of Sleeping Water.

"He's in hereabouts," shouted Mirabelle Marie, joyfully, as she came plunging into the pantry, "an' they say he'll git in everywheres. The ole Conservative ain't gut a show at all. Oh, ain't you glad, Biddy?"

"Of course she's glad," said Claudine, giving Mrs. Corbineau a push with her elbow, "but let her alone, can't you? She's tired, so she's quiet about it."

As it grew dark, the returns from the whole, or

nearly the whole county came pouring in. Men mounted on horseback, or driving in light carts, came dashing up to the corner to receive the latest news from the crowd about the telephone office, and receiving it, dashed on again to impart the news to others. Soon they knew quite surely, although there were some backwoods districts still to be heard from. In them the count could be pretty accurately reckoned, for it did not vary much from year to year. They could be relied on to remain Liberal or Conservative, as the case might be.

Bidiane, who had again retreated up-stairs, for nothing would satisfy her but being alone, heard, shortly after it grew quite dark, a sudden uproar of joyous and incoherent noises below.

She ran to the top of the front staircase. The men, many of whom had been joined by their wives, had left the dreary polling-place, which was an unused shop, and had sought the more cheerful shelter of the inn. Soft showers of rain were gently falling, but many of the excited Acadiens stood heedlessly on the grass outside, or leaned from the veranda to exchange exultant cries with those of their friends who went driving by. Many others stalked about the hall and front rooms, shaking hands, clapping shoulders, congratulating, laughing, joking, and rejoicing, while Mirabelle Marie, her fat face radiant with glee, plunged about among them like a huge, unwieldy duck, flourishing her apron, and making more noise and clatter than all the rest of the women combined.

Agapit was in, — in by an overwhelming majority. His name headed the lists; the other Liberal candidate followed him at a respectful distance, and the Conservative candidate was nowhere at all.

Bidiane trembled like a leaf; then, pressing her hands over her ears, she ran to hide herself in a closet.

In the meantime, the back of the house was gloomy. One by one the Conservatives were slipping away home; still, a few yet lingered, and sat dispiritedly looking at each other and the empty wash-tubs in the laundry, while they passed about a bottle of weak raspberry vinegar and water, which was the only beverage Mirabelle and Claudine had allowed them.

Claude, as in honor bound, sat with them until his wife, who gloried in including every one within reach in what she called her "jollifications," came bounding in, and ordered them all into the front of the house, where the proceedings of the day were to be wound up with a supper.

Good-humored raillery greeted Claude and his small flock of Conservatives when Mirabelle Marie came driving them in before her.

"Ah, Joe à Jack, where is thy doubloon?" called

out a Liberal. "Thou hast lost it, — thy candidate is in the Bay. It is all up with him. And thou, Guillaume, — away to the shore with thee. You remember, boys, he promised to swallow a dog-fish, tail first, if Agapit LeNoir went in."

A roar of laughter greeted this announcement, and the unfortunate Guillaume was pushed into a seat, and had a glass thrust into his hand. "Drink, cousin, to fortify thee for thy task. A dog-fish, — *sakerjé!* but it will be prickly swallowing."

"Biddy Ann, Biddy Ann," shrieked her aunt, up the staircase, "come and hear the good news," but Bidiane, who was usually social in her instincts, was now eccentric and solitary, and would not respond.

"Skedaddle up-stairs and hunt her out, Claudine," said Mrs. Corbineau; but Bidiane, hearing the request, cunningly ran to the back of the house, descended the kitchen stairway, and escaped out-of-doors. She would go up to the horseshoe cottage and see Rose. There, at least, it would be quiet; she hated this screaming.

Her small feet went pit-a-pat over the dark road. There were lights in all the windows. Everybody was excited to-night. Everybody but herself. She was left out of the general rejoicing, and a wave of injured feeling and of desperate dissatisfaction and bodily fatigue swept over her. And she had fancied that Agapit's election would plunge her into a tumult of joy.

However, she kept on her way, and dodging a party of hilarious young Acadiens, who were lustily informing the neighborhood that the immortal Malbrouck had really gone to the wars at last, she took to the wet grass and ran across the fields to the cottage.

There were two private bridges across Sleeping Water just here, the Comeau bridge and Rose à Charlitte's. Bidiane trotted nimbly over the former, jumped a low stone wall, and found herself under the windows of Rose's parlor.

Why, there was the hero of the day talking to Rose! What was he doing here? She had fancied him the centre of a crowd of men, — he, speech-making, and the cynosure of all eyes, — and here he was, quietly lolling in an easy chair by the fire that Rose always had on cool, rainy evenings. However, he had evidently just arrived, for his boots were muddy, and his white horse, instead of being tied to the post, was standing patiently by the door, — a sure sign that his master was not to stay long.

Well, she would go home. They looked comfortable in there, and they were carrying on an animated conversation. They did not want her, and, frowning impatiently, she uttered an irritable "Get away!" to the friendly white horse, who, taking advantage of one of the few occasions when he was not attached to the buggy, which was the bane of his existence, had approached, and was extending a curious and sympathetically quivering nose in her direction.

The horse drew back, and, moving his ears sensitively back and forth, watched her going down the path to the river.

CHAPTER XII.

BIDIANE FALLS IN A RIVER.

" He laid a finger under her chin,
   His arm for her girdle at waist was thrown;
Now, what will happen, and who will win,
   With me in the fight and my lady-love?

" Sleek as a lizard at round of a stone,
   The look of her heart slipped out and in.
Sweet on her lord her soft eyes shone,
   As innocents clear of a shade of sin."
                               GEORGE MEREDITH.

FIVE minutes later, Agapit left Rose, and, coming out-of-doors, stared about for his horse, Turenne, who was nowhere to be seen.

While he stood momentarily expecting to see the big, familiar white shape loom up through the darkness, he fancied that he heard some one calling his name.

He turned his head towards the river. There was a fine, soft wind blowing, the sky was dull and moist, and, although the rain had ceased for a time, it was evidently going to fall again. Surely he had been mistaken about hearing his name, unless Turenne had suddenly been gifted with the power of speech. No, — there it was again; and now he discovered that it was uttered in the voice that, of all the voices in the world, he loved best to hear, and it was at present ejaculating, in peremptory and impatient tones, "Agapit! Agapit!"

He precipitated himself down the hill, peering through the darkness as he went, and on the way running afoul of his white nag, who stood staring with stolid interest at a small round head beside the bridge, and two white hands that were clinging to its rustic foundations.

"Do help me out," said Bidiane; "my feet are quite wet."

Agapit uttered a confused, smothered exclamation, and, stooping over, seized her firmly by the shoulders, and drew her out from the clinging embrace of Sleeping Water.

"I never saw such a river," said Bidiane, shaking herself like a small wet dog, and avoiding her lover's shocked glance. "It is just like jelly."

"Come up to the house," he ejaculated.

"No, no; it would only frighten Rose. She is getting to dislike this river, for people talk so much against it. I will go home."

"Then let me put you on Turenne's back," said Agapit, pointing to his horse as he stood curiously regarding them.

"No, I might fall off — I have had enough frights for to-night," and she shuddered. "I shall run home. I never take cold. *Ma foi!* but it is good to be out of that slippery mud."

Agapit hurried along beside her. "How did it happen?"

"I was just going to cross the bridge. The river looked so sleepy and quiet, and so like a mirror, that I wondered if I could see my face, if I bent close to it. I stepped on the bank, and it gave way under me, and then I fell in; and to save myself from being sucked down I clung to the bridge, and waited for you to come, for I didn't seem to have strength to drag myself out."

Agapit could not speak for a time. He was struggling with an intense emotion that would have been unintelligible to her if he had expressed it. At last he said, "How did you know that I was here?"

"I saw you," said Bidiane, and she slightly slackened her pace, and glanced at him from the corners of her eyes.

"Through the window?"

"Yes."

"Why did you not come in?"

"I did not wish to do so."

"You are jealous," he exclaimed, and he endeavored to take her hand.

"Let my hand alone, — you flatter yourself."

"You were frightened there in the river, little one," he murmured.

Bidiane paused for an instant, and gazed over her shoulder. "Your old horse is nearly on my heels, and his eyes are like carriage lamps."

"Back!" exclaimed Agapit, to the curious and irrepressible Turenne.

"You say nothing of your election," remarked Bidiane. "Are you glad?"

He drew a rapid breath, and turned his red face towards her again. "My mind is in a whirl, little cousin, and my pulses are going like hammers. You do not know what it is to sway men by the tongue. When one stands up, and speaks, and the human faces spreading out like a flower-bed change and lighten, or grow gloomy, as one wishes, it is majestic, — it makes a man feel like a deity."

"You will get on in the world," said Bidiane, impulsively. "You have it in you."

"But must I go alone?" he said, passionately. "Bidiane, you, though so much younger, you understand me. I have been happy to-day, yes, happy, for amid all the excitement, the changing faces, the buzzing of talk in my ears, there has been one little countenance before me — "

"Yes, — Rose's."

"You treat me as if I were a boy," he said, vehemently, " on this day when I was so important. Why are you so flippant ? "

" Don't be angry with me," she said, coaxingly.

" Angry," he muttered, in a shocked voice. " I am not angry. How could I be with you, whom I love so much ? "

" Easily," she murmured. " I scarcely wished to see you to-day. I almost dreaded to hear you had been elected, for I thought you would be angry because we — because Claudine, and my aunt, and I, talked against Mr. Greening, and drove him out, and suggested you. I know men don't like to be helped by women."

" Your efforts counted," he said, patiently, and yet with desperate haste, for they were rapidly nearing the inn, " yet you know Sleeping Water is a small district, and the county is large. There was in some places great dissatisfaction with Mr. Greening, but don't talk of him. My dear one, will you — "

" You don't know the worst thing about me," she interrupted, in a low voice. " There was one dreadful thing I did."

He checked an oncoming flow of endearing words, and stared at her. " You have been flirting," he said at last.

" Worse than that," she said, shamefacedly. " If you say first that you will forgive me, I will tell you about it — no, I will not either. I shall just tell you, and if you don't want to overlook it you need not — why, what is the matter with you?"

"Nothing, nothing," he muttered, with an averted face. He had suddenly become as rigid as marble, and Bidiane surveyed him in bewildered surprise, until a sudden illumination broke over her, when she lapsed into nervous amusement.

"You have always been very kind to me, very interested," she said, with the utmost gentleness and sweetness; "surely you are not going to lose patience now."

"Go on," said Agapit, stonily, "tell me about this — this escapade."

"How bad a thing would I have to do for you not to forgive me?" she asked.

"Bidiane — *de grâce*, continue."

"But I want to know," she said, persistently. "Suppose I had just murdered some one, and had not a friend in the world, would you stand by me?"

He would not reply to her, and she went on, "I know you think a good deal of your honor, but the world is full of bad people. Some one ought to love them — if you were going to be hanged to-morrow I would visit you in your cell. I would take you flowers and something to eat, and I might even go to the scaffold with you."

Agapit in dumb anguish, and scarcely knowing

what he did, snatched his hat from his head and swung it to and fro.

"You had better put on your hat," she said, amiably, "you will take cold."

Agapit, suddenly seized her by the shoulders and, holding her firmly, but gently, stared into her eyes that were full of tears. "Ah! you amuse yourself by torturing me," he said, with a groan of relief. "You are as pure as a snowdrop, you have not been flirting."

"Oh, I am so angry with you for being hateful and suspicious," she said, proudly, and with a heaving bosom, and she averted her face to brush the tears from her eyes. "You know I don't care a rap for any man in the world but Mr. Nimmo, except the tiniest atom of respect for you."

Agapit at once broke into abject apologies, and being graciously forgiven, he humbly entreated her to continue the recital of her misdeeds.

"It was when we began to make *bombance*," she said, in a lofty tone. "Every one assured us that we must have rum, but Claudine would not let us take her money for it, because her husband drank until he made his head queer and had that dreadful fall. She said to buy anything with her money but liquor. We didn't know what to do until one day a man came in and told us that if we wanted money we should go to the rich members of our party. He mentioned Mr. Smith, in Weymouth, and I said, 'Well, I will go and ask him for money to buy something for these wicked men to stop them from voting for a wretch who calls us names.' 'But you must not say that,' replied the man, and he laughed. 'You must go to Mr. Smith and say, "There is an election coming on, and there will be great doings at the Sleeping Water Inn, and it ought to be painted."' 'But it has just been painted,' I said. 'Never mind,' he told me, 'it must be painted.' Then I understood, and Claudine and I went to Mr. Smith, and asked him if it would not be a wise thing to paint the inn, and he laughed and said, ' By all manner of means, yes, — give it a good thick coat and make it stick on well,' and he gave us some bills."

"How many?" asked Agapit, for Bidiane's voice was sinking lower and lower.

"One hundred dollars, — just what Claudine had."

"And you spent it, dearest child?"

"Yes, it just melted away. You know how money goes. But I shall pay it back some day."

"How will you get the money?"

"I don't know," she said, with a sigh. "I shall try to earn it."

"You may earn it now, in the quarter of a minute," he said, fatuously.

"And you call yourself an honest man — you talk against bribery and corruption, you doubt poor lonely orphans when they are going to confess little peccadilloes, and fancy in your wicked heart that they have committed some awful sin!" said Bidiane, in low, withering tones. "I think you had better go home, sir."

They had arrived in front of the inn, and, although Agapit knew that she ought to go at once and put off her wet shoes, he still lingered, and said, delightedly, in low, cautious tones, "But, Bidiane, you have surely a little affection for me — and one short kiss — very short — certainly it would not be so wicked."

"If you do not love a man, it is a crime to embrace him," she said, with cold severity.

"Then I look forward to more gracious times," he replied. "Good night, little one, in twenty minutes I must be in Belliveau's Cove."

Bidiane, strangely subdued in appearance, stood watching him as, with eyes riveted on her, he extended a grasping hand towards Turenne's hanging bridle. When he caught it he leaped into the saddle, and Bidiane, supposing herself to be rid of him, mischievously blew him a kiss from the tips of her fingers.

In a trice he had thrown himself from Turenne's back and had caught her as she started to run swiftly to the house.

"Do not squeal, dear slippery eel," he said, laughingly, "thou hast called me back, and I shall kiss thee. Now go," and he released her, as she struggled in his embrace, laughing for the first time since her capture by the river. "Once I have held you in my arms — now you will come again," and shaking his head and with many a backward glance, he set off through the rain and the darkness towards his waiting friends and supporters, a few miles farther on.

An hour later, Claudine left the vivacious, unwearied revellers below, and went up-stairs to see whether Bidiane had returned home. She found her in bed, staring thoughtfully at the ceiling.

"Claudine," she said, turning her brown eyes on her friend and admirer, "how did you feel when Isidore asked you to marry him?"

"How did I feel — *miséricorde*, how can I tell? For one thing, I wished that he would give up the drink."

"But how did you feel towards him?" asked Bidiane, curiously. "Was it like being lost in a big river, and swimming about for ages, and having noises in your head, and some one else was swimming about trying to find you, and you couldn't touch his hand for a long time, and then he dragged you out to the shore, which was the shore of matrimony?"

Claudine, who found nothing in the world more delectable than Bidiane's fancies, giggled with delight. Then she asked her where she had spent the evening.

Bidiane related her adventure, whereupon Claudine said, dryly, " I guess the other person in your river must be Agapit LeNoir."

"Would you marry him if he asked you?" said Bidiane.

" Mercy, how do I know — has he said anything of me?"

" No, no," replied Bidiane, hastily. " He wants to marry me."

"That's what I thought," said Claudine, soberly. " I can't tell you what love is. You can't talk it. I guess he'll teach you if you give him a chance. He's a good man, Bidiane. You'd better take him — it's an opening for you, too. He'll get on out in the world."

Bidiane laid her head back on her pillow, and slipped again into a hazy, dreamy condition of mind, in which the ever recurring subject of meditation was the one of the proper experience and manifestation of love between men and the women they adore.

"I don't love him, yet what makes me so cross when he looks at another woman, even my beloved Rose?" she murmured; and with this puzzling question bravely to the fore she fell asleep.

CHAPTER XIII.

CHARLITTE COMES BACK.

" From dawn to gloaming, and from dark to dawn,
    Dreams the unvoiced, declining Michaelmas.
    O'er all the orchards where a summer was
The noon is full of peace, and loiters on.
The branches stir not as the light airs run
    All day; their stretching shadows slowly pass
    Through the curled surface of the faded grass,
Telling the hours of the cloudless sun."

                              J. F. H.

THE last golden days of summer had come, and the Acadien farmers were rejoicing in a bountiful harvest. Day by day huge wagons, heaped high with grain, were driven to the threshing-mills, and day by day the stores of vegetables and fruit laid in for the winter were increased in barn and storehouse.

Everything had done well this year, even the flower gardens, and some of the more pious of the women attributed their abundance of blossoms to the blessing of the seeds by the parish priests.

Agapit LeNoir, who now naturally took a broader

and wider interest in the affairs of his countrymen, sat on Rose à Charlitte's lawn, discussing matters in general. Soon he would have to go to Halifax for his first session of the local legislature. Since his election he had come a little out of the shyness and reserve that had settled upon him in his early manhood. He was now usually acknowledged to be a rising young man, and one sure to become a credit to his nation and his province. He would be a member of the Dominion Parliament some day, the old people said, and in his more mature age he might even become a Senator. He had obtained just what he had needed, — a start in life. Everything was open to him now. With his racial zeal and love for his countrymen, he could become a representative man, — an Acadien of the Acadiens.

Then, too, he would marry an accomplished wife, who would be of great assistance to him, for it was a well-known fact that he was engaged to his lively distant relative, Bidiane LeNoir, the young girl who had been educated abroad by the Englishman from Boston.

Just now he was talking to this same relative, who, instead of sitting down quietly beside him, was pursuing an erratic course of wanderings about the trees on the lawn. She professed to be looking for a robin's deserted nest, but she was managing at the same time to give careful attention to what her lover was saying, as he sat with eyes fixed now upon her, now upon the Bay, and waved at intervals the long pipe that he was smoking.

"Yes," he said, continuing his subject, "that is one of the first things I shall lay before the House — the lack of proper schoolhouse accommodation on the Bay."

"You are very much interested in the schoolhouses," said Bidiane, sarcastically. "You have talked of them quite ten minutes."

His face lighted up swiftly. "Let us return, then, to our old, old subject, — will you not reconsider your cruel decision not to marry me, and go with me to Halifax this autumn?"

"No," said Bidiane, decidedly, yet with an evident liking for the topic of conversation presented to her. "I have told you again and again that I will not. I am surprised at your asking. Who would comfort our darling Rose?"

"Possibly, I say, only possibly, she is not as dependent upon us as you imagine."

"Dependent! of course she is dependent. Am I not with her nearly all the time. See, there she comes, — the beauty! She grows more charming every day. She is like those lovely Flemish women, who are so tall, and graceful, and simple, and elegant, and whose heads are like burnished gold. I wish you could see them, Agapit. Mr. Nimmo says they have preserved intact the admirable *naïveté* of the women of the Middle Ages. Their husbands are often brutal, yet they never rebel."

"Is *naïveté* justifiable under those circumstances, *mignonne?*"

"Hush, — she will hear you. Now what does that boy want, I wonder. Just see him scampering up the road."

He wished to see her, and was soon stumbling through a verbal message. Bidiane kindly but firmly followed him in it, and, stopping him whenever he used a corrupted French word, made him substitute another for it.

"No, Raoul, not *j'étions* but *j'étais*" (I was). "*Petit mieux*" (a little better), "not *p'tit mieux. La rue* not *la street. Ces jeunes demoiselles*" (those young ladies), "not *ces jeunes ladies.*"

"They are so careless, these Acadiens of ours," she said, turning to Agapit, with a despairing gesture. "This boy knows good French, yet he speaks the impure. Why do his people say *becker* for *baiser*" (kiss) "and *gueule* for *bouche*" (mouth) "and *échine* for *dos*" (back)? "It is so vulgar!"

"Patience," muttered Agapit, "what does he wish?"

"His sister Lucie wants you and me to go up to Grosses Coques this evening to supper. Some of the D'Entremonts are coming from Pubnico. There will be a big wagon filled with straw, and all the young people from here are going, Raoul says. It will be fun; will you go?"

"Yes, if it will please you."

"It will," and she turned to the boy. "Run home, Raoul, and tell Lucie that we accept her invitation. Thou art not vexed with me for correcting thee?"

"*Nenni*" (no), said the child, displaying a dimple in his cheek.

Bidiane caught him and kissed him. "In the spring we will have great fun, thou and I. We will go back to the woods, and with a sharp knife tear the bark from young spruces, and eat the juicy *bobillon* inside. Then we will also find candy. Canst thou dig up the fern roots and peel them until thou findest the tender morsel at the bottom?"

"*Oui*," laughed the child, and Bidiane, after pushing him towards Rose, for an embrace from her, conducted him to the gate.

"Is there any use in asking Rose to go with us this evening?" she said, coming back to Agapit, and speaking in an undertone.

"No, I think not."

"Why is it that she avoids all junketing, and sits only with sick people?"

He murmured an uneasy, unintelligible response, and Bidiane again directed her attention to Rose. "What are you staring at so intently, *ma chère?*"

"That beautiful stranger," said Rose, nodding towards the Bay. "It is a new sail."

"Every woman on the Bay knows the ships but me," said Bidiane, discontentedly. "I have got out of it from being so long away."

"And why do the girls know the ships?" asked Agapit.

Bidiane discreetly refused to answer him.

"Because they have lovers on board. Your lover stays on shore, little one."

"And poor Rose looks over the sea," said Bidiane, dreamily. "I should think that you might trust me now with the story of her trouble, whatever it is, but you are so reserved, so fearful of making wild statements. You don't treat me as well even as you do a business person, — a client is it you call one?"

Agapit smiled happily. "Marry me, then, and in becoming your advocate I will deal plainly with you as a client, and state fully to you all the facts of this case."

"I daresay we shall have frightful quarrels when we are married," said Bidiane, cheerfully.

"I daresay."

"Just see how Rose stares at that ship.

"She is a beauty," said Agapit, critically, "and foreign rigged."

There was "a free wind" blowing, and the beautiful stranger moved like a graceful bird before it. Rose — the favorite occupation in whose quiet life was to watch the white sails that passed up and down the Bay — still kept her eyes fixed on it, and presently said, "The stranger is pointing towards Sleeping Water."

"I will get the marine glass," said Bidiane, running to the house.

"She is putting out a boat," said Rose, when she came back. "She is coming in to the wharf."

"Allow me to see for one minute, Rose," said Agapit, and he extended his hand for the glass; then silently watched the sailors running about and looking no larger than ants on the distant deck.

"They are not going to the wharf," said Bidiane. "They are making for that rock by the inn bathing-house. Perhaps they will engage in swimming."

A slight color appeared in Rose's cheeks, and she glanced longingly at the glass that Agapit still held. The mystery of the sea and the magic of ships and of seafaring lives was interwoven with her whole being. She felt an intense gentle interest in the strange sail and the foreign sailors, and nothing would have given her greater pleasure than to have shown them some kindness.

"I wish," she murmured, "that I were now at the inn. They should have a jug of cream, and some fresh fruit."

The horseshoe cottage being situated on rising ground, a little beyond the river, afforded the three people on the lawn an uninterrupted view of the movements of the boat. While Bidiane prattled on, and severely rebuked Agapit for his selfishness in keeping the glass to himself, Rose watched the boat touching the big rocks, where one man sprang from it, and walked towards the inn.

She could see his figure in the distance, looking at first scarcely larger than a black lead pencil, but soon taking on the dimensions of a rather short, thick-set man. He remained stationary on the inn veranda for a few minutes, then, leaving it, he passed down the village street.

"It is some stranger from abroad, asking his way about," said Bidiane; "one of the numerous Comeau tribe, no doubt. Oh, I hope he will go on the drive to-night."

"Why, I believe he is coming here," she exclaimed, after another period of observation of the stranger's movements; "he is passing by all the houses. Yes, he is turning in by the cutting through the hill. Who can he be?"

Rose and Agapit, grown strangely silent, did not answer her, and, without thinking of examining their faces, she kept her eyes fixed on the man rapidly approaching them.

"He is neither old nor young," she said, vivaciously. "Yes, he is, too,— he is old. His hair is quite gray. He swaggers a little bit. I think he must be the captain of the beautiful stranger. There is an indefinable something about him that doesn't belong to a common sailor; don't you think so, Agapit?"

Her red head tilted itself sideways, yet she still kept a watchful eye on the newcomer. She could now see that he was quietly dressed in dark brown clothes, that his complexion was also brown, his eyes small and twinkling, his lips thick, and partly covered by a short, grizzled mustache. He wore on his head a white straw hat, that he took off when he neared the group.

His face was now fully visible, and there was a wild cry from Rose. "Ah, Charlitte, Charlitte,— you have come back!"

CHAPTER XIV.

BIDIANE RECEIVES A SHOCK.

"Whate'er thy lot, whoe'er thou be, —
Confess thy folly, kiss the rod,
And in thy chastening sorrow, see
The hand of God."
                        MONTGOMERY.

BIDIANE flashed around upon her companions. Rose — pale, trembling, almost unearthly in a beauty from which everything earthly and material seemed to have been purged away — stood extending her hands to the wanderer, her only expression one of profound thanksgiving for his return.

Agapit, on the contrary, sat stock-still, his face convulsed with profound and bitter contempt, almost with hatred; and Bidiane, in speechless astonishment, stared from him to the others.

Charlitte was not dead, — he had returned; and Rose was not surprised, — she was even glad to see him! What did it mean, and where was Mr. Nimmo's share in this reunion? She clenched her hands, her eyes filled with despairing tears, and, in subdued anger, she surveyed the very ordinary-looking man, who had surrendered one of his brown hands to Rose, in pleased satisfaction.

"You are more stunning than ever, Rose," he said, coolly kissing her; "and who is this young lady?" and he pointed a sturdy forefinger at Bidiane, who stood in the background, trembling in every limb.

"It is Bidiane LeNoir, Charlitte, from up the Bay. Bidiane, come shake hands with my husband."

"I forbid," said Agapit, calmly. He had recovered himself, and, with a face as imperturbable as that of the sphinx, he now sat staring up into the air.

"Agapit," said Rose, pleadingly, "will you not greet my husband after all these years?"

"No," he said, "I will not," and coolly taking up his pipe he lighted it, turned away from them, and began to smoke.

Rose, with her blue eyes dimmed with tears, looked at her husband. "Do not be displeased. He will forgive in time; he has been a brother to me all the years that you have been away."

Charlitte understood Agapit better than she did, and, shrugging his shoulders as if to beg her not to distress herself, he busied himself with staring at Bidiane, whose curiosity and bewilderment had culminated in a kind of stupefaction, in which she stood surreptitiously pinching her arm in order to convince herself that this wonderful reappearance was real, — that the man sitting so quietly before her was actually the husband of her beloved Rose.

Charlitte's eyes twinkled mischievously, as he surveyed her. "Were you ever shipwrecked, young lady?" he asked.

Bidiane shuddered, and then, with difficulty, ejaculated, "No, never."

"I was," said Charlitte, unblushingly, "on a cannibal island. All the rest of the crew were eaten. I was the only one spared, and I was left shut up in a hut in a palm grove until six months ago, when a passing ship took me off and brought me to New York."

Bidiane, by means of a vigorous effort, was able to partly restore her mind to working order. Should she believe this man or not? She felt dimly that she did not like him, yet she could not resist Rose's touching, mute entreaty that she should bestow some recognition on the returned one. Therefore she said, confusedly, "Those cannibals, where did they live?"

"In the South Sea Islands, 'way yonder," and Charlitte's eyes seemed to twinkle into immense distance.

Rose was hanging her head. This recital pained her, and before Bidiane could again speak, she said, hurriedly, "Do not mention it. Our Lord and the blessed Virgin have brought you home. Ah! how glad Father Duvair will be, and the village."

"Good heavens!" said Charlitte. "Do you think I care for the village. I have come to see you."

For the first time Rose shrank from him, and Agapit brought down his eyes from the sky to glance keenly at him.

"Charlitte," faltered Rose, "there have been great changes since you went away. I — I — " and she hesitated, and looked at Bidiane.

Bidiane shrank behind a spruce-tree near which she was standing, and from its shelter looked out like a small red squirrel of an inquiring turn of mind. She felt that she was about to be banished, and in the present dazed state of her brain she dreaded to he alone.

Agapit's inexorable gaze sought her out, and, taking his pipe from his mouth, he sauntered over to her. "Wilt thou run away, little one? We may have something to talk of not fit for thy tender ears."

"Yes, I will," she murmured, shocked into unexpected submission by the suppressed misery of his voice. "I will be in the garden," and she darted away.

The coast was now clear for any action the new arrival might choose to take. His first proceeding was to stare hard at Agapit, as if he wished that he, too, would take himself away; but this Agapit had no intention of doing, and he smoked on imperturbably, pretending not to see Charlitte's irritated glances, and keeping his own fixed on the azure depths of the sky.

"You mention changes," said Charlitte, at last, turning to his wife. "What changes?"

"You have just arrived, you have heard nothing, — and yet there would be little to hear about me, and Sleeping Water does not change much, — yet — "

Charlitte's cool glance wandered contemptuously over that part of the village nearest them. "It is dull here, — as dull as the cannibal islands. I think moss would grow on me if I stayed."

"But it would break my heart to leave it," said Rose, desperately.

"I would take good care of you," he said, jocularly. "We would go to New Orleans. You would amuse yourself well. There are young men there, — plenty of them, — far smarter than the boys on the Bay."

Rose was in an agony. With frantic eyes she devoured the cool, cynical face of her husband, then, with a low cry, she fell on her knees before him. "Charlitte, Charlitte, I must confess."

Charlitte at once became intensely interested, and forgot to watch Agapit, who, however, got up, and, savagely biting his pipe, strolled to a little distance.

"I have done wrong, my husband," sobbed Rose.

Charlitte's eyes twinkled. Was he going to hear a confession of guilt that would make his own seem lighter?

"Forgive me, forgive me," she moaned. "My heart is glad that you have come back, yet, oh, my husband, I must tell you that it also cries out for another."

"For Agapit?" he said, kindly, stroking her clenched hands.

"No, — no, no, for a stranger. You know I never loved you as a woman should love her husband. I was so young when I married. I thought only of attending to my house. Then you went away; I was sorry, so sorry, when news came of your death, but my heart was not broken. Five years ago this stranger came, and I felt — oh, I cannot tell you — but I found what this love was. Then I had to send him away, but, although he was gone, he seemed to be still with me. I thought of him all the time, — the wind seemed to whisper his words in my ear as I walked. I saw his handsome face, his smiling eyes. I went daily over the paths his feet used to take. After a long, long time, I was able to tear him from my mind. Now I know that I shall never see him again, that I shall only meet him after

I die, yet I feel that I belong to him, that he belongs to me. Oh, my husband, this is love, and is it right that, feeling so, I should go with you?"

"Who is this man?" asked Charlitte. "What is he called?"

Rose winced. "Vesper is his name; Vesper Nimmo, — but do not let us talk of him. I have put him from my mind."

"Did he make love to you?"

"Oh, yes; but let us pass over, — it is wicked to talk of it now."

Charlitte, who was not troubled with any delicacy of feeling, was about to put some searching and crucial questions to her, but forbore, moved, despite himself, by the anguish and innocence of the gaze bent upon him. "Where is he now?"

"In Paris. I have done wrong, wrong," and she again buried her face in her hands, and her whole frame shook with emotion. "Having had one husband, it would have been better to have thought only of him. I do not think one should marry again, unless — "

"Nonsense," said Charlitte, abruptly. "The fellow should have married you. He got tired, I guess. By this time he's had half a dozen other fancies."

Rose shrank from him in speechless horror, and, seeing it, Charlitte made haste to change the subject of conversation. "Where is the boy?"

"He is with him," she said, hurriedly.

"That was pretty cute in you," said Charlitte, with a good-natured vulgar laugh. "You were afraid I'd come home and take him from you, — you always were a little fool, Rose. Get up off the grass, and sit down, and don't distress yourself so. This isn't a hanging matter, and I'm not going to bully you; I never did."

"No, never," she said, with a fresh outburst of tears. "You were always kind, my husband."

"I think our marriage was all a mistake," he said, good-humoredly, "but we can't undo it. I knew you never liked me, — if you had, I might never — that is, things might have been different. Tell me now when that fool, Agapit, first began to set you against me?"

"He has not set me against you, my husband; he rarely speaks of you."

"When did you first find out that I wasn't dead?" said Charlitte, persistently; and Rose, who was as wax in his hands, was soon saying, hesitatingly, "I first knew that he did not care for you when Mr. Nimmo went away."

"How did you know?"

"He broke your picture, my husband, — oh, do not make me tell what I do not wish to."

"How did he break it?" asked Charlitte, and his face darkened.

"He struck it with his hand, — but I had it mended."

"He was mad because I was keeping you from the other fellow. Then he told you that you had better give him the mitten?"

"Yes," said Rose, sighing heavily, and sitting mute, like a prisoner awaiting sentence.

"You have not done quite right, Rose," said her husband, mildly, "not quite right. It would have been better for you to have given that stranger the go by. He was only amusing himself. Still, I can't blame you. You're young, and mighty fine looking, and you've kept on the straight through your widowhood. I heard once from some sailors how you kept the young fellows off, and you always said you'd had a good husband. I shall never forget that you called me good, Rose, for there are some folks that think I am pretty bad."

"Then they are evil folks," she said, tremulously; "are we not all sinners? Does not our Lord command us to forgive those who repent?"

A curious light came into Charlitte's eyes, and he put his tongue in his cheek. Then he went on, calmly. "I'm on my way from Turk's Island to Saint John, New Brunswick, — I've got a cargo of salt to unload there, and, 'pon my word, I hadn't a thought of calling here until I got up in the Bay, working towards Petit Passage. I guess it was old habit that made me run for this place, and I thought I'd give you a call, and see if you were moping to death, and wanted to go away with me. If you do, I'll be glad to have you. If not, I'll not bother you."

A deadly faintness came over Rose. "Charlitte, are you not sorry for your sin? Ah! tell me that you repent. And will you not talk to Father Duvair? So many quiet nights I think of you and pray that you may understand that you are being led into this wickedness. That other woman, — she is still living?"

"What other woman? Oh, Lord, yes, — I thought that fool Agapit had had spies on me."

Rose was so near fainting that she only half comprehended what he said.

"I wish you'd come with me," he went on, jocosely. "If you happened to worry I'd send you back to this dull little hole. You're not going to swoon, are you? Here, put your head on this," and he drew up to her a small table on which Bidiane had been playing solitaire. "You used not to be delicate."

"I am not now," she whispered, dropping her head on her folded arms, "but I cannot hold myself up. When I saw you come, I thought it was to say you were sorry. Now —"

"Come, brace up, Rose," he said, uneasily. "I'll sit down beside you for awhile. There's lots of time for me to repent yet," and he chuckled shortly and struck his broad chest with his fist. "I'm as strong as a horse; there's nothing wrong with me, except a little rheumatism, and I'll outgrow that. I'm only fifty-two, and my father died at ninety. Come on, girl, — don't cry. I wish I hadn't started this talk of taking you away. You'd be glad of it, though, if you'd go. Listen till I tell you what a fine place New Orleans is — "

Rose did not listen to him. She still sat with her flaxen head bowed on her arms, that rested on the little table. She was a perfect picture of silent, yet agitated distress.

"You are not praying, are you?" asked her husband, in a disturbed manner. "I believe you are. Come, I'll go away."

For some time there was no movement in the half prostrated figure, then the head moved slightly, and Charlitte caught a faint sentence, "Repent, my husband."

"Yes, I repent," he said, hastily. "Good Lord, I'll do anything. Only cheer up and let me out of this."

The grief-stricken Rose pushed back the hair from her tear-stained face and slowly raised her head from her arms.

It was only necessary for her to show that face to her husband. So impressed was it with the stamp of intense anguish of mind, of grief for his past delinquencies of conduct, of a sorrow nobly, quietly borne through long years, that even he — callous, careless, and thoughtless — was profoundly moved.

For a long time he was silent. Then his lip trembled and he turned his head aside. "'Pon my word, Rose, — I didn't think you'd fret like this. I'll do better ; let me go now."

One of her hands stole with velvety clasp to his brown wrists, and while the gentle touch lasted he sat still, listening with an averted face to the words whispered in his ear.

Agapit, in the meantime, was walking in the garden with Bidiane. He had told her all that she wished to know with regard to the recreant husband, and in a passionate, resentful state of mind she was storming to and fro, scarcely knowing what she said.

"It is abominable, treacherous ! — and we stand idly here. Go and drive him away, Agapit. He should not be allowed to speak to our spotless Rose. I should think that the skies would fall — and I spoke to him, the traitor ! Go, Agapit, — I wish you would knock him down."

Agapit, with an indulgent glance, stood at a little distance from her, softly murmuring, from time to time, " You are very young, Bidiane."

"Young ! I am glad that I am young, so that I can feel angry. You are stolid, unfeeling. You care nothing for Rose. I shall go myself and tell that wretch to his face what I think of him."

She was actually starting, but Agapit caught her gently by the arm. "Bidiane, restrain yourself," and drawing her under the friendly shade of a solitary pine-tree that had been left when the garden was made, he smoothed her angry cheeks and kissed her hot forehead.

"You condone his offence, — you, also, some day, will leave me for some woman," she gasped.

"This from you to me," he said, quietly and proudly, "when you know that we Acadiens are proud of our virtue, — of the virtue of our women particularly; and if the women are pure, it is because the men are so."

"Rose cannot love that demon," exclaimed Bidiane.

"No, she does not love him, but she understands what you will understand when you are older, — the awful sacredness of the marriage tie. Think of one of the sentences that she read to us last Sunday from Thomas à Kempis : 'A pure heart penetrates heaven and hell.' She has been in a hell of suffering herself. I think when in it she wished her husband were dead. Her charity is therefore infinite towards him. Her sins of thought are equal in her chastened mind to his sins of body."

"But you will not let her go away with him?"

"She will not wish to go, my treasure. She talks to him, and repent, repent, is, I am sure, the burden of her cry. You do not understand that under her gentleness is a stern resolve. She will be soft and kind, yet she would die rather than live with Charlitte or surrender her child to him."

"But he may wish to stay here," faltered Bidiane.

"He will not stay with her, *chérie*. She is no longer a girl, but a woman. She is not resentful, yet Charlitte has sinned deeply against her, and she remembers, — and now I must return to her. Charlitte has little delicacy of feeling, and may stay too long."

"Wait a minute, Agapit, — is it her money that he is after?"

"No, little one, he is not mercenary. He would not take money from a woman. He also would not give her any unless she begged him to do so. I think that his visit is a mere caprice that, however, if humored, would degenerate into a carrying away of Rose, — and now *au revoir*."

Bidiane, in her excited, overstrained condition of mind, bestowed one of her infrequent caresses on him, and Agapit, in mingled surprise and gratification, found a pair of loving arms flung around his neck, and heard a frantic whisper: "If you ever do anything bad, I shall kill you; but you will not, for you are good."

"Thank you. If I am faithless you may kill me," and, reluctantly leaving her, he strode along the summit of the slight hill on which the house stood, until he caught sight of the tableau on the lawn.

Charlitte was just leaving his wife. His head was hanging on his breast; he looked ashamed of himself, and in haste to be gone, yet he paused and cast an occasional stealthy and regretful glance at Rose, who, with a face aglow with angelic forgiveness, seemed to be bestowing a parting benediction on him.

The next time that he lifted his head, his small, sharp eyes caught sight of Agapit, whereupon he immediately snatched his hand from Rose, and hastily began to descend the hill towards the river.

Rose remained standing, and silently watched him. She did not look at Agapit, — her eyes were riveted on her husband. Something within her seemed to cry out as his feet carried him down the hill to the brink of the inexorable stream, where the bones of so many of his countrymen lay.

"*Adieu*, my husband," she called, suddenly and pleadingly, "thou wilt not forget."

Charlitte paused just before he reached the bridge, and, little dreaming that his feet were never to cross its planks, he swept a glance over the peaceful Bay, the waiting boat, and the beautiful ship. Then he turned and waved his hand to his wife, and for one instant, they remembered afterwards, he put a finger on his breast, where lay a crucifix that she had just given him.

"*Adjheu*, Rose," he called, loudly, "I will remember." At the same minute, however, that the smile of farewell lighted up his face, an oath slipped to his lips, and he stepped back from the bridge.

CHAPTER XV.

THE BEAUTIFUL STRANGER GOES AWAY WITHOUT HER CAPTAIN.

" Repentance is the relinquishment of any practice from the conviction that it has offended God. Sorrow, fear, and anxiety are properly not parts but adjuncts of repentance, yet they are too closely connected with it to be easily separated."
— *Rambler.*

CHARLITTE did not plan to show himself at all in Sleeping Water. He possessed a toughened conscience and moral fibre calculated to stand a considerably heavy strain, yet some blind instinct warned him that he had better seek no conversation with his friends of former days.

For this reason he had avoided the corner on his way to Rose's house, but he had not been able to keep secret the news of his arrival. Some women at the windows had recognized him, and a few loungers at the corner had strolled down to his boat, and had conversed with the sailors, who, although Norwegians, yet knew enough English to tell their captain's name, which, according to a custom prevailing among Acadiens, was simply the French name turned into English. Charlitte de Forêt had become Charlitte Forrest.

Emmanuel de la Rive was terribly excited. He had just come from the station with the afternoon mail, and, on hearing that Charlitte was alive, and had actually arrived, he had immediately put himself at the head of a contingent of men, who proposed to go up to the cottage and ascertain the truth of the case. If it were so, — and it must be so, — what a wonderful, what an extraordinary occurrence! Sleeping Water had never known anything like this, and he jabbered steadily all the way up to the cottage.

Charlitte saw them coming, — this crowd of old friends, headed by the mail-driver in the red jacket, and he looked helplessly up at Rose.

"Come back," she called; "come and receive your friends with me."

Charlitte, however, glanced at Agapit, and preferred to stay where he was, and in a trice Emmanuel and the other men and boys were beside him, grasping his hands, vociferating congratulations on his escape from death, and plying him with inquiries as to the precise quarter of the globe in which the last few years of his existence had been passed.

Charlitte, unable to stave off the questions showered upon him, was tortured by a desire to yield to his rough and sailorlike sense of humor, and entertain himself for a few minutes at the expense of his friends by regaling them with his monstrous yarns of shipwreck and escape from the cannibal islands.

Something restrained him. He glanced up at Rose, and saw that she had lost hope of his returning to her. She was gliding down the hill towards him, — a loving, anxious, guardian angel.

He could not tell lies in her presence. "Come, boys," he said, with coarse good nature. "Come on to my ship, I'll take you all aboard."

Emmanuel, in a perfect intoxication of delight and eager curiosity, crowded close to Charlitte, as the throng of men and boys turned and began to surge over the bridge, and the hero of the moment, his attention caught by the bright jacket, singled Emmanuel out for special attention, and even linked his arm in his as they went.

Bidiane, weary of her long stay in the garden, at that minute came around the corner of the house on a reconnoitring expedition. Her brown eyes took in the whole scene, — Rose hurrying down the hill, Agapit standing silently on it, and the swarm of men surrounding the newcomer like happy buzzing bees, while they joyfully escorted him away from the cottage.

This was the picture for an instant before her, then simultaneously with a warning cry from Agapit, — "The bridge, *mon Dieu!* Do not linger on it;

you are a strong pressure!" — there was a sudden crash, a brief and profound silence, then a great splashing, accompanied by shouts and cries of astonishment.

The slight rustic structure had given way under the unusually heavy weight imposed upon it, and a score or two of the men of Sleeping Water were being subjected to a thorough ducking.

However, they were all used to the water, their lives were partly passed on the sea, and they were all accomplished swimmers. As one head after another came bobbing up from the treacherous river, it was greeted with cries and jeers from dripping figures seated on the grass, or crawling over the muddy banks.

Célina ran from the house, and Jovite from the stable, both shrieking with laughter. Only Agapit looked grave, and, snatching a hammock from a tree, he ran down the hill to the place where Rose stood with clasped hands.

"Where is Charlitte?" she cried, "and Emmanuel? — they were close together; I do not see them."

A sudden hush followed her words. Every man sprang to his feet. Emmanuel's red jacket was nowhere to be seen, — in the first excitement they had not missed him, — neither was Charlitte visible.

They must be still at the bottom of the river,

locked in a friendly embrace. Rose's wild cry pierced the hearts of her fellow countrymen, and in an instant some of the dripping figures were again in the river.

Agapit was one of the most expert divers present, and he at once took off his coat and his boots. Bidiane threw herself upon him, but he pushed her aside and, putting his hands before him, plunged down towards the exact spot where he had last seen Charlitte.

The girl, in wild terror, turned to Rose, who stood motionless, her lips moving, her eyes fixed on the black river. "Ah, God! there is no bottom to it,— Rose, Rose, call him back!"

Rose did not respond, and Bidiane ran frantically to and fro on the bank. The muddy water was splashed up in her face, there was a constant appearance of heads, and disappearance of feet. Her lover would be suffocated there below, he stayed so long, — and in her despair she was in danger of slipping in herself, until Rose came to her rescue and held her firmly by her dress.

After a space of time, that seemed interminably long, but that in reality lasted only a few minutes, there was a confused disturbance of the surface of the water about the remains of the wrecked bridge. Then two or three arms appeared,— a muddy form encased in a besmeared bright jacket was drawn out, and willing hands on the bank received it, and in desperate haste made attempts at resuscitation.

"Go, Célina, to the house, — heat water and blankets," said Rose, turning her deathly pale face towards her maid; "and do you, Lionel and Sylvain, kindly help her. Run, Jovite, and telephone for a doctor — oh, be quick! Ah, Charlitte, Charlitte!" and with a distracted cry she fell on her knees beside the inanimate drenched form laid at her feet. Tears rained down her cheeks, yet she rapidly and skilfully superintended the efforts made for restoration. Her hands assisted in raising the inert back. She feverishly lifted the silent tongue, and endeavored to force air to the choked lungs, and her friends, with covert pitying glances, zealously assisted her.

"There is no hope, Rose," said Agapit, at last. "You are wasting your strength, and keeping these brave fellows in their wet clothes."

Her face grew stony, yet she managed to articulate, "But I have heard even if after the lapse of hours, — if one works hard — "

"There is no hope," he said, again. "We found him by the bank. There was timber above him, he was suffocated in mud."

She looked up at him piteously, then she again burst into tears, and threw herself across the body. "Go, dear friends, — leave me alone with him. Oh,

Charlitte, Charlitte! — that I should have lived to see this day."

"Emmanuel is also dead," said Agapit, in a low voice.

"Emmanuel, — good, kind Emmanuel, — the beloved of all the village; not so — " and she painfully lifted her head and stared at the second prostrate figure.

The men were all standing around him weeping. They were not ashamed of their tears, — these kind-hearted, gentle Acadiens. Such a calamity had seldom befallen their village. It was equal to the sad wrecks of winter.

Rose's overwrought brain gave way as she gazed, and she fell senseless by Charlitte's dead body.

Agapit carried her to the house, and laid her in her bed in the room that she was not to leave for many days.

"This is an awful time," said Célina, sobbing bitterly, and addressing the mute and terrified Bidiane. "Let us pray for the souls of those poor men who died without the last sacraments."

"Let us pray rather for the soul of one who repented on his death-bed," muttered Agapit, staring with white lips at the men who were carrying the body of Charlitte into one of the lower rooms of the house.

CHAPTER XVI.

AN ACADIEN FESTIVAL.

"Vive Jésus!
Vive Jésus!
Avec la croix, son cher partage.
Vive Jésus!
Dans les cœurs de tous les élus!
Portons la croix.

. . . .

Sans choix, sans ennui, sans murmure,
Portons la croix!
Quoique très amère et très dure,
Malgre les sens et la nature,
Portons la croix!"

— *Acadien Song.*

CHARLITTE had been in his grave for nearly two years. He slept peacefully in the little green cemetery hard by the white church where a slender, sorrowful woman came twice every week to hear a priest repeat masses for the repose of his soul.

He slept on and gave no sign, and his countrymen came and went above him, reflecting occasionally on their own end, but mostly, after the manner of all men, allowing their thoughts to linger rather on matters pertaining to time than on those of eternity.

One fifteenth of August — the day consecrated by Acadiens all over Canada to the memory of their forefathers — had come and gone, and another had arrived.

This day was one of heavenly peace and calm. The sky was faintly, exquisitely blue, and so placid was the Bay that the occupants of the boats crossing from Digby Neck to some of the churches in Frenchtown were forced to take in their sails, and apply themselves to their oars.

Since early morning the roads of the parish in which Sleeping Water is situated had been black with people, and now at ten o'clock some two thousand Acadiens were assembled about the doors of the old church at Pointe à l'Eglise.

There was no talking, no laughing. In unbroken silence they waited for the sound of the bell, and when it came they flocked into the church, packing it full, and overflowing out to the broad flight of steps, where they knelt in rows and tried to obtain glimpses over each other's shoulders of the blue and white decorations inside, and of the altar ablaze with lights.

The priests from the college and glebe-house, robed in handsome vestments, filed out from the vestry, and, quietly approaching the silken banners standing against the low gallery, handed them to representatives of different societies connected with the church.

The children of the Guardian Angel received the picture of their patron saint, and, gathering around it, fluttered soberly out to the open air through the narrow lane left among the kneeling worshippers.

The children of the Society of Mary followed them, their white-clad and veiled figures clustering about the pale, pitying Virgin carried by two of their number. A banner waving beside her bore the prayer, "*Marie, Priez Pour Nous*" (Mary, pray for us), and, as if responding to the petition, her two hands were extended in blessing over them.

After the troop of snowy girls walked the black sisters in big bonnets and drooping shawls, and the brown sisters, assistants to the Eudists, who wore black veils with white flaps against their pale faces. Then came the priests, altar boys, and all the congregation. Until they left the church the organ played an accompaniment to their chanting. On the steps a young deacon put a cornet to his lips, and, taking up the last note of the organ, prolonged it into a vigorous leadership of the singing :

> Ave maris stella,
> Dei mater alma,
> Atque semper virgo
> Felix coeli porta.

As the congregation sang, they crossed the road to the gates of the college grounds, and divided into two parts, the men, with heads uncovered, going one side, and the women on the other.

Above the gate-posts waved two flags, the union jack and the Acadien national flag, — a French tricolor, crossed by a blue stripe, and pierced with a yellow star.

Slowly and solemnly the long array of men and women passed by the glebe-house and the white marble tomb of the good Abbé, whose life was given to the Acadiens of the Bay Saint-Mary. The hymns sung by the priests at the head of the procession floated back to the congregation in the rear, and at the moment when the singing was beginning to die away in the distance and the procession was winding out of sight behind the big college, two strangers suddenly appeared on the scene.

They were a slender, elegant man and a beautiful lad of a clear, healthy pallor of skin. The man, with a look of grave, quiet happiness on his handsome face, stepped from the carriage in which they were driving, fastened his horse to a near fence, and threw a longing glance after the disappearing procession.

"If we hurry, Narcisse," he said, "we shall be able to overtake them."

The lad at once placed himself beside him, and together they went on their way towards the gates.

"Do you remember it?" asked the man, softly, as the boy lifted his hat when they passed by the door of the silent, decorated church.

"Yes, perfectly," he said, with a sweet, delicate intonation of voice. "It seems as if my mother must be kneeling there."

Vesper's brow and cheeks immediately became suffused with crimson. "She is probably on ahead. We will find out. If she is not, we shall drive at once to Sleeping Water."

They hurried on silently. The procession was now moving through another gate, this one opening on the point of land where are the ruins of the first church that the good Abbé built on the Bay.

Beside its crumbling ruins and the prostrate altar-stones a new, fresh altar had been put up, — this one for temporary use. It was a veritable bower of green amid which bloomed many flowers, the fragile nurslings of the sisters in the adjacent convent.

Before this altar the priests and deacons knelt for an instant on colored rugs, then, while the people gathered closely around them, an Acadien Abbé from the neighboring province of New Brunswick ascended the steps of the altar, and, standing beside the embowered Virgin mother, special patron and protectress of his race, he delivered a fervent panegyric on the ancestors of the men and women before him.

While he recounted the struggles and trials of the

early Acadiens, many of his hearers wept silently, but when this second good Abbé eloquently exhorted them not to linger too long on a sad past, but to gird themselves for a glorious future, to be constant to their race and to their religion, their faces cleared, — they were no longer a prey to mournful recollections.

Vesper, holding his hat in his hand, and closely accompanied by Narcisse, moved slowly nearer and nearer to a man who stood with his face half hidden by his black hat.

It was Agapit, and at Vesper's touch he started slightly, then, for he would not speak on this solemn occasion, he extended a hand that was grasped in the firm and enduring clasp of a friendship that would not again be broken.

Vesper would never forget that, amid all the bustle and confusion succeeding Charlitte's death, Agapit had found time to send him a cable message, — "Charlitte is dead."

After communicating with Agapit, Vesper drew the boy nearer to him, and fell back a little. He was inexpressibly moved. A few years ago he would have called this "perverted Christianity — Mariolatry." Now, now — "O God!" he muttered, "my pure saint, she has genuine piety," and under wet lashes he stole a glance at one form, preëminently beautiful among the group of straight and slim young Acadien women beyond him. She was there, — his heart's delight, his treasure. She was his. The holy, rapt expression would give place to one more earthly, more self-conscious. He would not surrender her to heaven just yet, — but still, would it not be heaven on earth to be united to her?

She did not know that he was near. In complete oblivion of her surroundings she followed the singing of the Tantum Ergo. When the benediction was over, she lifted her bowed head, her eyes turned once towards the cemetery. She was thinking of Charlitte.

The sensitive Narcisse trembled. The excess of melancholy and sentimental feeling about him penetrated to his soul, and Vesper withdrew with him to the edge of the crowd. Then before the procession re-formed to march back to the church, they took up their station by the college gates.

All the Acadiens saw him there as they approached, — all but Rose.

She only raised her eyes from her prayer-book to fix them on the sky. She alone of the women seemed to be so wholly absorbed in a religious fervor that she did not know where she was going nor what she was doing.

Some of the Acadiens looked doubtfully at Vesper. Since the death of her husband, whose treachery towards her had in some way been discovered, she had been regarded more than ever as a saint, — as one set apart for prayer and meditation almost as much as if she had been consecrated to them. Would she give up her saintly life for marriage with the Englishman?

Would she do it? Surely this holy hour was the wrong time to ask her, and they waited breathlessly until they reached the gates where the procession was to break up. There she discovered Vesper. In the face of all the congregation he had stepped up and was holding out his hand to her.

She did not hesitate an instant. She did not even seem to be surprised. An expression of joyful surrender sprang to her face; in silent, solemn ecstasy she took her lover's hand, and, throwing her arm around the neck of her recovered child, she started with them on the long road down the Bay.

All this happened a few years ago, but the story is yet going on. If you come from Boston to-day, and take your wheel or carriage at Yarmouth, — for the strong winds blow one up and not down the Bay, — you will, after passing through Salmon River, Chéticamp, Meteghan, Saulnierville, and other places, come to the swinging sign of the Sleeping Water Inn.

There, if you stop, you will be taken good care of by Claudine and Mirabelle Marie, — who is really a vastly improved woman.

Perhaps among all the two hundred thousand Acadiens scattered throughout the Maritime Provinces of Canada there is not a more interesting inn than that of Sleeping Water. They will give you good meals and keep your room tidy, and they will also show you — if you are really interested in the Acadien French — a pretty cottage in the form of a horseshoe that was moved bodily away from the wicked Sleeping Water River and placed in a flat green field by the shore. To it, you will be informed, comes every year a family from Boston, consisting of an Englishman and his wife, his mother and two children. They will describe the family to you, or perhaps, if it is summer-time, you may see the Englishman himself, riding a tall bay horse and looking affectionately at a beautiful lad who accompanies him on a glossy black steed rejoicing in the name of Toochune.

The Englishman is a man of wealth and many schemes. He has organized a company for the planting and cultivation of trees along the shore of the charming, but certainly wind-swept Bay. He also is busy now surveying the coast for the carrying out of his long-cherished plan of an electric railway running along the shore.

He will yet have it, the Acadiens say, but in the meantime he amuses himself by viewing the land and interviewing the people, and when he is weary he rides home to the cottage where his pale, fragile mother is looking eagerly for her adopted, idolized grandchild Narcisse, and where his wife sits by the window and waits for him.

As she waits she often smiles and gazes down at her lap where lies a tiny creature, — a little girl whose eyes and mouth are her own, but whose hair is the hair of Vesper.

Perhaps you will go to Sleeping Water by the train. If so, do not look out for the red coat which always used to be the distinguishing mark of this place, and do not mention Emmanuel's name to the woman who keeps the station, nor to her husband, for they were very fond of him, and if you speak of the red-jacketed mail-man they will turn aside to hide their tears.

Nannichette and her husband have come out of the woods and live by the shore. Mirabelle Marie has persuaded the former to go to mass with her. The Indian in secret delight says nothing, but occasionally he utters a happy grunt.

Bidiane and her husband live in Weymouth. Their *ménage* is small and unambitious as yet, in order that they may do great things in the future, Bidiane says. She is absolutely charming when she ties a handkerchief on her head and sweeps out her rooms; and sometimes she cooks.

Often at such times she scampers across a yard

that separates her from her husband's office, and, after looking in his window to make sure that he is alone, she flies in, startles and half suffocates him by throwing her arms around his neck and stuffing in his mouth or his pocket some new and delectable dainty known only to herself and the cook-book.

She is very happy, and turns with delight from her winter visits to Halifax, where, however, she manages to enjoy herself hugely, to her summer on the Bay, when she can enjoy the most congenial society in the world to her and to her husband, — that of Vesper Nimmo and his wife Rose.

THE END.

Formac Fiction Treasures
ALSO IN THE SERIES

By Evelyn Eaton

Quietly My Captain Waits
This historical romance, set during the years of French-English struggle in New France, draws two lovers out of the shadows of history — Louise de Freneuse, married and widowed twice, and Pierre de Bonaventure, Fleet Captain in the French navy. Their almost impossible relationship helps them endure the day-to-day struggle in the fated settlement of Port Royal. ISBN 0-88780-544-2

The Sea is So Wide
In the summer of 1755, Barbe Comeau offers her family home in the lush farmland of the Annapolis Valley as overnight shelter to an English officer and his surly companion. The Comeaus are unaware of the treacherous plans to confiscate the Acadian farms and send them all into exile. A few weeks later, they are crammed into the hold of a ship and sent south. In Virginia she patiently rebuilds her life, never expecting that the friend she believed had betrayed her and her family would search until he found her. ISBN 0-88780-573-6

By W. Albert Hickman

The Sacrifice of the Shannon
In the heart of Frederick Ashburn, sea captain and sportsman, there glows a secret fire of love for young Gertrude MacMichael. But her interests lie with Ashburn's fellow adventurer, the dashing and slightly mysterious Dave Wilson. From their hometown of Caribou (real-life Pictou) all three set out on a perilous journey to the ice fields in the Gulf of St. Lawrence to save a ship and its precious cargo — Gertrude's father. In almost constant danger, Wilson is willing to risk everything to bring the ship and crew to safety. ISBN 0-88780-542-6

By Alice Jones (Alix John)

The Night Hawk
Set in Halifax during the American Civil War, a wealthy Southerner — beautiful, poised, intelligent and divorced — poses as a refugee while

using her social success to work undercover. The conviviality of the town's social elite, especially the British garrison officers is more than just a diversion when there is a war to be won.

A Privateer's Fortune

When Gilbert Clinch discovers a very valuable painting and statue in his deceased grandfather's attic, he begins to uncover some of his ancestor's secrets, including a will that allows Clinch to become a wealthy man, while at the same time disinheriting his cousins. His grandfather's business as a privateer and slave trader helped him amass wealth, power and prestige. Clinch has secrets of his own, including a clandestine love affair. From Nova Scotia to the art salons in Paris and finally the gentility of English country mansions, Clinch and his lover, Isabel Broderick, become entangled in a haunting legacy. ISBN 0-88780-572-8

By Charles G.D. Roberts

The Heart That Knows

On her wedding day a young girl is suddenly abandoned. Standing on the Bay of Fundy shore she watches her husband's barquentine sail away without a word of explanation. Weeks follows days and she is left to face life as an outcast, scorned by her neighbours and family for being a mother, but not a wife. Over the years her son, like many sailors' children, grows up without a father. Confronted with the truth, the young man sets off to sea, determined not to return to his New Brunswick home until he seeks vengeance on the man who treated his mother so heartlessly.
ISBN 0-88780-570-1

By Margaret Marshall Saunders

Beautiful Joe

Cruelly mutilated by his master, Beautiful Joe, a mongrel dog, is at death's door when he finds himself in the loving care of Laura Morris. A tale of tender devotion between dog and owner, this novel is the framework for the author's astute and timeless observations on farming methods, including animal care, and rural living. This Canadian classic, written by a woman once acclaimed as "Canada's Most Revered Writer," has been popular with readers, including young adults, for almost a century.
ISBN 0-88780-540-X